THE MOON PINNACE

Other books by Thomas Williams

CEREMONY OF LOVE
TOWN BURNING
THE NIGHT OF TREES
A HIGH NEW HOUSE
WHIPPLE'S CASTLE
THE HAIR OF HAROLD ROUX
TSUGA'S CHILDREN
THE FOLLOWED MAN

THE MOON PINNACE

Thomas Williams

ANCHOR PRESS
Doubleday
NEW YORK
1988

All of the characters in this book are fictitious, and any resemblance to actual persons, living or dead, is purely coincidental.

Anchor Books Edition

Library of Congress Cataloging-in-Publication Data

Williams, Thomas, 1926-
The moon pinnace.

I. Title.
PS3573.I456M66 1986 813'.54 85-29255

ISBN 0-385-24247-6 (pbk.)

. . . so in love the heart surrenders itself entirely to the one being that has known how to touch it. That being is not selected; it is recognised and obeyed.

—George Santayana,
The Life of Reason

. . . American love of country has always been a curiously general affair, almost an abstract one.

—Henry Steele Commager,
The Nature of American Nationalism

THE MOON PINNACE

1

One June morning in 1948, in the town of Leah, New Hampshire, Doris Perkins watched John Hearne cross his backyard and her backyard, which met his, and lightly climb the woodshed roof to her bedroom window. She was waiting to hold the gray-gauzy curtains aside so he could slip through the small window head first, his hands on the wooden floor. Then, without a sound, neat as an acrobat, came the rest of him. Doris's mother and father and her younger sister would be getting up soon, so they didn't speak except in whispers.

She was seventeen and he was twenty-one. She had known him all her life, but this coming to her room in secrecy, this new interest he had in her, was strange, a wish fulfilled, but fulfilled, as all wishes were, in an unsettling way. She had admired him as long as she could remember him, when the children in the after-supper twilight played their games across the lawns as the dark came on too soon. Prisoner's base, kick the can, Red Rover, come over—now those games were played by younger children across other twilit yards. Once, when she was eight or nine, a little too small to be much of a player, he had chosen her for his side. He'd said, "I'll take Dory—she can run like the wind." No one had ever before called her Dory, or picked her anything but last. He had probably forgotten all about that time, but she never would. It was as if, during those evenings, or perhaps that very evening, something had become fixed in her way of seeing boys, and no other evidence seemed to matter, not even John Hearne's occasional later childishness, or her own. He must have been thirteen then, but she could see no real difference in him since that summer long ago, eight years ago, nearly half her lifetime.

He hadn't been the leader of the children in their games, though he was a force, and would often be captain of a side. He would say what was fair and what was not fair. He had once fought a boy in the schoolyard and it seemed to her a battle of Titans, perilous even to watch from a distance. Such anger and hitting. She had been so terrified she hadn't even thought to be on one side or another. Those eighth-graders were giants, godlike. There had been nose blood, or lip blood, the other boy's face gray as metal with hatred.

As he sat on her bed its cables and springs gave little twangs that made him grimace as a joke. His blond plain looks were what she thought a boy should look like, because conventional handsomeness didn't matter. She sat on the bed too, but up near her pillow. He seemed proud that he had dared to come.

"I said I'd come," he whispered, smiling at her.

"It's dumb," she whispered back. "Suppose someone saw you? Suppose my mother comes in here?"

"In that case pretend you don't know me."

It was funny, but it was not funny. She laughed silently and then stopped. She didn't like things to be this complicated, and she didn't think she deserved his new interest in her, because she wasn't pretty, so there might be something bad or cheap about his new attitude. Maybe it didn't matter much to him, but it mattered to her. She wanted him to be here yet she disapproved of her wanting him to be here.

Yesterday they were sitting on the old teeter-totter in her backyard talking about nothing—nothing! She couldn't remember a word of it. And then there was a silent moment and he came sliding down from his side and kissed her, saying something she couldn't remember. Nothing they said was what they were talking about, or had anything to do with what they were really meaning or doing. It was like a dance—something you did with yourself that wasn't really yourself. You almost watched yourself doing it.

They'd gone into his house to get a Coke. His house was all clean, with expensive carpets and wallpaper and polished wood. Union Street was richer than Water Street, the lawns wider, the larger houses fresh and bright inside as if ready for guests. No one was home, and in the kitchen he kissed her some more and put his hands on her back, his hands interested in her shoulder blades and her ribs. She was surprised by it all and felt just as if she were melting. The strange thing was that she couldn't disagree with anything he suggested. It was like a brand-new life that had just begun and she'd found herself in it, apprehensive or not, for better or for worse.

He poured their Cokes over ice cubes into glasses just like the ones at Trask's Pharmacy, special glasses bulbed at the top, with "Coca-Cola" etched into their sides. It seemed grand and yet frivolous to have glasses in your house just for Coca-Cola.

"This is only the third time I've ever been in this house," she said.

"That's because we weren't really contemporaries," he said. "But we are now, aren't we?"

He had always used words like "contemporaries" that others knew the meanings of but never used themselves. He hesitated, waiting for her assent, but she looked away; quite often she didn't answer questions that needed no answers. She was aware of this habit as a kind of doubtful obstinacy that sometimes disappointed people.

The large, bright kitchen didn't smell of food. The colors of cabinets and shelves matched the colors of electric stove and refrigerator. All hinges and pulls matched. She wondered if there would ever be any leftovers in this kitchen, in the refrigerator or on a shelf somewhere covered with a cloth. He showed her the rest of the house with all its surfaces that people must have had to worry about marring or soiling. There were framed paintings on the walls, of still lifes and landscapes, one of Mount Washington that was so old even the blue of the sky was more brown than blue. There were empty silver trays on tables, and no photographs anywhere, and a sunroom with curtains drawn against the light but themselves lighted yellow by the sun. There were tall lamps with linen shades, and everywhere the splashboards were so narrow the oak floors must never have been meant to be mopped. If you had to clean such a house you'd never know where you'd been. In the bedrooms upstairs the beds were high, rounded at the corners, and didn't sag in their middles. It was as if she'd come across the two backyards into another country. When she'd visited this house before, it was just for minutes, twice to the kitchen on errands, once to the front room when, as a child, she was invited in on Halloween and given wrapped chocolate candy instead of jelly beans and the like.

They came to his room. He had been flippant in showing her the house, not toward her but toward the house. He had some attitude toward it of disrespect that she had decided to ignore in order to make up her own mind. "And here," he'd said, showing her his parents' bedroom, "is the Grand Uxorium." But then, at the door to his own room, he grew nervous. She loved him but she really didn't know him. If it was love, whatever this melting was, much of it must come from history and not from what he was now. John Hearne had actually given her her name—Dory. He had named her for everyone she knew except for her father and mother, who called her Doris. Even her uncles and aunts called her Dory. But when she was in high school he was away in the Army and then at college, and when he was home they'd just said, "Hi, Dory," and "Hi, John"—neighbors across the way.

He opened the door and swept his arm around to present her to the room, or the room to her. His bed was unmade. Used clothing hung over a chair. Childhood relics, like the model airplane hanging from threads and the paper wasps' nest above a window, were in evidence. It was a corner room with windows on two sides (one window looked across the backyards, through leaves, to her window; she had known this for years). He must have been fond of the long bookcase in which the colorful children's books blended along the rows into the more solid, somber bindings of his growing up. In her house there were not five books in all except for schoolbooks and the books she had borrowed from her friend Cynthia Fuller or from the town library.

He sat on his bed and she sat on the arm of his leather easy chair.

"You don't say a lot," he said.

"I guess not."

"Most girls your age have all these idiotic expressions they think are clever."

She shrugged.

He stood up and came toward her. She felt risk, that she didn't really know him in these new circumstances. He was bigger and stronger than she was; his shoulders seemed a yard wide, his hips as strong and narrow as a tree. If it had been the other way around she could just say no, if she wanted to, and that would be that. But he was stronger and all she could do if she wanted him to stop would be to appeal to custom and law and the opinions of people like their parents. She didn't want him to stop, at least not yet, but if she had wanted him to stop her authorities would be distant.

His new interest in her had been so intense he'd trembled. She saw the tremor of his knee against his khaki pants. His warm blond head loomed before her, his open greenish eyes straight upon hers, so close everything blurred, including the feeling in her breasts and in the lower center of her, in which something seemed to drop down with a lurch as their mouths came together in that formal, folding way. She was curious about it all—about the feelings she was having and about what he really wanted with her. Maybe he just wanted to play with her.

But all he did was move his hands over her back and look very serious. In a way this was really happening but it was not right, because she couldn't figure out why this boy she had loved maybe since she was eight years old was suddenly doing what she had often imagined him doing. It was as if he were taking one of the most important of her fantasies away from her forever. It was all doubtful because in the fantasy she didn't look the way she actually did, which was plain, plain, her eyes too close together, her mouth too big and her straight hair a brownish tan color that reflected nothing. But all the time she melted. She had never felt such fine sandpaper as his face.

At the time it seemed that she must do everything he wanted; it was like falling. But after kissing her for a while he held her at arm's length and looked at her carefully for a minute, or part of a minute, and then they went for a ride on his motorcycle to Northlee and back, five miles each way, her arms around his middle. She wasn't afraid at all, but it was cold and she hardly saw anything but clouds and trees. He left her off in front of her house and made the joke, or dare, about coming to see her room the next morning before anyone was up. She had been so numb and invaded by so many new feelings it was as if she had lived a year on that one afternoon. And now he was here in her bedroom while through the small floor register at the foot of her bed the sounds and smells of breakfast came up from the kitchen—the squeezing sound of water not quite yet boiling, the odor of kerosene, the thud-clink of the refrigerator door and latch.

"Doris," her mother said in a normal voice, as if she were right there in the room, "you going to eat breakfast with us?"

"No, Ma. You go ahead. I'll get some later," she answered, shivering unpleasantly at the lie hidden in her words. At least John Hearne was startled by the closeness of her mother's voice.

Her mother and father would take Debbie to school on their way to work. A danger was that Debbie might want to come into her room for something, although she probably wouldn't. If she did, John Hearne would have to get in the closet, because she wouldn't refuse Debbie if she wanted to come in. She felt a surge of annoyance with him and then wondered why any critical feelings she had toward him seemed to demean her. Why was that? It was dangerous. Suddenly he was complicating and changing the life that she had lived mostly in anticipation of the future, its scenes and characters largely imaginary. She hadn't even studied practical things very much. She knew something about sex, about that compulsive attraction, but not enough about its mechanics and dangers. She had avoided the subject, leaving its parts and functions for some later time. There was the side view of the pelvic innards of a woman like curved sausage casings, tubes and clusters of little globules, but the murky picture in the book didn't seem to apply to her. At her period there was a spongy feeling but she seemed all of a piece up in there. Even the idea of "up in there" was new—she wouldn't have thought of it yesterday morning, but yesterday afternoon when he was kissing her something separate seemed to drop down like the stretching of a rubber band until it lost its ability to stretch any more.

And there was another symptom; she was acting the way he wanted her to act. She was not being herself. Among her friends she was considered a witty and caustic person. She never automatically agreed to anything. But his touch was a force she did not resist. If he pulled, she came forward before he had to use any strength at all, and if he pushed she faded before his hand like air. She didn't know how her body knew what step, turn, bend or fold his arms effortlessly commanded.

They were exaggeratedly immobile on her squeaky bed, waiting for the sounds in the house to go away. He evidently thought it was funny but when she frowned at him he stopped making faces at her. She sat Indian fashion in her pajamas, looking down the slope of the hammocky bed where he sat Indian fashion at the other end in his khakis and blue dress shirt with the sleeves rolled partly up over his smooth forearms. He'd slipped out of his leather moccasins and left them on the floor, but when he saw her glance at them he reached down with elaborate care, picked them up and put them under a fold of blanket. He pointed downstairs, made his fingers into a person walking upstairs, pointed to himself and then his pointing finger made a loop toward the underside of the bed.

"She could walk to school," her father said in his high but authoritative voice. He referred to Debbie, who was right there at the kitchen table. He knew about walking because he was a mailman.

"It's no more than two streets out of my way," her mother said. The subject came up most mornings, but what they did was, her father drove to the post office, got out of the car, her mother slid over under the wheel and drove Debbie to school, then drove back downstreet to her job at the Public Service Company. Debbie walked home from school but never to school, and it had been the same way with Dory. But it seemed that every chance he got her father brought up the subject of walking.

Knives clinked on the butter dish. Toast smells, light golden, near to char, wafted up into the air of the small room where she and John Hearne were immobilized in such tension right on the sheets and blankets of her bed. After a long time the sounds below diminished. The house opened out on voices, shut again, the car started and backed out the driveway with the light tearing sound of crushed cinders and they were alone in the house.

2

He was an only child, though that condition, being simply unalterable, rarely came to mind unless someone else brought it up. If it was a fault it wasn't his. Who knew what had kept him from the company of brothers and sisters? From what he knew of his mother he tended to think it was malfunction—in her or his father or stepfather—rather than choice, but he couldn't be certain.

In Leah it had been awkward that his mother's last name was not the same as his. No one else in Leah had the name Hearne; there were Hearnes in Northlee, according to the Northlee telephone book, but he'd never happened to meet one of them, and since his father came from the Midwest they probably wouldn't be related to him. His father, his mother had told him over the years, was in the far West somewhere, if still alive. He'd been a handsome man, a charming man everyone had liked, but he was totally irresponsible, just totally irresponsible. To John this had, even from the beginning, seemed too simple a judgment. He suspected, and as far as he could remember always had suspected, that on this subject anything his mother might say was untrustworthy, because she was not free of blushes and girlish self-flattery when she spoke of it. It was as if men, all men, were first evaluated by her as dancing partners. He supposed that most people were in the habit of self-congratulation, some more subtle than others, but hers was always obvious and bright, ego a coin forever new. Was his father then charming and popular because she had married him, irresponsible because she had divorced him?

Once, when he was seven or eight, he told her a dream he'd had, one he couldn't now remember except that there had been a great white mare on the ice, and asked her to tell no one. But it had been a cute dream, revealing, his mother had thought, superior imagination in her only son, and in his very presence she had told it to another woman. She could not understand his anger and sense of betrayal. She said that the dream was not shameful and the other woman was sympathetic, so why was he upset? Because you promised you wouldn't tell, he said.

She didn't understand. She was unhappy because of his anger, but her motives had been impeccable, hadn't they? In all ways she was kind and good to him, wasn't she? Gradually, through this sort of incident, he had come to believe that in her mind he did not belong to himself, nor did others to themselves, but all were the property of her charm.

His own vague memories of his father were of a tall, smiling man in another country, another world. They were living in a small hotel that looked like a painting by Edward Hopper, especially because in that country, southwestern Minnesota, the sky came down to the ground at all points of the compass. There were trees, but they grew against the sky. Buildings stood alone like children's blocks upon the plain. This was Winota, where he was born. It seemed another life, lost but still possible, an alternative to the realities of Leah, New Hampshire, where he was a singleton.

In some ways fate had been good to him. When he ran or jumped, or caught bouncing or flying objects, he thought no more about it than a cat. The act presented itself and was done. This gift had made his life fairly tolerable in Leah, that sometimes bloody jungle of violent, dishonest, fickle children, some of them bigger and stronger than he. It was their strange loyalties that he could not always fathom. When one brother was a crook, beware the one who was honest. Beware cousins and those of the same religion, those allied by poverty or by wealth. Beware those who were neighbors. What was right and fair might not be what was in contention.

But now he was twenty-one and a veteran; as the children grew up they lost the edges of their characters against the abrasions of responsibility. Savages became pale early fathers depressed by rent, by the mysteries of credit and payments on the cars they had so wanted when wheels had meant freedom. Now another generation of children glittered through the town, each no doubt a stunning character, dangerous or brilliant, dopey or queer or all of those, but their societies were as distant to him in his new adulthood as squirrels chasing each other through the branches of a high elm. He heard them down the street: *Lee me alone!* Three twelve-year-olds banging another over the head and shoulders with little fists, not little to the outcast, their noisy progress seemingly erratic. *Unfair, unfair* . . . The procession, its depressing precision, its call to guilt or desperation, passed beyond houses, yards and garages.

Leaving him alone in his room among the souvenirs of his own childhood—a dusty Stuka made of balsa wood and paper; books, guns, reels, pipes, knives, a vacant bald-faced hornets' nest, trophies and ribbons, scrapbooks, defunct fountain pens—shelves and drawers full of things once valued for reasons mainly of childhood's constant, boring fantasies in anticipation of reality. They and the room itself, which really belonged to his stepfather, hardly interested him at all. It was true that his plans for the summer were also rather childish; he would ride his ancient motorcycle from New Hampshire to California, that fashionable migratory destination the urge for which he understood but nonetheless allowed himself. He had wheels, untrustworthy as they might be, and some money he'd saved in the Army. His mother would defer to his wishes and his stepfather would be happy to see him gone, if anything could ever make his stepfather happy; the man had such a talent for rigidity, for embarrassment, for self-belittling rage, that even when John Hearne was a little child he had understood the pathological nature of such an existence and decided that it would impinge as little as possible upon his own fate.

Of course his real father, if alive, was out there somewhere in the easy West, among friends, charming, friendly, unawed by children, totally irresponsible.

Outside his window the new maple leaves were as pale as lettuce, small but quickly unfolding into what they would be in a week or two. Through them he saw movement, a figure against black earth in the Perkins's backyard. There was the lurch and stoop of spading, the flash of a bare arm, the hiss of the blade into stony soil. For a moment he didn't think to think who it was, and when he did look more closely, sliding his vision through the leaves, he didn't recognize whoever it was by name. It was a young woman in dungarees and a sleeveless cotton shirt, her back toward him. The difficulty of her work and the slimness of her body exaggerated each motion, so that at first he saw her as a system of thin beams and levers, a stiltlike machine operating near the limits of its power. Conscious of spying, he crouched by his windowsill to see her better. She stopped at the end of her row of fresh black earth and moved a slender wrist over her forehead to push back her hair, the color of which didn't matter because he saw her as form, as if all in grays against green and black. And now, as she stood for a moment to rest, she was so neat and sturdy and slender, so right to him that he must have invented, long ago, an idealized shadow form for the body of a girl. He hadn't known that he'd had this concept of perfection, but it must have been there all along, waiting until this girl with a spade happened to stand directly in its shadowy beam and make the design visible to him.

"What *is* this?" he said out loud. He was excited and felt the presence of danger, the marvelous kind that might threaten a change in the direction of his life. Yet he hadn't gone totally mad and was ready for disappointment. Maybe his eyes were wrong and she was a giant, or he was having a wishful hallucination as surprising as a fit. But then, with the deflating thump of the ordinary, like waking, he saw as she turned toward his window that it was Dory Perkins, whose mortal power slowly receded. There was her plain, pleasant, immature little friend-face, a smudge of soil on her round forehead. He had never really looked at her before without having known exactly who she was, and in fact hadn't seen her since Christmas vacation, and then only on the street when she had been wearing a large red mackinaw and leather-top boots.

She went back to enlarging her mother's kitchen garden, and he watched her from hiding. In a way it was reprehensible to watch every part of her like this. She placed the blade upon the segment of turf she wanted to turn, then jumped on the spade as if it were a pogo stick to make it slide straight down into the soil, an almost hydraulic, steady impalement. She pulled the spade handle back with all her strength and weight to lever out the bladeful of adhesive dirt and sod, then stabbed the chunks into smaller chunks. Small stones she picked out and tossed over to the cinder driveway. She would be determined to complete her task no matter how much effort it took; that he knew, but what else did he know about her? She had always been, after having been a baby, when he hardly saw her at all, a trim little girl who lived in back of his backyard in a house smaller and plainer than the house he lived in. One time when she was eight or nine, the neighborhood children playing kick the can or prisoner's base, someone had pushed her into the raspberry bushes and she'd cried, but they had easily cheered her up again in spite of her scratches and she'd run with them in the summer evening until the dusk fell like fog among the lilacs and juniper and her mother called her home. He had always felt somewhat protective toward that good-humored child.

Her sister, Debbie, had tended to whine; in Debbie's limbs, or psyche, or somewhere, was less of the unifying force that made for character. Debbie would have sulked if she'd had to labor with a spade, but Dory attacked the job with a sort of neutral fervor. She must be seventeen now, graduating from high school in a week or so, if his arithmetic was right. Most of the girls that age he'd known wouldn't much have liked to spend a sunny afternoon in June spading dirt, not with the new reality coming up, their new bodies radiating a more exciting power.

He really didn't know her very well; he couldn't know what she might want to do. He watched her use all of her strength. Though her struggles with the heavy, winter-packed turf and the rigid spade might be considered awkward, what he was seeing was the configuration, proved rather than refuted by each violent motion, of a woman beautiful to him. She was his childhood friend, his neighbor; all the childhood history of small important fears and insecurities was there between them, parents between them too, and even so he wanted to begin something with her. The desire was painful, wickedly near to child molestation.

He would have to go down and speak to her and see what this new creature was like. He had no idea what thoughts might come out of her head these days. Maybe she had turned into a silly idiot, and his toleration of that might sober him. He was nervous, but he did know that she liked him. One other asset he might have, the cautious or scheming side of him noted, was that because of her plain little face she might not be aware of her beauty.

"Hearne," he said aloud to his solitude, "what are you thinking of?" That was little Dory Perkins down there in her mother's vegetable garden.

3

It was she who had decided that she would spell her name with a *y* instead of *ie.* A dory was a small boat; a dorie was something vague or fluffy, diffused and cute, a feminine diminutive she couldn't apply to herself. She felt more like a good useful thing, tight in its seams, agile, made of good wood, maybe not too brilliant or pretty but well constructed. She knew where she began and where she ended. She could ride the waves.

She saw him watching her from his room. He might not even know that she knew he was home and that she often looked up at that mysterious window of his. She wondered if he might come out. When she finished the spading she went inside and washed her arms and face, quickly brushed her hair and went out into the sun again. She sat on the pipe fulcrum of the teeter-totter her father had made long ago. John Hearne was no longer at his window, but then he came out of his kitchen door and asked her if she wanted to teeter-totter. In their new adulthood this was a joke. How small the teeter-totter was; she remembered how high and scary it had once been, and how trust meant that the other person wouldn't get off and let you fall straight down with a terrible jar to your spine. Debbie had done it to her once, probably out of thoughtlessness; she'd just got off when her end was on the ground.

He had to sit in front of the handle on his end so they'd balance, and after talking about what they were not really thinking about, he'd come sliding down to her pretending it was an accident and out of the blue kissed her on the lips.

That was yesterday, and now here he was, actually on her bed, no one else in the house, and she wasn't even dressed yet.

4

At the other end of the sloping bed was this girl, strange because she had always been something other than what she was now. She didn't say much, but meanings were all different and her use to him was different, so whatever words they said, words that applied to a previous existence, did not mean anything. He could tell that she knew the words didn't mean anything, and that was why she didn't say very much. She had thin gold hairs on her forearms. Between the buttons of her pajamas he could see crescents of the pure skin of her chest; only thin bleached cotton covered her. The house was too-meaningfully quiet, and his bravado ebbed. She looked at him curiously, somewhat warily. She seemed to look at all of him while he found himself looking at parts of her, then guiltily shifting his eyes away from parts of her toward some general place he could not quite ever find. He was reminded by her bright look of the face of a waterfowl, that rightness and dignity seen before the strangeness counted, the even-gazing brown eyes, small and bright, and the wide mouth. As he watched, the face inseparable from its intelligence, he felt it imprinting itself upon his recognition of it, changing its meaning to him in dangerous ways.

"Well, you're here," she said.

So she had decided to talk about what was meant. He said, "Did you think I'd come?" which was evasive.

"I didn't know whether you would or not. I'm not sure what you want."

Silence. Then he said, "I'm not sure either." He thought this was perhaps a lie. "My intentions are honorable," he said as a joke, but she didn't smile.

"I always thought you were an honorable boy."

That was a stunning thing to say, and he considered it. In some strictly relative, more or less tolerantly interpreted way, there was some truth in it, and he was surprised by her authority. Hoping he didn't seem as nervous as he was, he moved on his knees to her, put his arms around her and kissed her. She was passive, quiet and unmoving, her hands still folded in her lap.

"Let's lie down," he said. After a moment of thought she lay down beside him.

In this small old house, everything faded brown from another age, stains on the wallpaper, the room heating up as the sun rose on the other side of its thin walls and roof, no attic over this room that was really a narrow dormer, he smoothed and straightened her pajamas. It was hard to believe that she had obeyed him. He really couldn't see a reason for it. His ordinary hands did not deserve this privilege. He shivered and burned, pleasurably constrained by his clothes. Beneath the thin gauze of her pajamas, the childish cloth, she was like miraculously firm water, smooth and cool no matter how his hands formed it, or it formed the undulations of his hands. He was very careful not to subject her to the possible necessity of having to say no, or to have to indicate no in any way.

They lay together as the room heated, time slowing, their seemingly languorous movements charged almost to pain with touch, repeated over and over, an anticipatory near-pleasure that could last forever. For an instant even their teeth touched, a risky light tick joining them bone to bone. Through the hazy ache of pleasure he observed other of his own symptoms: guilt to play with the nerves of this young girl; what about her feelings? At twenty-one he felt himself to be, with her, a jaded adventurer, oversophisticated, overexperienced. It seemed to him that the world was full of kind, warm girls who would risk everything on a bad gamble. To them it wasn't a game at all, but a future, and yet they gave everything, just so a boy could sample it. Thank God he hadn't been born a girl; his sympathy was real but overborne by his pride in his good luck in being male.

The sun heated the little room until they were slippery with sweat. Her hair lay soaked on her forehead. She said nothing. Her brown eyes were open and serene, as if profoundly studying him.

"Love in a steam bath," he said.

She smiled at that, but said nothing.

"Let's get out of here," he said. "Let's go to the lake. I'm supposed to open up the cabin anyway."

"I've never done this before," she said.

"Never done what?"

"Petted with a boy like this. Robert Beggs kissed me a lot after the junior prom, but that was sitting up in his father's car." She was still thinking about it all, looking at him.

"Do you like it?" he said.

"It goes beyond any kind of sense at all. It doesn't make sense. I don't know enough to know what I feel. I don't know what makes you like it so much. We've been lying here for two hours doing the same things over and over and not getting tired of it."

"It's a mystery," he said.

"It's not just funny," she said.

"No. I didn't mean to be facetious. I'm sorry."

"I don't know whether it's love or not, either. Is it?"

"You ask hard questions," he said.

"I think I've loved you ever since I was eight. I've always thought about you holding me and kissing me. It was always you, too. Never anyone else."

This startled him, and he felt himself turn a little cool. She saw it immediately, of course. His freedom was in danger; it was as if touch were thought itself, and in thought she was the stronger.

"Now I've made you nervous," she said.

"Well, it's a hard thing to accept. What can you say when somebody tells you that?"

"I shouldn't have blabbed it. I should keep my mouth shut."

But it had been said, whatever it meant, and if it meant what he thought it meant he didn't know if he could accept the responsibility. He believed what she'd said but he couldn't see why he deserved it. He remembered, too, that he wasn't really from Leah, but was an alien here —just a stranger passing through.

"What do you have to do at your cabin?" she said, and he saw that she meant to change the subject in order to calm him. His mood shifted mysteriously toward exuberance and he said, "Sweep up the mouse turds and find all the nests they like to make out of toilet paper and leaves, clean the pine needles out of the gutters, see if anything's drowned in the well, get the canoe out and all kinds of stuff like that."

"I could help you. I'm a good housecleaner."

"Bring your bathing suit."

"The water's still too cold, I bet."

"I'll jump in," he said. "I'll be showing off for you and I won't feel a thing." He could handle showing off and making fun of himself. He would jump into the cold lake because the caress of the water would be tender to his hardness. How he would preen and shine and flex his muscles! Even the musty air of the cabin and the greasy feel of damp shingles would be exciting and portentous because she had flattered him and made him nervous.

5

"The trouble with a motorcycle," he yelled over his shoulder, "is that you can't go slow! There's something dumb about a slow motorcycle! You look like a kid on a kiddie cart!"

She thought they must look handsome and brave on the motorcycle. She knew it was dangerous, and his old motorcycle, scraped and bent as it was, must have injured more than one rider, but she was with him and it didn't seem to matter. Like a dog, she thought; they'll go anywhere with you, just so they can go. Dory, beware—have you lost your brains? Why had she told him she loved him? It was as if she trusted him completely.

They climbed the long hills where the old highway followed the side of the Cascom River valley, then swooped down into the rich warm air along plowed fields and young hay, then climbed again past woods up toward the sky. She had never flown in an airplane but it must be like this to rise and descend with only the steady effort of the motor moving you.

The column of his back was hers to hold on to as she wished, with her hands on the muscles above his ribs, with her arms full around him and her breasts against his back, or with her hands at his waist. She was constrained not to hold him as firmly as she might have liked, and she was not sure of the reasons for that constraint. Nice girls didn't do certain things. They were always passive and gentle. She didn't remember having been told this, so she must have gotten it out of the air somehow. And of course he must believe the same thing and wouldn't like her to be too forward in the matter of grabbing him. He'd want her to be a nice, sedate, decorous pet. She wondered. Already she sensed a fairly basic difference between them. He was more self-conscious and less candid than she was. He was a little finicky about things like bathrooms and shutting doors and not farting out loud and all that. He was a little decorous himself. How careful he had been not to touch her in indecorous places; she could map his rules for his lips and his hands.

She was a little guilty about this analysis because it seemed a betrayal of her deepest feelings about John Hearne, that he was strong and wise and kind. Nobody was perfect, but she didn't want to be anywhere but with him, no matter what he did. This was obviously foolish, if not insane. He was surrounded by a goldish yellowy haze, as if a brighter sun shone on him than on everything else. That might be love.

But suppose he despised her and was secretly laughing at her? No, she wasn't that dumb. She did have some power over him. He did think she was a special person. She thought she was a special person too, but she didn't know how he could have found that out, because what evidence of it could he have seen?

They came up over Follansbee Hill and there was Cascom Lake below them, the little town of Cascom at its foot. The long green descent made her think of brakes—he seemed to let the machine go too fast, too long, but then they did slow down and they were on the lake road. After a mile or so they turned, blue glimpses through tall pines, onto a dirt road where they went slowly and twistily over the cracks and bulges caused by winter frost.

The cabin, on a foundation of large boulders, was gray-shingled, wide because of its screened porches, cool and dim under the pines. Over the door was a carved wooden sign:

CASCOMHAVEN
1918

Another dark cabin could be seen down the shore. This was the shaded, western, rocky side of the lake; the few sandy beaches and the public beaches were on the south and east sides. She had never visited this part of the shore with its private cabins set far apart on private land.

Inside, the cabin smelled of damp cloth and mildew. They opened all the shutters, windows and doors. The furniture was plain, old-fashioned, and didn't match. The inside of the cabin was more like the inside of her house than his. Few of the dishes, cups and glasses matched, and she supposed that what ended up here were the survivors of accidents, the old bridge lamps that were slightly bent or out of fashion, the Morris chairs, the rickety metal beds. This would be primitive living for his family, put up with for a weekend for the sake of the cool lake air.

They went beneath the cabin among the boulders and ledge that it was built upon. There, in the cellary twilight, beside the brick base column of the fireplace, he lifted the wooden well cover and they looked down into the silent, imprisoned water, the outlines of their curious heads looking up at them from that cool dungeon. He connected the plumbing, which had been drained for the winter, beginning with the connections to the well and the electric pump with its big flywheel and belt. She handed him wrenches and putty knives of goo for the threads. When the water was on, all traps sealed, they cleaned the kitchen counters and cabinets of mouse droppings, cleaned out a nest the size of a basketball, which she was relieved to find empty of white-footed mice, from below the sink. Another they found in a bureau drawer in one bedroom, and another was floating in the just-filled toilet reservoir.

She swept pine needles from the sills and steps while he crawled along the porch roof and threw them by handfuls out of the gutters. She vacuumed the rugs and floors with the upright Hoover while he let the dock back down into the water upon its chains and pulleys, replaced some shingles on the tool-shed roof and swept the longest porch with a wide push broom. They were busy, efficient at their domestic chores. It was hard work but useful, visible work, the kind she enjoyed, and she was happy.

The canoe was stored on the crossties in the tool shed. He stood on a stepladder and got it started and she guided one end of it as it slid down and became heavier than it looked. She was proud of her strength as they carried it, one on each end, down to the dock, where he examined it carefully, sighting down its keel, then turning it over so he could run his hands lovingly over its varnished ribs and gunwales and green canvas.

"This is a great little boat," he said, "but it suffered while I was away. One winter they just shoved it halfway under the porch. That's where I found it. Can you imagine that?"

"While you were in the Army," she said. Sometimes he seemed more her age, because he looked so young, but then she'd remember that he had been in the Army for more than two years.

"While I was gallantly defending our country they let my beautiful canoe crack and rot. I had to scrape it down to the wood and do it over. The only thing is, it's not my canoe. It is, as the Sylvesters would say, 'the Sylvester canoe,' just as Cascomhaven is 'the Sylvester camp.' "

"Your stepfather's."

"Not just his. His brother's, his sister's, his mother's, his uncle's, and on and on. He just gets to pay the taxes and piss and moan. But that's another story."

They secured the canoe upside down on what he called its summer rack, with a rope over it to keep the wind from taking it.

"There," he said. "We're grimy but we're done. You *are* a good housecleaner, and I thank you. The Sylvesters thank you. I don't know why I'm talking like this. You want to try the water? I'll get some soap."

She got their bathing suits and towels from the motorcycle's saddlebags and went into the cabin to change, wondering if she could make herself go into the cold lake. He was on one knee looking up into the fireplace and working the damper. Soot sifted down on his arm.

"I can see daylight," he said. "Maybe a fire would feel good after, if we're still alive."

She changed in the bathroom. Her bathing cap had turned sticky over the winter and she'd decided not to bother getting another, so she'd have wet hair and look like a fuzzy-wuzzy or a drowned rat—she could take her pick. There was a cracked full-length mirror on the back of the door, so you looked at yourself from the toilet, which was disconcerting at first glance. Her bathing suit was the official light blue one-piece Cascom Manor lifeguard suit with her Red Cross Senior Lifesaver patch sewn on the front. She had a more frivolous two-piece suit with lace around the skirt, but had decided, for reasons she could not logically explain, to take this one. Whatever the reasons, they had to do with impressing John Hearne.

He examined the Red Cross patch. "Save me!" he said. "God, you look good. Do you know that?"

"If you say so, but I'm pale as a fish."

"I mean it. I'm serious," he said.

They went down the steps to the dock. Even though the sun was bright, she was chilly already because it was the first time of the year in a bathing suit and because of the northwest wind that always seemed to sweep down from Cascom Mountain and smear the lake with white-caps. He grinned like an idiot and fell over backwards into the water, screamed as he climbed back out and then soaped himself furiously. "It'll take your breath! It's not fit for human occupancy!" When he was lathered all over, including all over his shorts and his head, he dove in and she dove in beside him. She was numb immediately. The water was like frozen metal and seemed to stick her muscles together. She thought of bare iron in winter that you should never touch with your skin. She got back to the dock, pulled herself out and rolled over onto the boards. He'd beat her out of the water.

"Soap?" he said. "Or would you prefer not to have to get stunned again?"

"No, I'll do it if you get a fire going." The soap was like a piece of stone, but she finally got some lather up and rubbed it over what he'd called "grime." This must be love, she thought, or I wouldn't murder myself like this. This water was not the kind you got used to in any way. She dove in again and made herself rinse by twirling her body violently under the surface before crawling out again. Her joints were slow; her blood seemed to have slowed.

He was standing by the beginning fire in a wool bathrobe, and he had a terry-cloth robe for her. "My step-aunt's, but she'll never know. Take your wet suit off if you want and put it on."

She hesitated, and he said quickly, "I don't want to embarrass you or worry you, you know. Do what you want, Dory. Okay?"

She took off her suit in the bathroom and came back feeling airy and naked under the white terry cloth, her towel in a turban around her head. "Suppose your step-aunt found us here like this," she said. The fire was too young to give much heat yet, but they stood formally in front of it.

"Nobody just drops in here. Let me tell you that the whole Sylvester family suffers from a kind of constipation of the impulses. Visits to this place are governed by a nervous, nauseating protocol in which no surprises are allowed. All schedules are published two weeks in advance."

She couldn't help but admire the clever words, though that tone, in anyone, had never sounded very pleasant to her. The fire grew and the bricks heated—tingly radiant heat against her ankles and calves and the feeling that she had nothing at all on under the skirt of the robe. She sat down carefully on the chintz-covered couch in front of the fire and he sat down on it too, at what he must have thought a proper distance away from her but not all the way at the other end. He was going to touch her and kiss her soon. A kettle whistled from the kitchen and he went to it and came back with two mugs of hot chocolate. "No milk, but it's sweet and hot."

They sipped their hot chocolate and looked at the fire.

He said, "I also found half a bottle of gin someone left here by mistake. I was going to offer you some but my theory is that your lips are more or less innocent of that sort of poison."

"I've had some," she said, defensive about her inexperience.

"Did you like it?"

"It was in grape juice and it was just sort of sweet. It didn't make me drunk or anything. Maybe I felt a little dizzy, but not much. I had some Beverwyck ale after the junior prom last year. It was bitter but I think I could get to like that."

"Come to think of it, it's illegal to ply a maiden of your years with alcohol."

Now he was bragging that he was twenty-one and not a minor. She said, "How does it feel to be twenty-one?"

He saw her point and laughed. She saw admiration in his laugh, and again she felt that melting, that dangerous pride in his admiring her. Surely he was going to touch her and kiss her soon. She wanted to urge him to get on with it, but she had no vocabulary or meaningful gestures that might with proper indirection signal her willingness. Limited willingness, because she didn't want, or was afraid, or thought it might harm her in his regard, to go too far. It was the unthinkable that she was actually thinking about when she thought "too far." But it seemed the more he approved of her, the more hesitant he became, and his energy went all into words. Or else he didn't want to pet her anymore—how could she know anything for certain? The danger was that he was becoming too important. She could feel the others, friends and relations, fading, losing their power.

"You're seventeen?"

"I'll be eighteen in September." That sounded, she thought, a little less reprehensible.

"High school isn't out yet, is it? How come you're not in school?"

She'd been wondering if he would ask this, because there was a warm little prideful thing she had been keeping to herself, waiting for it to be printed in *The Leah Free Press,* or for an opportunity to tell him, to have to tell him, about it. "I've got a pass for today and tomorrow because I'm giving the valedictory."

"Lord," he said, "I've been coming to the conclusion that you're smart, but are you the smartest one in your class?"

"I don't think so. I just did all my homework."

"You would. Yes, I can see that. And you're supposed to be writing your speech? And you've written it already, no doubt."

"Yes."

"What's it about?"

"Oh, honor, loyalty, honesty, kindness—the usual stuff."

"Actually, that doesn't sound too usual. Where's patriotism, for instance? Or good old simpleminded faith?"

"Well, I've sort of based it on Montaigne, and he's not too strong on those."

"I'll be damned. I'd like to read it."

"I'd be embarrassed. It's really the usual kind of thing. I looked over some of the ones they've kept in the office and they all give good advice and good wishes and a fond farewell. You know." Maybe she ought to write it over, differently, with more irony in it. When she wrote it she hadn't thought of him ever reading it. She hadn't thought of him at all, because she wrote it before he slid down the teeter-totter.

"Maybe I'll go to graduation and listen to you give your speech."

"Oh, no! Don't do that! I'd be too nervous!"

"Why should I make you nervous? Who the hell am I to make you nervous?"

She would not answer that; she'd already told him that she loved him.

He leaned over and took her by the shoulders. "Stop being nervous!" he said.

It was all right to wrestle playfully, pretending, even with considerable force, to get revenge upon him for teasing her. The result was of course inevitable and he had her pinned and lay on top of her, or mostly on top of her. She had never felt such kindly weight, or the quality of that weight as it slowly changed, as they stopped wrestling, to a force it was no longer part of a game to resist. She thought of the word "swoon" as she lay still. She thought of the wrong way she had once taken the saying "a needle in a haystack"—not the hopelessness of finding the needle so much as the danger of finding that impaling steel in the yielding hay, where you wouldn't expect it.

Time hazed and she melted into such honey there was a brief thought that the robe or the couch must be dampened by her, but along with the hazing of thought and time in this limbo of balanced forces was another part of her mind that knew just how far he was going. He was about to break his own rules, and as though she were emerging from a thick dream, streaming slow syrupy ropes of pleasure, she said, "Don't."

She would have allowed him to go ahead but he heard her and

stopped. It was like turning off an engine. They both sat up, embarrassed by their clarity of mind. She covered herself.

"Well," he said, "that was close." He covered himself too, but she had seen his penis for a startling moment. It was thick, reddish gold, absolutely vertical and enormous, much longer than she'd had any idea a penis could be. Its very size made her realize how she'd just escaped a kind of cataclysmic change in which she would have been stretched huge as a grown woman.

But he had stopped at one word from her, and she was so grateful she loved him even more, so that she was suddenly shy. She ran to the bathroom to change into her clothes.

6

When he came in his mother was in the kitchen stirring a pitcher of martinis. Her name was Martha and she was forty-two. Her husband, Amos Sylvester, was also forty-two. She was blond, "petite," and people said she was pretty. She wore yellow dresses more often than any other color, and she liked shiny red shoes. She liked perfume too, and you could smell her across the room. Amos Sylvester was a tall, thin man with a totally aberrant potbelly which didn't seem to belong to him, as though he were taking it somewhere to leave it. He was in the living room reading the paper and making loud crackles as he slammed the pages shut and snapped them out flat. Occasionally he spoke to no one, saying, "Assholes," "Shitheads," and the like.

His mother stopped stirring the martinis, a dramatic gesture, and looked at him, her expression an arch command for intimacy, implying palship and collusion. "So you were at the lake," she said.

"That's right," he said.

"You were observed heading in that direction with little Dory Perkins on the back seat of your motorcycle. Hmm." Her eyebrows stayed up.

"That's right," he said. His balls ached and he wanted to get to his room.

"Well, Johnny Hearne, I hope you aren't leaving any 'tracks' behind you. I mean, little Dory Perkins. Really."

"No tracks," he said, and went up the back stairs to his room, where he opened his clothes, lay on his bed with a handful of Kleenex, envisioned the dear sweet presence of Dory, entered his vision by her dark gate and, his hand become her, came. For that nerve-ruptured moment Dory was supreme, but then began a slow diminution.

A childhood warning, or joke, was that semen was gray matter—literally your brains—but it was just the opposite; what flushed out took with it recklessness and left the brain prudent and analytical. There was a sense of loss and at the same time relief at that loss, because it was the loss of madness. He mopped his fluids from his chest: careful maintenance, the odor of boiled egg and vague regret.

He did not know who or what he was except in minor ways, and here was this young girl, a virgin about to begin her adult life, over whom he had been given incomprehensible power. What about the intensity of her emotions? What about her honesty, which could stun him? He liked her, but the sex, the "love"—those things made him insane, and they would again, he knew. Right now Dory Perkins was all complicated by family, by embarrassing, clinging technicalities, by the inhibitions and taboos of childhood and adolescence—such as the very fact that she was a girl. Did he want to have to "own" that funny little face, to walk forever tied to that other? He would lose the freedom which, after the tyrannies of childhood, school and Army, he had hardly yet sampled.

But in a very short number of minutes she would begin again to smooth and glow, to move her perfect body through his demented imagination now reinforced by memory. O golden-meaned radii, ivory fulcra, amber hinges. She was here already.

He was drawn like an addict to the upstairs telephone in his mother and stepfather's bedroom.

Debbie answered. "Perkins's residence."

"I'd like to speak to Dory."

"Whom shall I say is calling please?"

She would say that; rote answers would sound expert to Debbie's class-conscious mind.

"You may tell your sister that it is John Hearne who is calling."

Debbie giggled and faded, calling for Dory. For a moment he worried that Mr. and Mrs. Perkins might think he was too old for Dory, but then, with a slight bit of snob guilt, he admitted to knowing that in their aspirations high school was terminal and the beginning of the breeding period.

"Hello," Dory said in the close, capitulant voice of a lover.

It was five-thirty. If his sociological data were accurate she would be eating supper in half an hour. Come to think of it, neither of them had eaten anything since nine in the morning, when they'd had toast and coffee at her house; they (or he) hadn't even thought of lunch.

"Hi," he said. "Are you tired?"

"Pooped."

He didn't want to see her tonight. He was too shaky, too cool. He wanted to see her tomorrow, not tonight.

"Are you doing anything special tomorrow? If it's a nice day, would you like to go sailing?"

"Yes."

"I'll pick you up at nine. We can bring lunch this time. Make yourself a sandwich."

"I'll make lunch."

"Okay. I'll bring a thermos of iced tea or something. Cold if it's hot, hot if it's cold. I've got this big jug." The thermos was for his trip West, his escape from what he seemed to be getting into.

"Okay."

The silence between them grew from fond-meaningful to oppressive as it lengthened and itself needed some kind of comment, which he couldn't think of. And so he would ignore it, revealing his lack of openness, or his confusion, or his lack of a sense of humor.

"I'll see you tomorrow, then," he said.

"Goodbye."

"Goodbye, Dory."

Farewells on the telephone always had frayed edges.

From downstairs came the louder voices engendered by dry martinis. He'd noticed on the way in that something was in the oven and that the dining-room table hadn't been set, so he changed into clean chinos and went downstairs to set it. When he was here such ordinary rituals were usually left to him to do, unasked, and he did them willingly because the alternative, getting enmeshed in their conversation, was to be avoided as much as possible.

Amos Sylvester was a Dartmouth graduate, a building contractor and one of those tall, handsome men whose faces are so pretty they are not accorded the dignity, or gravity, given to tall, handsome men lucky enough to have at least one or two redeeming blemishes. To make things worse, Amos wore a narrow black mustache along his upper lip, below a carefully shaved, classically fluted slope. The effect of this pencil line was so purely, almost touchingly, cosmetic, with none of the coarse naturalism of hair, as if each morning it had to be painted on like a whore's eyebrow, that it invited a patronizing response. Behind his back he was called, by some, "the Gigolo."

But then, John thought, he had never been very charitable toward Amos, even if Amos did aspire to resemble Warner Baxter, and even if his politics were right-wing prejudice and revenge, and even if his favorite poem, recited at length on any suitable occasion, was an interminable jingle called "Pete, the Piddlin' Pup," and even if he rarely spoke directly to John, but in his presence relayed all communication in the third person through Martha: "Tell him to watch his goddam mouth," and even if once, among many similarly painful episodes, when he found that John, aged sixteen, was earning a dollar an hour after school in a wartime woolen mill, declared him independent and threw all of his possessions out into the snow, and so on.

Since John's return from the Army, however, wearing on his blouse the usual undistinguished but colorful ribbons everyone was issued in the war, Amos's attitude toward him had seemed to change, and now there was an attempted joviality which John found edgy and uncomfortable. When he finished setting the table he went, warily, into the living room.

"So he's steppin' out with the gal next door," Amos said, still having trouble with direct address but signaling broadly with tone and grin that he was being friendly. "Just like in the movies."

"Yup," John said. As a concession to this mood he accepted from his mother a dry martini, a misted, stemmed glass with a Spanish olive sunk in a chilly chemical that seemed to leap directly into his metabolism through his mucous membrane.

"Little Dory Perkins," his mother said. "I find it a rather strange choice." Her expression clearly implied social, intellectual, chronological and aesthetic error. Not much left to poor Dory after that.

"A girl's a girl, Martha. Let our young hero have his fun. Ha, ha!"

"I think he'd better be very, very careful," she said, then laughed before composing her ladylike mouth to drink. When she drank she tipped her head over her glass.

How unfair was he being to these people? These observations, these summary judgments . . . Obviously poor Amos had been unable to cope with the child that had come with his pretty wife, and (here he went again) the pretty wife didn't mind that passionate rivalry. John often thought that he detected in her hysterical crying (such as when drunken Amos consigned him and his to the winter snow) the operatic fervor of a coloratura.

What he knew with certainty was that a wrong word from him could turn the coming meal into a riot.

So why did he come back here at all? Partly, he supposed, it was a sort of loyalty to his mother, who was always begging him to come "home." There were also those of his friends who were still in town, and it was a cheap place to stay for a week or two. Amos wasn't really around very much because he worked long, hard hours in a highly complicated, competitive and sometimes shady business in which the defections or incompetencies of his men or his "subs"—his subcontractors—might ruin him at any time. When he did come home he got semi-plastered and wanted his wife's uncritical attention. It had to be fairly competent, believable uncritical attention, though, and given that in her mind she, not he, was the center of the universe, she wasn't always convincing. Once her collarbone had been broken but that, she had always claimed, had been an accident. There had been other lumps, sprains and contusions, not all of them hers. He remembered their inexplicable pranks, their unstable hilarity, with an ineradicable sense of powerlessness and dread. And yet, Lord, in his short life he had coped with characters much more vicious than Amos Sylvester. As a child, though, the world had sometimes seemed to blow apart in an explosion of gin.

It had been after evenings like that—evenings not made tolerable by visitors, and he wondered how many children in the world prayed for guests at dinner—that he had reconstructed his father and his father's world out of fragments as meager as the shards of skull and thigh that were the clues of paleontologists. All he had were the words of his mother, and did these substantiate ape, mammoth or man? Amos, she told him with pride, had made her destroy all his father's photographs and letters and hadn't let her write to him. Then maybe his father didn't know where he was—a tempting thought, but improbable. And where was his father? Somewhere in southern California, when last heard from. "But where? What place?" "Johnny, that was years and years ago, and your father was always quitting his job and moving on. I can't remember the name of the town because it was just one of so many."

She would say, "He was such a marvelous dancer." Or "I was always such a little fool about a handsome man." Or "You took after me—short and blond. I mean, you're not short, but not really tall like your father." She said, "But then Amos came along. We met him at the builders' convention at the St. Francis Hotel in Minneapolis, and he just swept me off my feet. Your father was 'fooling around' with this girl,

Estelle Lundgren, and I knew it, so I was vulnerable. And Amos—he was so *satisfying.*" This information came when he was fourteen. What he got from her was always disheartening and untrustworthy, so he stopped asking.

His re-creations of his father's world were different, and each different from the last. The one consistent theme was a legitimate reason why his father could not get in touch with him personally. This didn't mean that his father's faithful servants, or his agents, or even sometimes his bosses, didn't keep a careful eye on John Hearne, Sylvan Hearne's son. Oh, he was being observed and judged; regular reports were being sent back to headquarters concerning his health, his intelligence, his proficiency at sports, his honesty and his honor. When the time came, all would be revealed. A faint aura of this theme still, occasionally, prevailed.

Amos had asked him a direct question, and he called it up from a more recent store of memory until it became clear: "Isn't the lass kind of young—what we used to call 'Concord quail?' " Concord meant the state prison.

"She's seventeen," he admitted.

"Then even if she's willing, it's close to statutory rape, and you'd better not forget it."

Amos's voice now had a derisive edge—challenge and a promise of nastiness. The question was, why would Amos want to do that? He always did it, and with everyone. People would always look at him askance, a quick look consigning him to a doubtful category. Think of that self-imposed exile from ordinary give-and-take.

In the kitchen the oven timer buzzed mutedly, as if to itself, and John was saved from having to make the demanded response. Dinner was a tuna-fish casserole, a money-saving dish Amos approved of. The subject matter at the table was, to John's relief, a supplier of Celotex who was a crook, the Democrats, the Cascom River Savings Bank, Jews (in passing, and more adjectival than substantive), lawyers, the federal withholding tax—all the programs and minions of the legions of bloodsucking unproductive sloth.

By nodding dishonestly from time to time John managed to stay neutral. In this company his responses had to be insincere, and Amos knew it; Amos had to know it. Did it please him to know it? In Amos's vision all of life was reduced to its fraudulent underside, its creepy adversiveness, its nasty motives. And of course there was enough truth there to work on, but why make a lifetime out of the seamy? It was a mystery.

For dessert they had plain raspberry Jell-O, one of Amos's favorites.

Perhaps it was the transparency that appealed—the mildest of pleasures to the tongue, but one perfectly expected and consistent texture, no surprises. Amos hated the profession at which he was successful. Sometimes he would come home and tearfully blubber about its injustices, even letting go so far as to shit his pants for his wife to clean up. On those occasions Amos's sibling had always made himself scarce indeed, but as he grew older and larger he often thought that if he and Amos had been actual brothers instead of the tangled thing they were, he might have gotten to know the man, or even have helped him. If only he had the right to tell him compassionately that he was being a stupid, flaming asshole, that might have been a start. But no one ever did that to Amos, and Amos wandered, forever unhappy, in a limbo of avoidance and hyperbole.

Ah, but in a week or so, or even sooner, as soon as his check arrived from the Veterans Administration, John would be free to leave here and to cross his country, a vast continental breadth he had seen only in part and intermittently from the windows of troop trains. This time its possibilities lay before him pure as a blank white page.

7

That night she held her pillow on top of her, slowly opened her legs and for a long time thought of the way she'd said, "Don't"—how she'd said it. Was it a flat statement? A request? A pleading request? And what did it mean to him? What if she'd never said it at all? For a moment she was breathless.

Her pillow had no weight; compared to his warm, gentle force that was to be gently met, her pillow was just dry bulk. He wasn't there.

In Leah, John Hearnes didn't marry Doris Perkinses. If she'd been popular and beautiful it might have been possible, but she was not one of those golden people who formed their own class, whose families could be rich or poor. Even then, that sort of marriage was considered strange and risky. John Hearne might be sort of a loner and not really a Sylvester, but the clothes he wore, or the way he wore them, the words he used, the way he walked, all kinds of things about him showed him to be of that class. He was in college, and would never stay in Leah, as she would. She had taken a lot of the college-bound courses, but mostly secretarial and home ec, bookkeeping and things like that. That she might somehow go to college had never been discussed at her house. No one in her family had ever gone to college. No one had ever considered the expense of college; it simply wasn't in her family's budget at all. That she was valedictorian hadn't changed anything. Valedictorians were just about always girls, usually girls who had taken easy courses, no languages, no math past algebra and plane geometry.

No, she would stay in Leah and work like her mother, keeping the books at the Public Service Company—something like that. And when, every few years, John Hearne came home from far, glamorous places to visit, she'd be here. She'd be his "old friend," whom he'd call up, take out to dinner and then for drinks at a dim hotel lounge in Northlee or Wentworth Junction and then . . . His sad, loving, forever hopelessly faithful woman. Except he'd be married and his wife would be with him and even that melancholy romance wouldn't happen.

He'd been surprised that she hadn't thought of going to college. That afternoon when they'd put their clothes back on they went down and sat on the dock in the sun for a while, until the shadows of the pines came over them. "Oh, you've got to go to college," he'd said, as if it were as easy as that. He'd always known, all through grammar and high school, that he'd go to college. It was normal to go to college. She'd told him that for anyone in her family it was just the opposite. "But you're bright. You're valedictorian, for Christ's sake! I know your parents don't think you have to go, but you ought to. Come to UNH and we'll do our homework together."

"Where would I get the money? I'd have to take another year of high school just to get in the requirements, and who'd pay for that?"

"You'd have a job part time," he said, but what he couldn't understand was that it was more than just the money, it was something like vertigo that the suggestion caused in her. It was out of the question, impossible. He became angry at her adamancy. "If you could afford it, would you go?" She shrugged. He shook his head, exasperated. She could understand his feelings, but he couldn't understand hers.

"Why is it so important to you?" she asked, and at that he seemed to grow shy, or secretive. She saw him choose not to give the true answer. "It's just a waste of intelligence," he said.

"I'm not so intelligent," she said, but she thought she knew the answer he hadn't given—that she had to go to college in order to be of his class, to be worthy of him. This was, if true, something of an insult and also a thrill, because it meant she might then qualify as a possible mate, with permanent status.

They couldn't discuss that. She put it out of her mind, calling it fantasy, dream stuff, foolishness. But if she was so practical, why was she going out with him at all? She wouldn't have said no to their going sailing tomorrow in a million years. Practicality or prudence had nothing to do with it; she wanted to. Maybe it was spring that addled her. She could smell the green, the moist humus of the garden, cool moonlight and new leaves.

High school was nearly over. There would be the prom, her date who else but Robert Beggs, class day at South Beach, baccalaureate, graduation and her valedictory, which seemed more and more just simple and marginally acceptable. As the end of high school approached it was as though it was all over already and "life" was about to start; she knew life's form and its schedules. A nine-to-five job someplace, marriage to some boy like Robert Beggs. She would find out the things she didn't know, like what it was to give birth and suckle a child. Her mother had grown old at what would happen to her—some good times and some joys but mostly work, and at home dishes, pots and pans, brooms, clotheslines, stacks of folded cloth, everything done and then undone, and done again, until you grew older and leathery and lined. Some grew fat, the flesh hanging down into hummocks around the shoulders, hips and knees. Some grew thin in the arms like her mother, the laboring muscles jumping out like ropes. You hoped your husband wouldn't be a drunk, you grew old and held your grandchildren and eventually you died of cancer and were buried in Homeland Cemetery.

Tomorrow—this whole episode with John Hearne—was time out and didn't count. Nothing would ever come of it. She would look at it that way.

And yet she was special. No one was as conscientious as she was. Show her what had to be done and she did it. No loafing, no halfway measures. She did it and did it right, and if it wasn't right the first time she started all over and did it right the second time.

That small note of pride lent her the calm to sleep.

She woke at first light remembering a dream more vivid than her window. She was at the railroad station in Wentworth Junction, standing on the platform next to a train full of Canadian soldiers, all of them blond, husky, smiling at her from the open windows and the vestibules between the cars. Their rifles all had canvas covers over the bolts and triggers (that must be a real memory), and over the public-address system came a deep, religious sort of voice, saying, "These are the lads who, combat-slain, shall never see their farms again." They didn't seem to hear the voice, but smiled on, all of them young and happy-looking. As the train pulled out they all waved at her. It was so sad and lovely she was crying. Her face was actually wet. She must tell John Hearne that dream, if she could do it without her eyes flooding.

After breakfast, her family gone, she made sandwiches of leftover pot roast, with mustard and horseradish, which she hoped he liked but he could always scrape off if he didn't. She boiled two eggs, chose from the cold-cellar two wintered-over apples that were in pretty good shape and two large dill pickles. He would be sustained by this food that came from her hands.

He came at nine and they rode, the hills rising and falling, to the now-familiar dark cabin. She worried a little about sailing in the small canoe, but at least the wind was light and the air was warm. She helped him carry the sailing rig down to the dock—sail, spars, sideboards, rudder and tiller. She knew something about this from Cascom Manor. The summer before last she'd learned to sail, and last summer she taught the city people how to sail, as she would this summer, besides being waitress, swimming instructor, chauffeur and nearly everything else. The two Cascom Manor sailboats were heavy, broad-beamed, no-class boats, but with quite a bit of sail, and turnbuckles on the shrouds you had to loosen and tighten whenever you came about. The canoe was simpler but its hull was so sleek and tippy she was glad the wind was light.

"This isn't what you'd call a scientific rig," he said. "I made it from a picture in a magazine before I knew what I was doing." Setting it up entailed lots of lashing and staying because, he said, he didn't want to make too many bolt holes or leave hardware on the canoe. The wooden sideboards, with their own wooden thwart, clamped on the gunwales; the rudder bracket was a V-shaped yoke that clamped on the stern, and the sail had sleeves that slid over the mast and boom. Once it was all set up, the little canoe danced and shivered at its mooring like a horse.

"Why don't you take her out," he said. "She runs downwind like a champ. Close to the wind she's not so good, but I've always made it back."

Because of the prevailing wind it would be easy to leave here and hard to get back—just the opposite of Cascom Manor, where you had to beat up against the west wind but could come running back with jib and mainsail spread. When they'd stowed everything aboard, he thought for a moment. "We can have lunch on Pine Island. How's that? I mean if the wind allows us to." Over their swimming suits they wore bulky old cork-filled life jackets that looked as though they'd survived the *Titanic.* "If the water was warmer I wouldn't take these," he said apologetically.

He got in the bow, facing her with his back against the mast, she carefully took her place at tiller and sheet and he cast off. They slowly gained sternway, she let the rudder bring them around, the sail filled to port and they moved smoothly across the blue lake.

"It might be better to go to the left of all the islands," he said. "The wind usually veers to northwest. You must know that, though."

"I'll have to jibe, then."

"You're the captain." He watched her, which made her conscious of how she placed her pale winter legs and how smoothly she ran tiller and sheet.

"Prepare to jibe," she said. He smiled and ducked his head, the sail came over and they pointed more to the northeast, neatly cleaving the small waves. The sun was warm and the water cold. Where they glided, suspended at that meeting of forces, all was crisp and precise. They moved without effort, expending nothing, hardly even thought, except for the minuscule commands of the spine in which they were one with the delicately balanced keel and with each other.

They were alone on the lake. Time passed. Only the small green boat with the white sail ran before the light wind. To the northwest, Cascom Mountain rose out of the long green hills and showed its patchy bald granite top, the fire tower a dot against the sky. As they came around Merrihew Island she knew they would enter its lee and the wind would become patchy and uncertain. That tingle of danger and responsibility made her skin taut and shivery, though she wasn't cold. He watched the passing land, the mountain, the sky, her. Had the sun already tanned his amiable smooth skin? She looked down at her pale legs. He looked at her legs and she saw in his expression what she wanted. She hoped they pleased him; her vanity was their shapeliness and she thought how homely women were always proud of at least some of their parts, as if parts could be detached and put on display.

The land moved past and they slowed in the quieter air. It would take them a long time in the sun to reach the broad lake's wind again. He said nothing, showing his trust in her skill and feel for the boat. He smiled because she had looked at him for so long a time, and as she looked away she remembered her dream about the Canadian soldiers.

The closed and boarded cabins on Merrihew Island crouched among their trees as if blindfolded, waiting for their people and boats, outboard motors, docks, rafts and the screams of summer.

Why Canadians? Always the north was purer, simpler, harder—or at least thought it was. She wondered if she believed that. The local people around the lake, who depended upon tourists from Massachusetts, Connecticut and New York, looked upon their guests with some disdain because they were summer people, a little flabby, careless with their money, and from the south. In a week she would be helping the crew prepare Cascom Manor for their arrival.

But those smiling soldiers—did they know they had been slain? There was something sad about their friendliness. They lacked force, or danger. There were no leers or shouts.

They could see Pine Island now. It was very small, uninhabited, less than an acre, but the pines that grew on it were as tall as the masts and spars of a sailing ship. To reach it they would have to cross the wind from the broad lake and she would have to sail on a beam reach. Now the wind was tricky, from no certain direction, coming in puffs. She saw whitecaps ahead, and nearer a smear of gusts darkened the water to blue-black. She nearly jibed as a gust overtook them, but then the sail snapped taut and they leaned, the wind showing its power. She was excited, in a kind of mild and distant dread, prepared to let the sheet out all the way, or to come into the wind—if the canoe would come into the wind. She sensed a tendency in it not to want to.

"The wind's come up a bit," he said.

"It's making me nervous," she said.

"Can you handle it?"

She didn't really want to handle it, but she said, "I'll give it a try."

"Just think of eating a wet sandwich." He laughed, but she could tell that he was nervous too.

As they came into the wind they heeled over a little too far, but she found that she could handle it, and then got used to it, gust by gust, until it was almost a pleasure to cut the waves and troughs, to steady the boat in three unpredictable dimensions at once, with lashings of fine spray that made them wince, but not from fear. Then, after that violent motion, they came into the lee of Pine Island and coasted in to its shore where roots held the bank together. Remembering the rough crossing was more pleasurable than the crossing itself had been.

He tied up on a thick root that made a ring, as if it had grown out of the brown bank, found nothing out there and grown back in. It was fairly calm here, but they could hear waves hitting the other side of the island, and high above them the wind hissed in the pines. "It'll go down in a while, I hope," he said. "Right now we'd have a couple of long, very wet tacks. But anyway, we're here."

They took off their life jackets and toweled off the spray, her hair in strings. They spread their towels on the pine needles in a patch of sunlight. The wind had shifted and came more from the northwest, stronger and colder. He opened the hamper and the always surprising formality of a picnic began. She approved of the sweet, hot tea he'd brought in his thermos and he approved of her sandwiches, but the wind was a shouldery presence they couldn't ignore. It came pushing and shoving out of a clear blue sky, invisible and senseless. The crash of waves on the other side of the island was so clear she thought she could feel the spray, yet that was invisible too and it was probably her imagination that caused those pinpricks on her shoulders. She felt bullied by that unending force. A small branch of green needles came whirling down from above and they looked up apprehensively at the twisting trunks of the pines.

"At least the island's not going to capsize. I think," he said. He suggested that they might as well enjoy their last meal. "It's been nice knowing you, kid."

"I am worried, really," she said. "How will we get back?"

"The wind's got to go down sooner or later."

"But how much later?"

"In a few days. Who knows?"

She thought of people worried, searching for them, and this was suddenly terrifying. "It's not that funny." Her anger surprised her. It was unjust and they were in no real danger, but she was cold and anxious and she resented his joking about it.

"Hey, Dory," he said placatingly. "It'll be okay." He put his arm around her.

"Don't patronize me," she said, jerking her shoulder. She had never used the word before and she wasn't sure of its pronunciation, which irritated her even more. He took his arm away.

She wasn't sure why she had shown him anger, but it felt justified. After a time of listening to the wind he said, "Our first fight." The way he said it made her have to smile, but she resented smiling. Inside her was a small but exceedingly hard little nut of resentment that had to do with him and his humor and college and his beloved canoe.

They sat side by side, chilly and miserable. Finally he said, "Let's try it back, Dory. It's the wind that's making us cross."

Us, she thought. Huh! But he packed everything up and she went with him to the canoe.

"I think the wind's going down a little," he said, but she couldn't see any difference. The pines tossed overhead and the lake was full of whitecaps. He handed her the wooden scoop that was the bailer and she took it. They wore their damp towels around their shoulders under their life jackets, and had a last cup of tea before he tied everything down.

"I'm scared and I don't care who knows it," she said. "Maybe we ought to wait."

"It's no fun here because we're worried. Hell, let's go. We can make it all right."

"Maybe we should go to the east shore, then."

"To tell you the truth, I'd rather keep into a wind like this. The waves get bothersome when they follow."

She was so anxious she was almost sick. She resented her willingness to get into the canoe. Why should she trust him? Why should she do everything he said? Another voice told her that she was insanely magnifying the danger, that the water wasn't really that cold, that they wouldn't capsize and even if they did they wouldn't sink and they could right the canoe and bail it out enough at least to drift ashore someplace. That voice made her get into the canoe, while the other shrieked in resentment and despair.

When they were out in the full force of the wind she saw that they would make it; it would be cold and wet and she would have to bail constantly, but they would make it. The waves didn't get any smaller but the slap and thump of the hull, the vibrations and reverberations, the tilting and planing, all grew repetitious rather than startling. Before they were halfway back she was ashamed of her fear. It was a cold and exhausting voyage, even worse on the starboard tack, but when they came, finally, under the pines to Cascomhaven's dock, the memory was exhilarating. Being safe again was worth more than the memory of fear.

"I'll decommission the boat later," he said. "Let's get dry and warm first."

Again she stood warm and airy in front of the fire in the terry-cloth robe of his step-aunt. She said, "I'm sorry about being in such a snit out there. I was scared. I don't usually act like that. I don't know what got into me."

"I was scared too, but of course I couldn't admit it in front of you."

She sat on the couch. "It feels good not to be drowned."

"It feels great," he said.

"It was tiring. All that . . . fright."

He sat beside her and put his arm around her, tentatively, making a joke out of her anger, but now she couldn't remember why she'd been angry. The passage across the lake to the wildly shaking trees, the flash of whitecaps, the water's heaving solidity and their lightness upon it were all that remained. She turned toward and into him. His green eyes seemed mineral. Hers closed, as if to say to her in the dusk behind their lids that it was none of their affair. He could do whatever he wanted because she trusted him and she was only half of what they were becoming. They were both melting, a disembodiment they both acquiesced to. It wasn't necessary to be responsible for a happening so vague and cobwebby, so diffuse and incomplete. Warnings had no force against this new wholeness, though they could be heard faintly, unconvincingly, shouting contempt. She might say, "Don't," again but she didn't want to. Existence was to accept what would happen without niggling reservations. But other voices frantically warned her that she could be used and discarded. There were all the stories of poor stupid girls who had been seduced and betrayed, lied to, smirked at, hushed up, and it was no different with her because all of those girls had trusted their seducers.

But she couldn't find a way now to care enough about all that because she was alive only within his interest and insistence. Their only attention was toward the one creature they were becoming. There was no idea of time, only an intensity that was forbidden yet soft, languorous and yet stretched. It was like stretching in the morning. After what had seemed a long time but may not have been, she did know, sharply, when the actual thing began. The strength and motion he used to pierce her was new and seemed involuntary. She really didn't care. It was like a pulled-at hangnail for a moment, a non-pain but as powerful and debilitating as pain because it was out of control, a surge and a contraction that brought her center all together upon him as if she were one fleshy vice. So this was what it was, this dreadful shuddery pleasure. If only she could deserve to have it feel so good. If only it could be forever, her power to contain him like this.

8

He sat on the couch with the brass-handled poker in his hands, more or less staring at the fire. He was depressed, dully and deeply heavy in the mind. They had dressed and Dory was down on the dock, sitting there looking out at the windy lake. He felt that he should comfort her or something but she didn't want him to. She was stuck down there and he was stuck up here being thumped over the head by hideously unworthy practicalities, each pulse a surge of shame and anxiety. Choices were so interesting before you acted upon them, and so awful afterwards. For instance, he had two condoms in his wallet; the Army had handed them out in connected segments, like tapeworms, and he still owned a string of them over a yard long. The idea of using one with Dory must have seemed, at the time, unworthy of their passion. That and something more stupid: he had wanted no film of rubber between them. That and something reprehensible: she might have had time to think of what she was getting into. And now she was confused, pensive, facing up to what must be to her such an important and dramatic change. Her delicate mortal balance must be in danger. That she might get pregnant—all that tawdry folk history suddenly possible to her. To her! But it was not just that. Three days ago he had looked out of his window and noticed a young girl spading her mother's garden and now that young girl was no longer a virgin and maybe in the irreversible process of becoming pregnant. It might be an old story but he was in this one and she was not like any other girl. This time he could not slide away from what he'd done.

He put the handle of the poker to his nose. Brass had an interesting odor, something like sweat, maybe the sweat of an old soldier, everything sour except his polished frogs and buttons. No, he couldn't get away from what he'd done. He'd been the person who did it, but he couldn't now understand the person who did it. Who was he, so incomplete he was still afraid of the dark, of the monsters his mind placed there, to initiate all this? Sex, flesh at its work, was generally forbidden except under circumstances he didn't yet want to be under. He remembered that the nerves at his skin had screamed for it, faintly but urgently, like a battle heard at a distance. In his life it had been the subject of willful, even gleeful misinformation, jokes told with a smirk that had seduced him to laughter, stern, perverted films in the Army of pus-globbed crotches and lesions of the throat. Love hovered elsewhere, whatever love was. And yet life's deepest command, in slime mold and in man, was to perpetuate itself, an order that couldn't be countermanded by anything as flimsy as foresight. Thus, perhaps, all the chaos and hysteria. Yahweh's name must not be spoken.

A child might ask why love and sex should ever be combined. He could have a certain amount of disdain for the chaos and hysteria, but he could have none for her, or for her feelings. He went out on the porch and looked down at her. She sat on the end of the dock, her back toward the land. Her head, her neck, her shoulders, her printed blouse, her dungarees, her gentle increase, waist to hip—the reality of her was beautiful and horrible. She was the treasure in a dark tale where a last wish must undo the first. Her thoughtful silence was also pitiful, and he had to find out how she felt. She could be crying, or angry—God knew what. He had to know, so he went down to her, but as cautiously as if she were a mine.

He came up behind her and said, "Are you all right?"

He thought she wasn't going to answer, but finally, still watching the lake, she said, "I don't know. I'm just thinking about it."

"Thinking what?"

"When I went to the bathroom to get dressed this stuff that came from you was running down my leg."

He winced, a shiver of avoidance, his former madness in his vision—strings of milk on the pale plane of her thigh. "Oh," he said.

"You asked," she said. "And I was thinking I don't want to go to baccalaureate or the prom with Robert Beggs or give my stupid valedictory address."

"You probably will, though. Won't you?"

"Probably."

"I'm sorry," he said.

"It's not your fault. I let you."

From behind her he looked down at her head, at those strands of straight, combed-out brown hair she thought drab. Her skull was round and small, held up by a narrow white column of bone and muscle, vein, gland, tendon, nerve—everything common and complex. It was this female organism, so ordinary and real and so full of instinct and worry about its existence, that he had invaded. Vaginal, uterine, ovarian—voodoo to a believer, words of almost repellent power. It seemed long ago that she was only a friend, and now she sat here in her dark mood thinking as a fuse might tick.

"It was both our faults, then," he said carefully. "I don't think I would have stopped even if you'd asked me to."

"I didn't want you to stop."

"It's dangerous, though. I didn't use anything."

"Did you have something to use?"

"Yes."

"But you didn't use it, so I'll get pregnant?"

"It's possible, but I think the odds are against it."

"Oh."

"You didn't know that?"

"I guess so. I just don't know very much about it."

That she'd let herself get into such a position, with so little knowledge, amazed him. Women amazed him—a whole half of the race so responsible in some ways and so mortally reckless in others. He put his hands on her head and face. Her jaws seemed tender as birds' bones. He felt the skeleton of her face, teeth beneath lips beneath his fingers, cheekbones, soft eye hollows. She turned her head as if to look up at him and he put his hands beneath her arms and lifted her up, his arms around her from behind so that they both looked out over the lake. She was exactly right for him, such a neat package, a charm, perfection.

"I know you'll never marry me," she said.

"Don't say that. I don't know that."

"Don't worry about it," she said.

They went up to the cabin, thinking that they were going to gather up their things and go home, but they stood watching the embering fire for a while as if each were trying to think of some summary thing to say, and their silence became mysterious and full of weight, more important than anything they could think of to say.

"Well," he said. "Well . . ." and kissed her lips. She was so passive he knew he could do whatever he wanted with her. This increased his dread of the future, but not enough. He began to take off her clothes and she, more efficiently, finished doing it. She said nothing, so he said nothing, just took his own clothes off, wondering if his erection, that gross opinion he couldn't hide, might be bad for her to see. He was embarrassed for it, wanting the moment to be more meaningful. Her body was very simple when it was naked, like a girl sculpted in white marble, from another century. Her narrow dark eyes looked at him. "I love you," she said. Her words were like manacles clicking onto his wrists and ankles.

He was going to do it again without using anything—a madman—but she reminded him, then watched, an interested witness to his "precaution," saying in the most reasonable and companionable voice that she'd heard them referred to as "safes." This let him pose as a man of experience, but also released in him, suddenly, a comradely tenderness that surprised him; he'd thought he was too horny and impatient to be tender—if tenderness was the glow of value and vulnerability that surrounded her. This didn't keep him from doing all he could to truly seduce her. He must make her so passionately ecstatic with him that she couldn't live without him; that was the object of his careful performance, his gentle restraint, his gigolo self-consciousness. But the more his seduction of her seemed too deliberate to him, the more she cried her love for him, and their separation was all on his side, a despicable triumph. Then he was surprised by what seemed to be a wind blowing through his nerves, and he was blown away, "dismasted," he thought, by the coming together of every quality of her that he used.

They were very cool and grave as they closed up the cabin and dismantled the sailing rig from the canoe. She was again thinking private thoughts, and he was shivery and apprehensive under the loom of the future. He kept thinking of her delicate little white panties, which she had no doubt bought in Trotevale's department store with her own earned money. Today she had taken them off for him, and they were part of his life now, girlish and slippery and secret.

That evening he called her, but the Perkins's telephone was in the dining room, where everybody could hear whatever she said, so she couldn't say much.

"How are you?" he said. He had to know if she was worried or confused.

"All right."

"Can I see you tomorrow?"

"I've got to be in school."

"After supper?"

"All right."

The next day his check for $110 came from the Veterans Administration. He took it to the Leah Savings Bank, bought ten ten-dollar American Express traveler's checks, then stopped at the bookstore and bought a Webster's Collegiate Dictionary, Fifth Edition. At home he wrote on the flyleaf, "For Dory on her Commencement. All the best, John." He thought long about writing, "Love, John," but finally came to the conclusion that "Love" wasn't quite right for a dictionary, love being the slipperiest word in the language. "Tender and passionate affection for one of the opposite sex" didn't quite make it. Then he looked up the word "patronize," and in the margin next to it wrote, "Even if it is pronounced ā as in āle, I apologize, J." He wasn't exactly satisfied with his wit, or with his gift, and didn't have any idea how she'd react. In a way this gift was like a threat: Dory, improve thyself. Something like that: the imperative of his princely vanity.

He picked her up after supper and they rode to the cabin. She seemed a little devil-may-care, as if she were a tragic heroine, and wanted to try the gin, which they did, straight over ice cubes because there was nothing to mix it with. It was hard to swallow that way but they each managed a couple of jiggers and felt it, watching the back of the sunset over the lake. She got a sort of twisted smile on her face and began to wrestle with him. She was very strong, for a girl, until she grew still, the wrestling having lost its increment of aggression. Then they "made love"—his quotes—and came back to Leah after dark, following the wavering yellow cone of his headlight. "Faster, faster!" she called into his ear. In front of her house he turned off his lights and engine and said, "I've got a graduation present for you."

She was still being the reckless lost woman, but even so she surprised him when she said, "Maybe you've already given me one."

He laughed, because it was the response her tone required, but he had a grave chill, a sympathy pain in the skin of his crotch.

He got the dictionary out of his saddlebag and she accepted it for what it was, all of what it was, and thanked him.

"You said you only had a pocket-sized one," he said.

"I appreciate it. I do," she said. She kissed him on the lips and went into her house.

She went to the prom and to baccalaureate, but skipped class day and spent it with him at Cascomhaven. When he was not with her he had twinges of yearning for the open road, single adventure, quest, space, *Zugunruhe,* but decided to stay until she had to go to work at Cascom Manor. Every day they went to Cascomhaven, wet through on one day it rained, and they had to dry their clothes on a clotheshorse in front of the fire. It seemed to him they'd been together for a whole season, as if he were living in a humid swamp of debilitating lust, in which time was inoperative and he was in thrall to a hydraulic sweetness whose power waxed and waned, then surged again with just as much power as before. Friends of his had come back to town but he never saw them, only her. He'd given up any other activity normal to a man and spent all his hours, it seemed, in the arms of this moist, naked girl who gave him everything. That he could put a name to the power invested in him didn't make it less mysterious. The word itself was mysterious. "I love you," she said, but never asked for the word in return.

She was often so quiet he hesitated to talk to her at all, as if by her silence she meant that now she was his, why should he bother to talk?

Once, after she moaned in what he thought was rapture, she grew still and her face was suddenly wet. Her lips turned sticky, as if they were dissolving. "Are you crying?" he asked, but she wouldn't answer. "Talk to me," he said. "Come on, Dory. Say something."

"There's nothing to say." The constricted words were those of a child in the paralysis of injustice or self-pity, and he remembered that ache in the throat very well.

"There must be something. You're crying."

"Why shouldn't I?"

He looked down at her child-face, her dark eyes, her lips now unhappy, and suffered a great hollow fear of loss. "I'll come back and marry you," he said, "and we'll live happily ever after."

"Why say that? You don't have to say anything."

"I do what I say."

"No, you won't. So stop being flippant. I love you and I'll do anything you want, so you don't have to lie."

Another time, in another mood, he asked her about the prom and Robert Beggs, implying light scorn and no jealousy toward that callow youth, that petit bourgeois whose father owned a grocery store. How could a high-schooler, a non-veteran, compete with the likes of John Hearne?

Actually he had acted like a spy and watched from among the sumacs and steeplejack on the riverbank across the street from her house. Curious, he'd told himself, to see this high school swain, cellophane-boxed gardenia corsage in hand, call for his date for the junior prom. Sweet virginal date that he, *he,* John Hearne (pulling on his villainous black waxed mustache wings, *Ha, ha!)* had seduced and deflowered. But when the prom couple appeared at her door and made their way to Robert's father's Plymouth, he could see only her, in a light blue formal dress of silk and gauze that looked insubstantial and, in a little-girl-dressing-up way, ill-fitting and tacky. Her mouth was too wide and natural to have been covered with stark red paint, her dark eyes too close together for cosmetic indignities that didn't work anyway. He wanted to take her away and remove all that stuff. He was embarrassed for her, protective, weak with pity.

"Robert's a nice boy," she said. "He gave me a charm bracelet. He wants me to marry him."

He thought they had a kindred scorn for Robert Beggs. "And I gave you a book full of mere words. Are you?"

"Am I what?"

"Going to marry him?"

She hit him hard on the cheek with her fist. He had to hold her still for a long time before he could trust her not to try it again. It was possible for him to understand that his question, seen in a different way than he'd meant it, without the collusion it had implied between the two of them against Robert Beggs, was insensitive and even cruel. But she would laugh at such things, sometimes. He could make her laugh out loud, even when she was in a mood like this, but she would hold her resentment, and even after laughing would still be angry. He couldn't understand how she did this. She would seem to be with him in jape and irony but her anger was still there, like fire underground. Then it would be gone altogether, and he was never sure when or why.

They went sailing once more, on a day when the wind, instead of increasing, died away in the late afternoon, leaving them becalmed on a wide reach of the lake. The light was odd, the sky filmed over with clouds that looked like fish scales, and they rode an invisible surface. When they looked down into it they saw a colorless progression into dark. He let the sail go and paddled leisurely toward the cabin, a mile away.

She told him the dream she'd had about Canadian soldiers, and his reaction to it was as irrational as a dream itself. He saw how she had been moved by the sadness of their journey into limbo, never to see their farms again, but he didn't like the dream and felt that she was in danger. He was also, irrationally, pricked by jealousy. There were too many of those young soldiers; their power of emotion over Dory was too great. He didn't trust them as she did.

"I don't like it," he said, and she was surprised.

"Why not?"

"I don't trust them."

"But they were all dead!"

"I guess I don't like your feeling so sorry for them."

She seemed about to smile, but didn't quite. "I remember when you left for the Army. I was afraid for you."

"You must have been thirteen."

"I told you I fell in love with you when I was eight or nine, so I'd been in love with you for maybe five years by then. I had my first period when you were home on furlough and I thought I was sort of catching up with you."

"You caught up, all right."

"I never thought much about being a virgin, but now it feels strange not to be."

"Do you feel any different, really?"

"I feel more real, like before I was mostly all one piece inside. Sort of rudimentary."

He thought he might be getting used to her candidness, as if she were giving him an education in the facts of life, or at least showing him how to accept them as matter-of-fact. Her curiosity had seemed a little unnatural at first. She touched and examined him, and herself, open-eyed, without any shame or shyness, expressing only wonder that it all "felt so good."

But beneath all of their talk, often muting their voices, were the ominous processes that might be happening in her body. Dory, as if she'd read his thoughts, put her hands under her bathing suit on her breasts.

"Do they feel sensitive?" he asked. They had discussed this before, in restricted voices, as if in the presence of a beast they might wake.

"It's because you're looking at me, I think," she said.

When they'd spoken of the possibility she'd said calmly, with a certainty, or maturity, more real than he thought his life to have as yet, that if she had a child, she'd have a child. What about abortion, or adoption, he'd asked, those solutions being modern and rational and acceptable to him. Abortion was illegal, she'd answered, the property of criminals and fly-by-nights, septic and dangerous. And to give a child away would be a betrayal; no person was interchangeable with another. He could say what he liked, but he knew by now that words could not change her. Her attitude seemed insane, and perhaps all he had was words.

But then she would grow quiet and sad in a way that hurt him because he imagined her to be in despair. She "loved" him, a power always accepted, after some initial wonderment, as a right.

This day they came silently gliding back to Cascomhaven, took a chilly swim and were again naked in front of a growing fire when he was overcome by the problem of her and turned a little brutal, strange to himself. He had her get down on her hands and knees and without a word, as if she deserved to have no opinions or feelings, took her from the rear—*inu-rashii,* or dog fashion, the Japanese called it. He observed the rise in her flesh caused by his entering her, her tea-colored anus, her position on knees and elbows perfectly subservient. If you can't understand it, he thought, gloating, fuck it. He came and was immediately dissatisfied, his orgasm tainted by selfishness and cruelty. What had made him come so soon was the act of humiliating her.

She turned around on the rug and looked at his eyes, which he didn't want her to see. He removed the condom and placed it in the fire, where it bubbled, swelled and made sooty smoke.

"It's all right," she said.

"What's all right?" he answered, lying.

"I don't mind your doing that."

He was cold with self-dislike, and looked away.

She said, "You can do whatever you want. I'll do anything you want." He didn't answer, and his anger began to slip toward her. She couldn't see this through his paralysis of expression. "What's the matter, John?" she asked. She was on her knees, facing him, and her body seemed to grow smoother and simpler, as though her breasts were accidental ceramic bumps, her neck the white neck of a ewer. It wasn't anger, it was a reduction, or an attempted one—attempted by a part of him he didn't care to know. She came toward him, on her knees, hesitantly, and offered herself to him. It was as if he broke strings to accept her.

Later she cried silently and apologized, saying she was just in a mood. He witnessed his own response, which this time was tender. She was valuable everywhere, everywhere beautiful. Of course he was ready again and it was that itch speaking. If he didn't use a condom he might make her pregnant and that would solve all this embarrassment and indecision. He'd marry her and get it over with. He was about to enter her but stopped, lifted her hips and kissed the wet maze of her vagina. He'd never done that and it startled her; he could feel the start in her thighs. His face was all wet with her, his tongue among clefts and edges.

She liked what he did, and said "oh, oh." She was so valuable, so present. He lifted her higher, to prove his regard, and kissed her budlike anus. Did that prove anything? Painful air surrounded his erection and he quenched it in her with no dull condom between them. She knew, and her eyes opened in surprise, but she said nothing.

They were both insane. Someone should stay sane, but that was a faint lost shout. When he came into her it felt as if bolts, nuts and washers hurtled out of him along with his spinal matter and the marrow of his bones. She still squeezed him as hard as she could and her own shuddering ended in a purr.

In the ensuing calm the subject of his recklessness surrounded them. "I must have been crazy," he said.

"I could have told you but I didn't care," she said. They were both in awe of their madness.

"If you get pregnant we'll get married," he said.

"I'll never marry anybody but you," she said, which gave him a deep but invisible convulsion of pity.

9

Her mother was quite aware that her life had changed. The long days with John Hearne hadn't gone unnoticed. They were doing the dishes, Dory rinsing and stacking the chipped white plates, her mother's hands red from the graying dishwater. Her mother said, "You better invite him to supper."

"To supper? Why?" She thought he wouldn't like to come to supper; she knew he wouldn't like it.

"Because it's a good idea. We ought to meet him."

"But he's just Johnny Hearne. You know him all right."

"I don't think he's just Johnny Hearne no more."

Since Dory was not given to lying she couldn't deny any part of what her mother meant. They had argued and fought in their lives, but she couldn't remember a time when they had misunderstood each other. She was not about to say, "What do you mean by that?" as Debbie would have.

At thirty-six, her mother had a few strands of gray in her hair, though her skin was pale and smooth, with a hard look to it, and she was too thin. She'd always been thin and busy, always going after a task or two, and maybe one more after that, she had to finish before she could sit down. Dory took after her in the matter of finishing things, while Debbie, who was bigger and stronger-looking than either of them, became weak from boredom at any job, and dawdled, not caring if it was ever done or not. Most of the time Dory and her mother didn't bother to ask Debbie for help, because it wasn't worth having her in the way of their purposeful hands.

Dory wouldn't lie to her mother, but she never made any confessions to her—not that she'd ever had any serious ones to make, until now. She was the daughter who never caused trouble, who, having given her word, came home on time, who got mostly A's in school, whose periods never made her slightly insane, as Debbie's did. She had heard her mother say to her Aunt Phyllis, "Doris never give me a lick of trouble." But she wondered if she was dutiful in part just to avoid trouble, sort of ducking everything that came along. Debbie never avoided any emotional confrontation, not even the horrendous ones, the screaming back and forth and the stupid, sarcastic rejoinders. "Don't get your water hot!" Debbie would yell at her mother across the table, her red mouth coiling and ugly with what seemed to be genuine hatred. Debbie would do odd, slobbish things, like drinking tea out of the teapot and leaving an obvious red smudge of lipstick around the white spout. Dory could understand the impulse to drink the tea out of the spout, but she couldn't understand not wiping the lipstick off afterwards.

Her mother said, without looking up from the dishpan, "I hope you know what you're doing, Doris."

There was no answer to that, so she made none. Her mother said, "He's older than you, he's a vet, he's been overseas, he's a college boy. He's probably . . ."

Her mother stopped there. This time she wasn't sure what he'd probably, so she said, "Probably what, Ma?"

"Been around plenty of women, is what I mean. What do you do out there at the Sylvesters' cabin all day long?"

"We go sailing and swimming and we talk."

Her mother didn't want to ask the real question directly. Maybe she didn't really want to know the answer to it, or she didn't want to put her honest daughter on the spot. "I always been able to trust you," she said. "I always thought Johnny Hearne was a good boy, but he ain't a boy no more, and you're not old for your age. I'd like to know more about his intentions, is all."

"Pa's nine years older than you."

"I was nineteen when we commenced stepping out, however, not seventeen. Even so, you know we had to get married. When the preacher said, 'Will you take this man?' you was already on the way. You invite him for supper tomorrow."

"I really don't want to. It isn't necessary, Ma, really!"

"It's 'necessary.' "

"Oh, Ma!"

Finally she promised to ask him. Even as she conceded she didn't think she could do it.

"Why don't you do it right now. Call him up."

"I've never called him up."

"There's a first time for everything."

So she did. Mrs. Sylvester answered the phone and said, "Oh, is this *Dory?* Dory Perkins! He's in his room. Just a sec and I'll get him for you, dear."

She already knew he was in his room because his light was on. What she read in his mother's voice was probably all in her own head, but she cringed at it. She must look up "patronize" in her new dictionary and make sure how it was pronounced.

John Hearne said, "Dory? Before you say anything you ought to know that my mother's still on the phone downstairs." There was a giggle and a click. "She's probably still on the line," he said.

"Meet me at the teeter-totter, okay?" she said.

"Okay," he said in a rough voice, imitating a tough guy.

The sky had clouded over, a heavy seamless vault over the town. It was only eight o'clock but the light was dusky, grass and leaves going gray, the arborvitae black columns. She wanted to move into his arms, now that they could put their hands on each other anywhere they liked, but someone might be watching.

"What's up?" he said. "Your father cleaning his shotgun?"

"It's my mother. She practically forced me to ask you to supper tomorrow."

"Hmm." The mosquitoes were singing. He stepped forward and pressed one against her forehead, then picked it off and flicked the tiny mess away.

"I know you don't want to come."

"Why shouldn't I want to?"

"Don't lie, Johnny."

"You never lie, do you, Dory? As long as we're naming each other, I'll admit, Doris Ella Perkins, that though I have nothing against your mother and father whatsoever, the prospect of being evaluated as stud, as it were, gives me one pure, cold grue. But I'll come."

"Around five-thirty."

"Black tie, Doris?"

"Shut up."

"Oh. 'Shut up.' I see, Doris."

"You're just nervous, so you can't be serious."

"You're getting to know me pretty well, Perkins."

She was still embarrassed about asking him to give a command performance. "My mother won't give you the evil eye, don't worry. She likes you."

"But she doesn't trust me, which shows that she's an intelligent woman."

"She thinks because you're older and a veteran and all, you've probably had a million women already."

"She's close—give or take a hundred thousand."

"Have you?"

"Only you, my sweet. I came to you pure as the driven snow . . ."

"Shut up, Johnny." When she was about to cry her face felt all pasty. She didn't like his flippancy and never had, but she wanted him anyway. It was just that it all seemed useless, something that could never come to a conclusion. All those frivolous, mannered little wisecracks. She'd rather have him in her, groaning.

He came up to her. "Hey," he said, his thumbs on her tears.

Oh, his voice was tender enough. He could be sincere. When he was sincere he turned warm and wise. His strength and kindness filled her.

But she felt that way one minute and resentful the next. She was a prisoner of these terrible shifts, these crack-the-whips. It depended upon his specific gravity, which changed constantly. He was real and less real, moment to moment. She felt like screaming, and abruptly left him and went into her house and up to her room. As she passed her family in the living room, the radio issuing the goopy, artificially sweet voice of Eden Abhe, her vagina felt used, heated by a mild irritation. They said nothing; with the probable exception of her father, they knew the reason for her moodiness.

She took off her clothes and lay on her bed as the dark fell. Distant heat lightning flickered soundlessly, printing her window on her eyes. When she moved her eyes the window's gray-white panes and black sash moved too as that ghost vision faded and another came, so that she saw two windows, and then another. The storm was to the west, and would come over Leah.

She accepted as inevitable her summer at Cascom Manor and his journey to California. Her summer would be hard work and fairly predictable, but his would be dangerous unto death—at least the going: he would sell his motorcycle out there and come back some other way, he said. She didn't understand the alien quality in him that looked forward to all that risk and discomfort, and she wasn't sure that he'd come back at all; he had the GI Bill and could go to college anywhere he chose.

So be it. One didn't scream at the inevitable, even if it had been the reason for her tears, the self-pitying child inside her sniveling in resentment for having been his . . . vessel. Her life had been all right until he had decided to use her for a week or so to while away the time until his check came and he could escape from her. She knew; she could read every jog of his mind. It was just that she couldn't control those quivers of hesitation and resolve.

In her own body a baby might be forming. That was what she was for, why she had breasts and organs and the opening that he fit, so there was no mystery about that and no reason why it shouldn't happen to her. She couldn't remember exactly when she'd had her period. There had been no reason to keep track of it, back in that other age when her best friend was Cynthia Fuller. Now she seemed to have no friends, just a lover, though he never used the word "love." Instead he would kiss her all over and tell her that she had a perfect body, that she was "edible," that her elbows were beautiful. Always it went beyond seriousness into self-mockery, where her heart would not follow.

Once she asked him why he had to go to California. He said he wanted to see his country. On the way he wanted to stop and see the town where he was born.

"But you grew up in Leah," she said.

"Leah!" he said. "Well, no, there are worse places, I guess. But I was born in Winota, Minnesota. That was another life. I had a father . . ."

She began to understand that his reasons weren't all frivolous. "Do you remember him?"

"Yes. I was five when I left there. I was in kindergarten. I remember a lot."

"Is he still there?"

"When last heard from he was somewhere in southern California—according to my mother."

"Are you going to try to find him?"

"No. Anyway, it would be like trying to find a needle in a haystack."

She thought of her own interpretation of that saying. "If you knew where he was, would you look him up?"

"I don't know. I wouldn't know what to say to him. What would I call him—Daddy? I'm a man now. I'm a veteran—even if I was in combat only three days. I'll be twenty-two in October and I don't need a father."

His statistics didn't seem to convince him. She wanted to comfort him, so she slid her arms around him and hugged him. He said, "I do think you're beautiful. You think you're homely, but you're not." He said that seriously.

Oh, she didn't know what to believe.

She couldn't believe she'd been asleep, but the air in her room was wild, her curtains and shade snapping and coiling, the storm assaulting the town in a nearly continuous flash and boom. She went to close her window and the floor and windowsill were already wet, the water cool but slimy-feeling because it was where it shouldn't be.

She dreamed he was thirteen and his father was whipping him with a dog leash while he danced in a corner crying, "Daddy! Daddy!" The cry turned into a tapping on her window and she woke, confused for a moment as cry and tapping separated from each other.

He knelt on the woodshed roof.

10

He and Dory spent the day apart, each getting things ready for their summer occupations. He did a lot of experimenting in how to lash his possessions on his motorcycle. As his journey neared it became more and more implausible, and as five-thirty approached his invitation to supper at the Perkins's felt more and more like an invitation to a shotgun wedding. Her mother was a formidable woman; although she'd always been pleasant enough to him, he'd seen her wrath exercised on others, especially on Debbie, whom he'd once seen whipped home, raised welts on her legs, her mother wielding a leather dog leash. Not that Debbie hadn't been expressly guilty.

He'd always said hello to Dory's father on the streets of Leah. The poor man had to nod and smile and say hello a thousand times a day as he made his appointed rounds, his bulging leather haversack hanging on one shoulder and then the other. He was a hunter, and long guns leaned in the dining-room corners. How he felt about John Hearne and his daughter, John didn't know. What name for him might come into her father's mind—fellow, boyfriend, suitor, sweetheart, son of a bitch? It was strange that he knew so little about a man so familiar to him.

The time came when he would have to cross the backyards and appear at their door. Front door, or kitchen door? He had decided to wear chinos and a clean dress shirt, no tie. He had decided to shave carefully in order to look as young as possible.

"Don't you look nice and clean," his mother said as she stirred the nightly martinis. "And you're having dinner with your girlfriend's family."

She meant collusion again, that Dory Perkins was a minor amusement and his visit to her house something like slumming. He felt a lurch of resentment against this attitude but said nothing. It was true that the Perkins's house was odd and interesting to him, and therefore he was tainted with the superiority of a cultural observer, but he didn't despise it the way he did the matched sets, the color codings, the displayed fabrics and the generally self-conscious decor of this house. The Perkins's house was full of accreted junk, but each piece was either functional or a memento.

"Are you two getting *serious?*" his mother asked lightly.

"I'm heading west tomorrow," he said.

"And I don't know why!" She turned quickly, so that her pleated dress would bell.

"Wanderlust," he said.

"But it's so dangerous on that motorcycle!"

"Where's my drink?" Amos called from the living room.

"I'll take it easy," John said.

The kitchen door or the front door? The kitchen door he'd entered as a child, for errand or Kool-Aid, and might make his visit seem less formal, but he had been summoned by a mother's decree, and that meant the front door, probably. He didn't want to begin this ordeal by startling anyone. No one's arms covered with flour, or doughy hands. He went around on the cinder driveway, past the prewar Chevrolet, to the front door, which he was about to knock upon when Debbie opened it.

"Hi," he said.

Debbie was grinning, and had been grinning; it didn't seem a response to him but to some earlier event. Maybe the earlier event was what had happened at Cascomhaven a few days ago, or maybe it was the circumstance of his being male and Dory female and all the libidinous implications of that. Or her father had made Dory confess everything and was about to confront him with two alternatives—jail or a wedding.

"Come in, Mr. Hearne," Debbie said. She stood aside to let him enter the small vestibule. The door wouldn't open all the way because of all the winter coats and mackinaws on pegs and the boots and overshoes on the floor below them, so he squeezed past her, his arm having to brush against a large breast bound in slippery aquamarine rayon. Debbie was almost as tall as he was, the sort of girl who had always been large, matronly even in grade school, and who in class plays was always someone's mother or aunt. She was noisy, sarcastic, subject to moods, a smoker, her inappropriate remarks causing boys to pick on her and think of names to call her. "Boobers," he had heard, was one of them. For all her emotional zigzags, her unfunny humor and her pride in borrowed jargon, he'd never thought her mean; but she was the sort of person you were more sympathetic toward when not in her presence. It was hard to believe that Dory, with her grave dignity and grace, was related to her at all.

He preceded Debbie into the small living room, where Mr. Perkins turned off the radio and stood up to shake his hand. "Sit yourself, John," he said. "Debbie, get us a ale. You like ale?"

"Sure," John said, and Mr. Perkins nodded once to Debbie, who still grinned and seemed pleased to wait on them.

Most of the room was taken up with furniture. He chose the overstuffed chair that matched the davenport, while Mr. Perkins went back to what was evidently his Morris chair, for handy to it were a wooden pipe rack and a humidor of tobacco. Small tables filled up all extra wall space, each covered with a crocheted doily, framed photographs of people, ashtrays, figurines, candlesticks without candles, ceramic match dispensers, glass-based table lamps with colored shades and on one table an enormous green glazed bullfrog. The photograph of honor, on top of the Motorola radio, was Dory's graduation picture in a folding gold frame. Her hand-tinted cheeks and lips looked like flower petals; her smile was so broad and joyful it went beyond mere cheerfulness and raised the question of what, at that moment, had so pleased her. He'd never seen such an unalloyed expression on her face. Again, art tried to widen the separation of her dark eyes, the rotogravure-brown tints not succeeding any better than her makeup for the prom, which he suspected in that case to have been applied by Debbie.

"Nice photo," Mr. Perkins said, glancing at John through fingers that filled and tamped tobacco into his pipe. He was a bony, angular man who gave the impression of great wiry strength. He'd changed out of his uniform into green pants and a white shirt, but still wore his regulation thick black ankle-high shoes that in spite of their high gloss were bent and squat from use. His legs seemed bowed from all his walking, and his long face wrinkled from all the smiles the townspeople demanded in return for their greetings. It must have been a chore, that constant exchange of mild affection.

"Genesee," he said when Debbie brought them the opened cans of ale. Evidently Dory and her mother were busy in the kitchen and dining room, which John couldn't see except for part of the silver-worn central floor register. His nervousness had subsided, although he wondered if Mr. Perkins had meant anything substantial by that quick glance through his fingers.

"I like a ale when I get off work," Mr. Perkins said. Debbie sat down on the davenport and looked from one to the other as if to say that she was there to listen to conversation.

John put the cold can to his mouth and the perfumy liquid's submerged bitterness reminded him of his first tries at beer and ale, when he was old enough to know someone old enough to buy it. It had been hard to get a whole can or bottle down then, but in the Army that sharp virginal fascination and revulsion had soon disappeared and for a while, on one post, he had come near to being a sot. He had a horror of soddenness, of potbelliedness; the animal he inhabited had to be, like Dory, quick and lithe. Right now if he had to he could dive neatly through the nearest window, taking with him at the most two lights of glass.

"I had a motorcycle once, when I was a young fella," Mr. Perkins said with the fond, savoring look of a coming anecdote. "It was a Indian, one-lunger, and you never seen such a mess of V-belts, pulleys and belt tighteners. In them days what worried us most was blowouts, though them V-belts could eat you up if you wa'n't careful. I recall . . ."

Debbie got up and left, her father ignoring her look of exasperated boredom.

". . . heading for Woodsville one night, must of been the summer of twenty-eight. There was four of us on two bikes—the other was a Gilson Chain-drive, you never heard of that make, I bet. Young hellions, we was. Woodsville in them days had a rep. It was a railroad town. Where them loggers and railroaders met was some wild goings-on, let me tell you . . ."

As Mr. Perkins told his story of the night ride, the paved and graveled roads, the weak, magneto-driven headlights, the hip flasks of Canadian booze, John came to believe that the subject of the evening, as far as Mr. Perkins was concerned, was not his grown daughter's relationship with John Hearne. Mr. Perkins was, after all, surrounded by emotional, authoritative and opinionated women and he was lonesome for a man to talk to. Machines, blowouts, the crazy exuberance of youth, a poker game in a whorehouse, everybody a character, a wonder. "Harvey Whipple, now—he owned the Gilson. What a heller he was in them days! Two cylinders and he never could get the goddam machine timed right, so it blew great fireballs each time he shifted, like a goddam Roman candle. Scare the living piss out of any car he passed, they believed they was being shot at!"

They were called to the dining-room table, Mr. Perkins still brimming with memory, to face the women and their food. There was Dory, in a neat print dress, his sweet and chilling reason for being at this table, and Mrs. Perkins, who was supposed to like him but whose smile was wary, as though she didn't want to give her friendliness away too cheaply. She must wonder about her daughter, he thought, then looked at her again. Their eyes met for one appraising moment: she knew.

She passed him the platter of boiled potatoes. "Here you are, John," she said. Not Johnny, as she'd always called him.

There was the clinking of knives and forks—individual preference in the preparation of potatoes for the gravy; the passing of the chicken platter, the baked meat separated from the bones; pickles sweet, mustard and dilled, bread and lima beans.

Lima beans. He took a few of them for politeness's sake. They never had them at Amos's house, and it was one matter of agreement between them. The fat, water-slimed gray-green of them, that taste of cement, bland but mealy and somehow wrong. Children hated lima beans; most people didn't like them, but there they were in stores everywhere, canned, dried and frozen. Who in cold blood, with freedom of choice, bought them? There must be a perverse underground of lima bean eaters, their tastes akin to geophagy, and here he was among them.

Mr. Perkins helped himself to a mound of them, their plump bodies little greenish half-moons that slithered down the sides of their own pile. Dory and Mrs. Perkins each had a proper share.

Debbie didn't like them; she took exactly four of them and he saw her hide one under a small peripheral gob of mashed potato, skillfully plastering it over and into oblivion. He decided not to try that; surely every guilty thing Debbie did was immediately discovered. He felt like a child, those no doubt nutritious leguminous presences accusing him from his very plate. What he did was to eat enormous quantities of everything else, trying to please. Weren't they examining him? Did he want to imply a snobbish disapproval of their food and thus their very lives? But there was no way to mask distaste for a certain food. He knew that if he chewed them the lima beans would grow in his mouth, but managed to take one and then another down like a bolus.

"Fella don't care for lima beans," Mr. Perkins observed, chuckling and giving him the cunning Yankee glance that signaled a friendly, or not so friendly, gibe. "They say you ain't a man till you like lima beans."

Mr. Perkins was amused by his remark and cocked his head this way and that. There was an interested silence at the table to see how John would take it. Evidently he took it all right.

Mrs. Perkins said, "Of course, *he* don't like oysters."

"Puh!" Mr. Perkins said. "I'd rather take a swig out of a spittoon."

"Pa, really!" Debbie said.

"Well, I would! Even if it was all one piece, as the story goes."

"That's disgusting!"

"So's oysters."

There were no ill feelings. Dory seemed to find her father amusing, as did her mother. They were also amused by Debbie's sudden propriety because of John's presence.

"Debbie, get me and John another ale," Mr. Perkins said. Debbie did this immediately, without comment. He wondered if Mr. Perkins was ever a dangerous child-man. Maybe he was a little spoiled by his females, but he didn't seem, at least in these circumstances, to threaten them, to be threatened by them or to be in competition with John for their attention.

"What you going to do, John, when you graduate college?" he asked.

"I'm not sure. I don't even have a major yet."

"The war slowed you down some." He added, philosophically, "Ayuh. I guess we all have to do what we have to do."

John could let them think that he had bravely sacrificed himself for his country, but he didn't want to have to sustain that idea. In retrospect he had mostly enjoyed the Army and it seemed to him that he was being overpaid for whatever services he had rendered. "I've got plenty of time and the GI Bill, so I can't complain," he said. "Anyway, I didn't mind the Army that much."

"You didn't mind the infantry?"

"No, not really. The training wasn't bad, and I was only in combat for a few days."

There had been an unpleasant combat-anticipation anxiety at times, maybe at all times, but against that was his escape from Leah, the general civilian admiration for servicemen and the great idea that he had become an adult at last, the uniform and the blue braid on his cap constituting absolute proof. He was good at everything they told him to do. Obstacle courses were legitimate ways of showing off; he shot "expert" with the M-1; he was never on shit lists. To try to impress Mr. Perkins with the hellishness of the Army, as he had perhaps done with others, would not be right. It was Dory, of course, before whom lies grew cheap. The opportunity to aggrandize himself was there, smelling of impermanence and dishonor, but she had changed him. She glanced at him across the platters, the pickles and condiments, too real to lie to.

But Mr. Perkins wanted information about that time. "I got questions about some of them weapons you had in the infantry, John. Maybe you can answer some of 'em, after."

After dessert, a chocolate cake Dory had baked, maybe to prove her domestic skills, Mr. Perkins took him back into the living room. The women cleared the table and did the dishes.

There was the filling and lighting of his pipe, Mr. Perkins's dark channeled face flashing in the match flame between hard sucks, an expectantly wide eye gleaming across this small Vesuvius. "Yup, yup," he said when his pipe was hot enough. "I ain't totally ignorant—for instance, I got a thirty-aught-six, Enfield, so I know something about the ballistics and all, but . . ." He puffed, the blue velvet smoke finding its way to the convective push above the iron central register. "Tell me about the Garand, now. Did you like it?"

Like it? An interesting question about an engine of war. The conventional attitudes of his college, for instance, would exclude such a question without a trace. Did he, John Hearne, like the M-1 rifle, which he'd had to disassemble, meticulously clean, never drop on pain of punishment, never lose or even misplace on pain of incarceration—that long, nine-and-a-half-pound weight he'd had to lug everywhere—did he *like* it? He didn't miss it. He had forgotten most of its serial number already, except for the shorthand last four digits—8825. Where was it now, his old partner? He could feel its weight in his wrist and forearm, the smoothed walnut and black steel of its balance point in his fingers.

"It was all right," he said. "Pretty heavy, though." But there was more to it than that, to be honest. He'd spent all of his eighteenth and nineteenth years in the Army, among men similarly occupied with steel, copper, brass and lead. With his M-1 he could at five hundred yards send deadly force into a circle as small in diameter as a man's chest. Not so much death as the elimination of imminent danger; the dead were anonymous, disarranged, dusty, inert. What could he have done with nothing but his hands? Though he hadn't, as far as he knew, shot anyone, the power had been there.

His feelings about that weapon must be allowed their complications. Shooting people, that gruesome rupture of tissue, was, as a general idea, insane, but he had been in a war that was as encompassing to his youth as the universe itself, and his rifle was his protection, his long arm. It happened to be more accurate than most, though it had its idiosyncrasies. It would half-extract a fired casing and crumple it in its breech unless its gas port and cylinder were cleaned more often and more carefully than most. It broke more firing pins than it should have, though they were easily replaced. Small, individual, accepted flaws. He explained these things to Mr. Perkins, who found them so fascinating his gaze was a totally unselfconscious stare. "Well!" he said. "God damn!" They spoke mostly of velocities, cams, grains, pawls, stops and feeds, terms they didn't have to define to each other.

When the dishes were done, Dory came from the kitchen and suggested to John that they walk around the block "to settle their supper." Mr. Perkins followed them to the door and put his hand on John's shoulder, a small gesture of friendliness, or of affection, or even of admiration, that he could not remember having received from an older man before. He thought how every man was supposed to want a son, someone presumably interested in motorcycles, tools, guns and the like —good hard things and finite processes. The light pressure of the older hand stayed with him.

In the dusk he and Dory walked down Water Street next to the weedy bank of the Cascom River. "I think your mother knows," he said.

"She suspects, but she won't ask me right out. She was pregnant with me when they were married and I guess she thinks I'm like her."

"You are like her in some ways."

"In some ways, I guess."

He asked her how she would like to live her life.

"I don't know. Is there any choice? As happy as possible."

"But where, how?"

"It doesn't matter where."

"In the country? In Leah? In a city?"

"Don't ask me that! What do you want me to say?"

She was angry, and as always her anger taught him that she was real and in her real danger couldn't afford this sort of moony theorizing about the future. She wouldn't be used that way. She was the only girl he'd known who wouldn't fantasize on his terms, for the possible benefit of his self-importance.

He looked down on her as they walked, the light fabric of her dress easy on her because she was so firm and trim, modest and ordinary. He put his hand on the small of her back, her graceful tensions in motion flowing up his arm like voltage. He would be responsible for the center of her, easy or not. What the hell? Sooner or later you made a choice and stuck with it. He said, "When I come back we'll get married, okay?"

"If you want to."

It was done. In the sudden absence of one of his anxieties he felt light on his feet. "Let's run," he said, and they ran down Water Street to Maple Street and stopped under the streetlight just as it came on—an omen. The motionless hard maple leaves overhead were greener than in daylight, the mown grass of the Pulsifers' yard the primary green of a child's painting.

They ran up Maple Street to Union Street past the shady yards and windowlights of houses, on the tilted slabs of sidewalk where he'd counted the cracks as a child, down Beech Street to Water Street and back to her house. He took her hand and led her behind some ancient lilacs, an enclosed place known from childhood games, and lifted her up against him. The sweat in her armpits and on her forehead was silky and endearing. When they kissed she had for him the shapeless power of water—not taste, but something deeper and more primitive, like the odor of that elemental fluid from which they'd both come. It was all consent, as if for once in the entire history of human intercourse an absolute mutuality, however temporary, had been accomplished. At those moments he felt his intelligence dissolve. Everything slipped, and afterwards he would have strange scuttling shadows in his memory, as if he'd been in the skin of one of his distant ancestors, some utterly unselfconscious, mud-colored skipper with external gills and just the one urgency.

A lilac leaf brushed his temple. Nothing caused such a delicate, creepy itch as the touch of lilac.

They went back into her house and played Monopoly with Debbie and her father. Her mother didn't like games. By ten o'clock Debbie had gone rather unpleasantly bankrupt. "Christ, Deb, it's only a goddam game," her father said, but he had all the utilities, and hotels on Marvin Gardens and Indiana Avenue that attracted their counters like magnets, so it was obvious that, with great satisfaction, he had won.

"Don't *gloat* over it!" Debbie said, and went stomping upstairs, which caused no general embarrassment. John thanked the Perkinses for his supper and he and Dory went out to the teeter-totter, officially sweethearts, to say good night. He would be leaving early in the morning and they had decided, or he had decided, that this would be their farewell.

"I'll see you in September," he said.

"All right."

"It's only nine or ten weeks. And listen, I'll keep in touch, and if you miss your period I'll come right back. I'll call you at Cascom Manor, okay?"

" 'No wind serves the man who has no port of destination'—Montaigne," she said.

"I know. I read your speech very carefully. But will you give me this summer?"

"It's not mine to give."

"You know what I mean. Don't keep on like this."

"All right. Goodbye, Johnny. Have a good trip."

It came to him that it was impossible for a man and a woman, tainted by love, to talk plainly to each other.

11

Her desk was a small oak table, originally a bedside stand for pitcher, washbasin and chamber pot. It was eleven-thirty and she sat there, the cone of light from her lamp yellowing the paper of her valedictory address—which John Hearne had read so carefully. His window was dark; maybe he had gone out somewhere on his last night in Leah. She didn't feel neglected because she felt that it was over, the whole freaky time with him in which she had been dreamy and unstable, as though great furls of satin were billowing inside her. They were so familiar with each other it was like being skinned and turned inside out, a domestic enormity, a rapture of guilt not at what they were doing but at the loss of sanity. The constant, sickish need for his presence she identified as love. No one liked to lose independence, to become an addict—at least she didn't, and that was why she got angry at times that surprised both of them.

Tonight he'd asked her how and where she wanted to live her life—

theoretical, of course, just for the purpose of discussion or confession. But she wouldn't be patronized, so she wouldn't talk about it. She must look up "patronize" in her new dictionary, and did, and her face flushed warm when she read his note in the margin. She had too many words she wasn't sure how to pronounce, words never to be said aloud. And so he had patronized her—he who knew how to pronounce the word.

How different was he from others, then? Suppose he went around telling that he had "made" her. Would he? Would she then get calls for dates from his friends? She had heard of such cases. She worried about Debbie in that respect; after the prom Debbie had been with a senior in his car, beer present, though Debbie had told her that nothing happened, "really." What was next to "really"? She knew the senior, Harry Morrow, and he would have told, or he might even make something up.

At least John Hearne would never do that. But where was he tonight, for instance? Where was his presence and warmth? He could be out with one of his old girlfriends, some woman his age, and they could joke about her. That empty ache was apprehension, helplessness, jealousy, the sick underside of love. She couldn't help having these spasms; they were part of the disease and out of her control. But she could put names to them, and what was named could at least be kept in context.

When John Hearne had read her speech he had been kind, noncommittal, pātronizing. He'd said, "Maybe you think we're all better than we really are in this country."

"I just meant that most of us know how things *should* be," she said.

"You and I do, babe, but how many of us are there?"

"Babe," he'd called her. She didn't like that. The unreality of it; the posing of it. Enough that he had given her the nickname that had stuck to her for all these years.

Everyone had gone to bed and the house was silent. The light still hadn't come on in his window across the yards, between the maple leaves.

There had been enough time since her family had gone to bed for the new electric hot-water heater to recover, so she decided to take a bath, a luxury that had been more difficult under the old system with the coil in the kitchen stove. Her mother had bought the new heater, using her employee's discount, and was now thinking of an electric stove, except that her mother couldn't understand why a person shouldn't get an electric shock when touching a metal pan on a burner. Even though they had tried to explain grounding, resistance and insulation to her, she was still bothered. Her mother was a capable woman who had dealt all her life with practical mechanics, having grown up on a hill farm in Cascom where they hadn't had any electricity but a lot of ingenious mechanical contraptions, some run by hand, some by water, some by animals and some by ancient one-lunger gasoline engines. Her mother knew the principle of a hand-cranked ice-cream freezer, for instance, but power enough to turn steel red hot before her eyes, from within, was too much. At least the hot-water tank was in the basement and the heating elements were drowned in water, out of sight.

It was a pleasure to fill the tub up higher than they had been able to before, the old level marked in indelible yellow. Just the fact of surplus warmed and enfolded now, where before the knowledge of the coming chill took the comfort away from lukewarm water. She removed the clothes from the body that was, with a shiver of cold or of embarrassment, no longer just hers, and eased into the hot water. She would wash her hair in the morning, leaning over the tub, rather than sleep with dampness tonight. After a while she ran more hot water, that new luxury, until the overflow vent glugged the water's surface away. Blood was pink in the water, along with a tiny squiggle of more viscous material like a knotted red string. Except for the first time, she had never before been quite surprised by the sense of fullness vented, the loss of something more than blood yet hardly stronger than an antipathy toward soilure. She was fairly sure, but not totally sure, that this was her period and therefore she was not pregnant. There was that little loss, then relief greater than she had let herself believe. She was herself—single, nimble, clever and quick again.

There was more than one strain to this relief, however; one was even a little flippant: Close call, Dory! Another was a feeling of unethical avoidance, not of pregnancy but of confrontation with the father of the now nonexistent child; she would never know whether or not she would have demanded anything from him. She thought she wouldn't have demanded anything, but now she would never be certain. Another was the feeling, shadowy and overwhelmed by the others, of possible inadequacy because he had placed within her, for whatever reasons, his sperm, and she hadn't conceived. The race was meant to multiply and she had not.

He told her once that he'd seen children killed by their own parents, who then killed themselves because they were afraid of Americans or they thought of themselves as soldiers and wouldn't surrender. He said from his distance he thought they were throwing their laundry off the cliffs, like old shirts and pants. He couldn't at first make himself see what he actually saw.

They'd all found out so many things during and after the war, things that had turned out to be real, actually real, not just rumor and propaganda. The torture and murder of millions. He said he knew the stink of terror because he'd had to walk through it. Thousands of civilians had hidden for days, almost shoulder to shoulder, in a small scrubby woods and his platoon had to walk through the woods afterwards. He said they prayed for no incoming fire because there was no room on the ground between the shit and they'd have had to dive into it. It was like the murmurous room in hell where the liquid was up to everyone's lower lip: "Don't make a wave, don't make a wave." They'd had no gas masks. It was so much the stench of their own fear, too, that they'd felt responsible for it. They could feel it coming through their clothes and skin, drowning them, and the woods seemed never to end. Then they came to the sea, and the laundry falling from the cliffs. Her blood bloomed like a pale cloud on its way to the drain.

In bed she lay quietly, letting sadness flow out of the ends of her fingers and toes, an old trick of hers. She'd been ready to accept the bondage of the child, that doubleness, but in her new freedom it was hard to understand the person who had made that vow. She was relieved, but nothing had been gained. She was just seventeen again, powerless, ordinary, and he was off in the morning on his separate quest.

She woke remembering fragments of a dream, but the dream had been so vast and the fragments were so small it was like trying to read a book with wind blowing the pages. She'd been on the lake in a boat, looking down into the water; there was a black '41 Buick sedan on the bottom of the lake among gray boulders. Somewhere else a maple leaf wind-walked along a granite slab, like a crab. She woke up all the way and the dream said farewell, farewell, you'll never know how important I was. She was a mess. Her mother and father had gone to work and Debbie was probably still asleep, her door closed. From the bathroom she went down to the kitchen for coffee, then heard his motorcycle out front.

She was wearing her mother's frilly, torn, baby-blue dressing gown she'd taken from the back of the bathroom door, where it covered the hanging hot-water bottle and its tube, so she ran upstairs and exchanged it for her plain bathrobe. She met him at the front door. He stood on the stoop, partly in uniform, in his Ike jacket and dungarees, looking rather blank and unsure of his welcome. She could still see where his corporal's chevrons had been sewn on his sleeves. The long red motorcycle leaned precariously at the curb, his duffel bag and other olive-green canvas things tied on the rear with lots of clothesline. He was so blond, square-shouldered and trim he looked like a character in a movie about great adventures, a charming young hero off to fight evil of some kind or another. But he didn't know who, exactly, he was, or where he came from—or thought he didn't. She didn't know why he wasn't from Leah.

"I thought I'd stop and say goodbye," he said, like a question, as if he were afraid of her. She thought how she could tell him or not tell him. Of course she'd tell him, even though it made it all seem artificial between them, like odds, or rubber. If you were lucky, hi-ho and away. Sadness and resentment; her throat refused to obey orders.

"Hey, Dory. I'll be back," he said. He put his arms around her and immediately she felt his desire to be free.

"My period started last night," she said.

"Whew!" He mimicked mopping his brow. "Okay. I'll still be back, you know. Of course, I may not even make it across Vermont on that spavined old critter. I may be back sooner than you think."

"Please be careful. I had a sad dream last night about a car under the water."

"Was I in it? In the dream, I mean."

"I don't know. I don't know whose car it was."

"No more Canadian soldiers?"

"Send me a postcard once in a while," she said, knowing that this cutting through of palaver to what was felt always upset him. He wanted everything nice for his grand departure. No hard feelings and now no threatening baby. He wanted to be free as a bird, his faithful woman ready and waiting in case he ever came back. Who wouldn't want it all ways like that? Just in case he didn't meet a beautiful, talented, educated girl in Minnesota or California he could always count on plain little Dory Perkins back in New Hampshire. She'd always be there, mispronouncing words and carrying her dim little torch for him. Self-pity, that degrading emotion, like slime.

"You'll see," he said unhappily.

"I'm sorry," she said. "I want you to do what you want. I just wish you were taking a bus or a train."

He was happy again, all illuminated and heroic and full of words. "A bus is a stuffy nose, and I've been across the country twice by train—Macon to Seattle and then San Francisco to Fort Dix, New Jersey. Troop trains, granted—sort of jails. Of course I'd rather have a car—say a Packard convertible—but I don't, so I've got to ride wide open, sort of naked, right *in* the country, so I can smell it and feel it. In a way I'm an exile, kidnapped as a child and taken to this mad dark state full of rocks and people you can't tell from the rocks. Not you, though you've got your share of granite in you too, come to think of it. That's all right . . ."

She kissed him on the lips to shut him up—to help him to shut up. "Well," she said.

"Well. I hope you have a good summer," he said.

"Take care, now, Johnny."

There was some more of that, and finally he turned and strode down the walk a little proud and swaggery, to mount his steed and do expert little adjustments and turnings-on of switches before the violent kick-down that made the engine begin its mouthy rumble, his arms wide on the handlebars. He saluted her, shifted with a clank and moved into balance and speed down Water Street to the corner. His engine sound faded behind houses and trees.

12

His motorcycle was an eleven-year-old Indian Pony, a beast that tended to lose its footing in hard places. The frame was bent, but he had learned to accommodate himself to that. The red fenders had been bent and straightened, bent and straightened again. The crash bar on the left side was worn half through from a long slide someone had taken on concrete. At least the tires were fair, and the old two-cylinder engine throbbed smoothly, as if in no pain. All kinds of breakdowns lurked, however, in the oily innards of the machine, where he hadn't the tools or the knowledge to find and repair them. But it ran now and could push him forward with a force that seemed willing and controllable.

The machine received him and made him nearly a free man again. She watched from behind the screen door, not coming out with him because she was still in her bathrobe. The kickstand went up with a hard clank. He turned on the ignition switch, retarded the spark with his right handle grip, made sure the butterfly stopcock to the gas tank was open, gave the engine a little gas with the throttle that was his left handle grip and kicked down the starter. The ragged old rumble began and he smoothed it down with the spark. The clutch was an iron rocker pedal beneath his left foot, the gearshift a knob on the right side of the gas tank. He eased into low and raised the engine's rumble. He waved to her where she was a vague, screened figure in the darkness of her house and then began to move the first yards of the thousands of miles. It was as though he didn't move but Leah moved past him as he sat steady and central in the gyroscopic force of his turning wheels.

He rode down Water Street to Maple Street, and as he turned, banking slightly, the town banked and turned around him. Oak Street, Beech Street and the other streets named after trees passed him, all the houses familiar, as were many of their histories and interiors. In that white clapboard house with green shutters there had been a tragedy once; a child had died and the family moved away.

He rode down Bank Street to the Town Square with its tall elms and octagonal wooden bandstand, deciding to circle it once before beginning, a centrifugal urge that would gently fling him west across his country. In the morning air that was so still and humid it seemed full of lethargy, a film on the eyes, the gaunt Victorian red brick blocks leaned back: Masonic Hall 1893; Tuttle Block 1901; Cascom Savings Bank Bldg. 1907. Then the Congregational church, white wooden Gothic; the colonial houses and wide lawns of the owners and formerly of the owners of mills and factories, houses he had visited as a false Sylvester. The small Romanesque library in tan brick and granite; then the colonial-style post office built in 1937; the Strand Theater, a brick box with a marquee; the Town Hall, a strange twin both Greek and Roman—square behind and round before; then around to the Victorian blocks again, stores below and dentists and such up long, straight wooden stairs that were always dusty and vast. The more he'd known the town and worked in it, the more it had become itself, separate from him. All these shapes were bound to their foundations and would stay here motionless, no matter how far he traveled.

The few morning people on the streets walked toward their eight hours of repetitious loafing and work. That white-haired man in a brown suit was Mr. Candless, who had taught him how to sell shoes and hats and to tie up a package without having to pin the first overhand knot with a finger. In Leah he had learned the small tricks of various labors and trades, enough to have made him aware that those minor skills were multitudinous and indispensable, the property of those he might sometimes be tempted to scorn because of his own vague but grander ambitions.

With a banking turn at speed, a gesture of superiority, bravado and farewell, he left the Town Square on Wentworth Street, which turned into the highway leading west. The engine revolved below him and turned the rear wheel by way of its great oily chain, the warmth of oil and seared cylinder vanes at his knees. For moments he forgot not to trust the machine because he was moving, passing not over but seemingly beside the land. He approached Vermont, its round hills over there, across the valley of the Connecticut River. He slowed to enter the wooden roadbed of the long covered bridge, the worn boards rising and falling like swells; the familiar *plimp-plump* of their flexing echoed among the barnlike rafters. Then he was in Wentworth Junction, in Vermont. On the main street he risked a moment to lean over and look down at his slightly unbalanced front wheel, spokes and brake drum, the tire tread bouncing over the dry asphalt. Just a glance, at real risk, his eyes quickly recovering and that picture of turning wheel superimposed upon the street ahead, the small railroad station, the general store, the Railroad Hotel, then the tenements and houses as he began the climb up out of town over the hump of Vermont toward New York State.

He was solitary now on the machine he held between his thighs, free and unlonely. The road was public and he had every right. He had been in thrall to the encircling desires of a girl, but now in his leaving she had already become vaguer, a woman, and he found it hard to believe his former assertiveness toward her. She had suggested at the moment of parting all women, women-in-power, mothers, teachers, and shaming, blaming episodes from too far back toward childhood. How could he understand her, them, women? They were so necessary and beautiful when they were happy, but a word could make their lives useless to them, and you saw hell smoking and burning in back of their shriveled eyes. In fifth grade when he'd had appendicitis a teacher had tried to comfort him in his pain on a couch in the teachers' lounge. She put her strapped and bound breast, firm as a basketball, against his cheek. He knew she thought that comforting, though he was ten, and despised that infantile comfort.

Now the wind cleared him as he moved away at nearly a mile a minute. Too fast! Then, oh, well, take the curve like a flier and make it. No, trust was dangerous, near faith; he should slow down to fifty. Perversely, he twisted his throttle and climbed past sixty. Why? Fool! He opened his mouth and the wind filled out his cheeks. He chewed the palpable wind.

At times the motorcycle hardly existed and it was only he who flew along the road past fields and woods. Then he would remember the machine which carried him and feel grateful for its power and loyalty. Good old Indian Pony. But it could break anytime; what would he do if it betrayed him? He could be stranded anywhere, miles from anywhere. Even now he was far from anyone he knew, his citizenship in this strange country tenuous. If Vermont was strange to him, what would the farther states do to his self-confidence? And the weather could turn back toward March at any time, with him as vulnerable to it as a fish naked in its element. His journey seemed absurd, his search a whim easily put by. But the engine kept moving him west and his danger was, for this hurtling existence and at least for now, stable. Cars and trucks came toward him—Chevrolets, Fords, Plymouths, Nashes, Studebakers—the constant involuntary listing of what was so early known—to suck the air from his side. He passed a pickup truck on a straight, the old Ford's fenders loose as a woman's skirts. Those others were enclosed in steel, he only by the fabric of his clothes, then his tender skin. He must foresee patterns and intentions so that he could pass safely, without a single touch, through each new conjunction of vehicle and direction. It was a constant divining of the immediate that he must repeat each yard for three thousand miles; again it all seemed absurd, beyond his powers. Sooner or later would come the possibly insolvable problem in vectors—his speed, traction, braking friction, the insane or at least unknown intent of a truck or car, with sand, oil or animals on the road.

At times his anxiety faded and there would be a mile or miles of peace and near-forgetfulness, the rush of the wind a kind of gray silence. A song which had been sounding in his head came to his lips; he had been considering it, humming it without words, the words embarrassing and mute, ever since he'd left Dory in the dim light behind the screen. He wasn't sure he could remember all the words. The wind in his mouth made his voice ghostly.

Can she bake a cherry pie,
Billy Boy, Billy Boy?
Can she bake a cherry pie,
Charming Billy?

She can bake a cherry pie
Quick as you can wink (blink?) your eye,
But she's a young thing,
And cannot leave her mother.

Last night he had, with a disturbing sense of disloyalty to her, gone to Futzie's Tavern, where he knew some of his friends hung out these nights between seasons and journeys. Davy Whipple was back from the

University of Chicago; John Cotter was going to Paris in the fall to take something called *Le Cours de la Civilisation Française,* courtesy of the GI Bill. All three were veterans, though Davy had never gone overseas. Their friendship had hard edges; they were all loners in some ways, contemptuous of Leah yet not quite certain about the rest of the world and what they wanted from its more important places. They had always competed with each other and among them was no buffoon, no comedian, no recognized type. Even in grammar school each had demanded an exact equality, and they had fought more than once over this principle. The war and their service in it had changed nothing. If there was one quality the three had in common it was, he thought, a sort of laconic candidness. Out of their natures, not much influenced by each other, they made a point of telling the truth.

John Cotter was short, dark and quiet, almost immobile at times, like a woods animal listening for danger. Davy Whipple was the handsome one, whose self-confidence was a wonder, who always, for instance, went out with those girls who tended to stun ordinary mortals with their beauty. His sister Kate was of this category; maybe that was the reason for his confidence.

When the three of them were together they were, as always, aware of potential judgments that might be unsaid but could never be ignored; each had more relaxing acquaintances, he was certain. That he should have met these particular friends on his last night, with Dory on his mind and his quest or flight ahead of him, was the sort of coincidence he associated with Leah, the town of eyes and ears. Or of conscience, though he attributed no particular virtues to Leah. "I was born in Minnesota," he said once in high school. "Land of the sky-blue waters; land of ten thousand lakes."

"Hey! *Really?*" Davy Whipple said.

John Cotter said, " 'When my father got me, his thoughts were not upon me.' "

Davy Whipple added, " 'When Adam delved and Eve span, who was then the gentleman?' "

Maybe they had influenced each other. Pretension, except for theirs, perhaps—their brand of it—would always be identified. One of them had discovered Isak Dinesen's "The Deluge at Norderney," and they could still quote from it.

> "Father," I said, remembering again how we had sailed together, "is Baron Gersdorff my father? Do you know the man?"

"Leave the women's business alone," he said. "Here you are, Jonathan, a seaworthy ship, whoever built you."

Last night his friends had been in a somber mood. They asked about his plans and were not inclined to scoff at his hints about the epic nature of his voyage. Each had his own romantic troubles. John Cotter's were well known; his girl, Jane Stevens, had married a hero of the submarines, a handsome, good-natured idiot who had been discharged while John Cotter was still in the Army. Davy Whipple was in love with a girl in Chicago who was six years older than he was. They all took this age business seriously; when he'd be twenty-five, she'd be thirty-one; when he'd be thirty, she'd be thirty-six; when he'd be thirty-six, she'd be forty-two. In other words he'd have this old lady on his hands, and yet he loved her. Letty was her name. Dark looks across the smoky room.

Futzie's Tavern was a workingmen's place few of their contemporaries ever patronized, though they might in later years when the flexible charms of youth wore away. Old men in work clothes ate hard-boiled eggs and drank draft beer at grimy and mismatched tables. Some played cards. None of the men spoke much, but from the radio behind the bar, never fiddled with but merely turned on, came romantic ballads, news, ads, whatever—a veil of sound that gave privacy. Futzie, an old man whose ethnic origins were vaguely Baltic, had been disconcerting when they first knew him because all of his communicating was done at the level of a yell, but he liked them and sold them beer after legal hours from a basement window out in back.

"On the other hand," Davy said, "my sister informs me that Johnny Hearne, here, is something of a cradle robber."

"In Leah everybody thinks they know everything," John said.

"She was at the lake and saw you and Dory Perkins sail by in your canoe. Now, does that mean everything? Is that prima facie evidence of everything?"

John Cotter looked from one to the other, reserving comment and even expression. Davy watched, waiting for some kind of answer but not about to force the matter. It would have been easy enough to indicate to them that the subject was closed.

"I guess I'm pretty serious about it, to tell the truth," John said.

So they were all serious about it. They gave him permission, for the moment, to be as serious about it as he wanted; that was what friends were for. "Maybe I'll marry her," he added. Saying the words made them official and the concept suddenly adult, generational in its implications, enormous, as though distant cathedral bells rang in a new life or tolled for lost boyhood.

"Well, good luck, Johnny, whatever happens," John Cotter said. "We're all going off somewhere and I suppose we'll all come back to Leah once in a while, for one reason or another."

"Funerals, mostly," Davy Whipple said.

"Lugubrious. Lugubrious," John Cotter said.

"Weddings, then."

"Concupiscence saps a man's juices, makes him soft."

"Afterwards, you mean."

"Soft as a daisy petal drooping with dew."

At closing time they briefly considered buying some beer from Futzie and continuing elsewhere, but no one had a subject to talk about. The general excitement, partly of the war and their having grown up, had faded now. They were veterans at twenty-one, but that claim, if made, would be for show, or for some other purpose not necessarily honest. It was a time to go off alone, probably; grand events, if there were such things, were controlled, or more likely uncontrolled, by their elders far away. As for John Hearne, he would try to find out where he'd been before he could speculate about the future. Best to head out alone.

As he rode across Vermont another phrase began to sound in his head, and he was surprised to find in it nostalgia. Was Leah, in some disputed way, home? Was he that far away from it already? The repeated phrase was Spanish: *agua caliente, agua caliente.* Every year in deep summer the old man who came with a scythe to mow the high grass along the road to the cabin sharpened his blade with a long stone, helve against his breast, the stone singing on the blade, *agua caliente, agua caliente.* The words, he finally discovered, came from a name he must have seen long before on a map, a place in Mexico called Hot Water, but before that definite information had arrived he'd heard them very plainly, over and over, in the old man's lifelong ritual of stone and blade. With the memory came the heavy heat of summer and the sweet new-mown grass.

Toward noon he was hungry in a dry, abstract way, the vibrations and wind a whole way of existing; if he stopped he might grow dizzy in that silence. He ought to stop in the next town, check his fuel and oil, and if he could swallow against the dryness in his mouth and throat, put something into himself. As he came to the summit of a long hill, almost a mountain, he saw weather ahead of him, a line of darkness approaching from the west. From his high vista the distant clouds with their blue-black roots seemed below him, but his road led down, and they were coming on.

The words *agua caliente, agua caliente* formed in his dry mouth, evoking the summer blue of Cascom Lake. The road descended past farms and fields, evergreen woods and groves of hardwood. He made his long, shallow descent toward the storm that would be the first of many. Wintry temperatures would return within that turbulence. He could be at Cascomhaven, the musty smell of winter not yet baked out by summer, a fire in the fireplace, watching a spring storm smear the water and bend the tall pines along the shore. Before he met this storm he must stop and put on his poncho, but to stop now might be dangerous to his resolve. At the lake, when he was alone there—and then with Dory—there were known rights and proper rituals. He deserved the cabin because he maintained it, but now he was leaving what he knew; there would be New York State, Pennsylvania, Ohio, Indiana and farther, where the people would speak differently and not know him. There was the question of his right even to ask to pay for food and shelter. He had never spent a night in a roadside cabin or a motor hotel, though in books and movies people did it without a twinge, as if it were an absolute right. And a motorcycle was not as respectable as a car. Wild and crude men rode them, oil-stained and wind-grimed people not to be trusted, who would soil the sheets and pillowcases.

He had with him a blanket bag and tarpaulin, so he could sleep out in an emergency, but among what plants and animals, poisonous or crawling? He would have no right to make the smallest fire on someone else's land, or even to stop there. Maybe in a desert among scorpions and rattlers, a place so forsaken and remote no one would care. But it was all maybe; he didn't know. Meanwhile he descended a long Vermont hill toward the storm.

The storm was a frontier. He could turn around and go back; though it would catch him he could run with it, not meet it head-on. Veils of rain hung from the distant clouds, curved swaths like blown gray curtains in a photograph. Lightning, behind the front, revealed higher cloud canyons that grew like geological uprisings to the west and south. Ahead and below him a mile or so, still not within the storm, was a little town, partly hidden by a fold of hill, white houses and the red brick of its business street gleaming in the last sunlight.

As he came into the town he heard the flat deep crack of thunder over the noise of his engine. The sun went out as if it had set, and twilight came sliding over the town as he stopped at a restaurant on the main street. He was unsteady on his feet as he set the motorcycle over on its kickstand. His ankles felt brittle, still tingling as if they had absorbed electricity from the magneto. It took him the few steps across the sidewalk to the old storefront restaurant to get his land legs again. It was the first time he'd stopped the engine since he'd started it with Dory watching, nearly a hundred miles ago, on a hazy blue morning in Leah.

13

Dory's responsibilities at Cascom Manor were great, but they were a little less worrisome because everyone else was so disorganized that her own arrangements were usually best. The person who presently owned Cascom Manor, or supposedly ran it, or who was merely its decorative hostess, was the Princess Ganz-Lengen. She had many Christian names, but her title was always used by the guests, most of whom were previous acquaintances of the Princess, or *Prinzessin,* or *Princesa,* depending upon the language spoken at the moment. Whether or not she was a real princess Dory wasn't altogether certain, because there was a sometimes frowsy exuberance about the guests that suggested make-believe. Or maybe it was her own feeling, that princesses existed only in stories, or back in history, dressed in strange costumes, and were the daughters of kings. There were, or had once been, principalities in Germany, she knew, and in *War and Peace* there were odd princes and princesses who had no thrones, but that was long ago. She hadn't asked direct questions because it seemed a matter of her own protocol not to be nosy, that asking might be construed as disbelief, and that one simply didn't inquire about royalty's antecedents, which were, in the end, all that royalty had.

The Princess was a slender woman in her forties with soft, powder-white skin. Her hair was so black that it seemed unreal until you observed that the silky hairs on her forearms, though so fine as to be invisible from a short distance, were also jet black. She never shaved; it was as if she had never heard of the custom. Some of the fine hairs on her legs were several inches long, and from the crotch of her bathing suit came a curl or two of coarser black. In a sleeveless dress or blouse her armpits flashed black fur.

Softness, though, was her most remarkable quality. Her fingers seemed to have no weight at all, but floated away from touch like waterweed fronds. Her skin took into itself the finest detail of a seam, even to the stitching.

Her accent was English, but the slightly harsher, or at least different, sounds of German came into certain words, like "bread," or "book." She smelled of spices Dory couldn't name—not the flowery scent of perfume but perhaps things like camomile, or sandalwood. She wore bright red lipstick, which made her face as striking as a flag—red, white, the pale blue of her eyes and black.

Before Dory had taken over, last summer, there had been "the Swede," a man who had acted as if he and the Princess were lovers, or ex-lovers. He drank, was surly, brutal with objects, dented the fenders of the Cascom Manor station wagon on the Scotch pines along the driveway and finally disappeared after having thrown the Princess on the kitchen stove. While the Swede was disappearing, Dory treated the mild burn on the Princess's hip and buttock with tannic acid. The elastic of her panties had cast its image deeply into her skin.

"He was so upset!" the Princess said. "So disturbed! One really worries about the poor man!"

Dory had been more worried about what the Swede would do next; his anger and frustration had a convincing intensity, as if they were justified. But he did disappear, driving off in his old car. Sometime during the winter he died, "by his own hand," the Princess wrote to her on stationery with a coronet and coat of arms. *Ex aequo et bono* was the motto beneath the coat of arms, which was a shield with quarterings, one a checkerboard, another a fish. The letter asked Dory if she would continue with the duties she had assumed on the Swede's disappearance. She would get an increase in pay to thirty-five dollars a week, room and board.

It had been while she applied the cool tannic acid solution to the Princess's soft white hem-etched hip and buttock with cotton batting that she'd thought more about the idea of one's antecedents. It all seemed un-American, yet she knew many people, including her friend Cynthia Fuller, who took great and continuing pride in their ancestors. Cynthia was a "*Mayflower* descendant," and this knowledge was always there for sustaining purposes whenever Cynthia might need it. Dory's own name, Perkins, and her mother's maiden name, Sleeper, seemed perfectly undistinguished, lines of amorphous toilers going back, back into the repetitious murk of time. But here was the Princess, her printed cotton skirt up to her waist, her rayon panties halfway down across her white buttocks, looking, from this angle at least, the most ordinary haired, pored and creased female. Still, she did seem more valuable, all of her, even the ancient crater there of a pimple, long healed; even the imagined manipulations of hand and toilet paper had a dainty grace about them, and the effect came from a veil of nobility that Dory could not quite remove from her mind. The Princess's accent was a specific difference between her and ordinary mortals, but in all the rest, even to her ignored wiry hairs, she was merely a forty-two-year-old woman with rather poor body tone.

The Princess had hummed a little and trembled nervously at what must have been minor pain, but was not modest or skittish at all about having her panties down and her behind revealed, maybe because Dory was a commoner, or servant, or New Hampshire peasant. She wondered about that; a note of Yankee Doodle disdain sounded faintly in her soul like a distant bugle.

But the Princess was amiable, in her distracted way. She didn't seem capable of anger, "rising above" leaky roofs, plugged plumbing, being thrown by a madman onto the black gas stove, its burners, though out, still hot enough to sear her regal skin. The Swede had been more impressed by his act than she was. After a while Dory had come to understand that the Swede, no matter who he was or how he'd come into the Princess's service, could not be fired because princesses did not hire and fire; it was as if their people were inherited, like servitors or populations. But the Swede had left her service "by his own hand," and this summer Dory would have to oversee hiring and firing, maintenance and provisioning, among her other duties. The Princess's cook, a man in his sixties named Kasimir, couldn't speak much English or drive a car. He could speak French, and Dory had built upon the slim knowledge of French she had gained in high school until she could understand his lists and even some of his conversation. On his day off she did the cooking.

On the day John Hearne left Leah her mother drove her out to the lake and around through the little town of Cascom to Cascom Manor, whose wooden sign and mailbox, she noticed, because she would have to fix them, had been knocked into the ditch by a snowplow during the winter. The long driveway was bordered by Scotch pines, aliens planted twenty years before by a previous owner. The lodge was a farmhouse of three stories that looked taller and more massive than it was because on each higher story the windows were smaller than the ones just below them. The roof didn't have much pitch to it, which caused leaking around the dormers that had been added in 1911, when the house had first been used as an inn. This sort of knowledge came from the research of curious and proprietary guests who wrote, some of them, long essays in the Cascom Manor Log, a thick blank book kept on the pine mantel in the library.

Her mother drove around to the front of the lodge, which looked through a frame of tall tamaracks to a broad field leading down to the wooded shore of the lake. No one else was here yet, but Dory had the keys. Before her mother could leave it was necessary to see if the telephone worked so that she could begin the process of awakening the old place from its musty winter sleep. Her mother came in with her, a little hesitant, quieted by this public place with its large rooms and with Dory's responsibility for it. "Them people," she always called the foreigners from the south. "When are them people going to git here?"

Dory was on the phone calling King's Garage in Cascom to have them bring the car battery, which had been in their care all winter, and install it in the '39 Ford station wagon. With the phone and the station wagon working she could begin.

"I'll pick up the Princess and Kasimir in Wentworth Junction Thursday," she said.

"The Princess!" her mother said, with a quick laugh; her strained belief was something like Dory's own.

It was a good clear drying day so her mother helped her open shutters and windows, and then, getting water from the old hand pump at the well, they made coffee, which was a little stale from its long winter in a paper sack, brought out wicker chairs and sat on the long screened porch. Her mother had to be back at work soon, but Dory felt in her a desire for questions and answers, the ritual giving of warnings and admonitions that made a mother feel that she had at least tried to do her duty. While the stale air of the lodge changed they sipped their black coffee and looked down at the lake. Dory searched the far shore, two miles across the water, for the cove where Cascomhaven was, but all she could see was a wall of black-green pines. Pine Island, where she had been so apprehensive of the wind, was closer, still sail-heavy but uncapsized. Today the lake was so calm and blue no one could be afraid of it.

"So he went out to California," her mother said. That he could be called "he" with no preamble meant that nothing could be denied.

"Yup," Dory said.

"Is he coming back, d'you think?" Coming back because of her, to make an honest woman of her.

"He's probably coming back, I'd say." But whether or not that meant anything, she didn't know.

"I know you ain't in trouble, Doris."

"No, I'm not in trouble."

"You might of been, though, God knows."

"Yes."

Her mother sighed and shook her thin shoulders, or they shook involuntarily. "Well, he's a nice boy in many ways, but if I was you I'd just go on doing what I had to do."

"I will, Ma."

"I don't know," her mother said. "You're young for your age in some ways, but here you are taking care of this big place. You're a lot like me. Of course, I never finished high school. Did you and him have much to talk about?"

"Sometimes. He wanted me to go to college."

"Huh!" her mother said. "You ever thought of going to college?"

"I never thought I could."

"Your friend Cynthia's going to college, ain't she?"

"I know."

"You're smarter than her."

"I don't know about that. Maybe in some ways, Ma, but maybe not college ways."

"Puh! You don't even talk like us. You already talk like a college girl, like that valedictorian speech you give."

Her mother was not chiding her for it. Things changed from mother to daughter, though the changes might be superficial. Her mother knew how superficial vocabulary was. And what her mother said about Cynthia was true, in a way. Cynthia never seemed to think of anything that was too deep or complicated to say out loud. What you heard seemed to be all there was to Cynthia. It was traitorous to think this about her friend, who was honest, clever and good-hearted.

Her mother said, "Maybe you ought to go to college. Northlee State, maybe."

"I don't want to think about it now, Ma."

"When do you want to think about it?"

"I couldn't afford it."

"I can help you with money."

"Ma, you worked the last ten years for your own money. You don't want to give it to me."

"Who's to say?"

They had no tradition of touching each other in affection, but she was grateful for this offer which she would never take. Never. She got up, went behind her mother's chair and shaped her mother's brown hair with her fingers, undoing and replacing a mother-of-pearl barrette. The dull hair was like her own—a sort of universal peasant pelt that was always limp, the color and texture nobody really wanted. Some strands were silver, evenly sown throughout the brown. Her mother's neck had begun to tilt forward, to settle into her shoulders, the bridging muscles at the nape seeming to grow higher each year.

"You ought to hold your head up, Ma. You're getting a stoop," she said, something she'd said before and which meant that not age but posture caused this slump in the bones. Her mother sighed in response.

Her mother's name was Sarah; her father called her "Sare" when he didn't call her "Ma." He called her "Sare" when he was defensive about something, "Ma" when the family was more or less in harmony. "Ma," or "Sare," her mother was never really in the wrong. She might be wrong about a fact or a process, but not morally wrong. In all her life Dory had never seen a time when her mother should have been guilty because of dishonesty or selfishness. She could not think of one time. It was strange even to consider that there might have been such a time. If her mother was ever unfair or unreasonable it was because of an excess of principle, never a lack of it. There were times when she was hard on Pa, and this sternness might not always have been so pure, coming as it may have from resentment or even cruelty. Sometimes she drove him to anger, but that was what people did who were not strangers, when hurtfulness came up as unawares as nausea.

Her mother took their cups into the kitchen and rinsed them out, using well water from the bucket. "You sure you don't need some help with all this?" she asked.

"No, Ma. There's a million little things to do but I can do them all right. The crew will be here this afternoon to begin on the rest."

"I know you can do whatever you make up your mind to," her mother said. "Will we see you much this summer?"

"I'll stop by when I can, Ma."

They went outside, to the black Chevrolet. "You need anything, you give us a call, now."

"Sure, Ma."

Her mother got into the car. "At least he ain't here to trouble you. You got time to think about it."

"It's all right."

They squeezed hands—proper at a farewell—and her mother drove in a half circle on the frost-heaved gravel turnaround and was gone.

She was familiar with what winter's long chill and pressure did to an empty house, so she got busy. Forgotten food, and paper unprotected from the mice was here and there shredded upon their trails and in their nests. The plumbing was simpler than at Cascomhaven but there was one bathroom downstairs and two bathrooms upstairs with all their traps and grimy porcelain to close and clean, faucets to check, the jet pump in the basement to prime and reseal, the gas water heater to start. The worst was bedding—dampish folded sheets heavy as bales, blankets bitter with the gas of mothballs. Then towels and tablecloths, throws and doilies, carpets, dust, dried water stains on sills and floors like topographic maps. Well, she had begun.

Old Mr. King came with the battery for the station wagon, pumped up the tires with a hand pump, removed the jacks and got the engine running. He thought she ought to bring it in soon for an oil change and grease job, which she promised to do. The dash compartment was a mouse nest, the registration chewed and stained with mouse urine but still legible. With it came a delicate white skeleton stuck to the paper with the now odorless glue of vanished flesh.

When the crew—three high school boys and the sister of one of them—hadn't arrived by four o'clock she called the home of the one who seemed to be their leader and got his mother.

"But, Dory, didn't they tell you? They all got jobs with the pine blister rust because it pays so much better." As for the sister: "Margaret decided she didn't want to do it again this summer."

One lived in a world of such people; she knew that well enough. Why should they bother to honor their word, unless punishment was involved? What was an agreement? In any case, she had a problem. The yards, the field, the hedges and flower borders—all the detritus and collapse of winter had to be cleaned up, mowed, raked, repainted. The boathouse and the boats, the beach, the fireplace wood, the docks and floats—she couldn't do all that by herself. And she needed a waitress. Here was an administrative dilemma. But she had contracted with the Princess to take care of such things, so she would.

She spent the next two hours on the telephone trying to find a crew. She didn't like the telephone much because she felt its preemptive ring to be an invasion of privacy, but she had to find some hands willing to work. It was late; school had been out too long and those of any competence had already made plans. Finally she called Cynthia Fuller, more for sympathy than anything else.

"I'm surprised at Margaret," Cynthia said. "She might have told you, at least. As for her brother, he's always been the sort of child who licked the snot off his upper lip. And now he's going to be a senior next fall, so he wants a *man's* job. So typical. Why don't you try Robert Beggs? He'll do anything for you."

"You know he's got to work for his father."

"Boy children don't always enjoy working for their fathers. Look, Dory. Let me do some calling. I've got some ideas. Trust me?"

She was tired, and grateful that some effort might be going on without her, no matter how little faith she had in it, so she thanked Cynthia, who seemed eager to hang up, and went on with her work. Tomorrow she would call the manager of the Community Center, who was also a Scout leader. Often there were notices on the bulletin board from kids who wanted work. She didn't think anything would come of Cynthia's efforts, but at least she had an excuse to stop using the telephone for a while.

She'd meant to go in to the general store in Cascom and get some supplies, but now it was too late. There were a few wintered-over cans in the pantry, one a No. 2 can of baked beans, so she heated that up. The sauce was grainy from having been frozen, but edible.

It was eight o'clock, the sun low and the air beginning to cool. Gold came through the western windows, held by the lively motes of dust her labors had stirred into the dark-cornered rooms—the dining room's empty tables and chairs, the chintz-covered couches, chairs and ottomans, the bridge lamps of the long living room, the smaller library through a plaster arch, where most of the books in the glass-fronted bookcases were an ancient red, faded rose. Some of the titles were: *The Vanished Messenger,* by E. Phillips Oppenheim, *The Boy Trapper,* by Harry Castlemon, *Paris Salons, Cafés, Studios,* by Sisley Huddleston, and *Word Pictures of Japan,* by Elizabeth Marker Willoughby. They seemed always to have been old, and to pick one out, take it to her room and read it, as she had done, seemed a journey into an alternate past, one that hadn't much changed whatever events had led to the present. In those books "the War" was another war, and the cultivated voices that spoke to her flattered and lied, implying that she was one of them. Cynthia would have been more comfortable with their assumptions.

Cynthia: when the pale, skinny girl had arrived in Leah in the fifth grade she had been accepted because in the fifth grade everyone was accepted, the children then still tolerant of unselfconscious foibles. Ten was a good age, before the second skin of conformity and self-consciousness hardened into dogma, before teachers and most adults became foreign powers. Cynthia was called upon to play her violin in assembly—to them then an interesting skill rather than a badge of queerness. Dory had been flattered when Cynthia walked home with her, as excited as a lover when this girl marked by talent chose her as a friend.

Cynthia still lived in the small, dim apartment with her mother and younger brother, downstreet on the square, above Trask's Pharmacy. Her mother was sickly, and didn't work; their money came from the father, who sent it through the mail. When Cynthia first used the word "alimony," Dory, because of the sound of it and the way Cynthia said it, thought it meant something like "a disease that was a crime to have," and that Cynthia's mother, having this alimony, had been sentenced to live in Leah, a place where she knew no one. They had come from Boston, where they had lived on Symphony Road, a name that was pretty and must have had something to do with Cynthia's violin. Though Dory had sorted these things out over the years, at some atavistic level that could not be reached for reassessment, she still half believed them.

In the later grades Cynthia had grown tall and rather gaunt, with bony shoulders and hips, but she had enviable golden hair—not silver blond but a true gold that could never be associated with the word "brown." She must have taken after her absent father, for both her mother and her younger brother, Dibley—called "Dibbles"—had dark hair, mouse-colored.

She did her fork and dish at the sink, put them away and walked, just as the sun set behind the hills toward Leah, down to the beach to look at the boathouse and the dock, which was now pulled up and stranded. If Cynthia called she would call again. The gravel path had been humped and disarranged by frost.

The lake was calm, for Cascom Lake, smooth little waves silently dematerializing upon the sand. The boathouse, formerly an icehouse, a barn improbably close to the shore, had survived the winter, its ancient tilt no more pronounced, she thought, than it had been last summer and the summer before. One double-hung window had fallen right out, probably into soft snow, for not one light had broken. She propped it up against the gray clapboards, to be replaced later. The lake was cool and pink, a corduroy of the reflected western clouds. Near Pine Island a boat trolled for salmon or lake trout, the sound of its inboard motor a slow pulse barely audible even down the wind. Faint hammering came from a cabin somewhere on Merrihew Island. She sat on the beached dock, not minding her solitariness in the falling dusk, though the lodge would be hollow dark when she returned to it, the ghosts of its long past quietly residing in the blackest alcoves. It was nonsense to be chilled by what could never hurt you, but it would be strange nearly to the verge of fright to be alone all night in Cascom Manor, all those rooms silent behind their doors.

Dew was falling, and she had left some windows open, so she went back to close them and turn on a lonely light or two. She could go home if she wanted to; the station wagon was there in the shed, a magical transport away from all this emptiness into familiar light and warmth. But she wouldn't go home. Larger concerns, or at least more real ones, always banished the ogres and grues (John Hearne's words). He must be settling in for the night, alone in some roadside cabin in Vermont or New York State. Maybe he was thinking of her, right now, at this very instant, just for a flash. If so, she wondered what he saw that he named Dory Perkins. If it wasn't good she didn't want to know about it. No, she did want to know. When did she ever not want to know?

At the lodge she shut the rest of the windows and then opened the damper of the living-room fireplace, receiving on her wrist the desiccated remains of a blue jay, the jaunty feathers he had worn still bright but detached from the weevily brown parts of him she pushed with the backs of her fingers into last summer's ashes. When she had a fire going she turned out the lights and sat before it in a deep wing chair, through doing anything.

She had never been one to mind being alone, but she said, "I wish he were here," daring with solitary speech the ghosts who might be tempted to answer. Nonsense, she thought, but the word was not as powerful as the dark spaces at her back. The fire grew and warmed her, her "loins"—did women have loins? He might know that sort of thing, and would do something odd and unexpected, no doubt, if she asked him about the word—something that should have been outrageous but instead would pass over into his new kind of whimsy. New to her, anyway, with the quickly passing shadow of possible resentment at being startled.

Now the ghosts were gone, because he was more dangerous than any ghost. There was the fear of loss and also the fear of handling him. He had too many advantages over her, was too ironic and slippery, and yet she wanted to be connected to him and have his children. She was too young and there was so much time she could almost wish it away. The firelight flickered down the long room, on the dull gilt frames of paintings, strange on the outsides of lampshades. Her warm thighs made her think of his solidity. It was a terrible surrender, too momentous because she could never separate her pleasure from his pleasure in that humid glandular merge in blood darkness which seemed the willing end of her as she had always known herself. That she'd wanted to do it all the time, anytime, was the measure of her thralldom. Even now she could imagine his presence in such detail that she responded to him.

There was another vision of them both, suggested by a picture she'd seen in *Life* of two ocean liners docked next to each other—first the high bow of one and then, behind it, even larger but dimmed by fog, the bow of the other. She thought of their two heads, just there in proximity, looking calmly at something outside of themselves, but forever a pair. That was the final judgment her self had made, which was to surrender to a dreamy idea of perfection she knew was not real life. But she did love him, a strange, ancient situation in which to find herself.

The telephone at the hall desk rang so hard she imagined it jumping up and down like a furious child. She went to it, turning on an overhead light that made her recent fantasies seem tawdry. The mouth (or was it the ear?) of the telephone looked like a black daffodil.

It was Cynthia, who said, "I've got you *two!* Two you'd *never* have thought of asking, so only I could have achieved this miracle!"

Dory felt apprehension. "Who are they?" she said.

"One is, of course, Robert Beggs—solid, steady, strong, boring—the perfect candidate. The other?" Cynthia paused dramatically.

"All right. Who?"

"Me!"

"You?" Every summer Cynthia went to a music camp where she played in the orchestra. "But what about your camp?"

"A short, sordid story. Daddy's had reverses, this being a depression, you know—or at least he says so—and what with college in the fall he claims he can't afford it. Mother thinks his current popsie—or is it poopsie?—is too expensive. So I must *labor* for my upkeep this summer. Are you pleased, or filled with consternation?"

"Pleased. But it's a lot of boring work, you know. You'll get awfully tired of dishes and mops."

"Paupers can't be choosers. What's the pay?"

"Twenty dollars a week, room and board."

"Lord! A fortune! I accept! But what about Robert—are you pleased by that?"

"I guess so. I'm sure he's a good worker."

"Hmm. He is your devoted slave, isn't he? I suppose a devoted slave in close proximity could be tiresome. But I suspect there are things you haven't told me, Dory."

"I guess you're right."

"I mean about a certain college boy you once confessed to having a crush on, who's been seen on the front of a motorcycle you were on the back of, so to speak."

"Yes."

"It is serious, then. I can hear it in your voice. If you don't want me to mention it again, ever, just say so."

Cynthia was kind, but she was a little hurt. She seemed to have no reticence and didn't like it in others, especially in Dory, who had been her best friend, after all, since fifth grade.

"I'll tell you all about it," Dory said, knowing that she couldn't tell Cynthia all about it, that she was lying. There were no words she would know how to use in telling Cynthia, and Cynthia might not want to know all of it anyway. She might think she did, but the real truth would only separate them. She didn't think Cynthia would like to have to take the part of the less experienced, the less engaged.

"Not over the phone, of course," Cynthia said, going into her "contralto" voice to try to make a joke of her curiosity. "But to get back to your immediate problems, I have a rather doubtful idea and I thought I'd better ask you before I asked him. 'Him' being Dibbles. The child is fifteen and rather strong in body if not in mind, and he's not going to his canoe-paddling and boondoggle-braiding camp this summer. What do you think? Could you use him?"

This was complicated. If she hired Dibley she would have to hire Debbie, who had asked her if there was a chance for a job. She'd tried to tell Debbie how much work was involved, but of course that didn't work. "Then I'll have to ask Debbie, too," she said.

"I didn't think of that," Cynthia said.

They were both silent, thinking, and then Dory, with the delinquent feeling, almost like an unexpected yawn, that meant she was trading bother now for trouble later, said, "All right. Maybe it'll work out. I'll come and pick you up tomorrow morning."

"We can handle it," Cynthia said. "I'll let our motley crew know. But are you utterly certain you want to take on Dibbles and Debbie?"

"Dibley's all right." Dibley was tall, bit his fingernails to the moons and was quiet to the point of soundlessness. The word he used most was a sort of "um," or "ahm," which could mean many things. It was one of the few words he ever said directly to her, but she felt that he would slowly and steadily do any task he was asked to do. Debbie, for all her protestations of industry and promptitude, was another matter.

"And Debbie?" Cynthia said.

"Yes. Oh, well . . . Lord, I'm too young for all this responsibility. How did I get into this?"

"The same way you get into everything," Cynthia said. "Instead of just talking about things, like the rest of us, you roll up your little sleeves and *do* them. You're condemned to be busy. All your life you're going to be busy-busy-busy taking care of slobs."

"Thanks."

"Don't blame me. I cannot alter the future, I merely predict it."

"Well, if you know what's going to happen this summer, don't tell me."

"Oh, Dory. We all love you and we'll do the best we can. We'll have some good times. You'll see."

When they said goodbye, Cynthia's reassuring voice suddenly gone, she was alone in the old house. She went back to the living room and put the screen in front of the embering fire—red eyes on a pillow of soft ash. Behind her was the wing chair, a presence with its wings like shoulders and its other human parts. From its thronelike hollow something might be looking at her back. When she'd come into the room she hadn't looked at the chair closely enough, and now it was too late to give that first easy look. She would have to turn.

There had been a suicide in the house; in 1915 a young girl had drunk lye and died two long weeks later. No one knew why she'd done it. That was what *The Leah Free Press* said, the yellow clipping in an old ledger in the library. Her name was Betty Salmon, from Cascom, and she'd been a maid. A strange word, "maid." Maybe the presence behind her was Betty Salmon, haunting the place of her agony. A chill of goose bumps passed over her arms and she turned, because she had to. The chair was empty of all but shadow, but in the shadow, vivid to some sense other than her eyes, was a form she could create in bone, fragmented garments and decay. Why had she always known that in life Betty Salmon was large and somewhat awkward, flushed with faint blue dapplings, those round watermarks that appear and disappear on too pale skin? Had she been seduced and betrayed, and died of shame, no longer a maiden, any death better than life? How horrible her life must have been to her, to drink lye! How stupid to drink lye, she thought, and her breath caught. She mustn't think that. The ghost girl, if angered, might open her ragged throat and screech at her. Who was she to judge that magnitude of despair?

She could go home tonight, but she didn't belong there now. If she were chased home by her own mind it would be a small but permanent shame, never forgotten. She would not live with that. She would have other, more tender visions of poor Betty Salmon, who had been so unhappy and was now all but forgotten, no more a force in this palpable world than a dead mouse or bird.

14

John Hearne, in bed in a place called Parthenon Cabins, in Tiresias, New York, has just created Dory, made her up of inner light and shadow, shaded in her pale thighs, changing his creation only toward a greater exactitude. He will make her as complete as he can stand. Her close-together eyes watch him, brown and amber, all of her independent judgments intact in them, except now he makes them change toward an avidity as simple as his own. He doesn't want to hurry, to waste this commanding pain. He could be with her but he is hundreds of miles away, making her small nipples grow and her arms reach out. As she becomes too complete she narrows to a use and he holds back, hoarding the pain he can lose any moment he chooses. She wants him now, but he waits, having her move and sigh. He will just enter her and then hold back. Against his will her fingers hook in his skin, his creation not obeying at all. She is ivory, and slippery silk, and he plunges and gushes, burning, then slowly cools. He is in New York State, alone in the small cabin, his semen like ice on his chest, and he has used her up. Whatever else is she now? A mist, an address far away, a separate female seen through old glass, doing sad and neutral things.

15

Poor Betty Salmon, she thinks, placating a ghost, or in a cowardly way trying to. She can't really enter Betty's despair because she has never felt anything like it. She is too practical. She can only come to a place where she can go no farther and has to think: How dumb. Even as she sympathizes she judges. She says out loud in the shadowy vacancy of rooms, "I do feel sorry for you," and the words hang madly in the silence, no answer seeming the most positive terrible answer.

Though she has a flashlight she goes by the safety of light switches upstairs to the small room that will be hers this summer, afraid all the way but afraid of the unreal, of nothing, so she goes anyway. "Nothing" has never had the power to stop her from what must be done, only to make her chilly and apprehensive.

Again she is a mess, so she gathers towels and tack and goes to the bathroom down the hall to take a shower, where she will be deaf and blind for a pseudo-dangerous time in the hissing water. Afterwards, as she washes out her things, she thinks that he wasn't overrelieved when she told him, but then in what feather-splitting ways does she want to judge his relief? And just how willing is she to think herself the sad used maiden? Not very, though she is sad, and used, and a little frightened.

16

He lay in bed in a small enclosure, the moving road still haunting his perspectives; where it had come toward him all day it now wanted to unwind, like a reel of film, so that the gloomy panes of the window moved away from him, as if he were hurtling blindly backwards in space and time. He shut his eyes on the gray lights of the window. The texture of the sheets informed him that he was alive and taut in his skin.

That day Vermont had flown past him, wooded hills and slants of velvet pasture, houses here and there companionably together in small hollows, then small towns under elms—Vermont in its deprived, conventional beauty. Motion, which always became more insistent than place, bore him on. In New York State he'd crossed the Hudson at Troy, a grimy and energetic city dangerous to him, where he felt invisible to cars, and searched for the eyes of drivers, trying to find recognition or intelligence. But all eyes seemed distracted, as if once removed by the prisms of periscopes, like the eyes of tank commanders.

Then had come U.S. 20, with its simpler mathematics of speed, and long hours to the west until the sun was low and directly in his eyes. The choices and complications of the night had come upon him, and he'd felt shy of ending his speed, as if stopping were to be truly in a foreign place, subject to its rules and silences.

It seemed that all his life he had played games whose rules were vague to him, like baseball, in which he was never quite certain when a play began and ended, when a base runner could take a lead, tag up, steal a base. So he had always waited and then run faster, right on past those rules that might have helped him, and because of some fatal laziness never did ask, or look them up. There were so many little things, little ignorances born of avoidance.

The land had begun to roll again, long farmed hills with wooded tops and wide valleys. There had been a glimpse of a lake, silver speckles far away in the glancing sunlight. TIRESIAS, NEW YORK—a small black-and-white sign came by him and soon he was on the main street of a little town, Victorian houses and high elms, a red brick church, ornate high storefronts, two gas stations and a streamlined diner, where he stopped, stiff and tingling in the ankles. He wasn't hungry, though he felt empty. He thought of treats, food supposedly bad for you, but even that echo of childhood couldn't cause hunger. He stood next to his motorcycle for a moment, looking up and down the street. The setting sun was dark orange on the old buildings. Soon he felt that he was balanced again in the steadiness of gravity. Lights came on in houses, and the diner was full of white light.

The Indian Pony creaked as it cooled, and gave off the odors of gasoline and scorched grease. The moving air of the town was fresh from the spring farmland. In the diner he went to the counter and sat on a high stool in the atmosphere of frying that he remembered to have been appetizing, the starved pale short-order cook all elbows and wrists as he scraped and slapped his grill, then brushed a little finger broom of oil over two frankfurters, their sweet-sour odor rising as suddenly as the hiss. The waitress was a thin blond girl wearing an apron as red as her lips, whose sullen face suggested possible beauty if she would ever smile. She must smile sometime, for someone, but not here. The three other diners ate in silence above fading smears of ketchup on white plates.

When he'd eaten and paid, leaving a tip for the unhappy waitress, he went outside, where it was night and the air was chill. He rode down the main street until the houses were farther apart and the black spaces of country came to the road. On his right a small red neon sign said PARTHENON CABINS. He stopped and put his feet down while he considered this incongruous name. Up a steep driveway was another flickering sign that said OFFICE, and then, as if it had just been placed on the small rise of land by magic, was a pale white edifice that was indeed a tiny Parthenon, set here among cedar trees on its own small Acropolis in Tiresias, New York. Tiresias was a person, though, not a place like Troy or Ithaca or Syracuse. Soon he would remember who Tiresias was, and what he had to do with Athena. It would come back to him. The fragmentary knowledge gave him confidence, so he rode up the steep driveway and stopped next to the red sign. As he dismounted a light came on between the wooden columns of the office portico, and a woman watched him through the window, her face framed exactly in one of the panes. He couldn't see her face very well, with the inner light at her back, but in her hand she held a stemmed wineglass. Around him, circling into the darkness, were other Parthenons, each with its wooden columns. The woman moved away from the window and opened an ordinary door.

"Come in," she said. She was at least in her forties, tall and slim, and wore a white dress that seemed formal, and gold bracelets on her arms. Over the dress was a dark apron, as if she had just left a party to prepare something in her kitchen. Her blond hair was dulled by white, and the flush in her cheeks seemed temporary. Her wineglass was now on a sideboard next to a gallon bottle of sherry.

"I'd like a cabin for the night," he said.

"That you will have, young man," she said. There was a practiced quality to her voice, as if it had been used much in public, and must charm, but it was a little out of control, a little contralto, as though she had just passed the degree of drunkenness which could be concealed. Formally, with both hands, she motioned him to a chair at a desk and gave him a pen and a registration form. When he had filled out the form and put six dollars on the desk, he stood up to find himself too close to her, just for a moment, before he moved toward the door. He'd had time to look straight into her blue-gray eyes, which seemed crushed, as if they'd lost clarity but not luster. She was nearly his height, and he thought she must have been striking as a girl, before age and perhaps wine had soiled her. No doubt she had fallen upon hard times.

"Take cabin number one," she said, handing him a key on a large ring.

"Thank you," he said.

"You appeared at my window like a centaur," she said, smiling and looking down with a youthful shyness that didn't go with her voice. She was a little surprised, he thought, when she found that her hand held no wineglass. She glanced at the sideboard, where her glass really was, and then knew that he had seen all of this. He hoped that his expression wasn't in any way judgmental, and then guessed that it wasn't in any way much of anything, because she decided to let it go. He saw the choices flickering across her attitudes of posture and expression, and then nothing, and with a familiar sense of inadequacy he moved to the door.

"Good night," she said. "Sleep well."

"Good night," he answered.

He pushed his Indian Pony over to Parthenon number one, a centaur unhorsed, feeling that there had been a response he should have made, that he was the drab prisoner of callow apprehension, and that her pride still fluttered indecisively.

It was after he had taken a shower in the small metal booth, brushed his teeth like a good boy, breathed the blue dust of a cigarette and squashed it out, that Dory appeared asking to be made vivid and more vivid. He slid his body into the clean coarse sheets with her.

He dreamed that night, fragment after fragment of dream. A car turned directly in front of him and he would have to hit it. He woke up with his hands and legs jumping at the controls—foot brake, hand brake, clutch, but too late. The lady of the Parthenon came to him and she was no longer old, but young and smooth as alabaster. She let her white robe fall from her shoulders and her breasts were full, her nipples red as lipstick, but below her belly she wore the small, tightly carved genitals of a male Greek statue, so it was wrong.

In the morning he remembered these two dreams, others fading into little pricks of color and feeling, then into the stream of the mostly forgotten. The first seemed obvious enough, but the second was somewhat startling. Was he slightly queer or something? This mama's boy who'd had no father since he was five? Those neat little balls and the boy penis had been clearly there, and at first hadn't seemed at all freakish or even unusual. A dream, after all, was clearly a fact. He'd never thought himself queer, and had always tried to put queers off without damaging them or their feelings too much. He decided, finally, that the lady's age was the taboo that the male genitals signified. Or else she was a god-goddess, willful and vengeful, accusing him of this coded shame. If he could play with Dory Perkins, power containing its inevitable measure of cruelty, perhaps the gods could play with him.

Tiresias, he now remembered, was blinded by Athena because he came upon her naked at the bath. What we do and what others do to us.

The morning was heavy with mist, the dark cedars and his motorcycle wet with dew, but the mist would soon burn off. He rode the few blocks back to the center of Tiresias, filled up with gasoline, checked his machine and went to the diner for breakfast. The pretty, sullen young waitress was there again, and though she didn't smile she recognized him. "You working around here?" she asked.

"No, just passing through," he said.

She shrugged and nodded, resigned to it all.

Later that day he came to the gray city of Buffalo and rode through busy, dangerously hazy streets with a glimpse of the blue lake to the west, a lake so vast it looked like an ocean. He was surprised to find himself surprised that his maps had told the truth, that the blue ink of the map approximated the blue curve of the great lake.

He traveled the long reaches of the Midwest, lucky in the weather, and made his way safely, though not without an edge of anxiety he would always recall when in the thick unhealthy richness of automobile and diesel exhaust fumes, through the cities of Erie and Cleveland. Out in the country again he took another highway, Route 6, which would let him avoid Toledo and South Bend, and instead pass through less complicated smaller towns with names like Bowling Green, Napoleon, Waterloo and Nappanee. Strange mixtures of history in the heads of founding fathers.

As he traveled west the sky grew larger and the land stretched. Farmhouses and barns were in the middle of vast fields, unlike New England, where the main road often led between house and barn. The distant farmhouses seemed unfriendly or even imperious in their isolation, like forts.

But then he would approach a river valley and hills would form again. Maples and oaks would cross the rounded elevations and he might have been in New Hampshire for several miles until the flatness came again. He had the feeling that he had come from a place ancestral to this and was moving forward in time, yet back toward his own past. The soil turned darker and deeper, more alluvial and unstable, as if the houses and barns, and even the business blocks of towns, might sink into the deep earth and have to be built again. Silos, already warped, twisted down into the rich soil.

He spent a night in Ohio, in a cabin made of painted cement blocks. Above the washbasin was a typed poem.

Patience Rewarded

There's plenty of hot H_2O,
The boiler's in the main house, though,
So it's got miles and miles to go!

He waited until the water warmed, washed himself and lay down on the bed, trying for downy flakes and the sweet somnolence his vibrating motorcycle's headlong rush had nerved him out of. This was near-exhaustion, and though his journey now seemed plausible, because here he was, somewhere toward the middle of the continent, it also seemed endless.

The next day he passed below Gary and Chicago, the sky to the north angry and sullen, as if a great battle were being fought there.

The cement highway was a narrow line floating on mud. Cars passed him at seventy or eighty, pushing him invisibly outward; then a force just as invisible pulled him inward—forces that were predictable yet never quite acceptable. When trucks came toward him at horrendous speeds it was like bashing through a wall to come out the other side amazed that he was still on the narrow gray line of rhythmical cement. Once two motorcycles came up on him from behind, one on each side, looked him over briefly and then sped off at nearly twice his speed. His night in a motor hotel in Illinois was a dream collage of velocities and near-disasters.

In Iowa, towns could be predicted by their silver water towers seen over the curvature of the earth, like the masts of ships hull-down at sea. Then the highway turned arbitrarily to the north, a right angle that had nothing to do with topography and must have been the jink of a surveyor's pen. Minnesota surprised him with its name.

MINNESOTA WELCOMES YOU
LAND OF 10,000 LAKES
HAVE FUN—DRIVE CAREFULLY!

He stopped beyond the sign and looked at the long fields and the scrubby roadside trees. Here he was; the land back there in Iowa was not home, and this land was. Only a child would see the difference, how even the roadside weeds were of home, a more benevolent green. Winota, his map informed him, was forty miles away. He would glide back in, unknown, to the place from which he'd entered all this feeling and seeing. Memories flickered within a more general one, of a long time when there was a child, a mother and a father so related in custom and law that from within the warm unit the outside world could be entered with confident pleasure. He seemed to remember a time when he was more generous and friendly toward strangers. Maybe the town was like that, or the whole state, and it wasn't just that he had once been a trusting child.

17

Dory watched Dibley for a moment. Either he knew she watched him, in which case he must have an eye in the back of his head, or he thought she always watched him. She had heard that he was fairly normal sometimes, but it was behavior she could never observe because when she was near he always knew it. What did he think? He was painting the sailboat they had unmasted and turned upside down on sawhorses. He was strong all right, as Cynthia had said—so strong that when he lifted the boat she'd worried that he might break his long thin bones or herniate himself.

But what did he think behind his silence? Lately she had begun to believe that she had the power to know what people really thought. She could see printed in the air the words they avoided, or hear and see little sounds and glimpses of words slithering out of choice in the mind as the spoken words were chosen. But Dibley gave her hardly any words at all, so it was hard to see the little tails of the hiding ones. Cynthia said that he liked her, but "like" didn't have the intensity of his muteness or the immobility of his face, his pale jaws hard as wood. She just couldn't get him to talk. Cynthia had lectured him on the subject, but like a prisoner of war he would give Dory his attention and very little else.

There must be fright in it; perhaps she gave him pain. She couldn't imagine why he didn't do his best to avoid her, but he didn't. If he had a "crush" on her, as Cynthia had also suggested, she didn't think he would be so sullen and unhappy-looking all the time. She couldn't read him, or find a scale with which to test his attitudes, but he worked hard, now painting carefully, each lapped strake of the hull creamed evenly white, his brush neatly saturated to its metal band and no higher.

Meanwhile the arrow of her regard seemed to pierce his Camp Washonee T-shirt, an invisible impalement she could not seem to undo. She would leave him with his constricted thoughts, whatever they were.

Up at the lodge, Robert Beggs pushed the lawn mower back and forth across the narrow front lawn. She went past him on one of his going-away laps, so he didn't see her, maybe, went to the kitchen and poured two glasses of iced tea and took them out front. "Ten-minute break," she said to him. He wore nothing but shorts and sneakers and was getting a tan, which made him look better. He had a good build, as they said; it was just his wheyish color that sort of grayed him out in the winter. They sat on the log that separated the lawn from the drive, in the shade of a tamarack. He glistened all over with sweat and looked over at the Princess, who sat with guests on the screened porch. He'd been looking at the Princess a lot, and Dory had begun to read something in his surreptitious glances. She knew the power of foreignness and of royalty because she'd felt them herself, not only with the Princess but with Cynthia when she'd first appeared in fifth grade, and in different ways with John Hearne because of his age and his house and the war he'd been a part of.

When Robert looked at the Princess he was puzzled by his feelings. Dory could read him well enough, and she suspected the Princess could too. The Princess charmed him, asked him favors, touched him on the cheek with her ethereal fingers; she knew how, maybe instinctively, to acquire allegiance. All this bothered Robert because his feelings were becoming stronger than respect and admiration. Dory wondered how it would turn out, and felt a small but ominous twinge of responsibility.

Robert had of course known about her days spent with John Hearne. Whenever a girl went out with a boy two or more classes ahead of hers, people became curious and proprietary. Depending upon their natures they thought it cute or something to smirk about. It was marriage time, sex time, just because you left the boys of your own class and went out with an older one. Robert had been hurt but knew he couldn't compete with a veteran. He'd been morose because it had changed his plans and that upset him, but they'd talked it over and were still friends—maybe more so because now marriage didn't hang over their heads like some big looming duty. They were honest enough with each other now for Robert to ask, "How old is she?"

"She was forty-two last summer."

"Wow," Robert said thoughtfully. "She doesn't look that old."

The Princess wore a white dress and laughed gently at something Ernst Zwanzig, the sculptor, was saying, her laugh never an interruption but a sort of encouraging applause, soft as splashing water. They couldn't hear it from here, but her bright red lipstick formed an O. As a princess she didn't quite exist in ordinary time.

"It's funny to look at a princess," Robert said.

"She seems to like you a lot."

He was stilled by pleasure and confusion. What she seemed to see was an infatuation Robert himself thought unnatural, and he was not the kind of boy to approve of anything so strange. She wondered if he ever even imagined the unnatural or the perverse.

"What's she really like?" he asked.

"She's always been nice to me. She never seems to get upset about things. Even when the Swede threw her on the stove."

He was still amazed by that story. "God!" he said. "Can you imagine that? To *her?*"

"He was a strange man," she said.

"Strange! Well, he did kill himself, I suppose."

"That's what the Princess told me," she said.

"Throwing her on a stove!"

He flinched as he said it. When he'd talked to her about John Hearne he'd scowled and flinched in almost the same way. He'd thought her at the mercy of an older man who could not be trusted. Robert really was a nice boy. All through school he'd never been in trouble. He'd always done his homework, as she had, and was always just there—solid, grayish and sturdy. No one, as far back as she could remember, had ever picked on him or teased him very much. When the time came for him to ask a girl to a dance he'd asked her, because they were so much alike. It wasn't that they'd ever gone steady; they hadn't gone out on any but scheduled occasions. She was the girl he asked to picnics and dances, and when it came time to think of marriage she was the girl who had come to mind. Eventually she would have agreed, too, if it hadn't been for John Hearne.

Robert might have been her husband. Strange that she had for him an affection as pure and bland as soapstone. His arms were solid as chilled meat, his kisses misaimed and shovy, like a lamb being bottle-fed. Or maybe it had been that she hadn't moved for him the way she did for John Hearne, so they'd always had little collisions. She was relieved that she didn't have to kiss him anymore.

She took their glasses back to the kitchen. It was two o'clock and the old man, Kasimir, was taking his nap. At four he would come down and begin his preparations for dinner. Debbie and Cynthia, having cleaned up from lunch and set the dining tables, were sunbathing on a flat dormer roof.

Things had been going better than she'd expected. Debbie, at least for now, would do whatever she was asked to do with a fair amount of cheerfulness. She was impressed by the foreigners and their strange talk, and by the long dresses the women wore, the "New Look" that was still rare in Leah, though they had all seen a thousand pictures of it in magazines, the women suddenly looking like tree trunks down to their separate ankles and feet. There was something peculiar about actually wearing this new uniform. It was not necessarily reprehensible but there was the feeling that its wearers were unreal, that those who showed themselves with no comment or apology in the decreed style were too easily led. But that was too stern a judgment, she supposed. What was, was. One didn't want to look strange, and if all the women painted their lips vampire carmine and their lashes black, stood themselves on stilts, padded their shoulders, enameled their fingernails to look as if they had just been dipped in blood, perfumed their innocent ears and . . . She skipped a thought, a breathless pause like a skipped heartbeat; those were John Hearne's thoughts, convincing and tyrannical, coming back disguised as her own.

She sat in the kitchen, alone for the moment with her yearnings and doubts. From the screened porch came murmurs that at their source were words, and some laughter. From across the long field leading down to the lake came the whirr and clash of gears and cutter bar as the farmer from across the road took the first hay. Loudest was the high, wheezing laughter of Ernst Zwanzig, whose amusement never seemed caused by anything Dory thought funny. It was said that he had been the last pupil of Rodin, had designed many heroic monuments, and that his works were displayed in great museums. The Princess called him "Maestro." Always, even while he ate, he had a cigarette going and he wheezed. His white hair was so thick it looked as if someone had carefully piled mashed potatoes on his head. When he worked, in a large shed next to the garage, he wore a blue smock, a red silk neckerchief and a beret. When not working he clothed his short, thick body in black suits with vests, gray spats and a string tie, as though he wanted to look like a posh or an "artiste" in a farcical movie or a comic strip. His clothes and manners seemed to her musty and used, as if both were theater properties too flamboyant for private use, the gestures as worn as the elbows and cuffs.

With him was his wife, Marta, who was Swedish and looked a lot like him. In bathrobes, from the back, it was actually difficult to tell them apart. Their thirty-year-old adopted daughter, Yvonne, was tall and quiet, with an occasional sweet smile. Yvonne, the Princess had once casually informed Dory, was the issue of a liaison between a Hapsburg duke and a French governess.

Also on the porch with the Princess was her nephew, Werner Ganz-Lengen, who hadn't ever been at Cascom Manor before. He was twenty, had been born in New York but had spent the war in Germany, having been taken there by his parents on the last crossing of the *Bremen.* He said that at sixteen he'd been drafted into the *Volkssturm* and was taken prisoner in May 1945 by the American Ninth Army. "Was I glad to see those guys!" he'd said when telling them about it, but there was something too shining and bright about his desire to be considered an American. He didn't quite stand or walk like an American, and he seemed too clean, blond and dignified to be an American of twenty. Debbie thought he was "cute." Maybe it was that an American with his narrow shoulders, plump face and pale eyes would have frankly looked homely, but Werner acted as if he carried in him some great unspoken superiority and was invulnerable and friendly to all. Cynthia thought he was "vile." "He says he has nothing against the Jews, for instance. How do you like that? It seems to me in questionable taste, at this stage of history, for a German to say *anything* about Jews."

"But he's an American," Dory said. "He was born in New York City."

"He's a creep. He makes me physically sick."

Debbie had listened to this conversation without comment. Around Werner she became almost demure, and had been seen to blush when he spoke to her.

As for Cynthia, Werner took her disdain as a challenge and tried to make up to her in all the wrong ways. No matter what she said to him he would never display anger, and this infuriated her. His fiction was that she was a charmingly temperamental girl whose animosity toward him was actually flirtation.

"I could knee that Hun in the groin and he'd still wiggle his invisible eyebrows at me," she said. "Doesn't his head remind you of a cantaloupe?"

So Werner was fascinated by Cynthia, Debbie by Werner; Robert cast awed glances at the Princess, and Dibley's vocal cords were paralyzed by Dory. Summer itself caused such tensions, she thought, because it was so short and complete, a whole life out of life with the warm breezes close to everyone's skin. There was someone's skin she would like to be close to, but he was not here. The brief summers around Leah were more like different countries than seasons. He moved through a summer far to the west, not this summer in which she had to be so constantly responsible. She wanted to put on him the duty of initiative; he could be here to use her and be used. Something belonging to her had been misplaced, maybe forever, but she didn't have the authority to go look for it. And now these people for whom she was responsible were all excited by each other. They took off their clothes, strutted and posed in shorts and bathing suits, excited by all that warm skin. Summer was so brief for them, and there was always the loom of infantile paralysis, half ignored, that vague terror no one understood but saw in the pipe-legs of children, and in the news of summer. In an iron lung the mirror was the face of the victim. A shudder, but misfortune and death had many forms, and life went on as long as it could. The breath of new-mown hay came from across the wide field and cleansed for a moment the kitchen's static odors of grease and old gas.

She got up to look at Kasimir's shopping list and decided that "8 kitchen boilers" meant eight broilers. "Kitchen" meant chicken; Kasimir was trying out his English more than he had last year. But she'd better get ten, because Kasimir tended not to count on seconds or on children.

The guests with children were a couple named Patrick who were so involved with themselves and their two small boys and baby girl that they lived a separate life concerned with manners and drool, cleanliness and toilet training. It was a case, as with some birds, where the male fed and taught the chicks as frantically as the female. The man and woman looked distracted and sweaty, and so disheveled that whenever they appeared they seemed to have just had sex and were still a little stunned by its compulsions. They seemed teeming and fertile, even as one or the other reached into a child's pants to feel for wet, or changed the jerking baby's diaper at the beach. They ate separately from the other guests, their table a little storm of hushed centripetal passions.

The Patricks were set and complete with each other, but her crew was not, and she was not. She felt incomplete, even anxious, and had little sympathy for the tensions the others found so interesting. Equilibrium was in danger, and whatever happened would in some measure be her fault, so she had to be alert. She would have liked to shut her eyes and drift through the summer in someone's care. Maybe she was too young for all that she knew and saw.

The great black gas stove with its many burners and ovens had a nameplate encrusted with baked-on carbon from the spills of the years: BETTY #3. She always thought of Betty Salmon, the suicide by lye, who was to her a presence in this house, a cautionary ghost whenever darkness spread through rooms and hallways. Dark was another season or country, with its own meanings. Betty Salmon's dumb trick of drinking lye—did she take something like Drāno, mix it with water and drink that churning mixture? What if she'd known all about the agony she chose? With darkness, when the business of the day was over, these thoughts came. She wanted to have sympathy for Betty Salmon, but the manner of her death overwhelmed any easy charity.

But now it was a sunny afternoon and she had an hour of freedom before Kasimir's alarm clock would send him with an old man's bleariness down the back stairs to the kitchen, his fringes of iron-colored hair in clumps he would douse with water at the sink and flatten with his hands. Then he would put on his white full-length apron and his tall starched chef's hat, another costume, like Ernst Zwanzig's costumes, that seemed more theatrical than real.

She went upstairs and out the window to the flat roof of the dormer, where she found Debbie alone, sunbathing on a blanket, her sturdy body gleaming with oil. Debbie had been naked and quickly covered up her lap and breasts with towels as Dory appeared. They were fairly frank with each other on most matters, but there had always been this modesty about nakedness, and Dory thought it might have something to do with their differences in shape and size, as if they were as different as giant and pygmy, or man and woman. With her big bones and broad round flesh, Debbie was sometimes arrogant about her body and at other times almost ashamed of its amplitudes.

"I thought Cynthia was up here with you," Dory said.

"She's there," Debbie said, raising up and pointing across the field, where beneath a pasture pine two bits of color could be seen, two people sitting on a boulder. "She's with Yvonne."

Dory had noticed that friendship beginning, even with a moment of jealousy she guiltily shrugged away. Cynthia was her friend and erstwhile confidante, but she hadn't been honest with Cynthia, and Cynthia suspected it. Think what she might have told her about the "real thing," a subject they had theorized about so much over the years. Cynthia had come as close as possible to asking her about it, too, but always with a way left open so that the real question could be evaded. And Dory had left it that way, saying only that she'd had idyllic days with him, sailing and swimming, kissing underwater, talking in front of the fire. When in reality they'd never talked much at all, just squirmed together smoothly in their skins. But talk had seemed inferior to what they'd meant; she'd wanted him to do what he wanted. She wanted to be as sweaty and fecund as Mrs. Patrick. She wanted to be flushed, inside out, fluid with his attentions, languid after excess. At least she would settle for that today, in this mood evasive of responsibility.

"Yvonne is nice," Debbie said slyly. "Don't you think so?"

Yvonne did seem nice. Though her plump cheeks were pale and grainy, she was pretty, and looked pleased by life. When she spoke her voice was soft and came from a little smile. Each word contained that smile, as if it were about to break in two with quiet mirth. She was as tall as Cynthia, but unlike Cynthia she was very narrow in the waist and her breasts were heavy, so that she seemed fragile in the stem.

"How come she isn't married? She must have been sort of pretty when she was young," Debbie said slyly. "Cynthia prefers her to Werner," she added.

"Oh, Debbie," Dory said. "What do you want from Werner, anyway?"

"I want him to marry me, what else? Then I won't have to go back to high school."

"All right. It was a dumb question."

"You know his family's got a castle in Uberbungenberg or someplace? A *castle?* Only the Communists got it."

They were quiet for a while, sweating on the hot black roof. Dory sat on the corner of Debbie's blanket, which was soaked, and felt a drop run like a spider down her spine. "I think I'll take a quick swim before Kasimir wakes up," she said. "You feel like it?"

"Sure."

She left Debbie on the roof struggling into her bathing suit and went down to the single room she had this year. Her window looked across the field, where Cynthia and Yvonne were slowly walking back. Cynthia was talking excitedly. She looked very happy as she spoke and gestured, while Yvonne smiled and nodded. Yvonne put her arm around Cynthia's shoulders and shook her playfully, and they both laughed.

The horse-drawn cutter bar passed behind them, the farmer high on his sprung iron seat. When Dory opened the sliding screen the new-mown hay was stronger in the room. She put her head out. "Deb and I are going for a quick swim. You want to come?" she called to them.

Cynthia nodded and came running across the gravel turnaround, but Yvonne smiled, grimaced and said something Dory couldn't hear.

"I'll lend you my other one! We're about the same size!" Cynthia called back to Yvonne.

Werner came out from beneath the porch roof and said, "Swell idea! Are men welcome?"

"Sure," Dory said. Cynthia came on, ignoring him, and Yvonne followed, blushing pink because, Dory thought, even though she was so much older, here she was, caught up in this younger exuberance and equality.

The Princess and the Zwanzigs decided to walk down with them, though not to swim.

Robert and Dibley were at the beach when they all got there, Robert so lathered up with Ivory soap he looked like a plaster statue. When he saw the Princess his chest swelled and he ran into the water and did a horizontal racing dive, then a few strong strokes that took him to the raft, which he lightly boarded in one motion, ignoring the ladder. He sat there looking nonchalant, but he was really so pleased with himself.

Ernst Zwanzig said, "Ah, Princess! So pleasing to look at all the young bodies!"

Marta Zwanzig said something like *"Zu vere imden flicka,"* and shook her husband's arm. He dropped his head and pretended to be contrite, then said, nodding toward Debbie, "A true Maillol. Everyone is a realist."

"Did you know him, Maestro?" the Princess asked.

"Oh, yes! We argued, though I was a young man, and very . . . importunate? He died a few years ago in an auto wreck. When you think he was born in 1861!" His strange, motiveless laughter blatted, ending in ecstatic wheezes. Dory could not find the principle of his humor. That automobiles didn't exist in 1861?

When he finished laughing—he still looked at Debbie, who was gingerly wading into the water, her balance shivery and delicate—he said, "The human form—why do we never tire of it? Is it beautiful? Who says so?"

They all stood as if posed, the Princess and the Zwanzigs standing in a row looking at the young ones. It was like a painting, everything hot but the cool lake. Yvonne waded palely, her large breasts compressed by Cynthia's red one-piece bathing suit. One of her buttocks protruded, caught at the wrong crease; there, she reached behind her with both hands and pulled the leg openings out, that unselfconscious gesture of beaches, a woman arranging her gifts. Cynthia, sinewy and spare, splashed in and got her hair wet, its gleams extinguished. "Damn!" she said.

Werner, his male bunch gleaming blue in tight rayon trunks, took three formal little hops, or false starts, before he ran into the water. His large legs were covered, as his upper body was not, with reddish-gold hair—one of those people whose halves simply didn't match.

Without his T-shirt Dibley was a structure of silvery white tendon and bone. He looked strong without muscle, as though his limbs were driven by his will. He looked at Dory once, then ran like a giraffe into the lake, his jaws hardening, or so she thought.

"Everybody to the raft!" Cynthia yelled, and Dory ran toward the mild shock of the water. She passed Debbie, who shrieked at the spray.

"To the raft!" Cynthia called. "To the raft!" Robert pulled Cynthia out of the water as the raft tilted, one rusty drum emerging, and they both fell back in. But soon they were all sitting on the hot planks. Robert reached quickly, self-consciously, into his trunks and produced the bar of Ivory soap, which they passed among them, each as aware of the others' positions on the raft as a single organism would be aware of its parts. Yvonne lathered Cynthia's back, Debbie Werner's. Dibley sat next to Dory, hugging his skinny legs and shivering miserably, while Robert, his hands immobile, preened manfully, interiorly, his superior muscles casting shadows upon themselves.

The people on shore seemed pleased nearly to the point of applause. Then, Ernst Zwanzig talking, Marta Zwanzig holding his arm, the Princess graceful in her long white dress, the spectators turned back toward the lodge.

Those moments on the raft were tense, whether of ecstasy, pain or apprehension, but soon they all had to slip back into the cool lake and go to shore.

In the days that followed Dory grew inattentive to the equation that seemed to have formed itself around her, *x*'s and *y*'s of emotion floating here and there—terms she was too self-absorbed to try to define. On her day off she took a sailboat and tacked across the lake to reach Cascomhaven. A car glinted behind trees and a woman lay colorfully on the dock among towels, lotions and magazines—maybe his mother. His little green canoe was upside down on its rack. Before she quietly came about she looked hard at the cabin, past the porch railings to the windows of the room in which she had been used as a woman and the sickness of this love had come over her. With a near-silent little rush of wake the boat turned away.

On other days, in the afternoon hiatus of Kasimir's naps, if no one wanted to learn to sail or children to swim, she walked alone or stayed in her room, writing him letters she wouldn't ever send. *Dear John,* they began, or *Dear Johnny.*

Desire was an itch, an anxiety; it wanted to become abstract, something that had no cause. It was distracting her from responsibility here where she believed she was the only responsible one. She did her duty, of course, but not with the proper foresight, and she blamed herself for this. His absence, after his promises, even though she hadn't believed he could keep his promises, seemed a betrayal.

All she had left was her mind, or that part of her mind she thought of as collector, or intellect. This was uncontaminated. She needed words and facts to feed it, as if she were preparing for a life-important examination, and she learned each new unit with an almost visible (through the backs of her eyes, somehow) flash of permanence. Hiatus: a break or interruption of continuity. Maillol, she found in the lodge's huge collection of old *Life* magazines, was a French sculptor famous for his big fat smooth graceful nudes. Rodin did "The Thinker," which had always suggested to high school students a man straining at stool.

"Dear John," she wrote on her lined tablet. "We were all on the raft and everyone but me was showing off for someone else. You weren't there."

There were two other guests. One was a Mr. Jean Dorlean, a young but bald and bearded little man who said he worked for the government. "Never mind which agency, my dear manageress. It's all just alphabet soup." He'd immediately taken this tone with her, and with it was a look that she could only think of as meaning "What have we here?"

Seemingly with him, although they were not always together, was a woman larger and taller than he, Kaethe Muller, who stood straight as a soldier. Her feminine clothes—chiffons and bright silks with pleats—and her habit of leaving her blouses open so low that the others could actually catch a glimpse of a great nipple big as a strawberry, seemed incongruous with her posture and her lack of any makeup.

Dory overheard strange sentences: "He thinks playing 'Love for Sale' over the radio is the height of sophistication."

"To sign his work with the numeral twenty! What pretension!"

"Have you heard of a weapon that has never been blooded in human flesh?"

"He made the death mask of Dollfuss and smuggled it out inside a bust of Schiller."

"I first met Labourie at Meudon in 1915; he was then a catamite belonging to the Duc d'Alva."

"Walter Ulbricht was General Gómez, responsible for the deaths of so very many of the Spanish people."

"You will see, in November, how at last the American people have come to their senses!"

"Catamite" was not in the dictionary John Hearne had given her. In the larger dictionary in the library it was defined as "a boy kept for unnatural purposes," which she took to be sexual purposes. Dollfuss sounded familiar. Schiller was "German poet, philosopher and historian." Walter Ulbricht was a blank. Poor little Labourie and the sodomite duke were mysteries that would remain mysteries.

In his studio-shed Ernst Zwanzig made quick pencil and wash drawings of Yvonne as she walked about, posed and did dancelike swirls with a long, gauzy scarf. This had been an exercise of Rodin's, it was explained—a model in motion—but it was startling to go by the studio and see that she was naked. On a table in the center of the studio, below the skylight, was a clay-and-stick structure that was going to be a larger-than-life bust of Thomas E. Dewey. After the inauguration Ernst Zwanzig would present it to Dewey at the White House. He had done the same with Herbert Hoover in 1929. Dewey's mustache, though, and the wide, squashed look of his face were major problems. Great as the leader was, that pubic *Schnurrbart* of his would be a challenge to the great Rodin himself. *"Das Bärtchen sieht aus wie Schamharre,"* he said. Nevertheless, Ernst Zwanzig would fashion a Noble Roman out of the American clay.

While Dory and Debbie were alone in the kitchen scouring black iron pans and crusted broiling racks, Debbie said, "You don't even try to understand Werner. You all treat him like he was a jerk."

"Cynthia doesn't like him very much," Dory admitted.

"Cynthia has a crush on Yvonne. But he's really hurt and nobody knows it."

"How do you know?"

"He told me. We went to his room and he even showed me his dirk."

"His what?"

"His dirk. It's sort of a dagger. It's all black and silver with writing on it." Debbie was bragging about this intimacy, yet beyond that she was very serious. "He said it wasn't his fault he was in Germany. He was only eleven when his family went back there."

"Nobody blames him for that," Dory said.

"I don't see why you all treat him like dirt. You hurt his feelings. He confides in me."

"He confides in you?" The word jumped dangerously in Dory's mind, its meaning unstable.

"He even cried. He said sometimes he even feels like falling on his dirk."

"You fall on a sword, not a dirk," Dory couldn't help saying, a bubble of totally unsought laughter caught in her throat like a water brash. She didn't at all feel like laughing.

"See? Everything he does you sneer at. I think you're cruel!"

"Me?"

"So goddam superior!"

Debbie, she wanted to say, this is me, Dory. What are you talking about? She reached to touch Debbie's shoulder, but Debbie jerked skittishly, red with anger. "It's because he looks kind of funny, isn't it!" she said.

"No."

"Just because nobody ever made fun of you!"

"Yes, they have, Deb."

"No, they haven't! You don't know anything about it!"

"Deb, no matter what he tells you, I don't think you ought to trust him too much. It's just a feeling I have."

"See what I mean? Who do you think you are—Ma?"

"I'm your sister."

"Oh, *God!"* Debbie said in utter exasperation, threw her Brillo pad into the sink and stamped out, shoving the screened door past its traverse so that its hinges complained like overflexed joints—a twinge of care in Dory for the fixable door, for her sister and their history of antagonism and intimacy. They'd had fights, screamings, poutings and making-ups so often, but the time she remembered most clearly seemed to be the one always recalled, when, years ago and for reasons now forgotten, she'd slapped Debbie three times so hard, so unexpectedly to her and to Debbie that the larger one, her sister, that loud, muscular vessel, collapsed to the floor. Her voice seemed all that had been left of her, a cracked clamor of despair so disorganized Dory had felt like a murderer. That she had been justified meant nothing, nothing at all.

Through the smudged window (that should be washed) she watched Debbie stamp across the field toward the woods, staggering a little in her disdain for the ordinary unevenness of the ground.

18

He rode toward Winota through the summer heat of his native state, anticipating the remembered in farmhouses, silos, barns and trees. The country was undulant only in distances of miles, trees along windbreaks higher than any rise of the land. A series of small signs passed on his right, each with two or three words.

PASSING SCHOOL ZONES

TAKE IT SLOW

LET OUR LITTLE

SHAVERS GROW

BURMA SHAVE

They had driven a lot. His father worked at the Winota *Herald,* as reporter, space salesman, columnist—how much of this was memory and how much was information given him by his mother, he could not be certain. There was the game of Zit: when you saw a white horse the first one to say "Zit!" got a point. His father's Chevrolet had a leaping greyhound for a radiator-cap ornament, and the ornamental greyhound was a little loose, so that while they were driving it moved around and pointed sideways. There was nothing to worry about, but to him the whole world was wrong and dangerous when the greyhound didn't point straight ahead. No matter how they tried to reassure him he cried and begged them to stop. His father did stop the car and took him out to the radiator and showed him that the radiator cap was tight, it was just that the greyhound was a little loose, but still it was wrong and he would not be comforted. He couldn't remember it happening again, so his father must have had it fixed.

Once his father bragged that on a trip to Sleepy Eye and back they had averaged thirty-five miles per hour.

Dust grew on the inside of the car windows, yellow-brown talcum that grew up the windows until the panes were soft and blank with it.

After, or before, they lived in the Park Hotel they lived in an apartment over the newspaper. Men came and asked for Hoover blankets, which were the brown paper wrappings from the rolls of newsprint. Every day men came asking for work and were given cabbage, potatoes, carrots and the like for their mulligans. Sometimes they were given coffee and a sandwich. The produce was barter given the paper in lieu of money. There were no jobs. The paper's cash came mostly from county legal notices. He had probably been told this. His mother worked at the paper too, and they had a maid who got room and board and two dollars a week. A hamburger at the Loup Qui Parle Diner was a nickel. Brierley's Orange Drink was a nickel. A small brown pot of baked beans was a nickel. In the evenings on the radio Kate Smith sang "When the Moon Comes over the Mountain." He sent a dime and a box top to Tom Mix and got back a huge wooden six-shooter whose cylinder turned. He also listened to Skippy and Tailspin Tommy, excruciating when the Atwater Kent squealed and faded as Skippy approached the haunted house, which was almost too frightening anyway. He dreamed that he was taking a leak on an old piece of wood and woke up sopping. Hot lead, silver as silver, the linotypist a man with two missing fingers on his left hand, the shiny stumps round and cataclysmic, a warning. He and Alice Giefer, a little girl with orange freckles, ate sand in her sandbox.

Once he went down to his father's office and asked for a nickel. His father looked at him seriously and said he guessed he'd have to get an allowance, which scared him because it sounded bad, but an allowance meant he'd get a nickel a week to spend or save as he wanted. He wanted a beautiful little pot-metal Packard, with real turning wheels. What was the name of those toys? It would come back.

As he came back. Silver mirages, mirrors of thin water on the cement highway. The water tower rose before the sign appeared. He stopped to look at both. Memory here? Maybe, but he wasn't sure.

Welcome to
WINOTA
El. 1560
Pop. 325ø1

Someone had crossed out the zero and added a one—a new father, come out to make the sign accurate?

His father wrote in the paper that when Johnny Hearne grew up he wanted to run a weed burner on the C.&N.W. Railroad. When his mother read it to him he was mortified, and couldn't remember having said such a thing.

Once his mother came and got into his bed and hid behind him under the covers. She said it was a game and if his father came looking he was to say she wasn't there. His father did come, open the door and ask if he'd seen his mother, and he obediently lied. But he lied to his father, and he knew it wasn't a game. He'd pondered why she'd made him lie to his father, and kept that happening in the limbo of the unexplained, where it still was.

In the summer evenings they would drive through the neighborhood of mansions and kept grounds, eating ice-cream cones, just to see the beautiful houses.

His mother and father knew a man in St. Paul, a wrestler, who strangled a burglar to death and was considered a coward because he killed the burglar out of fear when he already had him in his power. A lesson.

He got his Red Cross Beginner's Button at Loup Qui Parle Lake, from which the Loup Qui Parle River came and ran through town. Wolf who talks. He did the dog paddle from his father to his mother.

Sunfish fins could stick you. Punkinseeds, bluegills, crappies. When cleaned there were just two little pieces of yellowy meat. His father fried up a mess of them in an iron frying pan that was so heavy he couldn't lift it by the handle, even with both hands. No fish, ever after, had tasted so good.

A maid named Isabel let him get in bed with her and swim anywhere he wanted over her body, smooth slippery ivory. It was her belly he liked best. There was a sense of wrong about it, but vague. He never told anyone.

He would gag when they made him try to eat another carrot or lima bean, which made them angry, as if he'd just pretended to gag. He had to sit, in kindergarten, on his own bowel movement, which was, after a while, cool and plastic. Someone must have smelled it but no one said anything. He was too old for that, but he hadn't wanted to ask to go to the toilet. You paid for such reticence. When it happened again his father was very angry. When it happened again his mother didn't tell his father. Another lie between them.

His mother sat on a chair and jumped herself up and down in ecstasy, chanting, "Hoover's going to win, folks! Hoover's going to win, folks! Hoover's going to win, folks!"

They rode horses along the river, under the trees, his stirrups shortened to their last buckle holes. His father said, "Don't hold on to the saddle horn; that's for rope work." If he did grab the saddle horn, which looked so stable, he became unstable—another lesson in the theme of paradox.

A meadowlark stood on a fence post, black V on yellow breast, and sang a six-noted, falling, happy-wistful song he remembered with absolute clarity. There were no meadowlarks in Leah, New Hampshire; he'd never seen or heard one there, so this must be his first sweet pang of recognition.

He started his engine, the pulse, the intermediary thrust that had brought him all this way, and with a momentary loss of breath, as in a thank-you-ma'am in the road in his father's Chevrolet sixteen years ago, rode on into the town past shortened fields, bungalows, farmhouses now street houses, into the trees and onto the main street where soon enough the Park Hotel, dreamily the same but smaller, let a grid of other streets and destinations set itself softly down over what was here and now. The Loup Qui Parle Diner was exactly where it used to be but not as shiny. He didn't remember the Chrysler-Dodge dealership next door, but somewhere nearby had been a gas pump that his father cranked and the gas swirled up into a glass bottle marked with gallons. The Winota *Herald* was down the street and seemed very small. How could he, his mother and father and the lonely maid, Isabel, have all fit into that narrow upper floor?

He would eat at the diner, but first he rode down Main Street and turned at the street whose name he'd forgotten—Slayton Street—which led him past the Town Hall and the public library to the grammar school. The school was smaller, the playground tiny, the metal kid-propelled merry-go-round built for midgets. He didn't expect to recognize people, and didn't, at least not yet. The slope down to the river was less of a slope, and yet the town seemed concentrated, distilled, purified. The elms on the residential streets were lush tunnels, cool overhead. Some trees were a kind of massive poplar unfamiliar to his later knowledge. There was a care and neatness in the maintenance of cars, lawns, streets and houses he hadn't expected.

Impressed, feeling the erosion of an unexpected superiority, he rode back to the Loup Qui Parle Diner, leaned his oily machine on its iron leg, went inside and sat at the counter. Yes, the tables at the front, the booths at the ends, the chromed fittings. He had come here with his father for what his father called Wimpy hamburgers—that strange, strawish, sharp, easy taste. Ketchup and benign grease, a little bad for you in an appetizing way, hooky from greens and boiled things that grew in the mouth.

A waitress in a pink uniform with white, nurselike lapels and cuffs had been sitting at a table with another waitress and a young man, and now she came around the counter to see what he wanted. She was chunky in a blond, athletic-looking way, the kind of girl who would play a tough game of field hockey. Her pretty round face seemed so especially pleased, so wide open with extraordinary pleasure he thought for a second she must know him, or that for some reason this occasion was far out of the ordinary.

"Hi!" she said, her white teeth and crinkly blue eyes zeroing in on him. "What can I get for you?" She presented him with a glass of water and stood back, her smile moderating just enough to partly cover her teeth.

He was unable to crank his face into an answering expression, or at least to smile with anything like her voltage. "A hamburger and a small Coke," he said, his voice sounding strange until with a cavernous flutter his ears popped open.

"Anything on your hamburger? Onions, relish, green peppers, lettuce, tomato?"

"A little raw onion," he said.

"Oh-oh! Your girl won't like that!"

"My girl?"

"Your breath! Of course you could take a Sen-Sen!" She laughed lightly, companionably, nothing in it but good nature.

"My girl's about fifteen hundred miles from here," he said.

"Oh, that's too bad," she said, a shadow of sympathy on her brow. "Where is she now?"

"In New Hampshire."

"New Hampshire! Did you ride your motorcycle all the way from New Hampshire?" She wrote his order on a pad, tore off the page and put it on a spike at the window to the kitchen, tapping a bell with her palm. This was done in what seemed one expert motion, and she was back. "How long did it take to ride all that way?" As he thought about this she turned to get him his small Coke from the machine.

"Four and a half days," he said, finally having figured it out.

"Four and a half days! Did you stop over at night? Of course you must have. I've never in my life met anyone from New Hampshire! What's it like there?"

A simple question, he thought, searching ledges, cellar holes and hill-shadowed mills for a simple answer. "It's all hills and mountains," he said. "Mostly woods."

"And pretty little towns with village greens?"

"Some. It depends on the angle you're looking from."

She went a little blank at that, but brightened again. "What town are you from?"

"Leah."

"And what brings you . . ." she began, but the other waitress called her.

"Gracie? Why don't you two join us?" The other waitress was slender and dark, with glasses and a long neck that gave her a rather courtly or scholarly look. No other customers were in the diner and she and the young man leaned casually over their coffee.

Gracie blushed, her pale skin washed with rose. "Would you like to meet my friends?"

"Sure," he said. The bell pinged and his hamburger appeared on the shelf. Gracie went to get it. "I'll be right with you," he said, and went to the men's room, knowing where it was without thinking. At five he'd had to urinate in the toilet bowl, but now he had the choice of two urinals. He washed some of the road grime from his face and hands, thinking what a mysterious welcome this was, this friendly curiosity that seemed entirely motiveless. Perhaps it was totally innocent, Minnesota and his half-memories, half-fantasies of the sky-blue land identical. Strange, because his real memories were not idyllic. His father could grow angry, a tornadic storm could blow down trees and even houses, children could fight, but it was always his father, and his native state, where, after anger, came justice and fair skies. There was another constant, he now remembered: his father was always welcomed. Always the people grinned their welcome to him and made the sounds and gestures of pleasure.

Gracie had been about to ask him what brought him to Winota, which gave him an interesting sort of Faustian choice he didn't yet want to make. In a way he had no particular desire for company and would be happy enough to look around Winota through a nice romantic fuzz of nostalgia before moving on, still an observer. If he lied, saying for example that he had relatives in North Dakota . . . what was its capital? Bismarck . . . whatever happened in the present would be tinged irreversibly with inconsequence, whether or not he might later change his mind. But if he told them the truth he would immediately be a special case, intimate with them in a way he could foresee being over-involved and cloying, the power of his secret lost. In adventure the hero, the picaresque wanderer with a dark yet somehow noble past, comes drifting into town as a heroic catalyst to ordinary lives, his secret his power, his exit lonely. The trouble was that he had been resisting adventure, fading away from it toward a quest he wasn't ready to define.

At the table they made their introductions while he ate his hamburger. The other waitress was Loretta, the young man, Miles. In Loretta's attitude toward Gracie he detected something of the matchmaker and chaperone—a fond, protective look, a touch on Gracie's strong forearm. Miles was tall, sandy-colored and rather pleasantly vague about things. In his unbothered cheerfulness he resembled a dog who depended more upon his nose than his eyes, the scent dim but pleasant.

In their clear midwestern voices, no modulation for hesitancy or embarrassment, they would tell their stories and have his. Miles was twenty-three. During the war he had been in the Navy, Stateside, for three years and four months, and was now going to the University of Minnesota, off and on, not able to decide what he wanted to major in. Gracie and Loretta had gone to school together all their lives. Gracie's father couldn't stand Miles, which seemed irrelevant because she wasn't going with Miles. Loretta's mother and father were separated and her father lived in Mankato. She and Gracie were both nineteen, Gracie two months and five days older than Loretta. Gracie, three days each week, was doing an internship in physical therapy at St. Luke's Hospital. Loretta had no intention of going to college. Miles had a '39 Mercury convertible, the black one out there. Loretta's last name was Pachek, and she was a "Boheemie," which didn't seem a term of belittlement; her grandparents had come from Bohemia, which was now part of Czechoslovakia. Gracie's last name was Lundgren—a name his mother had used: Estelle Lundgren, whom his father had "played around" with. "Playing around" had seemed an odd thing for grown people to do. He saw them playing catch, or throwing stones at tin cans, now here, now there. He wondered if he might, if he really wanted to, ask Gracie if she was related to an Estelle Lundgren, but let it go.

Their desire to give him information about their lives seemed smoothly normal to them. Perhaps he'd been infected by Leah's self-consciousness—superiority combined with self-doubt. Did you blab everything? And who would be interested in all those details? These people seemed to believe that everything about themselves, large and small, must be fascinating to a stranger—a kind of innocent vanity as American as all get-out; he felt as if he had been in exile for a long, long time.

Gracie's sister, Irma, who was really a knockout, had to get married in February to Gus Rasmussen, and she was barely eighteen, which hadn't improved her father's temper. Loretta had a '41 Ford coupe, the dark green one out there. Miles and Loretta were more or less engaged, but she wasn't sure; for one thing, Miles's father was a lawyer and his mother was kind of snooty, to be honest, and Loretta's father worked in the furniture factory in Mankato and her mother was a hairdresser—sort of the wrong side of the tracks to the high and mighty. Loretta's mother had a boyfriend, an old farmer with gray hair. Gracie thought they were kind of cute together. Gracie had a heart murmur, though it wasn't serious; Loretta was allergic to chigger bites and her father was sort of an alcoholic. Gracie had a little dog named Jo-Jo, part whippet. She and Jimmy Webber went steady for a while this spring, but had stopped now. Gracie's father didn't like Jimmy, either. He had a hardware store and she simply would not work there. Winota Hardware, down toward the grain elevator.

When two salesmen from the Chrysler-Dodge dealership came in, Loretta went to wait on them while Miles got up to put a nickel in the jukebox: "Heartaches," the sweet whistler and the running, swooping melody that had been part of the background for a year now, even in Leah.

"So, John," Gracie said, "what brings you to Winota? Are you visiting, or just passing through?"

Oh, well. As usual, he didn't feel up to lying, but his voice was a little constricted as he said, "Actually this is my hometown. I was born at St. Luke's."

"What?" She was ecstatic. "Loretta! Miles!"

So he told them what he knew. When he'd left, so many years ago, Miles had been seven, Loretta and Gracie three, so they marveled and wondered but had no memories of him or of his family.

"And you don't know where your *father* is?" Gracie said. "That's terrible!" She squeezed his hand with both of hers, broad warm hands with light golden fuzz on them, and he found himself answering precise questions, giving the sort of information he thought, or had thought until their sympathy charged him with nervous emotion, irrelevant or even vaguely degrading. It was as if he were answering the questions on a form, and as the categories were completed he began to see how comprehensive was the emerging definition of John Hearne, white male, English-Irish-Welsh, etc., twenty-one, nominally Protestant, single, five foot ten, 155, hair light brown, eyes green, light smoker, infantry veteran, college student, only child of broken marriage . . . They would have their facts, and even as he reserved the vaguer aspirations of his uniqueness, his talents, the indefinable difference between statistics and potential, their expressions of concern, superficial or not, cut through his judgmental reserve to touch the quick.

Loretta kept looking at him as if she were about to nod her head, agreeing with herself that her first impression of him had been correct. Then she looked at Gracie. Lord, that familiar surmise. He looked at Gracie with Loretta's idea in mind—marital, genetic, theoretical. A pretty face, symmetrical and clear in the universally admired way, her corn-silk hair Scandinavian clean. With her sturdy shoulders and good strong back he and Gracie could produce plenty of happy, strapping towheads to continue the work of the world. Anyway, it was flattering that Loretta thought so.

"So you're going to stay in Winota for a while?" Loretta asked.

"A day or two," he said.

"You can bunk in with me if you want," Miles said. "I've got a spare couch."

It was explained that Miles had his own apartment over his family's three-car garage. So that was settled. The weenie roast at the reservoir was Loretta's idea. Miles would bring his guitar. Jack and Laura were called and would meet them there. Potato salad from the German grocery on Third Street. Some beer, which the boys would have to get. Tasks and schedules were briskly arranged; it was already nearly five.

John followed Miles's '39 Mercury convertible across the river to the neighborhood they used to drive through and admire on summer evenings, thinking of a future among trimmed dark hedges, lawns like putting greens, trees like Sherwood Forest, the arched and shaded formality of big houses more lushly satisfied with their wealth than the houses of New England.

Miles, instead of going to his apartment, did an unexpectedly formal thing; he took John into the main house and introduced him to his parents, who were having drinks on a shaded patio.

"I remember your father well," Miles's father said. "Everybody liked him. He was a clean man."

Miles's mother agreed. "Yes, Syl Hearne was a clean man."

John had never heard that expression, and its strangeness, its impossible simplicity, even though tested by eye for the sincere or the patronizing mode, was a puzzle. He couldn't ask them what, exactly, they meant by it, so he let that hygienic comment slide into the limbo of the unexplained.

Miles's apartment, a large room with a bathroom and kitchenette, was airy and modern, with a sliding glass door onto the balcony of the outside stairway. John took a shower and changed into clean but wrinkled chinos, thinking that now he, like his father, was a clean man, though not a compulsively clean man, or a man who wouldn't talk dirty, or whatever they'd meant.

Miles had turned on the radio, and Dinah Shore sang, "Oh, how we danced on the night we were wed," the volume low. "Help yourself to anything you want," Miles said. "Have a drink." He opened the cabinet doors of a compact bar that even had its own little refrigerator. "Loretta sure took a shine to you, arranging a date with Gracie." He shook his head, as if this were very odd, poured himself a few gurgles of Southern Comfort, added an ice cube and took it with him into the bathroom.

John examined the bottles, those glittering Sirens who promised everything and delivered sogginess. Still, he had an extra edge of brittleness, so he poured himself some Hennessy and sat back on the couch in the laving of the radio's constant celebration of love. On Miles's walls were tennis rackets and casting rods, sporting prints of pheasant and quail, a mounted bass thick as a thigh. On his bureau was a color photograph of Loretta, smiling and pert-breasted in a frilly white dress, her eyes large through rimless glasses.

John chipped in for the beer and they picked up Gracie and Loretta at Loretta's mother's small bungalow in a neighborhood of such houses. This way Gracie's father wouldn't be subjected to the sight of randy boys.

They passed, on the way out of town, a Shell station where a bright red-and-silver car, mangled beyond the immediate identification of its make, had been towed and was on display. Several people stood back a few feet from it, bending, as if over an invisible railing, to peer inside.

"That's Roger's car," Gracie said as they passed, turning away from it. "I don't want to see it."

He and Gracie rode sedately in their places in the back seat, the top down though the evening was cooling quickly in a northwest wind that must have come from the Dakotas and Canada. "I just don't want to see it," Gracie said.

"It's a '48 Pontiac, but you wouldn't know it from the front," Miles said. He drove with one hand casually on the wheel, his right arm along the back of the seat, ready to turn and talk when he wanted to, as though he were controlling something as uncritical as a sailboat on a lake.

"Miles, would you watch the road?" Loretta said. Miles laughed and turned back to his driving.

As they left town on a narrow concrete highway, Miles drove faster, so that wind isolated the two compartments of the car and John and Gracie moved closer together, a blanket around their shoulders. The late-setting early-summer sun descended at their left as they passed immense fields of pale young corn like sparsely planted new grass. He asked Gracie what had happened to Roger.

"Dead," she said. "He killed himself on purpose."

Though they had lived in different parts of the country they had in common the deaths of contemporaries in torn and folded automobiles.

In the front seat Miles and Loretta were silent. Loretta stared ahead, her dark hair in a ponytail with its long fringes, after the tight ribbon, blowing against her regal neck in that reverse convertible wind.

Gracie adjusted the blanket so that it went over their heads, and in that insubstantial cave told him about Roger and Alice. The story was, in its main events, known. Alice wanted to stop going steady with Roger. She had decided she really didn't love him, but agreed to go with him one last time to the parking ground at the reservoir because she still liked him and felt sorry for him. He strangled her, and when he saw what he had done he left her body there and drove for hours through the night in the new Pontiac he had bought in part to impress her. At three in the morning he stopped at a telephone booth in Perch Lake and called his older brother, who was married and lived in Minneapolis, and told him what he had done. His brother talked to him for a long time and finally convinced him that he should give himself up. When Roger promised, the brother called their parents, a lawyer—Miles's father—Reverend Griswold and the police and told them all to meet Roger at the police station, that Roger was coming in to give himself up. But Roger drove the rest of the night on the country roads and at dawn into a cement bridge abutment at eighty miles an hour, the speed still registered on the smashed speedometer of Roger's new red Pontiac.

"Nobody ever thought Roger would do anything like that," Gracie said. "Roger was a nice boy, and Alice was a nice girl."

So, he thought, a cautionary tale, close to these people. Alice stopped loving Roger, so he killed her and then he killed himself. Of course, John Hearne believed himself immune to such insanity. Gracie Lundgren, this girl, rode beside him, compact, contained; to touch her would be like touching something as consistent along any part of its surface as a basketball, he thought at first, before they did touch. She was too husky for him, but her nerves were on her skin and to her he seemed a marvelously exciting force. Even the dime-store perfume behind her ears sent a poignant message of crushed petals and ethyl acetate wafting to him like a plea. Girls who wanted to please were all alike—extremely pleasant—yet they were always having to find forgivable ways of saying no to reckless and importunate boys. But he did feel demeaned, somehow, by his inflexible estimation that Gracie was too sturdy for him, and when, later, in the woods when it grew dark and the fire died down and she let him put his hand beneath her blouse on the wide, bare mounds of her breasts, the sweet acquiescence with which she let him commit this impropriety caused him to feel protective toward her, as though he ought to tell her that she shouldn't let strange boys do what he was doing.

"I never let Jimmy do that," she said wonderingly. "It feels so *strange.*"

But that was later, after the weenie roast, the potato salad, the beer and the singing ("Careless Love," "Down in the Valley," "The Wabash Cannonball"). Miles had a few chords and a clear tenor voice that was unexpected, his bland speaking voice suddenly amplified when it turned to song, so they mainly listened to him. The other couple, Jack and Laura, though pleasant, said very little and didn't sing at all. Gracie told him that they had been going together since junior high, that they were practically married.

They all disappeared into the shadows as the fire died down. Once, when the fire blazed up for a moment of its own accord, John raised his head to look and found Loretta's head up like a periscope, checking them out. Miles's arm came around her and pulled her back down, but her eyes, smaller without her glasses, remained on John as long as they had time to.

"Loretta's keeping an eye on us," he said to Gracie under their blanket.

"She's always worrying about me," Gracie said fondly. "She's my best friend."

"Does she always take care of you?" he asked.

"Sometimes I think everybody takes care of me." She meant to indicate wry exasperation, but he thought he also heard the pride of the infantile, the cute. For a moment his kind feelings toward her turned cool, though his hand was on her breast, and he wondered at his being here disguised as an adult in the damp summer woods. He lay touching another organism suddenly reduced in his mind to its components—veins, glands, white expanses of skin over flesh. This momentary vision didn't exclude his own morphology; two strange organisms lay here inexplicably entwined.

"My father's the limit. And then there's my mother—and even Irma, but she should talk," Gracie said.

He said, "Did Irma want to marry the guy she had to marry?"

Gracie thought about it. He could feel through her skin the general pause for such a large consideration. "I don't know. Irma's always been mad for boys, but Gus Rasmussen? I don't know."

The waste, the aftermath of passion. Well, there was that other question he might ask, in this mood. "Do you know anybody named Estelle Lundgren?"

"My aunt used to be Estelle Lundgren. Now she's Estelle Hilberg. She works at the *Herald.* Why?"

"I think my father used to know her, that's all."

"Go ask her tomorrow. She's nice."

"Maybe I will."

Maybe he wouldn't.

"Oh," Gracie said as he idly touched her nipple. She squirmed toward him and kissed him, her tongue long, changing the subject.

He moved his mouth back from hers and said abruptly, "What are you going to do with your life? What do you want?"

If she recognized this as aggression she didn't show it. She told him of her internship in physical therapy at St. Luke's, of new techniques for getting old people to move their atrophied limbs, to help crippled children and accident victims of all ages, to make them well again. Hydrotherapy, massage, special exercises—how wonderful, how exciting to help people! Did he know how terrible it was not to be able to walk, to take care of oneself, to do the little things we never even think about, like being able to go to the bathroom without help?

He supposed he really didn't know. "I can imagine," he said. "But are you going to get married and have babies and all that?"

"Oh, sure, someday," she said gently, guardedly, and pulled his head down to hers.

From the other sides of the fire came murmurs and the chink of bottles. She allowed him more and more of her skin, and her hums and sighs of pleasure grew quieter and more intense. "Don't," she whispered. "Don't." But her fending hands were so weak he couldn't believe them. She didn't signal that she wanted to get away because she didn't want to be anywhere else or to be doing anything else. "Oh, oh," she sighed into his ear. Why do this? he thought. You approach the edge of a cliff just to look over the edge, not to jump off, so maybe it was all right. No, there was a mean strain here. Examine that. A memory: once when he was five or six he was petting a cat, and its silken flanks evoked some dark proto-urge or other. He'd wanted to go on petting the cat when the cat wanted to go somewhere else. Of course the cat won, but that brief moment before the cat turned into needles and fishhooks—no confusion in its desires—struck him forever, a permanent memory to be sorted out later, if possible. He'd known and feared the strength of giants, because he was so small, but for that one moment, before the reality of needles and teeth and the cat's unalloyed will took over, he'd had an eerie intimation of the pleasure of cruelty.

Her slacks were now off and he touched her slippery places. She didn't seem to hear him when he whispered that he was prepared; in his wallet were those devices—ghost white, mythy, clinical—so it would be all right, or at least safe. This she would not hear. If she were to submit there wouldn't be any cold-blooded pause for that sort of thing. There would be no mind here, no collusion; what she would accept was her own unconditional surrender or nothing.

She was about to let him, no precautions at all, and he was amazed. This was very bad judgment on her part. She must be mad. This was what happened to her sister—did it run in her family, this blackout of sense? Did it run in the state of Minnesota? He suspected that she really was without guile, and he felt sinful and avaricious, but when had he ever denied himself what he could have?

He should not accept possession; he would have no moral passport out of here. His later indifference would be purely cruel. She wouldn't understand his coldness. She would wonder what she had lost.

But with the dreamy quiescence of her flesh she said yes, she said now.

Unless he was a monster, he created his life second by second. He could quench this burning by immediate immersion, but not without the knowledge of consequences. One consequence might be a later memory of pleasure tainted by cruelty—seduction as a kind of rape. There was also the shamefully interesting fantasy of leaving one's progeny scattered over plain and valley, each with a sad little mother, and then would come the pity and blood love for those abandoned strangers.

That he was no longer an irresponsible child was in part his own idea, undocumented. Once, a grown child in his bath, looking down at himself engorged, he marveled at what had risen from his body and been endowed by the dark reaches of evolution with shaft and glans for the one purpose, to penetrate the silken sheaths of women, those difficult, soft, flighty, dangerous, vulnerable creatures of his race. He was made to fit all of them. They were all his, fat or thin, short or tall, all were created to be his scabbard. Gracie seemed to be in a swoon. Sense, the thicket of care and fear, had burned away and his lower motors hunched him like a goat, but still he didn't enter her.

"Gracie! Gracie!" Loretta called across the embers. "What are you doing?" Then Loretta was over them and pulled his head up by the hair. "What are you *doing?*" she cried. The interruption was intense enough so that some glimmer of consequence came back to Gracie. Loretta was not just trying to wake them from their madness. With all her wiry strength she tried to peel them apart, and did. Gracie was contrite; as they sorted out their complications of limbs and clothing her healthy leg searched desperately for the entrance to her slacks.

At this point Miles threw his guitar into the fire. Loretta ran over and snatched it out, whereupon Miles erupted into apparently dangerous violence. He punched the air near Loretta, though she was not fazed and he never quite hit her. He took the guitar out of her hands, threw it down and jumped on it, its compression like the last scream of a small bony animal. Upon its remains Miles danced slack-handed and slack-footed, a comic imitation of a marionette, and John saw that in Miles there was no real danger, that his object had been simply to gain Loretta's attention. Miles threw the remains of the guitar on the fire and they watched as it caught, the sudden light making columns of the trees, whose branches spread high above them like the ribs of a Gothic ceiling. They listened to the crackle and plink as the fire detuned what was left of the guitar.

Loretta found her glasses and stared through them at Miles, as if better vision might enlighten her. Jack and Laura were the last to emerge from their privacies. Their faces rose from the dark of their hollow as if from the underworld into the light of the burning guitar. They looked; it was only Miles, so they descended again.

Miles ran off into the woods, down the slope toward the reservoir. They listened, Loretta's arm outstretched like a conductor's to hush them, and heard Miles crashing around down there in the dark.

Out of the blankets the night was cold and still. A thin moon seemed to have quenched the wind. Loretta shrugged and raised her eyebrows above the lenses of her glasses: what could you expect of such a nincompoop? Lord, did she have to live her life in a world of fools?

From down by the water began jungle screams and screeches—giant macaws and gibbering monkeys, baboon hoots and shrill soprano staccatos that were surprisingly real, or real for Tarzan of the Apes. Then came a splash, and more splashes, as if Miles were beating the water with a branch.

"I'll get him," Loretta said with disgust.

John helped Gracie carry things to the car—blankets, bottles, food and wrappings. When they were through picking up they stood next to the car, waiting. There seemed to be the necessity to speak, though he feared what they might say. Gracie finally said in a small, almost babyish voice, "Did we?"

"No," he said hastily.

"You could have."

"Yes, I guess so," he said, looking back toward the fire as if preoccupied with Loretta's and Miles's whereabouts.

She moved up to him in the semi-darkness, her pretty face round as a clock, and felt for his hands. Her short presence was massive and thermal. "You guess so?" she said.

"Yes," he said coolly, to suggest that the subject had been adequately covered.

"You could get a job here. You don't have to go to California."

He told her, with a creaky shifting of tone, that he had to see the rest of his country, that he had to travel on—a compulsion, certainly irrational, but there it was.

Gracie understood perfectly and let go of his hands. "I just lost control," she said. "I'm glad you didn't lose control, John." His name on her lips was possessive.

"Yes," he said.

"You could have taken advantage of me, but you didn't. I guess I fell in love with you."

For that word Roger had strangled Alice, thousands had died.

Gracie said, "I felt sorry for you about your father and I guess I didn't have my guard up. Here you are, a handsome stranger and then it turns out you're really a local boy and I could tell you were upset, so I guess I just let my guard down. It was pretty serious between me and Jimmy—I guess you don't know that. One of the reasons we broke up is I wouldn't let him do anything, and then the next thing I know you've got my bra off and then practically everything else and I didn't even try to stop you. I must have been in a crazy mood. Maybe it's a rebound, or something like that. It doesn't feel like it, though. But why didn't you, when you could have? Jimmy would, all right."

"I might have. I don't know," he said, feeling vile and ungenerous.

"It's because you're a nice boy. I know. Loretta thinks she stopped it, but you could have done it anytime. I must have been in an absolute trance."

Loretta came back with Miles, the now passive buffoon. He walked behind her, chuckling, a little drunk, a little stunned but nonchalant, jaunty in his disgrace. He was covered with swampy muck, so Loretta wrapped him in a blanket and made him get into the backseat. "A blanket can be washed," she said disgustedly—disgusted with all of them. "Gracie, get in front. I'm going to drive."

As soon as they were in the car Miles reached forward and took Loretta's thin neck in his muddy hands. "Break her goddam neck!" he said exultantly.

"Miles! Mi-*yuls!*" Loretta yelled.

"Break her goddam neck and take her while she's still warm!"

"That's enough!" Loretta said, disengaging his hands and throwing them back over her shoulders. *"God!"*

The ride back to town was cold, but Loretta wouldn't stop to put up the top. Miles asked her once, then lapsed into what seemed to be indifference. He and John were let off at Miles's place. The car would be at Loretta's, the keys under the floor mat. Loretta was stiff with disdain, her glasses glinting.

"Good night, John," Gracie said.

"Oh, shut up!" Loretta said.

"But, Loretta," Gracie said as the car whined down the driveway in reverse.

"Jesus, take it easy on the transmission," Miles said.

In the bathroom John was scrubbing at Gracie's pink lipstick when Miles came in behind him. "I love her," Miles said. "I can't help it. So why do I always do something that pisses her off?" He put one mucky foot, sock and sneaker still on it, into the toilet and flushed. Before the cascade ended he substituted the other foot. John was startled but then he had to admire this innovation. His countrymen, as far as he'd had a chance to observe them, were always difficult to classify. He doubted if Loretta would admire such originality, however.

"Oh, we'll get married sooner or later," Miles said. "She's such a domineering bitch nobody else wants her."

"How come you do, then?"

"I don't know." Miles shook his head. "Love, I guess. By the way," he added, "did you nail Gracie?"

"No," John said.

"Just asking," Miles said lightly. "Just asking."

Later, in his sleeping bag, the muted radio crooning its fantasies but timed to go off soon, John had one more thing to do in order to relieve an ache similar, he thought, to that of impalement. With his hand and his immediate visions of the sturdy blond girl, he entered her as deeply and opportunely as would the reckless, vivid rogue it was not his talent to be. But as his fluids gathered she became, against his will, Doris Ella Perkins, of Leah, New Hampshire, whose passionate synchronous desire, unencumbered by flesh and circumstance, welcomed him into thin air.

19

One evening at dinner Debbie dropped a large porcelain gravy boat, a vessel that looked like a pitcher and a saucer but was really all one piece. It cracked on the table edge and sloshed an extraordinary amount of *sauce duxelles* into the Princess's lap.

"Robert, would you help me?" the Princess said calmly.

Robert put down a tray of *oranges glacées,* and using the lap of the Princess's dress and a napkin they walked the hammocky mess out of the dining room. Debbie was mortified, tongue-tied and sullen in her apologies. In a little while Robert and the Princess were back, the Princess in another dress, and the meal continued. Debbie had disappeared, and didn't show up for cleanup, either.

Dory supposed she was in the room she shared with Cynthia, but when everything was done for the evening and she went up to look for her, she wasn't there. Daylight was fading out of the dim old room, the window like the entrance of a cave seen from the inside. She had a chill, partly from embarrassment for Debbie but also, unexpected in these circumstances, from fear of the dark. It could come on very quickly, its intensity surprising her into involuntary twitches of flight that she resisted but not until her skin jumped and chilled. Betty Salmon, just behind her, or in a chair or beyond a shadowed doorway, might stare at her. The strength of Dory's disbelief in apparitions was, strangely, an ally of cold fear. But never mind; she controlled herself and walked carefully out of the room. When she turned on the lamp at the end of the hall she was safe again.

Debbie wasn't downstairs anywhere, either. The guests were in the living room, some having brandy and coffee, a stratum of blue haze from Ernst Zwanzig's cigarette dipping toward the fireplace and its open damper. Yvonne wasn't there and neither was Werner.

"It won't be long before the Bolsheviks have the bomb . . ." Jean Dorlean was saying, pleased into mirth by this possibility.

"That was his largest mistake," Sean Patrick said, interrupting him.

"That *Teppichfresser?* That madman?" Kaethe Muller said in her high, harsh voice.

"That's what he said, the columnist; that the New York City Fire Department could take on the whole Russian Army. Can you imagine?" Ernst Zwanzig said this to the Princess, who didn't seem especially amazed.

Dory checked the library, but no one was there. She found Robert sitting on the porch railing where he could look into the living room and catch glimpses of the Princess.

"Have you seen Debbie?" she asked in a low voice so as not to betray him.

"No," he half whispered back, acknowledging her judgment.

"I don't know where anybody is," she whispered. "Have you seen Cynthia?"

"She and Yvonne went down to the lake."

"How about Werner?"

"Haven't seen him."

"Dibley?"

"In our room. He's making a ship model and the place stinks of airplane cement." He got off the railing and motioned toward the field, and she followed him. When they were far enough away from the open living-room windows, he said, "Can I ask you something?"

"Sure."

"What does she want from me? She's always touching me and I don't know what she means by it. Does she like me a lot, or what?"

"She likes you—that's pretty obvious."

"But what does she want me to do? Touch her back?"

"You might try it."

"But I can't! I swear she'd have to ask me straight out, or put it in writing or something. It's not that I don't *want* to, I just don't dare."

"If she didn't like it she could just say so."

"But she's a princess. I can't get over that."

"Wouldn't you rather find out and get it over with?" Dory said, wondering why she seemed to be encouraging trouble.

"I think I'd explode," Robert said. "Listen. What happened at dinner —I've got to tell somebody or I'll go nuts. We went out to the kitchen and scraped off most of the gravy and then she sort of led me by the arm up to her room and had me help her peel off the dress 'cause it was still a little mucky and she didn't want to get gravy on her hair and all . . ." Then he said wonderingly, "I never noticed how small she is. I always thought she was taller, but she only comes up to my chin."

"So?" Dory said.

"The gravy had seeped through onto her slip, so then—I still can't believe it—cool as a cucumber she asked me to help her off with that, so I did, and there she was, practically naked." His voice had subsided, from awe. "I mean she wasn't exactly naked—she had on some stuff. You know. Anyway, she got out another dress and had me zip it up in back. But before we went downstairs she squeezed my arm and looked at me, kind of smiling. God, I wish I knew what she wants!"

"Why don't you just ask her?"

He laughed miserably. "I could no more ask her that question than I could jump over the moon. You know me." He looked over at her, then straight ahead. "I'm not exactly your John Hearne type, you know."

"I know, Robert. I wish I could help. I shouldn't have gotten you into all this in the first place."

"Yeah, but I . . . I feel funny but it's not something I want to *not* have." He thought this over, shaking his head. "I feel sort of queer about it, she's so old, like with my aunt or something, but it doesn't seem to matter."

They walked along, crunching stubble, heading down toward the lake parallel to the gravel path. The air was warm and completely still, and mosquitoes sang around their ears. Heat lightning, so far to the west it might be in Vermont, flashed silently behind the shoulder of Cascom Mountain.

"Storm sometime tonight," he said.

"I guess," she said.

"She gives me those looks, but I can't read looks. I might be dead wrong. If she'd just say something—I mean one word more. The way I feel about her, I don't want to wreck anything. I think I'm a goner, Dory. I'm all hot and bothered and I can't think straight. I guess I'm in love."

"So am I, if that's any consolation," she said, and they both laughed with a sort of bitter softness she'd never heard from either of them before.

When they came into the pines above the beach she wondered if they had meant to come all the way to the lake. Out near the raft, in the very last of the light except for the silent stutter of the heat lightning, was a silvery gleam of wake where a white arm and shoulder rose out of the black water.

"Who is it?" Robert said quietly.

A slow swirl appeared next to the first swimmer and Cynthia's laugh came very clearly across the water.

"Cynthia and Yvonne," Dory said. The swimmers approached the shore and stood up to wade. Yvonne's large breasts, unhampered, swung heavily.

"Hey, they're skinny-dipping," Robert said, and without further comment they turned and faded back through the trees.

When they were nearly to the lodge Robert said, "They sure are close, those two."

"I guess they are."

"I don't know if it's unhealthy or not," he said, "and I guess it's none of my business."

She had been wondering about that, too, unwelcome visions of the two female bodies pushing rudely into her mind. She wasn't sure what constituted unhealthy—what caresses or writhings or what. It was a vague, sweet, hurtful area she didn't want to think about.

She decided to enlist Robert in Debbie's case. She had to trust somebody, even though she might not deserve his loyalty.

"Robert, would you do something for me?"

"Sure. What?"

"Would you make an excuse to go up to Werner's room? I'm worried Debbie might be there."

"Deb? And that blivet-head? Sure. Anyway, he's been trying so hard to be friendly it makes my teeth ache."

"She feels sorry for him. If she thinks I'm butting in I don't know what she'll do."

"She better be careful. There's something slimy about that guy. He's too polite. He reminds me of a little kid with a load in his pants."

While Robert went up to Werner's room she went to the rolltop desk in the front hall where she kept accounts, schedules and the ledgerlike checkbook from which she made out checks for the Princess to sign. By the schedule she was to give swimming lessons to the Patricks' two little boys tomorrow afternoon. In the morning she would have to go to Leah for supplies. Kasimir's day off was Thursday, so she planned a hamburger or barbecued chicken cookout at the beach, if the weather was good. The laundry truck was coming tomorrow; she'd have to announce that at breakfast.

Robert came back and reported in a conspiratorial voice that Werner's room was empty.

"Then where can they be?" she said.

"How about the car? I'll go and look," he said.

"Then there's the two empty rooms on the third floor, and the dormer roof."

"And the boathouse and a zillion acres," Robert said. "They could be anywhere. But why do they have to be together? Maybe she's so ashamed of slopping gravy on the Princess she hitched home."

"She'd be more ashamed to do that. I thought she'd just be sulking in her room and now who knows where she is?"

"She'll be all right, Dory. She's pretty tough."

"She acts tough. Sometimes."

They went through the kitchen to the shed where the station wagon was. It stood below the dark old rafters empty and innocent, its modern curves meant for speed.

They came back around the lodge to see whose windows were lit up. The heat lightning had spread across the western horizon and flickered constantly, reddish-yellow rooms of it as large as townships, but still without sound. The hills and the mountain seemed to jump to their heights each time and then not be there at all until the next flash and the next. When the sound would come the wind would come with it, but now the air was so warm and still no leaf or needle moved.

"Their room's still dark," she said. "And Werner's."

"Old Kasimir's still up."

Mrs. Patrick came out on the porch and looked toward the west, shaping her belly with her hands. The hemline of her light, loose dress was several inches higher in the front than in the back. Then, as if she had made up her mind about something, she turned around and went inside. Though they weren't twenty feet away, and were perfectly visible in the porch lights, she hadn't seen them.

Something moved behind them, first felt as vibration under the feet, then heard. They both turned smoothly and involuntarily toward the heavy concussive sounds—thuds that had the authority of mass but were not really startling. A horse had come running from the field and had stopped short at the border of grass and gravel. It looked at them as if astounded, its eyes white all around. As they went toward it, it turned nervously, with exaggerated stampings of its rear hooves, so that it was sideways to them. Its dark coat was wet and it drooled a loop of foam. One hoof touched the border log and withdrew so quickly the gesture seemed one of great distaste.

"Hey, boy, whoa now, boy," Robert said soothingly as he went up to it. "You belong across the road, now, don't you, boy? Hey, steady, steady now."

Dory had ridden horses and helped harness them and she always had the feeling that a horse was two creatures in one great vulnerable body, that a horse's basic fear was that it was going to be eaten. This horse wanted to run away but also didn't want to run away, and out of this turmoil came glossy, violent muscular spasms, a kind of warning to the omnivores.

But the big skittish farm horse did in some measure want reassurance from them, and allowed Robert to take its tether in hand. Like molasses its dark gray penis spilled slowly out of its body halfway to the ground, then commenced an equally slow retraction.

"I'll take him back," Robert said. When he tried to touch the horse's neck it shied and jerked the tether from his hand, but it didn't run away and Robert simply took the tether again.

"It's going to storm soon," she said. The horse didn't like the flashes, which made its eyes startle in their whites.

"I'll get him home," Robert said. "He needs to be in the barn."

Robert led the horse down the driveway and she went inside. In the living room, sitting aside from the others in a shadow, Mrs. Patrick now nursed her baby, her blue-white breast rolled out of her dress, the baby's mouth centered at an almost separate brown hemisphere. As Dory passed she heard the slight ticking of valves.

The library was still empty. The talk in the living room was hard, bitter-seeming without her really listening to the words. "So one wog bumped off another wog," she heard on her way back to the kitchen. They were talking about Gandhi. She took the back stairs, which led only to the second floor, then the main stairwell to the third, where a lower ceiling flattened the same spaces. The table lamp at the end of the hall contained an ancient bulb of clear glass in which long orange filaments wavered fragilely. The wallpaper, vertical columns of twined vines, stained and watermarked, had once been another color but had dimmed to rotogravure. The two empty rooms, as yet unmade-up for guests, were in the back, shaded in daylight by large maples that reached over the eaves. Now the rooms were vault black, and if she entered them the sudden, all-revealing flash of ceiling light would violently change whatever thing or event each contained.

Debbie might be in one of them. She might be alone, agonizing in her horribly intense and disorganized fashion, or she might be with Werner and in that case it would be like entering a brawl. By what authority she would engage in that conflict she didn't know. Older sister, parental proxy, reminder of law, boss of the crew—none of these seemed quite authoritative enough to challenge Debbie in her wrath. Though she was barely sixteen, Debbie seemed able to swell like some kind of freakishly evolved fish into twice her bulk and even age; her violence of emotion could be daunting, even if you knew her.

Should she knock, asking the possibly empty rooms to respond? To ask a question of the vacant dark always caused an answer, the more silent, the more terrible. But she had to ask, and stepped forward on the warped floor to knock. There was no answer, but in her mind it was as if she had disturbed a school of minnows so that they swirled in common alarm through the room behind the door. Then she went in and clicked on the light. The room was empty, full of air; her eyes hurt from the instant clarity of their search.

She went into the second room more easily, or recklessly, then out the window to the roof in the flashes of the coming storm and found only a blanket Debbie had left there to get soaked or to blow away. She took it in. As she went down the long hallway the bothered darkness followed behind, touching her with its fingertips. She went down the stairs without looking back.

Debbie was somewhere, troubled or in trouble, as she usually was, but there seemed a more nasty edge to this time and this place. It came from the voices of the guests, a kind of predacious knowingness that excluded them from contemplation or wonder. Even the atomic bomb appealed to their sense of humor, and the mildness of the Princess and Yvonne, because of their bland acceptance of whatever was said, didn't seem a counter to this tone but complementary to it. Of the other women, Mrs. Zwanzig was old enough to have a license to practice sarcasm, but Mrs. Patrick was brood stock, to be used and not heard. Kaethe Muller, with her sergeant's bearing, was both man and woman, a soldier in mufti. Perhaps in the world beyond Leah, in the great cities, a bitter smirk infected all human intercourse.

At last she reached her room. With relief, and also the sense of dereliction of duty, she went inside, turned on the lights and locked the door. She was tired of anxiety. Her care for Debbie was in danger of turning into simple exasperation, so how strong was that love in the first place? She should go down to the boathouse and see if Debbie was there

—go quickly before the storm began—but she was tired of having to confront Debbie. She was tired of the anticipation of finding her. She sat in her room's musty, chintz-covered easy chair, feeling small and for a moment even weepy. Well, she *was* small. Everyone in the place, except the Patricks' children, was bigger than she was, and in the worst sort of finality that was what counted. All the little rules and laws that created order could be lost in an instant, and when that happened she would have no control at all.

Her door, behind her, sounded with a tapping she at first thought came from inside her room, and for a moment she felt invaded, but the tap was Cynthia's—two quick nail taps with one finger, repeated.

She had to get up and undo the turnbolt before she could open the door. Cynthia indicated the strangeness of this with a quick glance, but said nothing about it.

"We haven't talked much," Cynthia said tentatively. She wore her bathrobe over her candy-striped pajamas, and had been drying her hair with the towel that was draped over her shoulder.

"Not much," Dory said, grateful to see her.

Cynthia sighed theatrically, and with an inquiring but then evasive flick of a glance, as though her mind had changed in that tiny part of a second, sat on the bed. "Yvonne," she said, getting it over with, deciding to plunge into and over that subject, "has led a terrible life. You know she's a bastard? Bar sinister? The Zwanzigs adopted her."

"I know."

"You do?" Cynthia was really surprised. She frowned at this secret Dory hadn't told her.

"The Princess told me once."

"You didn't tell me."

"It never came up. I don't pay much attention to that sort of thing anyway."

"I guess you don't."

"It's because I come from common peasant stock," Dory said.

Cynthia had to smile, but she didn't want to and the smile went away. "We've known each other so long, haven't we? Childhood and all that."

"Since fifth grade," Dory said.

"Best friends," Cynthia said. She seemed tired, worldly. "I remember how nice you were to me when I first came to Leah."

"I was nobody," Dory said. "I thought it was you being nice to me."

Cynthia looked away, toward the flickering window. "There's no reason we have to admit everything to each other, though, is there? You won't tell me about John Hearne. I mean you won't admit anything and it's really none of my business."

Dory could think of nothing proper to say, so she said nothing, but Cynthia's mood was proof against her silence. "You wouldn't believe some of the things she's told me." Cynthia stared gravely off into this knowledge. "Like at the age of nine . . . God, you're so *little* when you're nine! She was . . . She didn't even know what was happening. One of her father's pupils took her on his lap and she felt this *thing* and he pulled aside her underwear and just *did* it to her. Can you imagine? She never told anyone. They were alone for a few minutes and it hurt a lot but she didn't dare cry or anything because she hadn't lived with the Zwanzigs long and she was afraid to cause any trouble. Her mother had died and she didn't have any other place to go. The pupil never came back but she was scared he would for a long time, until they moved to Zurich and then to New York. She used to have nightmares about him. One minute he was smiling and dandling her on his lap and the next he was hurting her like hell and snorting like a pig. Christ, what a monster! Can you imagine it? Nine years old! You're so *small* when you're nine. You're small all over. And she didn't tell anybody about it. Nobody ever knew. The Zwanzigs still don't know about it. Can you imagine feeling you can't even cry because you're so scared you'll get kicked out?"

Cynthia registered hatred, her fingers even curling into claws. "God!" she said, her jaws so constricted the word sounded German. "She says the most important thing about life is you never hurt people. It doesn't matter what you do, there's just the one forbidden thing—hurting another person. Instead you should love people and make them happy. She used to be a Catholic and she was going to be a nun but that didn't work out, and then when she was nineteen she married a friend of the Zwanzigs' who was twenty years older than she was. They were in Vienna when the war began, and he simply disappeared, totally. Later she saw a photograph in the New York *Times* and there he was in a German uniform standing with a bunch of other German officers under the Arch of Triumph in Paris. As far as she knows he was killed later in the war. She says she's sorry for him but she never loved him, she just married him to please the Zwanzigs. She was pregnant and she had the child in New York. It was born with part of its spine uncovered and it died two days later of meningitis. It was a girl." Cynthia's voice had quavered at the last, and she sat quietly, her eyes moist. "And she's such a beautiful person."

Dory felt that she ought to say something. She was moved by Cynthia's emotion more than by Yvonne's story, which seemed so foreign and so far in the past. It was ancient history because it had happened before she became aware of history, a story of foreign perversities in which a child, or a million children, could be raped, and a husband could be a Nazi. Of course, all their histories would one day be ancient, and the old griefs would mean little. Like Betty Salmon's. But now a real storm was coming and she didn't know where Debbie was.

"Have you seen Debbie?" she asked, finally.

"No," Cynthia said, startled out of her sad reverie into concern. "What's the matter?"

"She and Werner seem to have disappeared."

"Oh-oh. She likes him."

Someone walked down the hall past the closed door, and they looked at each other. Cynthia went lightly to the door, opened it without a click and peeked down the hall, then shut the door carefully. "It's only Mrs. Patrick," she said. "With the baby. Poor Mrs. Patrick—why does she have to wear those dresses that look like they came out of the dust bowl?"

"He doesn't seem to mind," Dory said.

"Oh, him. I mean she's got the 'new look' and all that, but hers looks like 1936. And he looks like his battery's run down. I mean they both practically drip libidinous fluids, don't they? Maybe they don't get enough sleep."

Then Cynthia was looking at her with a kind of reckless intensity, about to say something she hesitated to say right out. "You and John Hearne," she said quickly. "Did you?"

If Dory answered, "Did we what?" it could remain unadmitted, or nobody's business, but Cynthia was her old friend and up till now they'd had no secrets. With a kind of relief she said, "Yes."

"Wow. More than once?"

"Yes, a lot more than once."

"Did you . . . like it?"

"I love him," she said.

"But did you *like* it?"

"Yes."

"Really? I mean a *lot?*"

"Yes. A lot."

"So do you have any kind of understanding? About the future, I mean?"

"I don't know. Anyway, it wasn't his fault."

"He seduced you!"

"It wasn't hard."

"You're only seventeen! Are you pregnant?"

"No."

"Well, thank heavens for that. But he did take advantage of you. You've always had a crush on him and now he's had his fun and taken off for California."

"Fun?"

"Yes, basically, I suppose. He had this lust so he just used your body."

"Cynthia, do you know all that much about it?"

"It's pretty simple, isn't it? When you cut out all the palaver and the moonbeams he had this urge and you were handy."

"He said he was going to come back and marry me."

"Huh! I'd get it in writing, kid."

"You sound like my mother, only she's not so . . . vociferous."

"Your mother *knows?*"

"Yes, she knows."

"Did you tell her?"

"No, she just knows. What's so strange about that? She had to get married herself. In my family we know what happens when a boy and a girl spend a lot of time alone with each other. She didn't have to be Einstein to figure it out."

"Ah, yes. Folk wisdom. I keep forgetting your peasant origins."

"Well, that's why I'm worried about Debbie. All the Perkins women have round heels."

"Are you offended? Dory!"

"I'm worried, that's all."

"I'm sorry," Cynthia said, taking her hand. "I didn't mean to be so . . . vociferous."

The dry, tanned hands enclosed her hand and her first instinct, though she didn't allow her hand the slightest pulse of motion, was to withdraw. This touching was new, something Cynthia had learned from Yvonne.

Cynthia said, "If they're out there somewhere the storm will bring them in."

Lightning was continuous in the west, and they heard the first faint tinnitus of thunder.

"I've got to go," Cynthia said. "Oh, how things have changed, Dory." She seemed again emotion-weary, a lady in romantic decline. She sighed. "I haven't practiced for three days—I might as well have left my violin at home. Anyway, I'm no Fritz Kreisler, so what's the use?"

"You're good," Dory said.

"What good is good? Oh, I'll keep it up, I suppose. I'll go and crank out my exercises. Every genteel young lady should have a minor talent." With that she got up and went to the door. She was acting now, going, as Cynthia would, from emotion to its dramatic imitation.

"Don't worry too much about Debbie," she said. "She'll come back." With a sad, brave, encouraging smile she said good night and slipped out the door with something of a dancer's controlled fluidity.

Dory turned to the window, toward the storm. A tiny pattern glittered at the bottom of her screen, a geometric arrangement of squares that seemed deliberate, and she went closer to look. In letters four squares high, each square touched with, probably, a dab of Duco Cement, were the words I LOVƎ YOU. The porch roof ran along a few feet below her window, but she'd never thought to pull the shade. Dibley. Dibley, she thought immediately. Dibley trying to write backwards, remembering to reverse the L but not the E, making the letters so small no one might ever see them. But that he'd had to make the message concrete when he could never say it aloud—that he'd had to turn the idea into action—seemed as premonitory as the coming storm. Had he hunched there in the dark while she undressed, not five feet away, black eyes in his white face?

Cynthia tapped her tap on the door and opened it. "You'll be relieved to know she's back," she said. "She and Werner sailed out to Pine Island and had to paddle all the way back in the calm. Creepy as that Hun is, I don't detect any major hanky-panky, if you get my drift. Okay, Dory?"

"Thanks, Cyn. Thank you."

"Are you okay, kid?" Cynthia asked. "Listen, I didn't mean to be so hard on John Hearne. What do I know about it? Do you miss him terribly?"

"I'm afraid he'll get hurt, and I'm jealous, too. I'm nervous all around, Cyn."

"Listen, Dory. We all love you. Your loyal crew. We may be a little screwy but we love you, okay?"

Before she undressed that night she pulled down the shade, then put it up again when her light was out. The storm passed with high bursts of wind and thunder, but little rain or damage. The electric clock in the hall lost only a half hour during the night, less of an outage than most storms caused, or would cause.

20

He woke not knowing where he was, examining carefully, as if his eyes were scouts on the point, a square of light upon which leaves or their shadows danced. The square, cut by a vertical line, was too even and straight to be organic. He was in the Army, on bivouac—the rough wool of his blanket bag insisted upon it—but the tall lighted square didn't belong. He felt for his rifle and his hand dropped over the side of what was suddenly a bed. As the light became the sliding door of this room in Winota he was whirled over years and faces to land here smeared with guilt he would have to remember and classify. He'd monkeyed with other lives, is what he'd done, the irresponsible little shit. For someone who didn't believe in God he had a bad case of looming judgment.

So he was twenty-one and his country was full of women to charm and hurt, to nuzzle and abandon. For Gracie he felt pity, awe at her candidness, shame at his unloving seduction. How could he have undressed her? Shame for his priorities, his self-indulgence. Everyone seemed more real than he could ever be, yet he could delude them into thinking him real. Life went on everywhere else, people having real feelings for each other, real unto danger, while he treated them as objects upon which to test some kind of cruel aestheticism. Even here in Winota, where he'd been a real child, and in Leah, where Dory, her clear gaze noting all of this, still claimed she loved him. Her resignation when he left had been part of that knowledge.

"I'm too nervous," he said out loud, a kind of groan.

"What's the matter?" Miles said from across the room. "Hey, John, you having nightmares or something?"

"I'm afraid I made an ass out of myself," he said. He was anxious, breathless with unfocused fear and embarrassment. Everything frightened him, including his motorcycle.

"You? What did you do? You were nice as pie," Miles said.

"Screwing around with Gracie."

"What's wrong with that? Anyway, you said you didn't slip it to her, right?"

"Right."

"So what's the problem?"

"I don't know. I just feel bad about it."

"Shit. You ought to have Loretta to deal with. You want problems? All I *think* about is putting it to her. Jesus, I go crazy thinking about it. I'm supposed to be taking courses at UM and all I can think about is Loretta opening her knees. I get so goddam hot and bothered I practically explode. It took me six months to get her to give me a hand job and sometimes she won't even do that. She says it's too messy. I tell her, okay, I'll put a sock on it, and she gets mad. I tell her let's get married before I get an internal hard-on and fuck myself to death, but she can't make up her mind. Other women don't interest me, honest to God. I'd rather jack off thinking about her than screw anybody else. I have just plainly got to have her. So you got problems? Your girl in New Hampshire—you got problems like mine?"

"No, not like yours. She likes to fuck."

"So what's your problem?"

"It's me, not her. She's real enough."

"Real enough? This got something to do with you looking for your dad?"

"I'm not really looking for him."

"Okay. I'm no psychiatrist, but he abandoned you, so you think you don't exist? Did you think you existed on Okinawa?"

"Yeah. I could tell by the piss in my boot."

"Ha, ha! Oh, shit. Life's complicated, ain't it? I tell her, 'Look, all the dumb things I do that piss you off I wouldn't do if I wasn't suffering from a terminal blue-steeler, so if you'd just lie back and relax . . .' She says she's going to be a virgin on her wedding night, but she's driving me ape and that's why she can't make up her mind to get married in the first place. So you got problems? You going to marry your girl in New Hampshire?"

"I think I might."

"She want to marry you?"

"Last time we talked about it."

"So she's waiting for you, huh?"

"I guess so."

"I still think you should have humped Gracie. What the hell! There's got to be a first time for everything. Sooner or later somebody'll get into her skivvies, so why not you? Stick around for a while and do it right."

"She doesn't appeal to me that much. I mean there wouldn't be any future in it."

"So break her in. Do some guy a favor. Hell, do *her* a favor. She might look a little butchy but I'll bet she's got the muscles to pump your bilge, man. Drain your brain. So teach her the drill. There's enough goddam virgins as it is. Any virgin over fourteen is a crime against mankind."

Though he didn't agree with Miles's theories they were widely held and he found their expression, at least, somewhat comforting. Because he'd been alone, out of that sort of company, its side of the equation had faded into the shadows where it no doubt belonged, but that world existed and expressed no guilt.

"Christ, it's four A.M.," Miles said, yawning as audibly as a dog. "I don't know what she's got that gets to me. I mean *Gracie's* got a prettier head, for God sakes. It's something else, like those long bones. Long neck, long legs, heart-shaped ass, a kind of horsy, snooty look. Even her goddam glasses."

John woke again in the heat of the morning. Miles was already up. "Let's go get some breakfast," Miles said.

They went on the motorcycle to pick up Miles's car, and then John followed him to where he didn't expect Miles to go—the Loup Qui Parle Diner. He thought as he parked that maybe Loretta and Gracie didn't work today, but there was Loretta's Ford. Miles was already at the door and motioned for him to follow, so he didn't have time to object. They sat in a booth and Gracie, smiling, healthy and friendly, came to wait on them. Loretta, behind the counter, gave them one cold look and turned away.

"I told Loretta nothing happened last night," Gracie said, "but that only made her mad at me."

"We're all in the doghouse, huh?" Miles said.

"She said if you came in this morning the cook's got a gumboil and she was going to get him to spit in your eggs."

"I've seen her madder than that," Miles said. "I'll have her eating out of my hand again in no time. Tell her I want to take her away from all this. Tell her I want to be the father of her children. Ask her how many she wants. Tell her I want to eat her . . ." But Gracie, having seen that he was maundering, had gone to get them their coffee.

When she came back with the coffee she said to John, "I saw my Aunt Estelle this morning and told her you wanted to ask if she knew your father."

"I did?" John said.

"Didn't you? What's the matter?"

"Nothing." This was like his mother. You mistakenly told a woman something and she immediately translated it into action.

"She'll be coming in for coffee in a while. Anyway, she says she remembers you and she wants to see you again."

Maybe he could escape right now. He could zip back to Miles's place and get his gear.

Gracie looked at him, frowning—a frown worried for him. "She's not going to eat you, John."

This exchange had interested Miles. "The question, me boy, is, is you interested or is you ain't?"

"I is nervous," John said. He was moved by their concern but had a small reservation concerning curiosity, or the documentary urge. They might have expressed the same alert interest while watching a pinball game, and he was not much used to, or taken with, the idea of being the center of attention. In Leah he could fade into the trees.

Miles ate ham and eggs, spit or no spit, but John had only an English muffin, its blandness necessary. When Estelle Hilberg came in and Gracie brought her over to the booth, Miles had finished eating and tactfully went to sit at the counter.

Estelle was a handsome woman of about forty with wide, freckled jaws and long teeth. Her reddish-gold hair was done in reverse-curled glamour-girl style, a tube of it across her forehead, and her eyes seemed smashed into diamond and blue fragments that glittered with delight, as if lighted from inside. Her tan linen dress was so pressed and crisp it rustled as she moved.

"Johnny Hearne," she said. "You were knee high to a grasshopper when I saw you last. How's your mother? Is she still pretty as a picture?"

"She's fine," he said, remembering a large force of light and enthusiasm that might have been Estelle when he was five. "I remember you at the paper, I think."

"I was twenty-two and just out of college when your dad got me a job on the *Herald.* I remember you just as plain. You were a bright little guy and we all thought the world of you, Johnny. And now you're grown up. My! I'm trying to figure. You were in kindergarten, so you must have been five, and I was twenty-two and now I'm thirty-eight so that must have been sixteen years ago and you must be twenty-one. Lord, how time flies! For the last ten, eleven years I've been writing the column he started. 'Just a Ramblin',' by Syl Hearne. Now it's 'Just a Ramblin',' by Estelle Hilberg, but so many people remember your dad and all the nice things he had to say about interesting people and happenings all over Lou' Qui Parle County."

Gracie brought coffee and Estelle said to her, "You should have seen Johnny when he was five. He was the cutest, brightest little guy. Of course, you were only three or four. I was telling Johnny how people still remember his dad with such affection. He was such a nice man. He was awfully good to me, I'll tell the world. Nineteen thirty-two was a bad year anyway and in August my dad lost his arm in the binder. Walter had his own family to support, so that ten dollars a week kept us afloat."

When Gracie had gone Estelle said, "My niece thinks you're the cat's pajamas, Johnny. I guess you must take after your dad." This, by her lowered voice and soberer expression, was a delicate subject. "Your mother thought every woman in Lou' Qui Parle County was after him, and maybe some were, but he was a straight arrow and I'll proclaim it from the housetops. She even thought we were up to something." She stopped short and gave him a quick glance to see what he knew. Their eyes met and they both looked away.

"What do you hear from your dad?" she said. "Is he still in Tulaveda?"

"Tulaveda?"

"I haven't heard from him lately and I just wondered. He does like to move on, doesn't he?"

"I haven't heard from him ever," he said. He hadn't meant to say such a simple, vulnerable thing, and the words brought on a surge of anger and self-pity he did his best to resist.

"Johnny! Is that true? Gracie didn't tell me that!"

"Yeah. The guy my mother married evidently vetoed any communication at all."

"And Martha went along with that? It doesn't sound like her, unless she really wanted to."

"I guess she did, then." He could see that Estelle wondered how much could be said about his mother.

"Do you think Syl knew where you lived?"

Syl again; he hadn't got his mind around "Dad" yet. "I've thought a lot about that," he said.

"Bless your heart, I bet you have. I don't understand it. All these years and you wondering about your dad and never hearing a word? It defies comprehension." She became very still, making a decision. Then she went into her handbag and kneaded its contents until she came out with an address book, a fountain pen and a spiral notebook. "Here," she said as she wrote, then tore off the page and handed it to him. "I haven't heard from him since around February or March, so he may not live there anymore."

Sylvan Hearne
c/o Forester
601-B Los Robles
Tulaveda, Calif.

"February or March," he said, looking down at this document. Robles meant oaks. Oak Street. Tulaveda was near Los Angeles. He'd looked at maps of California and had evidently learned them without trying, as he had war maps in high school. But this plain, ordinary address—it was as if, on a navigational chart as big as the West, two finely drawn lines had intersected, a fact once and for all ending speculation and its choice of inaction.

"We've always kept in touch," Estelle said. "A card or a note once in a while. Once I didn't hear from him for two years and it was during that time I married Sonny Hilberg. I always thought he'd come back to Winota, he liked it here so much, but he never mentions that anymore." She sighed at the changes wrought by time. "I can't understand why he never got in touch with you, Johnny. Your mother . . ." She pressed her lips together as if to say no to the comment she had been about to make.

"What about her?" he said neutrally.

"I don't want to say anything and I shouldn't, but I don't think it was the right thing to do. It doesn't matter how good a father the other man was to you—the man she married. Your own father is your own father and I think you ought to know each other. I know he thought the world of you. I just disapprove all the way around, even if it isn't any of my business. Are you going to look him up?"

"I don't know."

"For goodness' sake why not if you're going all the way to California anyhow?"

"If somebody doesn't want to see me, they don't see me," he said, and the pronouncement-like accident of phrasing made his throat tense.

"I don't know what Martha told him or you," Estelle said. "Forgive me, but sometimes your mother and the truth were barely on speaking terms."

He remembered how when they came home at night he'd pretend to be sound asleep in the car so his father would have to carry him up the stairs; he wondered then why his father never knew he was really awake. Obviously his father could be fooled.

"Well, I'm headed that way," he said. "I'll see what happens when I get there."

Estelle went on, reciting information and requesting it. She knew about his father's cousins in Minneapolis and St. Paul, his father's brother in Seattle—all this a vague rumor in his mind. His mother's family came from St. Cloud, he knew; his grandparents on her side were still alive, but were strict Lutherans still icy about the scandal of divorce all those years ago. He'd seen a picture of them in which they stood two feet apart and noncommittal under a maple tree. She asked how long he would stay in Winota, and did he have a place to stay? His exact Army and college records went into the files, as did Amos Sylvester's vital statistics. Who was he, he thought, faced with the warm energy of her interest, to look down upon this form of knowledge?

Estelle herself had two girls, twelve and ten, and Sonny Hilberg was kind to the three of them. Winota was a nice town, a friendly town, a good, solid, hardworking town. There were worse places in the world, Johnny, to settle down. With his college background he could get a job on the *Herald*. It wouldn't pay much at first, but the opportunities were good. Think about it.

Estelle looked at her tiny gold wristwatch. "Goodness, I've got to get back to work! I may be the publisher's wife, but the presses must roll." She stood up and he stood up with her, bent a little because of the constrictions of the booth. "Don't be a fool," she said, blushing so that her skin turned as tawny as her freckles. "Make sure you find him." She kissed him on the mouth, a depth of perfume, and lips smoother than he expected; then she had to wipe her lipstick from his mouth with a paper napkin, a motherly act, her left hand holding his chin steady. "You keep in touch, now," she said. "You can always write me at the *Herald*. I may hear from him anytime, so if you can't find him, please let me know." Estelle, this lively woman whose eyes searched for his father in him, had to be telling him that she was more than his father's friend, and that her connection, unlike his mother's, would not be broken.

"I want to know what happens to you in your life. Will you write and tell me?" She meant it, literally.

"All right," he said, feeling that he lied, that slight twinge.

"Do you mean it?"

"I think so."

"You're a lot like your father," she said, and gathered her things. "I just wish you were taking a train or a bus, but both you guys are always out of control. I know. Goodbye, Johnny."

Gracie, Loretta and Miles, together at the counter, watched all of this, Loretta seeming to have forgotten her anger. She leaned against a stool in such a way that her arm touched Miles's arm.

Estelle went to the cash register, a jaunty sway in her hips, and as she paid she said something to Gracie that made her look at him; then Estelle turned to look at him, too. She waved as she left.

He decided to leave Winota today, and when he told them he was surprised by their vehemence. "Not today!" Gracie cried.

"Come on, John," Miles said. "We're just getting to know you, as the song says. Stick around. Take a break. The girls are off this aft and we're going swimming out to the lake. Come on with us."

John looked to Loretta, that authority, and found her looking at him sternly, thinking hard about him, his character, his motivation. Finally she nodded. "Stay another day. You need it," she said.

"Stay forever!" Gracie said.

So in the late afternoon he lay on the white raft next to slim Loretta, Gracie and Miles having a race to shore. Gracie swam like a torpedo, faster than her arms and legs seemed to propel her. The lake water was so warm it was no shock at all to enter it.

"Your girlfriend in New Hampshire," Loretta said. "Are you serious about her?"

"You mean I'm not about Gracie."

"I know that. It's too bad. She's such a generous, loving girl."

"How about you and Miles?"

"Miles is a child. I'm waiting to see if he ever grows up."

"I remember this beach," he said. "I got my beginner's button here."

"I'm grateful you didn't go all the way last night. She got an instant crush on you as big as a house. She just doesn't let boys do things like that. Please believe it."

"Okay."

She turned onto her hip and looked at him to see if he believed it, and they faced each other as closely as lovers for a moment, long enough for her clear skin and graceful pose to give him an erection, which seemed in such bad taste he rolled into the water to hide it.

He was to leave early the next morning, the sun behind him. That evening they danced at the Lakeside Casino to a brassy local band. "You belong to my heart . . ." Gracie was a little bundly and awkward to dance with, her pretty face blissful. She hadn't once asked about his girl in New Hampshire.

In the morning Miles got up to see him off, and just as he was about to start his engine Loretta and Gracie arrived in Loretta's green Ford.

"Come back and see us," Loretta said.

"Send us a postcard from California," Gracie said. "You've got friends in Winota, just remember that."

"Take care, buddy," Miles said.

The town had become new because a new part of his existence had taken place in it, but at the moment of leaving the older memories came back as flicks of emotion, nudges of feeling.

"Did you ever know an Alice Giefer?" he asked them. "When she was five she had bright red hair. She taught me to eat sand in her sandbox."

They were silent, perplexed. "But . . . ," Gracie said.

Miles said in a voice gentler than usual, "She's eating sand right now, Johnny."

"She was Roger's girl," Gracie said.

It was like a stitch, the crushed bright red Pontiac, that closed past to present, the knowledge vivid but not as sad to him as they thought it was. After all, he'd only known Alice for a short time, long ago, about as long as his father had known him.

After he'd started his engine Gracie ran to him, hugged him with her field-hockey strength and kissed him on the lips. "Goodbye! Goodbye!"

He left them because he was pushed, or pulled, by the technicality of his having said he would leave. He ran that way—affection-proof, sorrow-proof, a ghost of what they thought him to be.

"We'll miss you!" Loretta called over the urgency of his running engine.

He left Winota on a narrow white highway, the wide land smelling of fecundity. To be on the motorcycle again was an act that had stretched him out past weariness with distance and the fear of breakdown or crashing. His wheels continued to vibrate as they revolved, the slightly bent frame to twist his back, the wind to desiccate his skin. Winota receded into time as the miles passed and he achieved a kind of second wind of boredom. He stopped to eat in South Dakota in a little town whose name he'd missed on entering and never knew, then went by steps west and south into Iowa and then into Nebraska.

He saw from its first ominous hump a storm rise over the horizon like a mountain range, palpable as lead, yet it could not be mountains because the Rockies waited for him around the curve of the earth. The flatness of the land, the views too far and too level, made him uneasy, suggesting an unexpected phobia, not quite pathological. Fear of flatness? Of nothing? Zerophobia? There must have been a name for it, but the name would not help his apprehension. Surely he had expected flatness.

Only the storm approached, with no trees or town or anything in sight but the mirage-smeared highway, telephone poles and low grasses that seemed half alive, or ragged signs proclaiming obsolete powders or teas, a collapsed shack and perhaps a pile of bones a mile off, or ten miles off. Occasionally he would glimpse a starved brown river, weedy green along its banks, a phrase coming from some memory or other: Too wet to plow, too dry to drink.

Then the lead-colored storm, thousands of vertical feet of dingy, coiling mayhem, came over the land like a shutter and he had to stop, put his poncho over his head and wait while it doused him and pried at him with a wind that was like a horizon-wide blade and then a punching, hammering series of small but vindictive blows. In his blindness he thought of tornadoes that drove straws through steel, and waited for impalement. But the storm was a roar and a force that grandly passed, disdainful of what it had not bothered to destroy. A yellowish, sickish light, a thousand miles of puke-colored light, grew and smoked and was gone eastward away from the sun.

The land didn't know what to do with the sudden water, grass and earth armored against it and bright with it, so that it would go to waste. The sun and wind would suck it back and the land would go on starving, or nearly starving, not green enough for eyes used to the green of New England.

He went on toward the evening as the sun began to blind him, looking for a town. The Indian Pony seemed to be losing power, which worried him until he remembered that he must be climbing, the whole land a hill, plains and prairies tilted up toward the Great Divide, where everything would be a mile high, the sharp young mountains rising from that base up into moonlike snow—geology, geography, the matter-of-fact of school. It turned cold as he climbed, cold as March at home. It turned by the mile colder as the sun fell toward a sealike horizon, until his fingers were thick and slow with it. He didn't want to stop and break the toleration of the stiff ache of riding, but he finally had to stop and put on his wool hat and gloves and another sweater under his Ike jacket before he went on. If it was this cold here, he would not have enough clothes for the real mountains. Even now his ankles and calves seemed banded by ice, and his knees were so numb he wondered, as he rode, if they would ever straighten. The cold that told him he must soon stop also insulated him, as if he were in numbed suspended animation, a part of the machine. He found himself traveling right on through a wind-blasted, barren, twilit town called Cinch, where there was a post office–store but no obvious place for travelers to stay. The sun turned right and left with the narrow highway he saw sometimes through blood-red refractions. Then the sun was gone, the plains a blue, planetary emptiness with a white penumbra that faded quickly into dark.

In his headlight, a shaky, shallow hole of yellow light, the road came under him, the worn white centerline skimming inches under his left foot. Eyes or bottles gleamed past on the shoulders that went back forever to ominous dark behind him.

A few miles on, no town lights ahead, a brown animal jerked across the asphalt in front of him, the quick vision of long ears and the squatted body said rabbit, a fixed picture like a photograph taken in panic and examined later. The next one he didn't see but felt, *k-thup-thup* as his wheels passed with a percussive shake over its body. He twisted his throttle down, holding his handlebars rigid, dependent upon luck and gyroscopic force to keep him from the disaster of falling. Then his rear wheel locked and slid out past him, tilting over. As the rear wheel and frame took control, the rigid, forward-pointing handlebars were meaningless and his light turned as the motorcycle lay over and down, the yellow light seeing shoulder and sparse grass, a cone of field, then the road again, but the road he had already passed. He swirled on the crash bar in a bow wave of bright sparks and finally the world stopped turning.

His engine had stalled, the headlight dimming quickly under battery power. He dragged the machine to the shoulder, stood it up and turned off the light. He wasn't yet sure that he wasn't hurt, because shock and the cold might have masked even drastic wounds.

Instantly he was among the stars. They seemed to begin at his feet, on all sides of him, defining by their billion white points a globe that was not just a hemisphere but the black, endless space of the universe. He could see the wheel of his own galaxy, the infinitude beyond. No shadow of a hill or tree cut into that void to remind him of the homeliness and presence of Earth.

Gravity held his feet to the hard dirt; that was evidence, but at first gravity was untrustworthy, coming at him unsteadily. He recognized the symptoms of fainting and bent over for a while until the force was again vertical. He was here, somewhere, and had immediate earthly problems. In his toolbox was a small metal flashlight he'd meant to buy new batteries for, but hadn't. He felt his way to it past buckles, torn canvas and rope, and in its sick dim ray found that his rear tire was flat. He could possibly repair it, if it was only punctured and not blown, but not in the dark. His flashlight, as if in remorseless agreement, or in collusion with rabbit and general malfunction and the cold that numbed his fingers through his gloves, then dimmed to a filamental glow far inside its lens.

The wind was not strong but was like the current of a river, steadfast and cold. It came great distances and would go on toward continental, hemispheric distances. He could feel in it the ice fields and high barrens of the distant mountains, but he must not let loneliness and fear, or the paralysis they might together cause, take his precarious dignity from him.

There was no doubt that during the night cars and trucks would pass along this highway. He might try to flag them down, but he didn't want, really did not want, to leave his possessions here and go as a supplicant, a passenger, passive and in need. His instinct was, he thought proudly and fearfully, to stay alone, survive this wilderness and its cold, and cope like a traveler from another century who had nothing but his own hands and skills. Men had done it. So he half dragged his motorcycle farther off the road, across a shallow ditch, into the tall weeds where passing headlights might not see it, and in the dark, with the instantaneous flash and blown-out void of matches, made himself a nest of his wool sleeping bag, ground tarp, poncho and warm clothes in which he might not be comfortable but would survive.

In his sleeping bag, beneath the stars that seemed to grow clearer, closer and yet, with a click of the mind, recede with the speed of light to proclaim the vast, killing and implacable distances of space, he found that what crept in toward his concern were the weeds, grass, the lumps of earth beneath his bones and whatever creeping or crawling locals, fauna alien to him, might want to invade his small space. He didn't want to light a fire, even if he could find fuel. Invisibility and the frigid, hidden stasis of time passing was what he wanted. He wanted morning and light, knowing that even if he slept, and slept well, too many hours would have to pass. And he wouldn't sleep well.

He hadn't eaten since the little town in South Dakota, hundreds of miles and a whole other geological climate ago. His thirst and hunger were strange and exhilarating, real for perhaps the first time in his life.

When had he ever really been hungry and thirsty, and was he really that now? Maybe when he was a baby and mewled for the breast or the bottle, but even in the Army he had eaten mainly because someone had insisted that it was time to eat, or the hour had vaguely suggested it, and the urge was little more than habit, or the hardly more than passive inclination toward a minor pleasure.

Some food was pretty good and some wasn't so good. He had eaten Dory's chicken and potatoes, but those slate-green lima beans had been a chalky paste on the tongue. In his present hunger, though, the idea of having to eat any food merely out of politeness was beginning to be a difficult thing to remember. Deeper than flavor and texture was perhaps a primordial knowledge of nutritional function. A dog or a cat knew, and if it was the fuel of a carnivore, took it. To a cow or a deer, or a rabbit, meat was as interesting as a fence post or a stone.

He would eat those lima beans now, with a little butter and salt and pepper. Protein and carbohydrate, trace minerals, the essence of each a little lightning flash on the tongue, a squirt of tooth-lubricating saliva, a communiqué from the central cortex via the stomach's craving network of nerves and avid acids. Also cool water, tepid water, *agua caliente,* puddle water, any water. The desire was wonderful and amazing.

It was also welcome because its reality cleanly excluded the fears of the child. No Paiutes, Apaches, Comanches, wolves or rattlers were really going to attack him. Maybe rattlers, but he really didn't think so. Or scorpions. He thought both were more southern creatures. Real problems tended to eliminate the well-fed fantasies of middle-class children. If he was really hungry he could scout, by the flicker of matches, back along the highway, find the rabbit that had scuttled him, skin it, eviscerate it, half cook it over a fire of dry weeds and gnaw its bloody bones. In a way he would be interested in feeling that kind of hunger.

A boon came—had been gradually coming and he recognized it now: the earth, unlike the moving air, was warm, heated all day by the high summer sun. The warmth came up through his tarp, blanket bag, clothes, skin, flesh and bones. Let the stars' inhuman light tell him of the absolute zero of space. He was at least warming a little, his pulse slowing, his bruises minor. He could now reach down and separate the tear in his pants from the scrape below it on his knee, and feel the weepy but not very bloody abraded skin, which stung a little and would grow a little taut as it dried, but didn't really hurt.

But all fear of the dark hadn't passed. He woke often in the night, once believing that the bulky snout of some large animal was an inch from his face. He dreamed that he climbed a mountain highway that kept rising toward the vertical, so that soon he would lose traction altogether and fall backwards, wheels over handlebars, for all those hundreds of feet where only centrifugal force had held him to the surface of the road. There were too many hours before dawn; after fragments of sleep he spent the still-dark hours worrying, with the feeling of breathlessness, about his rear tire. There was the axle to unbolt, the chain to remove, the brake linkage, fender braces, brake rod, the clincher rim to pry out, the limp gray tube coming out of the crack like the intestine of a dead pig. Was it a blowout or a puncture? Would he have to leave all his things and hitchhike, trying to find one of the nearly obsolete clincher tires? Nothing could be decided or done until light came. He yearned to have all of the problems solved and be again independent, everything snugged down and shipshape, moving on.

Dawn came as if the prairie were a sea, as he had seen dawn come over the Atlantic, horizon-wide. Telephone poles, stunning in their monotony, came from their vanishing point in the east and went forever on to their vanishing point in the west, the looping wires no doubt alive, but silent as the poles. The dusty wind was cold, but the sun was warm as soon as it was visible below his level gaze toward the eastern rim of the world.

The tire was punctured but with no mere nail hole. After nearly an hour's work he pumped up the tube and air hissed from a ragged tear as big as a nickel. Something rattled around inside, and when he worked the foreign object out through the tear in the collapsed tube, it was a jagged shard of bloody bone, part of the jackrabbit's thigh.

He used most of his patching-kit material on the tube and the rest on the inside of the tire casing. When he had pried and pulled, stretched rubber and arranged recalcitrant folds, the valve stem finally straight in its hole, he pumped up the tire and reassembled everything. It had taken him more than two hours.

He glanced back down the highway at the dead rabbit, a brown lump that was the only flaw on the miles of asphalt that in the distance melted off into wavering mirage. He sacrificed a torn T-shirt to wipe the bulk of black grease from his hands, and thankful, stiff, lucky, hungry, tough and spare as rawhide, he rode on to the west.

Nebraska would never end, nor would the road, the level-seeming railroad tracks, the long freights with several engines, their great mass slowed by the western climb, the trucks pulling more slowly to the west, the eastern-bound speeding toward him to blast him with their turbulence. He gassed up and ate standard food in one little town, stayed at a tourist home when there were no roadside cabins in another, wondering if his torn, dusty and windblown self would do in the lace-fringed room in the genteel house, but the middle-aged lady was friendly and curious to the point of irritation; what would she ever do with the names of his parents, his mother's maiden name, the exact population of Leah, New Hampshire? It was not the information that was important, but the ritual of its transference. He couldn't help liking her, feeling that she was, in some way valued by God, pure in heart, but he was so glad to finish the huge breakfast she made him of shredded wheat with cream and brown sugar, fried eggs, toast, grape juice and milk and to be on his way.

Finally he left Nebraska and climbed into Wyoming, lucky in weather. Distant mountains seemed permanently in winter, but a warm sun heated his back in the mornings. The names of towns were to him as vaguely historical and romantic as those of Africa or India: Cheyenne, Laramie, Medicine Bow, Bitter Creek. The climbs and descents were so long that braking or gearing down took hours, parts of days. The Rockies were on either side of him, the foothills and the Wyoming Basin a sometimes bitter land that was too glaring and chromatic, vertical and unanchored. He had read in school once that the mountains of the West were like great caterpillars crawling toward Mexico. The evergreen trees seemed simpler than those of Leah, primitive as ferns, and stood too far apart from each other, jealous and starved. There were great openings of grass or earth the trees of New Hampshire would never have allowed, as if blight had fallen here upon random acres and valleys. It was a land of gawky, raw distances, the air so clear there seemed to be no depth in its vastness, like a picture postcard taken under optimal conditions. Wherever he looked he saw miles-long vistas of conventional beauty, unmysterious.

He stayed the night in a log cabin with a tin roof, where a sign over the washbasin said not to drink the tap water, but to fill his canteen at the office. He had no canteen, but planned to buy one of the canvas water bags he'd seen tied to the bumpers of cars, where evaporation supposedly cooled them. He would soon descend the other slope of the continent, where what water there was ran west and south. The Uinta Mountains to his left, he would enter Utah and the Great Salt Lake Desert.

The next day, south of Ogden, he saw what he thought must be the Great Salt Lake, miles away, the caustic inland sea looking like real water. He came that evening into Salt Lake City, thinking of the Mormons. From a wide, clean avenue, the streetlights coming on, he saw what must have been the Tabernacle of the Choir, a building with the look of faith and pretension. The city itself seemed stable and clean. Cleanliness and neatness were his impressions of the city, or at least of the brightly lit wide avenue he followed. The traffic flowed along, civilized and decorous, the cars all clean and seemingly full of shining faces untouched by the corrosions of excess. This was a delusion, he suspected, based upon an Army acquaintance, an equanimous pure-eyed religious who had tried to convert him from the slough of smart-talking agnosticism to the Church of Jesus Christ of the Latter-day Saints. But the city, as he passed its buildings of clean gray stone and invisible glass, was burnished in the alien way of a church—for miles until the pride seemed to run out and he came into sparser purlieus where, amid vacant lots and industrial sheds, he found what he could only call a horizontal hotel, cars nudging its separate doorways, a red neon sign saying HOTEL-RESTAURANT-BAR.

Later, as he sat in the restaurant-bar with a beer and his maps, he was recognized by a familiar spirit, a pale man in a pinstripe suit a degree less than clean who sidled toward him with eyes like beacons and asked him if he knew about the Mormons.

He said he knew something about the Mormons, whereupon the sidler, with the glee of a conspirator rather than the normalizing tone of a homosexual, told him the dark secrets of the ceremony of "investment," in which the young Mormon is, in the presence of the Elders, broken in to the acceptance of polygamous sex. By such gleeful yearners he had been taught what Jews did with all those foreskins, the ways of priests with nuns, etc., and he sometimes thought he attracted this sort of education, sinister moth to innocent flame, because he must seem to these teachers unfinished, or in some remediable way pure. In any case, they came across rooms, past others, to him.

As for the Latter-day Saints, he had no inclination to defend their beliefs and he had learned that the sidlers wanted nothing more than to teach, so this one, having given his lesson, went away.

In the morning he bought and filled a canvas canteen, fashioned a sun hat of sorts with a bandanna knotted at the corners and rode south toward Provo. Though no weather had ever really daunted him he thought of the crusted eyes and swollen tongue, the last lurch toward mirage of an actor on shifting dunes, under a white sun. But his endurance had always been easily at hand, even when spent soldiers had lain like drab, exhausted birds along the roads. He had six hundred miles of semi-desert and real desert to cross, but on his map was a highway marked with names—a hundred miles from Provo to, say, Fillmore; a hundred miles farther to Cedar City; a hundred and fifty more to Las Vegas. If his machine remained faithful, if he kept to the road, and if the sun and the hot rush of air didn't desiccate him like a dying leaf, sooner or later the long push would end and he would be left with an address in Tulaveda. He would go toward a choice, but that didn't mean he would have to make it.

The distances, miles out of Provo, were mineral, alkaline, the scrub not quite green; at the horizon lay the dead ranges of the moon.

At noon he stopped at a lone gas station and restaurant, several mismatched, paint-cracked buildings inaccurately pushed together, where a Greyhound bus had let out its passengers for a rest stop. He was about to enter the restaurant when he saw the sign over the door: NO COLORED. The colored; could they eat or take a leak in this land? In this desert, you sons and daughters of Ham, seal your orifices. This issue was dangerous in him and had caused him much trouble. He rode on, avoidance familiar and demeaning. What could he do in this godforsaken place, its conviction hung over the door? The air was like a blowtorch, but whatever thirst or hunger he felt was minimal, not even comforting.

In Bunkerville, Nevada, it was 109 in the shade. He put a dime in a slot machine and won two dollars and thirty cents, enough for a bowl of chile, a piece of bread, a Coke and a tank of gas. He paid five dollars for a closet of a cabin through a surprisingly cold night. He wasn't seeing his country, he was seeing a highway, everything else peripheral. The Mojave Desert was ahead, but it would also be a highway. This urgency of travel was as far beyond his control as psychosis. He was sick of the machine he rode, yet impatient if not riding toward the liquid of the distance—*agua caliente* that was boiling highway, and that only in the mind.

But when he finally crossed the drab Mojave after Las Vegas and Barstow and came down the west side of the San Gabriel Mountains into a pretty, tended land of palms and orange groves, all stems and leaves kept and gaudy, as if each had been washed that day, he seemed to have entered the Land of Oz, although orchards and towns faded at their edges as if singed. In the late afternoon he came into Tulaveda on a street of little lawns clipped and green, little bungalows neatly aligned amid foliage that must have originated elsewhere, in some Far Eastern jungle, in New Guinea or the Solomons. The royal palms along the boulevard strips seemed fabricated and placed, their guy wires invisible. On the streets were strange, self-conscious automobiles—overpolished Fords with their roofs and windows too low, too small, and skeletal Model A's with open, chromed long engines and motorcycle fenders. Hot rods—so that was how they sounded, at intersections, when they painted the cement with black rubber. The air was clear to the bluish sky, yet not quite clear, and there was no wind. A still picture with machines in motion, like a cheap animated cartoon. His own beat-up

Indian Pony with its torn luggage was a stock contraption obviously foreign here. The people seemed to be on vacation; in this setting life could not quite be real. They must all return sometime to a working, blemished world. Winota had been frugally neat on its deep soil, and Leah grew twisted and slow on granite crevices, but here lushness seemed rootless, cosmetic and cheerful.

The street turned as the houses grew in size and the green yards grew into small parks, palms in rhinoceros skin, borders of plants sharp as broadswords, spears, the back fins of stegosaurs. Next to Spanish Mission was Victorian next to Gothic, the Gothic in adobe, the Spanish in stucco. Each lawn seemed to be having its private sprinkling, and the humid zones in the baked air were like familiar breaths of his own distant country.

He stopped at a four-way intersection, where everyone was supposed to stop, then go—an invitation to the odds, because some, depending on the others to obey, didn't bother to stop. If life was a hard gamble elsewhere, here in this strange garden it was merely a sport. He pulled over to the curb and turned off his engine, one foot on the boulevard grass, the better to observe this carefree roulette. Down the sidewalk came a thin little man sitting in a child's stroller pushed by an identical little man. Both wore white seersucker suits, rope sandals and white straw hats with cherrylike red pompons dangling all around the brims. Ancient twins. They both smiled and said, "Cheery hi!" as they passed, their leathery but delicate faces creased with goodwill.

"Hello," he answered in his own language.

A girl in plaid Bermuda shorts, sandals and a halter made of two tied-together red bandannas followed the twins. "I definitely approve of your hat," she said, and tweaked the knot in her halter with a bright silver thumbnail nearly two inches long.

He took his bandanna from his head and looked at it.

"They're super-handy," she said, smiling as if for a camera, her broad healthy white teeth shining on and on until, he suddenly thought, they must have had time to dry. Her hair was of two colors, gold streaked with orange, and she seemed to have a little knife on the end of each tanned finger.

"Yes," he said.

"I bet I've got thirty of them," she said. "You can make halters like this." She cupped her breasts, her nails clicking together. "Or even a two-piece swimsuit, or a pickaninny hat like yours, or a pokey-poke and about a godzillion things."

"You can even blow your nose in one," he said, but she didn't seem to hear this.

"You go to TJC?" she asked.

"What's TJC?"

"Tulaveda Junior College, of course," she said, and waved her glittery hand toward the prosperous hedges, walks and low Spanish-style buildings across the street. "Summer session. I'm taking Secretarial Studies one and two."

"Can you type with those fingernails?"

"Oh, these aren't *mine!* They come off."

"What are they made out of—aluminum?"

"They stick on with clear nail polish. Just a dab of nail-polish remover and they slip right off!" She was so pleased to explain all this—so pleased to make explanations—he asked her if she knew where Los Robles Street was.

"Los Rowbles is how we say it. What number you want? 'Cause, you see, all the numbers under five hundred are below Buena Vista and all the numbers over five hundred are above Buena Vista."

"Above?"

"That way, toward the mountains. Below is toward the ocean."

"It's 601-B, so I guess it's above Buena Vista, then. Where's Buena Vista?"

She laughed merrily. "You're *on* Buena Vista!"

"Last time I looked it was San Jose."

"San Jose *turns into* Buena Vista, so now it's Buena Vista. Anyway, Los Robles is three blocks, maybe four blocks."

She was interrupted by a great zooming and blatting of engines from two hot rods that had lined up at the intersection. They bragged at each other with their exhaust pipes, their huge rear tires like coiled haunches, and then burned rubber, blue smoke hovering at the spot where they had disappeared. She gave the blue cloud a brief glance and said, "See you around, now."

"See you around, and thanks," he said.

"My bunch hangs out at Jimmy's Palace, on Concha, case you might want to drop by sometime. My name's Dianne, but they call me Streaky 'cause of this dumb hair. There's no bleach or anything in it."

"My name's John. Maybe I will."

"Saturday nights, mostly."

"Okay."

"Bye now, John." She took a few steps and turned to wave and smile, catching him looking at her, and smiled a little more at that.

"Bye, Dianne," he said, and she walked on knowing that he looked at her tanned legs and strong bare back, her sexy swing of a walk, her garish hair that gave her a name. She'd put her hands on her breasts and looked at him with large, simple eyes, pretty-as-an-unfinished-picture eyes that gave him the suspicion that she was purely and playfully innocent, and that to go to Jimmy's Palace on Concha, whatever it was, to see her again and try to charm her, was not in the mood of a man, or child, looking, or half looking, obliquely looking, for his father.

He would find Los Robles and ride past 601-B, then look for a place to stay, or temporarily stay. After that he had no plans. He turned onto Los Robles, seeing no oaks but lots of mulberry trees, which he had seen in the Army in Georgia. Unfamiliar little warblers caused their own private racket among the dark leaves. The houses along the uneven-numbered side of Los Robles had deep porches, some duplexes sharing a long veranda, the front doors side by side. Lawns here were a little less tended, scorched at the edges. There was 599. He saw 601, a dark brown shingled duplex, and then a car was broadside to him. There was no time to touch his brakes, or any controls other than to jerk his handlebars to the left. He rose in the air and his own taillight and license plate passed beneath him. He seemed to be in the air for a long time while the folded motorcycle continued its somersault below.

In the air before his return to the pavement his mind was imprinted by the slow, graceful movements of the machine below him as the world revolved. Then vision was a faster, nebulous spiral, a vortex in which he was an imperfect ball. He rolled and rolled, amazed by the force that his mass contained. Each contact with the street caused his inner lights to flicker as he was stunned and stunned again. He could not stop rolling and hurting. He dreaded the ghost wall or tree or car that would stop him and probably kill him, and heard nothing but the thudding of his joints. But finally he did stop, or had stopped sometime earlier, and with the light of day dingy he stood up to find his motorcycle on its side right next to him, so he pulled it over to the curb and stood it up to keep its fluids from bleeding out. His fluids, too, seemed unstable, sloshy.

"Are you all right? Are you all right?" a woman asked in a voice so fearful he wanted to reassure it, but then a red filter came over the light and he was, time having passed, looking up from the street at the wide, frantically caring face of a woman who knelt beside him, her hands clasped together in the attitude of prayer. "Dear God!" she said. "Dear God! Dear God!" In spite of the distortions of her anxiety she was smooth and large, her wide face full of a soft light that had no texture and made him seem small. He tried to get up, but she carefully pressed his shoulders down. Something had been put under his head and from it came perfume—something of her. All around, now, people had gathered among the grinning faces of cars. He turned his head aside, embarrassed, and vomited easily into the street. She wiped his mouth with an aromatic little handkerchief.

"You stay still," she said. "I backed right smack in front of you and it's all my fault. I always look and I don't know why in heaven I forgot this one stupid time."

"I'm all right," he said.

"No, you're not. You look like death warmed over. It's a miracle if every bone in your body isn't broken. We'll just wait for the ambulance and then we'll see." She looked for the ambulance and he watched the smooth skin under her jaws and chin, feeling the largeness of her and her seamless warm light.

He was not all right; his knees and elbows were numb, and though tentative messages along the lengths of his nerves didn't quite signal broken bones, except maybe something in one knee, he had been hammered on too hard. Something was wrong with his sense of the vertical and even of dimension, because this smooth giantess covered the sky above him, her dark hair a cloud. Or he had grown small in his weakness. She looked down upon him and caressed his face and neck, her hands as familiar and matter-of-fact with him as a mother's with a baby. She was as vast as a movie, someone he must have seen acting out grand emotions on a screen. If he could think he might even give her a name, like Loretta Young, Myrna Loy, Joan Bennett—a name somewhere among those flawless American goddesses never to be seen in the flesh.

"Who are you?" he asked. "Should I know who you are?"

"I'm Bonnie Forester," she said, "and I'm going to take care of you."

21

One evening the members of the crew were all together at the beach. The sun had just gone behind Cascom Mountain and the rest of the earth—grass, stone, wood, sand, water and the almost palpable air—all was still radiant of the heat left by a summer day. They passed a big bar of Ivory soap among them, soaping off the grime caused by whatever tasks they'd done. In spite of their odd loyalties and infatuations, for the moment they felt that they were natives and that the guests of Cascom Manor were foreign to the valley and the blue lake. For one thing, none of the guests worked. None mowed, washed, sawed, dug, painted, scoured; none was, at least for this moment, as real as the crew was to itself.

Dibley watched Dory until the last moment before her eyes could touch his, then his shied off. She thought how "shy" seemed a clear and honest attribute, but whenever you met the shy they were always shy in impure and creepy ways. There was that writing in her window screen;

love as irritation, as a sickness. She couldn't be absolutely certain that it had been Dibley, or even that the words hadn't been there for a year or more. There was not enough proof of his skulking on the porch roof to accuse him, to disrupt, with unpredictable, possibly frantic results, his difficult life.

He was a good worker, though, and knew how to do things, unlike the Princess and her guests—except for Werner, who did know how to sail. He and Yvonne were coming about between Merrihew and Pine islands now. The Princess couldn't swim, Kasimir carboned the bottoms of pans, the Patricks couldn't sail because, in some vacuum of conception, they couldn't understand the leverage of moving air. She'd found the Princess trying to screw in a light bulb backwards, turning and turning the bulb the wrong way in a live socket. None of them except Jean Dorlean knew how to drive. Mrs. Patrick plugged a toilet and hadn't the sense to do anything but run for help while her children crawled in the overflow and the ceiling of the library turned soggy. Jean Dorlean bragged about not being able to understand machines, as if that simple knowledge were contemptible. She didn't despise their ignorances but couldn't understand why they were indifferent to them, or even proud of them, as if they felt superior to competence.

Debbie kept looking out to the lake, where the sailboat came about again in the mild wind. Yvonne had asked Werner to take her out because she wanted to talk to him, Cynthia said, about his attitude toward Debbie. He bullied Debbie, but she wouldn't stay away from him. He pushed her off the dock, turned her upside down in the water until she came up choking, turned her over in her fleshy helplessness to reveal red finger marks on her thighs and a buttock freed from her swimming suit, yet she sputtered and laughed, and even though she looked flushed and unhappy she never got angry at him. She wanted his attention but what she got was rough treatment and jocosity, not the seriousness she wanted. When Dory asked her why she took it, Debbie inflated in wrath and said, "Mind your own business! Take a powder!"

Maybe there were times when Werner didn't treat her like that, but never in the presence of others. He treated her with contempt, calling her German names she didn't know the meanings of, always with laughter, as if he were embarrassed by her devotion.

When they'd all soaped up, as if by general agreement, or by tradition, they swam to the raft.

The water sped along her arms and thighs, high summer and the water her element, cool as her blood, fluid as John Hearne in his absence, she the lake he swam in. These moments came upon her unexpectedly, even in the midst of worries or pending decisions. Jealousy and sex, actual parts of him. She'd never thought of parts of him like that before when she wanted him. Now she allowed his tall flushed penis, silken, fluid, deep in her. Too far in, to the limit. Did she want to be hurt by him? Then she would know he was there.

On the raft she knew that Dibley shivered near her not in discomfort but in ecstasy. To be here in the clear air, nearly naked, near his beloved . . . . Ick, sick, the sick virgin boy dying of rapture. She slid into the water and swam the few strokes to where she could stand and walk to shore.

Werner brought the sailboat in, raising the centerboard as the bow slid against the sand. "Werner," she said to him without quite knowing what she would say next. She, too, would talk to him about Debbie.

Werner stood at attention in the tippy stern of the boat, saluted and said, "Werner Friedrich Joachim Roland Josef Graf von Ganz-Lengen, at your service!"

Yvonne, in Cynthia's red bathing suit, stepped out of the boat with hippy grace and waded toward the raft. She turned back to Dory and gave her a sweet, worried smile before sliding forward to swim.

"Werner," Dory said. "I want to talk to you."

Werner pulled the sailboat farther up on the sand and again stood at attention, or nearly at attention; his ordinary posture was such that it was hard to tell what he meant by this pose. He said, "Of course, I jokingly gave you my full name and title. Here I'm plain Werner Ganz-Lengen and proud of it. In Germany I'm what you call a 'hereditary count,' even though my family's estates are in the Russian Zone, so it's cheerio to all that. Not that we're paupers, you understand, or without influence. I'm not complaining in the slightest. It's A-okay with me just to be alive and in the good old U.S. of A. Bet your boots!"

"It's about Debbie," she said.

He waved this away with a smile. "Just a little teasing, a little kidding around. Nothing to take seriously."

"She has a crush on you. I hope you won't . . . ."

Werner laughed. They began to walk up the path toward Cascom Manor, Debbie no doubt watching them from the raft.

"I was just a child," Werner said. "I didn't want to leave my friends and my school and go to Germany. I played baseball and football and basketball. What did I know about Germany? I had such an American accent it made my mother angry. I was just a plain American boy." He looked at her as if wanting a verdict, his little blue eyes waiting for a sign. "My heroes were the Yankees—Joe DiMaggio, not Adolf Hitler."

"Yes," she said, wondering what it was in Werner's nature that made it difficult to feel sympathy for him. When he pled he was imperious;

when he bragged he spoke as if to total agreement. He was unhappy now, but the sympathy she felt was floating, and wary.

"I never volunteered," he said. "I was simply sent to Klagenfurt and enrolled, mainly because of my father and my title and the respectability this was supposed to have lent to those fanatics. Did I decide to be a cadet? I was even underage! But my father held the Knight's Cross with oak leaves and swords when he fell at Rostov, and you can bet your bottom dollar he was an honorable soldier, first and last. The *Liebstandarte* was under Army command, remember—crack troops, an elite formation, nothing to do with Uncle Heini's *Totenkopfverbände* and all that *Völkisch* drivel!"

"I don't know what most of those words mean," Dory said.

"They mean that the *Waffen SS* had nothing to do with the *Allgemeine SS,* the *Sipo* or the *SD.* Nothing! My father was a soldier first and last!"

"What's all that got to do with you?"

"What? What? Me?" Werner stopped and looked down at her, standing straight in his bulgy blue trunks, the reddish fur standing out of goose bumps on his husky legs. She thought she saw a glimmer of fear in his pale eyes, just a wash of it. "We were always Christians! My great-grandfather was a bishop! It's our sacred honor, my family's sacred honor that has to do with me!"

"That's not American," she said. In the way he said "honor" was something immaculate, impersonal and cruel, like a blade—like the blade of the "dirk" he'd shown Debbie.

"I'm an American," he said. "This was decided. Don't you think it was decided at the interrogation camp? I was only seventeen! All we'd been given were *Panzerfausts,* finally. Twenty rounds in all for a *Trupp* of twenty children. We were just children, but that didn't mean we couldn't die!"

"But you didn't die," she said.

"They made us walk among the corpses. Do you know the stench? No! As if we had anything to do with it! Who are you to judge me, anyway? A girl? What did you do in the war? Did you freeze and go hungry? Did you hear the Katyushas?"

"I thought you were captured by the Americans."

"You can think what you like! I am Werner Graf von Ganz-Lengen! What do I care what you think?"

But he wouldn't leave her, and he seemed sustained by his prideful words. He became friendly and confidential again. "No, Dory. You simply can't know how complicated it all was, but American Intelligence understood. The CID and the CIC—they understood. The world is very complicated now, you see."

"Who is 'Uncle Heini'?"

Werner laughed. *"Reichsheini? Reichsführer-SS* Heinrich Himmler. My father called him 'The Sleazy Eminence'—in a letter! And do you think anything happened? Nothing. In my father's regiment no one used SS titles. They wouldn't think of it. My father was a colonel, never a *Standartenführer!"* He laughed, and kept laughing too long, alone in another context in spite of her silence. *"Reichsheini!"* he said. "An insult, a nickname for the chinless little conniver!"

Himmler. She saw bones sticking from the inside into starved skin grainy as dirty canvas, stacks of corpses always in her mind gray, as if the sun never shone in Germany or in Poland. She'd been fourteen when all that had come into its gray light and been real, actually real—the slime of it, infecting the race she was born into. Even in her guiltlessness and helplessness there was a film on her own hands, an invisible grease no soap could cut. Imagine that intoxication with death, a sort of honey lust, cloying but seductive, their insignia the death's-head. She felt cruel, perhaps unfair. "What do I care for your sacred honor and all that?" she said. "What do I care for your German honor? I don't like the way you treat my sister and I want you to leave her alone. Is that too complicated?"

"Then tell your fat sister to stop showing herself to me. Does she think she's attractive? She acts like a slut."

She left him and went on to Cascom Manor.

She didn't have to look for Debbie, who came to her room in a rage. "What did you tell Werner?" she yelled, tears making her voice harsh—the voice that had the discordant volume of struck bronze. It was an assault, her voice, her big body and breasts too mature for her emotion. She was too big for the sympathy she ought to receive, always. Dory could think of nothing to say that wouldn't insult her and hurt her even more.

"Well?" Debbie yelled. Surely she could be heard all through the house and over the grounds.

"I told him I didn't like the way he's been treating you."

"What the hell do you know about it? What the stinking hell business is it . . . yours! Why can't you leave me alone? Who asked you to butt in?"

"He said you keep showing yourself to him. What does that mean?"

"Oh, you *bitch!* You dirty *bitch!"*

Yes. How could Debbie ever forgive that? A brutal description of what she must have thought charming, flirtatious, secret. Her ugliness revealed. But Debbie wasn't ugly until she screamed in injustice and pain.

"Deb, I'm sorry," she said, but Debbie's momentum of anger and passion took her out the door, which she slammed so hard plaster dust sifted down each side of the frame.

Now what would Debbie do? It would do no good to go to her, at least for a while, until she calmed down a little. She had stamped down the hall toward her and Cynthia's room, so that was probably where she was sulking and brooding now, maybe packing her things to go home, maybe not. It all seemed so unnecessary, and Debbie was always in some overwrought state or other. Always. No, that wasn't fair. Not always.

Even so, there were things that had to be done—tomorrow and the next day and the next—duties she had taken on. She went downstairs to the hall desk where she kept schedules and lists. It was dark outside now, so she turned on the lamp over the desk. Sometime tomorrow she would have to go into Leah for supplies.

Jean Dorlean came out of the living room. "Ah, our most efficient manageress," he said. "Come in and talk to us."

In the living room he and Kaethe Muller were alone. From somewhere upstairs came the melodious whine of Cynthia's violin. Jean Dorlean wore a polo shirt and khaki Bermuda shorts, his legs unhairy only at the knees, as if the curly brown hair had been worn off in just three places—his two knees and his forehead. Kaethe Muller wore a beige skirt and blouse and no bra, her blouse as usual open nearly to her waistband. She was so big she made Jean Dorlean look like a hairy little spider, one of those males a quarter the size of its mate. They were a pair; Dory had seen her go into his room late at night.

"Please sit down, Dory, if you have a minute," Kaethe Muller said. Her *s*'s were *z*'s and her *v*'s were *f*'s. All of the guests had accents except Jean Dorlean, though his name sounded French. Werner almost didn't have an accent. The Patricks sounded English, but there was an Irish lilt in their voices, especially Mrs. Patrick's.

"How politically conscious are you, Dory?" Jean Dorlean said. His accent was American, all right, but the question seemed foreign. And she smelled the patronizing tone of it; her consciousness of that was developed enough.

"How do you mean?" she said neutrally. She sat in the wing chair, facing the two of them on the chintz-covered davenport.

"For instance, are you a Republican or a Democrat? I suppose being from New Hampshire you're a Republican."

"I can't vote yet. I don't know what I'll be when I'm twenty-one."

"But you're quite sure you will know when that magic number arrives?" He was amused by his question, as was Kaethe Muller.

Dory didn't answer. One impulse was to smile and let herself be led into the patronizing humor of a guest, and the less conventional impulse was to be irritated.

Jean Dorlean said, "But about Dewey and Truman—do you think 'Maestro' Zwanzig will get to present his monster bust to Dewey at the White House?"

"I'd rather have Truman win," she said, knowing that this preference had really come from John Hearne.

"Not a chance!" Kaethe Muller said. "Too bad for you, Dory!"

"Yeah. Too much going against old Harry, I'm afraid," Jean Dorlean said. "The American people just won't accept this civil-rights legislation of his. Imagine that kind of equality for the Negro! Too much history there, and anyway, the whole thing was Eleanor's idea. Then the Roosevelt-Truman Supreme Court throws religious education out of the public schools! I mean, Dory, who's going to vote for Harry S. Truman? And now he wants a peacetime draft and racial integration in the armed services! What next? He's got some nerve even running."

"He may not get elected, but you're wrong about the other things," she said.

Jean Dorlean turned to Kaethe Muller, pleased. "See?" he said. "I told you she was something, didn't I?"

Kaethe Muller shrugged and smiled knowingly, her unadorned lips like big healthy pink muscles, which they no doubt were. All of her was large, healthy and German, and Dory couldn't help thinking that if they had all been that large maybe we wouldn't have won the war. She wondered what sort of German Kaethe Muller was. Some Germans had been against Hitler, but most of those were Germans first and anti-Hitler in their spare time, on leave from their units. Where had she studied this? Why had she studied this? *Boche, Hun.* Winston Churchill said, "The Hun is either at your throat or at your feet." But what did he mean—a race? Ike Eisenhower was German—his name was, at least, and no one could be more American. But why was he called "Ike"? His name was Dwight David Eisenhower. Maybe "Eisenhower" sounded Jewish to his West Point classmates, so as a joke they called him "Ike." Did our national hero get his nickname because of a Jew joke? Hopefully she was wrong. But then, Jewish actors and others, even, changed their names; they must know something about her country, too. Joseph Goebbels said that if his arguments about the Jews got out into the world they would do their work, like a disease. There were two Jewish families in Leah. One ran a junkyard and the other a haberdashery. She didn't know the children because they were older. But she knew who they were. She was aware of them as Jews, who knew how?

"What?" she said to a question, to an expectant look.

"I asked you what Werner told you, that's all," Jean Dorlean said. "What did he say about his career, if anything?"

"He said something about being a cadet."

"About Klagenfurt?"

"He said that name."

Jean Dorlean and Kaethe Muller looked at each other quickly.

"Anything else?"

"He said his father 'fell' at Rostov, and that he was in the *Waffen SS.*"

"Do you know what that is?" Kaethe Muller said.

"Yes, I think so."

"Well . . . what?"

"Black uniforms. No prisoners. The Malmédy massacre."

"Oh, they weren't all like that!" Kaethe Muller said.

"Well, that's all right," Jean Dorlean said. "But why don't you go talk to Werner, Kaethe? He did seem very upset."

"I asked him not to bully my sister," Dory said.

"*Ja.* He should stay away from your sister," Kaethe Muller said. "I shall go to him and talk."

When she'd left, Jean Dorlean got up to replenish a brandy glass Dory hadn't noticed before, lit a cigarette, sat down again and leaned toward her as far as he could without falling off the davenport. "What do you know, and what do you not know?" he said as if to himself, looking at her. He glanced conspiratorily around the room, then leaned toward her again. "We are at war. You understand that, don't you? The real war goes on. It was always between Bolshevism and the West. The Nazis were an aberration, totally disorganized fools with their insane *Führer* and his idiotic racism. Bad luck for everybody except Stalin, in the end. And the Japanese with their toy navy and their stupid, suicidal racial arrogance! No, Dory, the real enemy is organized, ruthless and determined to destroy us."

He seemed pleased to have given her this information, and was about to continue when Mrs. Patrick came into the room. In her dowdy way she was dressed up, with lots of lipstick and pancake makeup that faded her reddish freckles. She didn't acknowledge their presence but went to a bookcase and stood looking at it. Her large breasts seemed swollen, her belly swathed in the loose, flimsy material of her green dress. She was posing, sucking in her belly and standing up straight, as if stretching. Mr. Patrick came in, following her. He paid no attention to them either but went up behind his wife and stopped. He leaned over her and placed his hands on the bookcase, but she bobbed under his arm, as if doing a curtsy, and moved away from him. He followed, stopped behind her and leaned over her again. They seemed to be in a trance of some kind, or as if they followed rules, and then Dory recognized their purpose, which she had seen in birds and in other animals. It was a ritual of pursuit and coy avoidance. She and Jean Dorlean watched openly, without feeling that the Patricks were aware of them at all.

When Sean Patrick approached his wife again she preened, and when he stopped behind her he placed his arms around her. Only then did she bend at the knees and twirl out of his arms. He was tall and broad-shouldered, but seemed washed out, somehow. He wore a loose summer suit of cotton, a light, faded blue. He seemed as simple as the simple desire his actions revealed, and she, too, seemed to have been made simpler and tackier by her coy mincing. Soon she left the room, and he followed.

Jean Dorlean looked at Dory and raised his eyebrows. "One can practically smell the musk," he said, his urgent political tone having disappeared. "Tell me," he said. "Are you a virgin?"

She didn't answer.

"Perhaps you think that wasn't a proper question," he said. "But I'm curious. Honestly, now. Are you?"

"It's not a proper question," she said, getting up.

"Just curious, that's all. I don't know too much about the mores of these latitudes, but you weren't too greatly offended by my question, were you? From my observations you and I are the most intelligent people in this nest of clowns."

"It's none of your business," she said.

"I beg to demur. It's my business to ask questions. It seems to me that you and I are natural allies. For instance, you're worried about your sister and you're worried about your friend Cynthia and you're even worried about the calf-eyed swain, Robert, Her *Altesse,* the Royal Tease, having chosen him for her summer's amusement. I happen to know more or less what's going on around here, and I suspect you'd like more information than you have. But how mature are you? How politically and socially sophisticated? How much do you know already? You can see that my naughty question does have some relevance aside from the unavoidable fact that I'd like to get into your pants. Oops! Pardon me. There I go again; my defect is candor. As a matter of fact, that idea just jumped into my head. Does its implementation interest you at all?"

"No," Dory said, and went toward the door.

"Wait!" he called with enough urgency to make her turn and look at him. He came up to her and said in a low voice, "Let me give you something as a bit of earnest. Here's something I know about 'Maestro' Zwanzig. Did you know that he's been known to sell those wash drawings he makes of 'La Gioconda' as genuine Rodins? Signs them 'A. Rodin' and sells them? How anyone could be fooled by his talentless line is a mystery, but there it is."

"Why should I want to know that?" she said.

He appeared to be startled. "Because it's information!" he said.

She shrugged and turned to go. At the doorway he caught up to her and held her by the waist. "Wait," he said. "I don't understand."

She tried to shrug out of his grasp and was astounded that he wouldn't let her. "Wait a minute," he said. "Don't be in such a damned hurry!"

She felt no fear, but his breath was sickish sweet from alcohol and she tried to pry his hands from her body, fighting the male fingers that were much too strong for her and holding her breath. Finally she took a breath and said, "Let *go* of me!"

"Calm down," he said, "I'm not . . ." In an involuntary spasm of escape her head swung back and jarred against his face. "Ow!" he said. "That hurt! That wasn't so funny!" There was an edge in his voice that gave her the first little fringe of fear. To fight against what could overpower you was to risk more than imprisonment, said that fear, and that this man was irrational enough to break laws. Maybe she was in a situation beyond law; she was not so far removed from childhood, that legal vacuum, even to be certain about what laws he might be breaking.

"You'd better let me go," she said. "There are things I have to take care of." It was demeaning to have to justify her release, and there was a taint of crying in her voice that she despised but couldn't help. She could feel, as if it were a suction, the parasitical enjoyment her body was relinquishing to him, and also the cruelty. She hadn't called for help. He must know why she hadn't—or maybe he was so stupid he thought she didn't want to get away and was playing a game of resistance for him. The vagaries of human pleasure had been revealing themselves this year, most with the logic of nightmare, and this one, for all her desperation, had in it elements of repetition.

"It's all right. Take it easy and . . ."

He didn't finish what he was going to say because Dibley appeared, reached over her and took him by the beard and the hair on the back of his head. Dibley said through closed teeth, "Break your neck!"

She was caught between them, feeling the daunting strength they both possessed. Then she ducked out under Dibley's long arms and was free.

"Christ almighty!" Jean Dorlean said, gargling the words. "All right! Get your goddam knight-errant to let go of me, all right?"

"Dibley," she said, and Dibley let him go.

"What is he, your goddam bodyguard?" Jean Dorlean complained, rubbing his hairy face. "Jesus!"

Dibley kept himself between them and looked down on the short man, flexing his long muscles, his legs trembling. He was just a boy and he must have been awed and even frightened to fight a grown man.

"You wouldn't let me go," she said to Jean Dorlean. "You can't do that. Why did you do that?"

Without answering he pushed past them and went toward the stairs. Dibley turned toward her, squinting as if in strong light. She took his arm, which turned him as immobile as wood. "Thank you for helping me, Dibley," she said.

"Urr!" he answered, meaning that he was still angry. She began to tremble, and came all over with sweat that immediately turned chilly. Just for a moment Dibley looked straight at her. There was something primitive and pure about his slate-colored hair, white skin and black eyes. He was all angular and sharp at the edges, all in black, white and gray, as if the sun hadn't touched him at all. She was grateful, and he seemed so whole and simple in what he meant and felt that she hugged him. He was as rigid as a plank but the tremors she felt in him were of a frantic ecstasy that made her quickly let him go. Distaste and guilt about her power and his freakishness and youth were all mixed up and unsortable.

As she went to her room he stayed at her side, inches closer to her than anyone ordinarily would, so close she wondered if he would leave her voluntarily. She began to feel shadowed, and stopped at her door, saying, "Did you write on my screen?" She really didn't want to hurt or embarrass him and wished she could take the words back. But she did want to know. He turned away from her so violently it looked like a military about-face.

"Well, did you?" she asked.

He spoke to the hallway. "I never spied on you."

So he had crept along the porch roof outside her window, because he "loved" her. But what was that love? What was its power? From the cruel race came this force that was not cruel, but not always kind, that could be exploited, that could change in a second to hatred or disdain.

"All right, I believe you," she said. But she didn't, because she had no way to get the truth.

"Good night, Dibley," she said.

He wouldn't look at her, but bowed, nodding, to the empty hallway as she went into her room.

22

The young doctor and the older nurse with the mother-of-pearl stockings both agreed that it was a miracle his head had never touched the pavement, that he must have tucked it in like a snail. His kneecap was a little out of place, and they spent a lot of time with Q-tips and a kind of medical soap taking grit and fiber out of his knees and elbows. "Ah, youth," the nurse said. They'd been informed by the police that according to the marks left by the motorcycle he'd rolled one hundred feet.

He was bandaged, stinging and stiffening up when Bonnie Forester arrived. The nurse was impressed by her size and glow, the silken sheen of her dark hair, her high heels, sheer stockings, a flag of chiffon at her neck mauve against rich navy, coral and silver. She was stunning, the clear expanses of her handsome jaws so wide as to seem, at first glance, almost indecent exposure. But it was more an exposure of feeling, each variant of friendliness, commiseration, clear and rightful sympathy coming and going like a flash of light. The nurse came into her influence immediately, encircled by her power. Such pure good nature, such spiritual cleanliness—even her musical, continental American voice, so ordinary and transparent, was full of unintimidating power.

"I'm Bonnie Forester and it was all my fault!" she said to the nurse. To John she said, "I've seen the police and the doctor and I'm taking you home with me!" Then she consulted the flattered nurse about the care of his wounds—dressing, antisepsis and manipulation. She seemed to treasure each technical term the nurse used, and repeated it aloud as proof of the nurse's superiority in knowledge and in nobility of occupation.

The nurse brought him a pair of crutches and taught him how to use them, first demonstrating their use with a stiff right leg, her mother-of-pearl stocking like a glimpse of lucent shell between the flat white of uniform and shoe. He'd used crutches before, but saw that he should ceremonially take the lesson the nurse wanted to give in front of Bonnie Forester.

He could move his right knee a little bit, in spite of the bandages, but there was a deep, puncturelike ache that admonished him to be very careful. The knee, that improbable, complicated joint known for its unreliability, spoke to him. The crutches adjusted and tried, he was finally declared capable of locomotion, but from all the bearing surfaces he had instinctively used to protect his head from the street came the beginnings of the reckoning. The nurse, seeing him wince, said that he might not be doing much walking, even on crutches, for several days.

Bonnie signed him out and the nurse wheeled him in the mandatory wheelchair to the parking lot, where the two women gently helped him, with a tentativeness about his discomfort that was his life's memory of women, into Bonnie's Ford. His knee had to bend, which made him think of the semi-raw joint of a cooked fowl, one of those joints with a vague, tendony correspondence to a human joint, and he was given a deep, badly focused pain that caused a flutter of nausea. He hadn't been consulted about going home with Bonnie, or about anything else, for that matter. He was evidently the ward of her best intentions, as if his wounds had deprived him of opinion along with mobility. He felt that he would heal soon, but in the meantime he would be incapable of evasion.

As they drove, in the hazy benign sunlight of late afternoon, along a curving avenue beneath palms, she straightforwardly acquired his vital statistics, one fact after another, each in an order that suggested the official organization of a dossier. All he knew of her was her name, but it was Forester and she had probably been backing straight out of the driveway of 601-B Los Robles. His own name had no special effect on her that he could see.

"How tall are you, John?" she asked. "It's hard to tell 'cause you're so crabbed up."

"Five-ten or so, normally," he said.

"Then you're just my height! I mean in bare feet, of course."

There was a statistic for him, though he rarely asked questions of fact because, he had often thought, he was not that curious, or was too self-involved to be curious. Maybe it was that the presence of another gave him too much data as it was—a thousand glinting, purring shocks to his senses that could never be put into any sort of order. From her he received all at once the cluster of specifications that meant beauty, glamour, age without her being especially old. Her eyes seemed larger, bluer, whiter than other eyes, unblemished by anything they had ever seen, and she insisted on looking into his while she spoke, which, in his tender condition, made him wish she would pay more attention to her driving.

Having asked him all sorts of statistical questions she volunteered her own, a monologue that seemed in its clarity and organization rehearsed, or composed especially for an audience whose attention might wander if fact were diluted by any complication other than good news.

"I was born in Omaha twenty-nine years ago in April and I came to California after high school because of this talent contest put on by the Delbekah Shrine and the Junior Chamber of Commerce. The winner (me!) got to be an apprentice at the Tulaveda Playhouse, which is often visited by Hollywood scouts and has a fine reputation all over the country." Her history sounded like a brochure. She had enjoyed her apprenticeship; it was great fun. No Hollywood scout had plucked her out for stardom but she'd had bit parts in several movies: *The Pearly Gates,* with Constance Bennett and Fredric March; *Saturday Morning,* with Barbara Saxton and Bert Parks; *Farewell, My Darling,* with Teresa Wright and Sonny Melton. Right now she was mostly modeling, but who knew what could happen, even if she appeared mostly in catalogues and trade journals? But of course a year ago she'd met Oval Forester (no relation, by the way, just a coincidence that they had the same name, one of those mysteries of this life) and through Oval's teaching she had found Christ Mediator and was doing further study at the Church of the Science of the Way, or CSW, and was living at the parsonage, which was 601-B Los Robles, from the driveway of which she had backed out in front of him without looking and caused all of this pain and trouble. But she *always* looked before she backed up, and there was no logical reason in the world why he wasn't killed, or made into a paraplegic or something. It had to be part of the Divine Plan. "This ministry," she said in the pleased and kindly tones of certainty, "teaches that there is an all-encompassing Power for Good, the Plus-Power, or Godhead, or Divine Intelligence, or Universal Mind (there are many, many names for it, in all religions), and if, through Christ's mediation, you tune into It, you will prosper abundantly and live a life of love and happiness!"

They had given him a shot of some kind in the emergency room and later a green-and-black capsule. Now, to his surprise, he felt the change; caution began to slide away. Her gaze, too long upon him and not the road ahead (but who cared?), was as wide and benevolent as her faith. Her perfume was of flowers, a multitude of flowers enhanced by a fascinating and valuable ferment something like a swamp, and he was saddened by his skepticism, his built-in, lifelong, dull, ungenerous skepticism. Maybe there did exist, in this garden of primary colors, this mainland Papeete or Moanalonga, this land of pampered herbiage and engines, sweetness without irony. Without, too, he dazedly considered believing, now that he felt no pain at all, the necessity for consciousness.

"You're so tired, John," she said. "Would you like to put your head in my lap? Would that hurt?"

"Nothing hurts," he said, and descended past the giant-spoked steering wheel to her thighs that seemed to hiss creamily like warm surf.

He awoke in bed, in a dim brown room in which soft varnished gleamings made no urgent claims for identification, being as they were the tops and rungs of furniture. There were memories of being helped by Bonnie and another person, a short man, up wooden steps, across a sunlit porch, down a hallway, of cool soapy moisture on his face and chest. Right now his consciousness was a small creature peering from the pilothouse of his vast, extended body. Controls were at this creature's command but caution said to be very careful with relays and levers. He moved a finger and then a hand, but the elbow was not pleased that the message had been routed through that area. One by one he found that his connecting places had been overextended by his rolling and falling, even the gristle of his ribs. Sludge had congealed in his gears and pistons, his universals and suspensions, and he was actually the prisoner, for the first time in his life, of the body he had always taken for granted. He and his Indian Pony, now somewhere nearby, were both immobilized and this hadn't been his plan. He had intended to ride on past this address, to look at this house, to have options, and now he had none.

The door opened and in came a person about four feet high and nearly that wide, who opened the blinds upon daylight and turned to him with an immense yellow smile. "Ith Thelma!" it said, and he saw with the instantaneous judgment of the normal that this short being, or person, was feebleminded, a mongoloid trapped into all of its configurations by whatever Divine Force implemented such horrors. "Ith Thelma!" It—she—said again. Her teeth were at first glance all one piece, like the dental ridge of a turtle, but then he saw that whatever she had last eaten, perhaps peanut butter, had smoothed them together.

"Ith Thelma!" she said. Her mouth was full of the humped tongue she spoke past, her lips moist and thick below her bridgeless nose, her eyes dropsical yet humanly blue under the telltale folds. Her pleasure was so intense as to seem detached from any circumstance.

"Thay thumthing, John," she said, which shocked him, because she had chided him, and her amusement was now at his expense. He said in his shame, "Hello, Thelma," and they understood each other.

"You hurt?" she asked.

"A little," he said.

She nodded and nodded upon the axis of primitive ears set into the top of her short neck. She smelled of bleach. Her blondish hair had been cut short, perhaps for reasons of hygiene.

"You hungry?"

"Not really," he said.

"Not weally?" She pondered this, her lip drooping and shiny. Over her pink, tentlike dress she wore a gray bib dampened in places. She seemed all at once shy, and took from behind her back, where she had been holding it, a piece of white cardboard and put it directly on his face.

"Thith ith for *you!*" she said.

He managed to get his hand, at the expense of pain, to the cardboard and hold it away from his face so he could see it. On it was a drawing in pencil of a motorcycle—his motorcycle. There was the horn with its Indian head, the slope of frame, the spoked wheels and the twin cylinders with their cooling fins. The accuracy was amazing, but even more impressive was a confident delicacy and variety of line. He could even tell how much the front fork had been bent by the crash.

"Did you draw this?" he asked.

She nodded, looking down and away, nodding and grinning in a shy fit of pleasure and pride. When she pulled up her bib to wipe her chin the pink dress came up with it, so that he had to see how the amorphous, hairy flesh of her thighs sagged half over her knees.

"This is very good," he said. "This is my motorcycle, all right." She shook and giggled with pleasure, spraying him a little, and he thought only of getting out of here, that he couldn't take this, that he was too sensitive, that he couldn't deal with this much longer because, disarmed by sympathy, he would in some monstrous and unthinkable way become her.

His leg jerked, an involuntary twitch of escape that dealt him purifying pain. When he opened his eyes Bonnie Forester had appeared, tall and shimmery in a white nightgown. "Thelma," she said mildly, "I thought I heard you giggling in here, you naughty girl! You went and woke John up and it's only six o'clock in the morning!"

"Thix o'cock!" Thelma said happily.

"And she showed you her picture of your motorcycle? Isn't she clever? A God-given talent!" Bonnie said as if he were the normal sort of person who could cope with enthusiastic mongoloids.

"Yes, she sure is," he said.

"Does aspirin upset your tummy? The nurse said to give you aspirin."

"Not that I know of," he said, so she tipped aspirin from her warm palm into his mouth and produced a Dixie cup half full of water.

"Do you have to go to the bathroom?"

"Not urgently."

"Go to the baffoom!" Thelma said.

"That's right, dear." Bonnie sat carefully on the bed, in order not to jar him, and in the most abstracted and impersonal way began lightly to massage his shoulders, neck and chest. Her hands were on his skin and over him was the glamorous loom of her, her classic breasts visible to his ill-at-ease X-ray eyes. At her bosom was a decorative, non-functional little tielet of blue ribbon. "Does that feel good?" she asked. "Pretty soon the aspirin ought to start working and then we'll try to get you up. How do you feel?"

How did he feel? "Pretty good," he said. How did he feel? Anxious, immobilized, and yet invested by involuntary and inappropriate lust.

"How you feel, John?" Thelma asked around her swollen tongue.

"Okay," he said, his voice surprisingly calm. Add a demeaning dread of the harmless, the abomination. Meanwhile Bonnie's gentle hands soothed and scorched him, and next to her power was Thelma, flesh gone wrong, bladders beneath the pink dress big as oddly hung basketballs above the spread nominally of a woman but here blown up into a cosmic smirk at the expense of everything human and female. She must have, along with her obvious good nature, ovaries and tubes and womb and all the rest of a mammal's business, here skewed and parodied—what the rest of the race passed with averted eyes. They died, mostly, he had heard, in the gruesome joke of their own adolescence.

But he lay helpless within his temporarily wounded but perfect body with an erection mind and good taste and will disowned, to no avail, when there came a muffled, nudging knock on the doorframe, and a short man in a brown suit stood there burdened with a golf bag full of hooded and tasseled clubs and what, from its weighty pull on his arm, seemed to be a cased bowling ball. The skin of the man's face was smoothly pink, as if he had pressed his head into a thin diaphragm of flesh-colored rubber, with eye holes, nostril holes and a mouth slot. He seemed shy, but the set of the slit of his mouth indicated determination.

"Oh, Urban!" Bonnie said. "Don't tell me you've figured it out again!"

"Yes, I'm afraid so," the man said. "I want to give Oval these, and the deeds to my church, and my car keys and green slip."

John saw then that there were raised striations under his chin and ears and that he wore a mask of healed tissue. His face had once burned.

"All right," Bonnie said. "But when is it going to happen?"

"Tomorrow morning at five o'clock, Pacific Standard Time."

"Are you sure, now? Remember last time."

"Oh, yes," he said, his syllables growing rounder through the slot of his mouth. "That was a miscalculation, pure and simple. This time is the Time and the hydrogen and the oxygen will catalyze. The oceans will rise and burn, according to Ecclesiasticus in the Apocrypha, Daniel 12:7 and 12:11 and the Second Law of Thermodynamics. I'm certain this time!"

Bonnie said, "Well, you can put everything in Oval's office. Put them over by the window, all right?"

"All right. Thank you, Bonnie."

"Hewwo, Ooban!" Thelma said.

"Hello, Thelma, dear."

To John, Bonnie said, "Urban helped me get you to bed yesterday."

"Oh. Thank you," John said.

"John," Bonnie said formally, "this is Urban Stumms, pastor of the Church Ovarian Apocalyptic, over on Alta Vista. Urban, this is John Hearne, from New Hampshire."

"Howdy!" Urban said, then added, "Well, there's so much to do . . ."

"You go right along, then, Urban. And good luck, now!"

"Geggod bleggess yeggou," Urban said. *"Heggis weggord beggurned leggike egga leggamp*—Ecclesiasticus 48:1." Urban went on down the hall.

"What did he say?" John said.

"Oh, they speak that language—Ovarian," Bonnie said. "I mean when they quote scripture or mention the name of the Lord."

"Oh," John said.

"Poor Urban! The last time he predicted the end of the world he lost more than half his congregation, you know. I hate to think what will happen to him if he's wrong again."

"Yeah," John said. Pondering the Apocalypse evidently had a neutralizing effect, along with the aspirin, so that when Bonnie helped him out of bed, he in his olive-drab GI shorts, he was not unduly embarrassed by himself. She and Urban Stumms had retrieved his duffelbag from the bent motorcycle, which was now leaning against a tangerine tree in the yard, and she carried his musette bag containing razor, toothbrush and such, while helping him toward the bathroom. He could use one crutch as a cane of sorts, but progress was slow. Thelma wanted to help, but her stubbed, thick fingers pulled with unsynchronized force, and her huge thigh pushed the crutch out from under him twice before Bonnie made her stop. He wondered, shame overcoming revulsion, how much he had contributed to that awkwardness. Thelma was genuinely unhappy, and seemed about to cry, so Bonnie had to hug her and take her to her room. He leaned on crutch and wall until Bonnie came back. Thelma, she told him, that poor child of God, was seventeen years old and Oval Forester's daughter.

The parsonage was all in browns, full of dim furniture with an old but unused look, like the furniture of churches. The toilet reservoir was an oak box up near the stamped-metal ceiling, with a long chain and a wooden pull, and the lavatory and tub were leggy and coarse-grained—the institutional facilities of 1920, Bonnie told him, when church and parsonage had been built heavily and well by Lutherans. The church itself was of gray stone, and faced the next street, Villa Mesa. It was a small church, with a small congregation, and Oval Forester had to work at another job to support it.

When he was propped against the lavatory, his musette bag at hand, he assured her that he could carry on by himself, though he was not quite certain he could. The anesthetic power of modesty.

"All right," Bonnie said doubtfully. "I'm going to go get dressed, now, but if you need any help, John, you just holler."

Whether out of desperation, his desire for independence and solitude, or from youthful resiliency, when he'd finished washing up and had managed to shuffle carefully back to his room, the news from his synapses was cautious but optimistic. He got back into bed by himself, chirping only once from pain that came as a surprise rather than a calculated risk, but then couldn't reach down for the sheet. While he tested his articulations, unfamiliar small birds outside the open window swooped and sang. After a while Bonnie, carefully dressed and made up, with a frilly apron over an expensive-looking silk suit, came in with breakfast on a tray.

"Can you sit up? Can you eat by yourself?" Expressive modulations of sympathy rose and subsided in her voice. "Are you mad at me for backing out in front of you? Do you feel angry, John? I wouldn't blame you!"

"It was an accident," he said. It hadn't occurred to him to be angry. As he chewed his toast he wondered how he had managed to strain even his jaw muscles.

"But I wrecked your motorcycle, too! Phil's coming to look at it to see if it can be fixed—Phil's in the Church and he's a mechanic. But here you are, you can hardly move, and it's all my fault! You must have some anger, and I don't blame you."

What a strange way to put it—that you "had" anger when angry. Bonnie looked at him earnestly and he glanced at her for a second and was almost blinded, or at least caused to look away, flinching at her perfection. Every standard of beauty he had been brought up to admire she possessed in such measure his first reaction had been to consider her a sort of freakish ideal, not to be touched. But she insisted upon touching him, and even if she didn't consider her touch a caress, in his life he had rarely touched another out of mere affection. She sat on the bed, one hand steadying the tray and the other lightly on his hip, and he remembered with anxious nostalgia the infatuations of childhood, and began to greet as he took them the delicious little steps toward that sweet insanity.

She was eight years older than he and of other worlds. Her beliefs were perhaps ludicrous but her presence was beyond anything he had ever considered attainable. He thought suddenly of a boat, a Chris-Craft, comparing her to an expensive and beautiful boat. There were those who owned Chris-Crafts of dark mahogany and chrome and powerful rumbling engines, but he had never planned to desire one. They were to be admired, but without yearning. He didn't want to cope with the desire for something so rich and dramatic, and so never had.

Maybe it was Dory Perkins, back in New Hampshire, whose name meant a kind of boat, who suggested this comparison. Dory seemed pale and dim, her smaller symmetries now remembered cerebrally, in grays, with only a faint shadow of disloyalty.

"Finish you owange joosh!" It was Thelma, standing at the door, pretending to look stern. She held a piece of white cardboard across her short forearm, and looked down to it, drooling lightly as she manipulated her pencil. "Ith drawing you, John!"

"Thelma," Bonnie said, "I don't want you bothering John today. He's got to rest."

"Dawing pichure!" Thelma cried, hurt by this injustice. She came closer and drew faster, giving him quick, desperate looks, through tears, and the injustice of her condition, which she probably knew about, gathered in him as a horror of all female unhappiness. She—*it,* his revulsion said—was seventeen, Dory's age, and whatever was fearsome in women was in Thelma exaggerated beyond his tolerance. At first he wouldn't consider admitting his cowardice, but Bonnie watched him, and a shamed nod admitted that he couldn't stand it.

"You can show John your picture tonight, when I get back," Bonnie said, gathering up the tray. With a firm arm around Thelma she moved her toward the door. Thelma was still drawing and trying to see him, the liquid snot of unhappiness like shellac over her mouth. "We love you, Thelma. Jesus loves you. Oval loves you. We all do," Bonnie said. "And, John? I've sent out a call to our Healing Echelons, and today they will aim their prayers at you."

Alone again, he arranged his legs and trunk in order to get out of bed, which he just managed to do, and moved on sludgy joints to the window, where freedom was, where the small birds swooped and clamored in the vines. Just below him a tricolored cat had caught a brown lizard, which thrashed in its stiff, limited way until its tail came off, right off without any blood at all, and while the tail kept on wiggling all by itself the lizard escaped—he saw it work, that trick. The cat with fierce interest watched the tail, and hooked it fussily, fascinatedly, its fooled eyes gleaming.

Freedom from what? he thought. From imbecility, from the sweet delusions of this simpleminded church and from the chance of finding out why your father's last known forwarding address was 601-B Los Robles, Tulaveda, California.

But his joints were not ready for freedom yet, so he carefully returned to bed, whereupon Urban Stumms knocked on his door and came in.

"You think I'm a nut, don't you," he said, his face of pink scar tissue exoskeletal, teeth and eyeballs moving behind it. "Bonnie told me you're a veteran, so okay, buster, let me tell you something. Let me tell you something, dogface. Let me tell you something. You think I'm some kind of pansy fruitcake pastor going around praying and asking the people to be sweet to each other, huh? Is that what you think? But he's got a screw loose somewhere because he thinks the world's going to burn? Is that it? Huh? Is that it? So what did you ever see? You look too young anyway. You ain't been kissed yet, I can tell. You ain't got the look, buddy boy!"

So Urban was also this fellow, then, when not the theologian speaking "Ovarian." He was a GI, a vet, buster. One of the wisecrackin' normal guys. Take no shit. Tough titty. John felt no danger in Urban, but he could be wrong.

Urban said, "All right, all right. I'm here to tell you when I saw Heggim. It's getting late for us. Late, late! I've already seen the burning—that's not the question. The question is, will it come in time? Heggow leggong, eggo Leggord?

"So you think I'm crazy. Listen to me, then, and ask what a man is made for. Here's what I was doing. I'll just give it to you straight, statistics and all. It's March 9, 1945—around twenty-four hundred hours, a few minutes after midnight, so it's March 10, and I—me—this ordinary young shmoe—where am I? I'm at an altitude of around six thousand feet, airspeed around two hundred and ninety, and I'm over the second-biggest city on earth. And for what purpose? Doesn't it seem strange to you that I'm there for the purpose of killing the people of that city? How should a man be used? What's he for? Who in hell put me in that airplane with six other guys and nearly twenty thousand pounds of bombs? Our eggs. We're laying our eggs at low level, incendiaries with maybe a few HE mixed in to stir up the omelette. We're frying gooks, man, we're making a firestorm. The plane's humping all over the place in the turbulence from the fire. It's getting to be one solid fire. There's three hundred B-29s over the city and more coming, and we're all there for the same purpose. Man-given purpose. We're going to kill ninety-seven thousand people that night, and wound a hundred-twenty-five thousand more, and burn out the homes of a million, two hundred thousand. We found all that out later, but we knew what we were doing. Then we're going to turn around and fly more than a thousand miles back to Guam, if the Franks and Tonys, Jacks and Oscars don't get us. I'm scared shitless. We're all scared shitless, but not of Geggod's wrath like we ought to be. We're scared of flak and twenty-millimeter cannon shells, which have already holed us in about six places. Before he got it the tail gunner said it was Jacks after us, Mitsubishis, but what I saw was a Tony, a Kawasaki Ki-61, with the radiator fairing under the cockpit. All the others had radial engines—that's how you could tell 'em apart. I was at the port central aiming blister and all we had was one ventral turret, because the other turrets, guns and ammo had been taken out so we could carry more incendiaries, a new type—magnesium and jellied gasoline. The turbulence was so bad I thought the wings were going to come off, they were flapping up and down. The radio operator lost his helmet and got coldcocked on a frame member; he didn't find all his marbles till we were halfway back to Harmon Field on Guam.

"We didn't have Iwo then, so it was fly all the way home or swim—you wouldn't want to bail out, now, would you, over Nippon? It was bright as day, all this time. Tokyo was like the sun, like we were flying over the sun, the light coming up from below. But it was all nasty, is what I mean. We were just burning houses, that's the reason—just people and where they live, so if we got caught what the hell could we say? That was the whole purpose of the mission and we all agreed, so if a Tony shot us down or rammed us? Who cares about the Rape of Nanking or the Death March or Pearl Harbor—those poor bastards are burning down there, little kids and mama-sans and old ladies, everybody, in the firestorm. The ones that don't burn first suffocate first, and the other way around. Who are we and who in hell's domination is General Curtis E. LeMay to make that judgment? *We have made a covenant with death, and with hell we are at agreement.* Isaiah 28:15. *Woe unto them that call evil good, and good evil. Weggo eggunteggo theggem theggat ceggall eggiveggil geggood.* Isaiah 5:20.

"Then we're past the turbulence and there's a Tony flying along with us, just under the port outboard engine. I don't know how I can see him so plain. There's his rising sun on a white square. He's got a red spinner and a red tail with white lightning painted on it, and he's just cruising alongside. I figure he's going to ram and I'm in a panic trying to get the twin fifties on him, and then I do and I'm just creaming that guy, I can see the tracers going right through him, into his engine, knocking off hunks of his exhaust ports, and glycol and pieces of him flying back in his slipstream. I'm murdering the guy, I don't know what's keeping him there. My slugs are killing him, I can almost see the solids between the tracers, like it's all in slow motion, and I'm in a panic to get him out of there before he can ram us, but I can't seem to finish him off. I just want to plaster him, wipe him out, and there's the fear and also a kind of exultation in the terrible damage I'm doing.

"Then he slid back his canopy and looked at me, and I looked into his eyes, we were that close, and there was a radiance about his head, and nothing between us but understanding. Then came the white fire and the heat and I saw nothing more of this world for three nights and three days until they dared to open my eyes, with surgery, on Guam. But he had spoken to me and I knew that he was Jeggeseggus Chreggist, that he had appeared over all that agony, over the fiery furnace, in the turbulence of burning human grease, in the stench of lost human souls, to tell me something, and what he told me was that the sons of man had gone too far. *They crucify the Son of God afresh, and put Him to an open shame. Theggey cregguceggifeggeye thegge Seggon eggof Geggod egg-afreggesh, eggand peggut Heggim teggo eggan eggopeggen sheggame.* Paul to the Hebrews 6:6.

"They had exceeded on that very night Geggod's allotment of agony, registered in Cruces: the allotment of pain and agony caused by man since Creation had that very night been used up, and it was that very night, March 10, 1945, that man was given the final knowledge, for it wasn't four months later that he exploded the first atomic bomb, at Alamogordo, New Mexico, and the second less than a month later, over Hiroshima, and the third three days later, over Nagasaki. We killed more people on March 10 than either of those, but the knowledge they contained was that here was the primer for the real egg, the final egg, the awful knowledge of how to blow up the whole world. When has man ever not done what he could do? And tomorrow morning at five hundred hours, our time, at an island in the South Pacific, man in his Satanic Pride will detonate a bomb a thousand-thousandfold more powerful that will cause the waters of the earth to burn, the oxygen and the hydrogen to catalyze. *He maketh the deep to boil like a pot. Hegge meggakeggeth thegge deggeep teggo beggoil leggike egga peggot.* Job 41:31.

"In the Book of Daniel it is written: *How long shall it be to the end of these wonders?* And the question is answered: *It shall be for a time, times and an half.* A year, two years, and half of a year: three and a half years. The time is now. This is the Ova of Armageddon! And the Church Ovarian Apocalyptic teaches that for every Crucis of agony caused by man since March 10, 1945, will each and every man at the Great and Dreadful Day of the Leggord suffer seventy and seven megatimes, and so do we beseech Theggee, eggo Leggord, Let the day come soon, let us abide Theggy punishment as we deserve! Let it come soon!"

Urban's stiff mask, dark with passion, tilted toward his chest, and he stood silently as red splashes and deltas drained and faded from it until it was again all pink. Then, having said the last word, he turned abruptly and left.

John Hearne, while pondering this message and all of its implications, found himself in a state something like suspended animation only partly caused by little warnings, little *cruces* issuing from his connectors here and there. To him religion of any kind could be, he thought, rather precisely defined by the term "culture lag," although he supposed the word "lag," indicating that culture was somehow improving, could be called a religious impulse, an optimistic one not too well supported by hard evidence. Okay, he thought, play around with glib phrases in order to make yourself imperviously superior to the tortured man who had just left, a man wounded by fire and by an immensity of guilt it's true you yourself ain't yet been kissed by, buddy boy.

Ovarian Apocalyptic: Jeggeseggus Chreggist. And right now he lay in broad daylight in a bedroom of the parsonage of the Church of the Science of the Way, which at least didn't sound very apocalyptic. But was the Atomic Energy Commission going to explode some god-awful bomb tomorrow? In any case, something was wrong with Urban's calculations: March 1945 to June 1948 was three years and three months, not three years and a half. Maybe the world had until September but Urban couldn't wait, or couldn't count, or had made some arcane corrective calculation based upon Daniel's calendar, and the goddam world was going to go in a chain reaction. Water was H_2O, wasn't it? And hydrogen bloody well burned, as the *Hindenburg* found out at Lakehurst, and oxygen was what was needed for combustion. Oh, cut out all this shit. All he had to do was wait about seventeen hours and find out. Meanwhile he would heal, he would concentrate on that, and get his legs under him that had once let him run like a deer from such and other complications.

His next visitor appeared at noon, asked him if he wanted some lunch and introduced himself as Hadasha Kemal Allgood, visiting the Church of the Science of the Way as biblical scholar and lecturer. He was a thin, stooped man in his forties whose skin had an almost cyanotic blue glow and whose Adam's apple was so large it looked painful. "Bonnie asked me to look in on you," he said. Though his voice seemed normal midwestern American he looked as though he had tried to swallow something as uncompromising as a broken goblet. Between the bow of his glasses and his head were two yellow pencils, and fountain pens and other pencils stuck out of his vest. On his shirt sleeves he wore black arm garters that suggested a nineteenth-century stationmaster.

"A sandwich? Can I get you something? I'm not terribly practical about such things, my being more at home, so to speak, with Greek and Aramaic. Do you want a cigarette?"

John accepted a thin cigarette with gold lettering on it that said "Houri," and Hadasha Kemal Allgood produced from a vest pocket a small silver ashtray, which he put on the bed.

"You haven't met our pastor," he said, pulling up a chair and seeming to have forgotten about lunch. He lit their cigarettes and the funky odor of Turkish tobacco preceded even its visible smoke throughout the room.

"No, not yet," John said with a shiver of apprehension.

"Oval Forester is a saint," Hadasha Kemal Allgood said. "A teacher.

You will be aware of his power immediately. He has subsidized my work, given me time for my scholarship when the Huntington Foundation, in their ignorance, turned me away. So far I've found and corrected one thousand eight hundred and ninety-eight major errors in the New Testament alone. Of course, I do have the advantage of possessing seven ancient scrolls given to me by my grandfather and unknown to the general scholarship. Some of the errors are quite obvious: Matthew 19:24, for instance. The Aramaic word for 'camel' is the same as their word for 'rope,' and doesn't it seem more logical, more analogous, to say that it is easier for a *rope* (rather than a camel) to pass through the eye of a needle than for a rich man to enter into the Kingdom of God? A *thread* will pass, but a rope will not!"

"It does sound logical," John said, and then added, because Hadasha Kemal Allgood seemed fairly sane, "What do you think of 'a time, times and an half' in the Book of Daniel?"

"Oh, yes. Urban Stumms. All I can say is that the Bible is a power. I might once have scoffed at the Apocalyptics' penchant for such calculations, but no more. They perceive an ending, and it's hard not to perceive an ending. Oval Forester has taught us *never* to scoff at passion. But as for the meaning of 'a time' in Daniel, it could mean a decade—the way we refer to, say, the twenties and the thirties as separate 'times.' And, in that case, counting from the hour of Urban's extraordinary and powerful vision over Tokyo, we've got till 1984. No, I do *not* scoff at Urban, nor at his strange tongue. I, too, have felt the sting of the supercilious: the Huntington Foundation, the Gideons, the sanctimony of the elders of my former church, and more, more. But they will see. When each and every Holy Book in each and every church, in each and every seminary, in each and every domicile, in each and every court of law—yea, in each and every top dresser drawer in each and every hotel room—is shown to be rife with error and only the Allgood translation proved, Book by Book, chapter by chapter, verse by verse, line by line, word by word, syllable by syllable, letter by letter, to be the true Word of God—*then* see if they scoff!"

Hadasha Kemal Allgood trembled for a moment and then grew vague, his eyes shifty and preoccupied. "My work," he muttered. "My work. My work, you know. Well, goodbye." He took with him his little silver ashtray and their cigarette butts.

Oh, well, John thought, he could do without a sandwich.

He would rest easy and heal. He wondered if the prayers aimed at him by the Healing Echelons were hitting their mark, or if his cynicism acted as a shield. Okay, Healing Echelon aimers, three clicks to the right. There, fire for effect.

He went to sleep; that is, he'd been asleep, just for a moment, maybe, knowing it in the sensual fuzz of dozing and waking. Bonnie Forester might enter his room, in her sheer nightgown, her hair like midnight, and her name would be biblical, her belly like a heap of wheat set about with lilies, her two breasts like two young roes, that are twins, which feed among the lilies, and she would say to him, "Make haste, my beloved, and be thou like to a young hart upon the mountains of spices." For the lips of a strange woman drop as a honeycomb, and her mouth is smoother than oil, and he lusteth after her beauty in his heart, and let her take him with her eyelids.

A piece of cardboard banged down on his nose, and it was Thelma, her gray bib all wet now, moist heat radiating from the gross injustice of her body. "Thith ith for *you,* John!" she said against the will of her tongue.

At first glance the picture was of two smiling persons. Below it she had printed a word in block letters with falling and tilted lines. Strange that her drawing from life should be so precise and the symbols which made up a word so inexact. The word was recognizable as LOVE.

The two persons were Thelma and himself, both vivid, bright, smiling and holding hands as if they posed on a happy occasion for whatever loved friend or relative was about to snap the picture. But of course all except the authority of likeness and of line had changed, and he thought of the earliest pictures the Japanese had painted of Occidentals, where it seemed as if they didn't quite know how to draw such round and characterless eyes, so that while other, more obvious characteristics, such as clothing, were plainly foreign, the eyes always hinted at the Mongolian fold, as his did here. Thelma had no doubt drawn her own likeness in front of a mirror, because it was her, though slimmer and taller, more like him, as if they were kin, brother and sister. But it was still her, and he wondered how, out of the dulled neurons, the fudged genes, the errors of creation, the skewed glands, the signals unreceived or badly sent, came this one undamaged talent, a sort of genius peering out of the doomed vessel.

But in the picture there they were, John and Thelma, smiling happily from the Peaceful Kingdom.

He looked into her creation rather than at the soul who breathed and exuded heat into what had become a hot day, tongues of heat wafting from the open window, and her smell of bleach, or ammonia, along with flowers.

Thelma took the drawing from his hand, propped it on the varnished bureau next to her other present to him, and in the silence, smiling thickly and secretively, because she had been naughty to disobey Bonnie's orders, said, "G'bye, John," and went away, leaving the door open.

He willed healing fluids to his slow joints. Thelma's condition was of course an accident of the chromosomes, a shake of the dice never to be recalled, and was not, at least for people other than John Hearne, catching. He could, he thought, catch anything, a symptom being a compulsion to imitate her congested voice, the swollen, imbecilic droop of her eyes and mouth. He couldn't help an empathic horror of becoming, but it was not physical; his body had never really let him down. Even now he could feel his gristle healing. Any other body, he believed, would have let its bones break and its head smash in that trajectory along Los Robles. The entrance to his life was sympathetic, and his pain was for the trapped, the cheated, the helpless—every kind that by his gifts and luck he wasn't meant to be.

He didn't know what day it was, however, and he didn't know why accident had put him into a position where he would appear to be looking for his father, or what he wanted his father to be.

> "Father," I said, remembering again how we had sailed together, "is Baron Gersdorff my father? Do you know the man?"
>
> "Leave the women's business alone," he said. "Here you are, Jonathan, a seaworthy ship, whoever built you."

But was he? And who had he, in his youth, ever sailed with? The sailor's metaphor was the vessel in which he sailed, which he was, now beached on an exotic coast among the bingo-bongo trees, the natives, as far as the spare voyager from New England could perceive, not unfriendly, though he found their rituals strange. Strange but familiar, as if he had once in a previous incarnation accepted certain premises.

His father had taken him to church in Winota. What church it was he probably never knew, but he remembered being impressed by the ceiling and the singing, and somewhere he had learned a version of the Lord's Prayer: *Our Father who aren't in heaven, hollowed be Thy name,* and this version seemed to conform to something his father must have told him—that God the Father is here, everywhere, not in some faraway place called heaven. No, He aren't in heaven, and His name is hollow; God is hollow because we are inside Him and He is all around us. The biblical exegete at four or five years old.

Now the beached ship, or sailor, rerove his rigging and remembered a green canoe sailing swiftly over a cold blue lake, a canoe that wouldn't have existed except for him and yet was not his, and at its helm was a slight, winter-pale girl whose claims upon him, even at this continental distance, could be felt. They were like fine webs that might easily be broken, quietly broken and forgotten.

23

The summer grew into its green and heat, the heavy kind that forbade much physical effort, but all major projects had been completed. Debbie had subsided into a sullen but steady worker. She didn't want to go back to Leah and have to look for another summer job, so she just stayed on. Werner spent most of his time sailing, alone. He told Dory, when their anger at each other had cooled, how the *Bremen* had steamed first to Murmansk, in Russia, and then slipped through the British blockade and arrived safely in Germany on December 13, 1939, its captain, Commodore Ahrens, a hero. That year his family lived in a beautiful house in the Grunewald, and he sailed his own small catboat on the Wannsee. He could sound pleased and straightforward, as if in one of his moods, or poses, he were still eleven or twelve. But then would come the self-satisfied arrogance. "So you see why I'm so good at handling a sailboat."

Dory's window faced toward the southwest, so the still, heavy dawn came over the house behind her and lighted the far shore of the lake and the tops of the pines on Pine Island. She had an hour before the Big Ben alarm clock would clatter, so she left the window and went back to her bed. In the window screen were the tiny words I LOVƎ YOU. So she was loved, the E backwards. When Dibley could, he came near her, without volunteering to speak, as if proximity were enough for him. It no longer made her feel so uncomfortable.

Cynthia was bright and happy, talking all the time. She and Yvonne sometimes held hands, and Dory thought how Cynthia had never considered Leah, New Hampshire, to be the real world. Like John Hearne, she had been brought here as a child, against her will. She'd never thought to stay and had never cared very much about Leah's judgments. She was headed for the city, for "culture," where all foibles were forgiven. It had been Robert who wondered if Cynthia and Yvonne's relationship was "unnatural," and that had made Dory think of it that way, too, a vision of female bodies in a naked embrace, hands and lips who knew where. Again came that sweet wrongness, like a sense of loss.

She thought of love, and sex, and touched herself; it was and had always been him. He was still two persons, the John Hearne she had imagined all her life and the real John Hearne who melted her and pulled her inside out. She loved them both. But why should he come back just because she yearned to have him back? She lay naked and alone in the sultry morning air, smooth as if she glistened with oil, languorous, having him here now, his smooth weight, the surge of his concentration upon her. She did bend him and move him, just so, now. There was the turning in her, but soon it was just her own hands and imagination. He was not there. With this, her small room was suddenly a strange place, suggesting anxieties and responsibilities.

Robert was the one who had changed the most. He had always been honest, phlegmatic and dependable, but he'd grown nervous and odd. He'd lost weight. He always seemed to be thinking about something other than what he was doing, so that he became awkward and had accidents. He broke one of the iron wheels of the reel lawn mower by running it straight into a boulder. He cut his finger with the sickle and bumped his head on a low tamarack limb. He wiped one dish too long, until Debbie took it from his hands and suggested he try a wet one. He thought it wrong to do what he wanted to do with the Princess, but she acted as if everything was "just plain nice," he said. She would touch him and then be sort of sweetly indifferent to him. He couldn't talk to Dibley about it, so he tried to talk to Dory about it but was embarrassed. "I'm afraid I'm going to do something terrible," he said. "Sometimes I think I don't like her anymore. She acts like the feelings I have had never been invented." But the Princess remained affable and normal, in her own fashion, to everyone. Dory had no idea what the other guests thought was going on, except for Jean Dorlean, who gave her knowing, smirky looks, as if they were allies after all. Dibley had been worried that he might be fired for having grabbed Jean Dorlean's beard, but of course nothing came of that.

John Hearne was going to finish college and go somewhere, everywhere through his life without her. There was no reason, ever, to be unrealistic. The world was the world and she was alone in it except for those she had to look out for. That was the clutter you possessed in this life—the addled and the helpless, the enthralled and the blind. She couldn't think of a way to interfere with what the Princess was doing. She couldn't say anything to the Princess, and what could she say to Robert?

Harry Morrow, the senior in whose car Debbie had drunk beer after the prom, showed up one Saturday night, with two of his friends, wanting to take Debbie out, or for a ride. Debbie said no and they drove away. "See?" she'd said to Dory. "You know what they want. That never happened to you, did it? Where'd they get the idea I was the town pump? Maybe I let him feel a little after the prom, but that's all. What did I ever *do?*"

She could think of no way to suggest to Debbie that her raucous laughter, her sarcasm, her smoking, her slang, like "town pump," her arrogant sway of the hips—all those flamboyant gestures of hers added up to what the Harry Morrows thought. It would be like telling Debbie to change her life, and there was no way to change a life.

"What did I ever *do?*" Debbie said. "I can't help how I look, how I got big boobs. Sometimes I want to be dead."

"Oh, Debbie."

"It's always like that, isn't it? 'Oh, Debbie,'" Debbie said.

"I'd like you to be happy," Dory said, but that was so easy to say and she felt helpless. She felt helpless because she couldn't make herself have the energy to enter into Debbie's life, and she was close to tears.

"Dory, I don't hate you," Debbie said. "I know you've got your troubles, too, and I'm sorry if I called you names before. I'm just like that. I'm an asshole." Then, embarrassed, Debbie had turned and left her.

John Hearne might be with a girl right now. He would think only of that pretty girl, there, wherever he was, in sunny California, on a golden beach with a golden girl. He'd be tanned all over too, his hair bleached nearly white, and their golden skin would shed little grains of sand, one jewel at a time, and he would touch her gently, falling in love with the most beautiful girl in sunny California, in the warm sunlight. He would transfer to UCLA, where she went to school.

She had expected at least a postcard from him, but none ever came.

She went down to the kitchen to get the coffee going; that was what she could do. It was degrading to be jealous. The coffee was perking when Robert, looking peaked, came in and sat on a stool. "God, it's hot," he said. "A weather-breeder. I think I've aged ten years this summer already. By the end of August I'll be as old as she is."

"You've changed," Dory said. "We've all changed, though."

"I swear," he said, "I think I'm beginning to understand the Swede."

But Robert didn't throw the Princess on the stove, or end his life "by his own hand." That afternoon Dory came up from the boathouse and sensed a general consternation as soon as she entered the living room, where all the guests except Werner and Mrs. Patrick sat looking at each other.

"This affects much planning," Ernst Zwanzig said without his usual punctuating laugh. "Who can talk her back to sense?"

Then Mrs. Patrick came in and gave a report on the Princess, who was in her room having hysterics, saying in coherent moments that she was going to close Cascom Manor and return to New York.

"What happened?" Sean Patrick said. "She's not the flighty sort."

"It was the boy, Robert," Mrs. Patrick said. They all looked at Dory, who turned and went up to the Princess's room, knocked on the door and went in without waiting for an answer. This was the largest bedroom, with three windows, wardrobes and an antique canopied bed, upon which the Princess lay on her side under a crumpled sheet, her black hair a disorganized tangle. Lipstick was smudged over her mouth and chin. She moaned and turned, kicking the sheet to rearrange it, billowing it out to reveal a flash of her black pubic hair. Her silk slip was bunched up under her arms and she was fever-wet, gleaming as if varnished.

"Oh, oh," she moaned.

"What's the matter?" Dory asked with a tentative amount of sympathy.

The Princess looked at her, wanting something Dory couldn't yet identify. It was a defined, not hysterical, look. But she moaned again, "Oh, oh." She sobbed, those breathless, hiccupy noises that were strange unless you uttered them yourself.

"What happened?" Dory asked, with the feeling that in her own impatience and even exasperation she was breaking protocol, as she probably had by coming into the room without permission. "Was it Robert? What did he do?"

"Yes, yes! He forced himself upon me! He overpowered me and violated my body!" Then she shuddered and sobbed, tears running from the outsides of her blue-white eyes that even now looked at Dory with an intelligence independent of outrage; she was examining Dory for judgment.

There was a light knock on the door. Dory went to it and it was Robert. Dibley waited a few feet down the hall. She let Robert in and the Princess whimpered with an edge of possibly real fear.

"I'm sorry," Robert said. He was beyond worrying about whether Dory or anyone knew what had happened. There was a smear of incriminating lipstick on his mouth. "We were straightening the picture," he said, glancing at a gilt-framed landscape with cows that hung between the windows.

"You were what?" Dory said.

"We were straightening it for half an hour," Robert said. "She stood on the chair and I had to hold her and then we'd go sit on the bed and see if it was straight, but it was never quite straight, and then I lost my mind. I'm sorry."

"And you . . . did it to her?" She was afraid she would have to ask incriminating questions all her life, like her mother, but somewhere deeper than worry was a painful pressure of laughter, like air caught in the throat, or below the throat.

"I went crazy," Robert said. "I don't know. I just lost control of myself."

The Princess cried, "I couldn't stop him! I struggled with all my might! He hurt me!"

"Listen," Robert said, blushing. "I kind of thought she wanted me to. I didn't know it would hurt. I thought because she didn't have anything on underneath she wanted me to. I saw it, you know, and . . ."

"I might become pregnant! He is a beast! I thought he was a kind and gentle boy, not brutal, not an animal!"

"I never did it before," Robert said. "Honest to God, Dory, I didn't even know where it *was.* I thought it was more on the front. I thought she wanted me to and I thought her being old and all she'd be prepared or something."

"He opened his trousers!" the Princess cried.

"Anyway," Robert said, "it only lasted about three seconds."

"He penetrated my body!"

Dory said to the Princess, "He's only seventeen, and you had him in here, alone, and you had nothing on but your slip . . ."

"I am the victim, and now I am being accused!" the Princess cried with trembling eyelids, tears and whimpers. She seemed as consistent in this mood as she had been in her old one of imperturbability.

"I'm awful sorry," Robert said. "I'm disgusted with myself."

Suddenly Dory wanted to hear no more of it. She was only seventeen herself, and she had to try to make sense of these giant children. "Oh, be quiet now," she said. A horrid bubble of mirth was caught in her throat like waterbrash, and she hated that mirth and where it came from; this was not how it was supposed to be. Wasn't all laughter, like this within her, born of violence and misfortune?

At the door appeared a delegation from downstairs—Mrs. Zwanzig, Mrs. Patrick and Jean Dorlean. The two women went to the Princess, one on each side of her bed, and began to care for her. Mrs. Zwanzig arranged her pillows so she could sit up, and Mrs. Patrick took a silver comb and began to straighten out her hair. With Kleenex and cream, Mrs. Zwanzig then began to cleanse her face of makeup. The Princess accepted these services without comment and looked apprehensively at Jean Dorlean, who stood at the foot of her bed.

"There is, Princess," he said, "a certain ambivalence among your guests as to the assignment of culpability in this unfortunate affair, and also a strong desire not to have their plans disrupted. They have chosen me, if Your Highness has no objection, to act as a sort of mediator, or referee." He, too, contained his sardonic humor.

"Again I am being accused! Oh! Oh!"

"Hush, now," Mrs. Patrick said. "Hush, now, dear."

Jean Dorlean looked at Dory, raised his eyebrows and tilted his hairy face as if to say that his expectations had been confirmed.

From the Princess and the two women who sat tending her came a pulse of feminine heat, cosmetic and musky. The Princess was subdued now, and wary. Her pale face, cleansed of red, seemed succulently fragile, like cauliflower. She was afraid of Jean Dorlean, that was clear. There were levels of authority Dory hadn't quite been aware of, things she really didn't want to know.

Jean Dorlean said, "We also agree that Werner shouldn't be told about this." He looked at Dory and Robert to see if they had heard him.

What business was it of Jean Dorlean's that Werner not be told? Shiftings in her perceptions bothered her. Dreams that weren't night dreams were dangerous. The world, which she was powerless to control, began to slide beyond her understanding.

"When you play with fire, you often get burnt," Jean Dorlean said. "Did you intend to make a big hullabaloo over this?"

The Princess said, with self-pity, "I didn't intend anything!"

"You didn't intend anything but the boy's delicious frustration, you mean?"

"Cruel!" Mrs. Patrick said.

"Well, what have we here?" Jean Dorlean said. "The seduction of a minor? Or rape? In any case, it is my understanding that you wish, Princess, to break your contract with your guests, close this place and return to New York. Might I remind you that there are certain kinds of freedom royalty does not possess, especially, in the light of the recent, dubious past, Austro-German royalty."

The Princess said nothing. Mrs. Zwanzig turned, looked hard at him and barely shook her head.

Dory was astonished by his tone; no one had ever treated the Princess this way. Someone could have, maybe, but no one ever had.

The Princess cried calmly.

"I concede that Robert will have to go," Jean Dorlean said.

"Don't worry about that," Robert said. "I'll be gone all right."

Dory could see Robert's great relief—maybe he'd expected reform school, or at least the notification of his parents.

Jean Dorlean turned to Dory. "You see? There are some very strange alliances in this modern world. Your friend Robert rapes a princess and gets off scot-free. In the not so distant past he would have been lovingly flayed alive, drawn and quartered. But now? For the dark deeds of the past, for justice and its punishments, substitute the politics of the hour."

"Ah, go away and leave her be," Mrs. Patrick said. "It's disgusting, this posturing about."

Robert was certainly eager to leave the room, and Dory followed him. Jean Dorlean came along too. Once the door was closed he chuckled and made other small sounds of satisfaction. "Well, Robert, my lad," he said, "I suspect you can always say that you lost your cherry on a princess. Oh, ha, ha, ha! Listen, as far as I'm concerned she got what she deserved. What is the term—prick-teaser?"

Robert blushed.

After supper, at which the Princess didn't appear, Dory drove Robert and his things to Leah. "I'm sorry about all the trouble," he said. "Dibley can handle the mowing and the heavy stuff, though. He'll do anything you ask him to do."

"It'll be lonesome not having you around," she said. "I don't see much of Cynthia anymore, Debbie's still down on me and Dibley's practically mute."

"You've been a pal, Dory. I mean it. You've always been a pal, even when you found out I was a . . . I mean . . ." His voice had grown strained. "I mean *rape!* My God! I can't laugh about it like that creep

Jean Dorlean. It was weird, and it's weird to remember. It's all wrong and shameful and puky, but it felt too good, even the part when she was saying no and I went ahead anyway. You know me—I'm not one of those hammerheads that get a kick out of hurting people. You know that, don't you?"

"Yes, I do, Robert."

"She said no, and I knew she meant it. There's something really screwy about her, you know. I knew she meant no and I didn't stop."

"It was her fault, too," she said.

"I'll tell you one thing, Dory. I better get married soon, or I'll go crazy."

She envied Robert's leaving. She was so tired of Cascom Manor, of the constant repetitive tasks, everything undone, done and undone again. It was life but it was no way to have a life, and there were dangerous secrets among these people. If she could get Debbie and Cynthia and Dibley safely away, the season over—for all their foibles and odd habits, Cynthia, Debbie and Dibley were American, undevious, understandable.

24

A truck, by its sound, passed his window in reverse gear. He reached the window in time to see four men pick up his Indian Pony by main sinewy force and slide it into the truck, one long handlebar over the side of the bed like an arm.

"New Hampshire!" one of the men said. "He got pretty far at that!"

"Till he run into Rita Hayworth there."

"Aw, shut up, George." This last was meant, but said with tolerance, an admission of its possible humor. He supposed the last speaker was Phil, who was in the Church. The men got in the truck, a black Ford with no hood, the chromed engine meant to be seen gleaming behind its chromed radiator, and left, one man in the rear with the drably bent motorcycle.

Things were out of his hands, and the somewhat disrespectful reference to Bonnie Forester disturbed him in an interesting way, as though the rules here were subject to change, perhaps toward threat. It was as if he had believed her to be a sort of vestal virgin, and had taken her sweet openness for all of the truth, and now there was a doubt, a smirk somewhere upon the premises.

For the first time in a month he thought of a girl he'd last seen in front of her family's tenement in Manchester, New Hampshire—Virginia Hadar, who, in the middle of his mild, friendly goodbye, suddenly leaned over his motorcycle's gas tank and kissed him on the mouth. Dory had somehow caused Virginia to be wiped out of his thoughts completely, even that final kiss that was her declaration of love. She was Lebanese and looked Oriental, so much so that one of his friends had asked him if she was Japanese. She was firm-armed, and had such a narrow waist her hips and legs seemed bravely independent of the rest of her body. She liked Stan Kenton, and was a little ashamed of her father's atonal folk records. He hadn't known her for more than the last part of the semester, but this weekend she had him come to her home and that Sunday he'd gone to Mass with her, her father and mother, brother and sister. After the Latin, the sonorous litanies, the placing and raising of chalice and other objects, all of which he saw as emotionless repetition, the priest gave such a fulsome sermon upon the glories of mothers and families he'd wondered for a moment if it hadn't been directed at him.

Then back to her house for Sunday dinner and her father's twangy records, primitive strings and whistles too simple and immigrantish for her, and they'd gone to her room to hear her Stan Kenton records, her modern sounds. She'd never let him enter her, and didn't then, but was so wise and sweet in saying no. She was lovely and impervious. But of course he'd gone away that afternoon to Leah, where Dory appeared through the young leaves, dirt on her forehead and a spade in her hands. And now he hadn't even wondered how Dory was doing at Cascom Manor, or thought to send her a postcard from along the way. Perhaps he took after his father. He didn't understand these things; he must know that others' lives passed without his presence. It seemed to him that he wouldn't always be like this.

Time passed slowly for him in the brown room, tropical green heat at the window. In the drawer of the night table beside the bed he found some literature, small folders and stapled pamphlets he read with a strangely erotic edge, as if he might learn here the secrets of Bonnie, whose saintliness had been called into question.

> All aspects of our metaphysical Being are divine when motivated by love. Says Kahlil Gibran in his book *The Prophet,* "I would have you consider your judgment and your appetite

> even as you would two loved guests in your house. Surely you would not honor one guest above the other; for he who is more mindful of one loses the love and faith of both." Be tolerant of yourself. Leave the door open wide between your physical and spiritual desires. Let them blend into One Desire. With love as your motivation, you can never do wrong.

Hmm. It wasn't that he didn't honor the two guests, it was that the guests didn't approve of each other. He read on. "We must open our hearts and pray that the Wayshower cleanse us and awaken us into our divine integrity . . ."

That was interesting, that bothersome though refreshing shower one was bound to run into along the journey. Then he came to "the day of at-one-ment," and some readjustment in expectation occurred. Christ Mediator was the Wayshower, who didn't shower but showed the way, obviously, that chastising rain not meant. As for the general message of the Church of the Science of the Way, Oval Forester wrote that Paul "took the torch from the Master and wrote: 'Now abideth faith, hope, love, these three; but the greatest of these is love.' " The "science" part had to do with faith healing, a sort of Christian Science without going all the way. They believed in microbes and doctors.

But if the collection of literature he'd found in the drawer meant anything, they seemed to believe, or at least to tolerate, just about anything. Or else why did he find here the School Bulletin of the Prenatal Astrobiology Academy, of Monrovia, which "applied Solar System Energies as Natural Heliocentric Astrology as Science," and taught, among other things, "Prognostification of Psychoeconomical Cycle Happenings" and "Marriage Compatibility Comparison Analysis"?

> The analysis is based on mother's conception of both partners. The conception status reveals all particular planets in their birthchart sections as well as all planetary angles in a given birthchart. For the women it is also important to know how her uterus will react in marriage relations. And the male partner must know something about his love ability because such facts are mostly ignored before marriage and bring disaster by finding out the disability of making love or to reproduce.

Well, there was marriage in a nutshell, he guessed. Ten lessons by mail for fifty dollars. There were also pamphlets from the Rosicrucians, AMORC, the Seventh-Day Adventists, the Church Ovarian Apocalyptic, a brochure on the lectures of one Prince Grégoire Ushant, who was ninety-five years old but had the body of a thirty-five-year-old and would reveal his secrets, and a picture of the Cathedral of Gladness, Church of Love and Triumph, Biosophic, Pastor: G. Oswald Rittheuber, D.D. The parking lot would accommodate one thousand cars.

Actually the literature of the Church of the Science of the Way itself was literate, clear, and contained a sort of Western directness, a humorless but unassuming candor unashamed of love, goodness, courage, goodwill, harmony—all such abstractions.

Late in the afternoon Bonnie came in and found him reading a magazine called *Avatar: A Quarterly Devoted to Metaphysical Thought,* and was pleased. "Oval has an article in that issue—did you see it?"

"Yes," he said. The article was titled "Keep Your Eye Fixed on God!"

She'd changed into a man's shirt and very short shorts, and tied her dark hair back as if she were going to do some kind of physical work, which he found she was. She put scissors, gauze, adhesive tape, a sponge and a towel on the bed, then went out and came back with a basin of water. Her beauty was more severe, ivory, tethered. "Now," she said, "let's find out how good a nurse I am!" She pulled down the sheet and looked closely at his knee, seeming very curious about what might be under the bandages. "I'm supposed to change this one. How does it feel?"

"Better," he said.

"This might hurt a little."

"Okay," he said, falsely signifying bravery he knew there was no necessity for. She snipped the tape and gauze until she had everything loose except a tart-sized area of red-yellow gore over his kneecap.

"Should I just sort of worry it off?" she said.

"Sure."

"I don't know if I can. I'm afraid I'll hurt you."

"What's a little pain?" he said. He didn't like pain at all but was anesthetized by his showing off, as he had been when he jumped into the cold lake in front of Dory.

"You're very brave, John."

"Aw, shucks, ma'am," he said, and she laughed, then grimly and slowly peeled the scabby congealed gauze away from his knee. It hurt.

"There!" she said. "It looks awful but it doesn't look infected. Actually it looks like the hole in a baked apple."

"It does, at that," he said.

She washed him gently around the wound, the water like cold fire, dapped him dry with the towel and redid the bandage. The bandages on his other knee and on his elbows seemed all right, so she didn't change them. When he thanked her she moved impulsively to him, put her arms around his bare skin and kissed him on the cheek. "I'm so glad you weren't killed!"

"Me, too," he said. His arms had come around her, and were slow to disengage themselves. This reluctance made her blush, and she sat on the bed with her hands demurely in her lap.

"How come you're not married?" he said, not changing the subject and feeling a little brash about it.

"Oval asks me that, too. I don't know. It isn't anything I ever decided."

"You're so beautiful they're afraid of you."

"Beautiful!" she said.

"You are, you know."

"I'm too big! Anyway, this is a ridiculous discussion," she said, but she wasn't displeased by the subject.

"I'm not exaggerating," he said, feeling shy, his voice constricted. She blushed, the skin below her eyes darkening, her breasts seeming to rise.

Part of him had also risen, but the sly host, anticipating that obstreperous guest, had already pulled the sheet back up to his waist. "I'll be able to walk by tomorrow," he said. "I'm healing up pretty fast."

"That's youth, as the nurse kept saying," Bonnie said. "Oval won't be back till Sunday, so I won't allow you to leave till then, no matter how well you can walk. You've got to meet Oval. Until then you're my prisoner! Anyway, I called Phil and they're looking for parts for your motorcycle and it won't be fixed before next week at the earliest." She kept talking, and as she talked she glanced quickly at his eyes and away, again and again, so he knew the idea had grown that he might not be just a boy. That thought had infected her, and made her keep talking. "I had a beau once, a long time ago. We were going to be married, I think, but then I won the contest. He was Prom King . . ."

"And you were Prom Queen."

"That's right. Everything was so simple and nice then." They were silent, she thinking of the departed past.

He said, "Oval has a job so he can support the Church?"

"Yes. It's a shame because it tires him so. He has this machine he built to freeze things, but it isn't exactly perfected yet. He's gone to Seattle to get some aluminum trays he needs 'cause the others broke, and pretty soon the lima beans are going to start coming and they've simply got to be frozen. Mostly they put them on pushcarts, but that's not enough and too slow."

"He runs a freezer?"

"He works for the Tulaveda Produce Co-op, where they freeze food, you know. Everything. Orange juice, beans, spinach, everything that grows, practically. But it's the lima beans that take so much out of him because they come in all at once, and he's no longer young, you know. He's nearly fifty."

His lack of real curiosity about Oval Forester had to do with the dread of meeting this saint, this teacher, and her insistence that he meet him. That, and having to be the man's guest. Oval Forester could not be pleased with the situation. And what had John Hearne, the sinner, to do with saints, anyway? The whole idea of saints made him itch. Even lima beans, coming up like that, out of nowhere, made him feel vaguely defensive, like a child trying not to swallow, or trying to swallow when he couldn't.

"I wish Oval were here," Bonnie said. "I can't help worrying about Urban tomorrow morning. He depends on Oval a lot more than he thinks."

"I'd forgotten about the world coming to an end," he said.

She smiled, then was ashamed of smiling at Urban's expense. "It's very real to him. We mustn't laugh."

"Maybe he's right. He came and sort of preached to me about it."

"Did he? I hope he didn't disturb you. He does get angry when people doubt him, but he's not as bad as he used to be, and all because of Oval. That's why I wish Oval were here." Bonnie looked around the room and noticed Thelma's new drawing on the bureau. "Thelma!" she said. "So she did come and bother you!"

"She just brought me the drawing," he said.

Bonnie got up to look at it. "Isn't that sweet. And so good! Do you mind her, John? I know some people are . . . sensitive that way. It's just one of those things."

"I'm not proud of it," he said.

"No, of course not. You're good. I know."

"Well . . ."

"No, I mean it. Do you know the kind of men I have to deal with in my line of work?" Her face turned bitter, revealing the planes and contours of its non-beautiful distinctiveness, so that it seemed ordinary and knowable. The end of her nose seemed to grow into an asymmetrical bulb, flushed and white-edged. For a moment it was a face capable of ugliness, but just for a moment.

"You mean acting and modeling?"

"Yes, all that. You can't believe what they take for granted. Even the sissy boys want something from you. No, they're not scared of pretty girls—not out here. Pretty girls are a kind of . . . produce. You begin to think it's the rules or something. But then I found Christ through

CSW, and Oval's teaching, which revealed my Christed self. We are all one with the Divine Spirit, John! It's so beautiful!" She had smoothed again into a simpler form. Beauty as simplicity, he thought, or purity of emotion, the way we wanted it in our fantasies. But the religious spirit wasn't his fantasy, and his baser guest couldn't help wondering if Oval Forester, the fifty-year-old saint, wasn't getting something more tangible from this beauty than abstract love and emulation.

"Well," he said as a form of confession, "you've got me all wrong, I'm afraid."

"Oh, no, I haven't!" she said as if teasing him. "When we are one with Him we perceive the soul-forces of the innermost being wherein God's harmonies, the celestial symphony of Truth and Love, are heard. I see all of you, and you are good. Maybe you don't think you believe, but that's just background noise. Deep down, you believe."

He believed she was a nice person, but anyone who could stomach all that jargon couldn't be too bright. That was what he believed, even as his green eyes gazed levelly into her beautiful blue ones. What he was thinking was that if it were at all possible, without making a lot of trouble and unhappiness and embarrassment for everyone concerned, he could fuck her, that would be marvelous. Did she not perceive *that* in his soul-forces? Did she perceive the blue-steeler he tried to disguise by having raised his knees against a lesser pain?

"I believe you're beautiful," he said, the shy constriction in his voice again. "Beyond that everything is fuzzy as hell."

"Oh, *John!*" She laughed, kissed him swiftly on the cheek, gathered up her nursing equipment and left.

Something swirled in her wake, a soft film of color in his vision of this place where she lived. Even that quick look at bitterness, and a disdain for her theology, couldn't clear the rainbows of infatuation. He could say she was too big, as she'd said of herself, and therefore not for the likes of him. Also too old, too this, too that. He could think "fuck," that diminishing word, all he wanted, but still he saw her through the prismatic haze of a lens.

She came back later, Thelma peering contritely around the doorframe behind her, and asked if he needed help washing up for supper. He said he was healing fast and could make it, thanks to the Healing Echelons. This bantering tone came from their new near-intimacy and the mention of his belief or disbelief, and she recognized it for what it was, an invitation to further efforts at discussion and conversion, now that they knew where they stood.

They ate supper in the large kitchen, grace said by Bonnie, words like "Lord" and "thankful" passing through his ears. Thelma's spoon was like a dowsing wand, never wanting to turn where she wanted it to, pieces of macaroni and cheese slipping out of it in a way that made his wrist ache for her thick wrist. Hadasha Kemal Allgood said hello enthusiastically, but during the meal he read a small, flexible, leather-bound book as he chewed each piece of macaroni separately, like a Fletcherite, ten times or more before swallowing what was left of it, his fork, always in his left hand, primed with one more segment. There was something pelicanish about his head and the foreign object of his larynx.

After supper Hadasha Kemal Allgood went away and Bonnie washed while Thelma wiped, seriously concentrating on her task. The dishes were plastic, though Thelma didn't drop one. He sat at the table and could hear her moist breath. She had the habit of turning her head as if she had to see something up in the corner by the ceiling, and he wondered if she actually looked up there, or if the movement itself was all she was impelled to do.

When the dishes were done the three of them went into the brown living room, he stiff-legged but without a crutch. Tomorrow he would be able to walk even better, once the morning stiffness had been worked out. This thought gave him the ease of his coming freedom but also the bother of its choices. Bonnie snapped on amber lights in brown sconces around the walls, over the heavy furniture, also illuminating a portrait of a handsome Anglo-Saxon-looking Christ. Over the oak mantel of a small fireplace was a brass cross. The cabinet radio, which Thelma turned on, was of brown veneer, with a small amber dial, its loudspeaker defined by a Gothic arch. Crooning music grew slowly out of it, to which Thelma bounced, her parts out of sync with each other.

"Why don't you draw a picture for us?" Bonnie asked her, meaning that her attempts to dance and be graceful in the happy wash of music were not good to look at. Not understanding what Bonnie really meant, because she couldn't understand everything, she went off happily to get her pencils and posterboard. Bonnie gave him a sad look. When Thelma returned she made him sit next to Bonnie on the horsehair settee, then took his arm strongly, as if it were a log, and placed it over Bonnie's shoulders.

"Thath *ni'!*" she said, and as he and Bonnie moved, using all their learned skills in such matters in order to be more comfortable with that burning arm, took her pencil easily in thumb and fingers and deftly began to draw.

The radio murmured, rattled tympanically, crooned and occasionally wailed or moaned, nothing it did important because of its lack of volume and because all of the songs were familiar and nothing to him. He and Bonnie didn't talk, not because they were posing but because, he thought, of his arm and his hand that was now around her waist, resting easily on her hip. That meant enough to think about, at least for him—what his arm encompassed.

Thelma finished soon, or what seemed soon to him, and submitted her drawing for surprise and praise. She had placed herself—her not so gross but still recognizable self—between them, so that they cuddled her. His revulsion at the idea of this embrace was surprisingly strong, almost of a moral intensity, of taboo—as if all the while he'd been having lustful thoughts not of Bonnie but of Thelma.

They praised her drawing, which deserved wonder.

After a while Bonnie made them hot chocolate, a marshmallow foundering in each cup. He smoked a cigarette, which made him think of a beer, but there seemed no occasion for alcohol in this place. Without his asking, Bonnie told him more about Oval.

"Daddy!" Thelma said when she heard the name. She pointed at Bonnie and said, "Sister!" and at John and said, "Brother!"

"Oh, Thelma, you haven't got a real sister or brother, but we love you just as much as if we were!" She turned back to John and said, "Oval doesn't talk much about himself because he's always taking care of other people and all they want to talk about are their own problems. But every once in a while I'll ask him something about his life. He was in the Navy, but that's just about all he'll say about *that* subject. At the Co-op he's an engineer—that's his title, I guess. He invented and built this freezing machine of his, I know that. He was married . . ." She nodded surreptitiously at Thelma, who was working at the drawing again. "And I guess she couldn't take . . ." Another nod. "So that didn't last very long. Actually he's not the kind of person you quiz like that, not because he's hard to talk to, though. He just doesn't seem that interested in himself."

"That's a very strange person," John said. He hadn't removed his sneak-thief arm, but now decided that he should, and did.

"I truly believe he saved my life," Bonnie said. "I was so bitter, John, so cynical and bitter. I couldn't give love. I'd been treated rotten and all I felt was hate, the ego-Satan in me was in the ascendant. I had lost Christ."

"A man was rotten to you?"

"A man, men, but that's all gone. All the hatred and resentment are all gone, just gone! It's such a wonderful feeling! You must give love and only love! Oval quoted Glenn Clark in one of his sermons. Someone asked Dr. Clark what would happen if someone refused to take your love. Dr. Clark answered, 'Increase the dose.' Isn't that lovely?"

That night as the air cooled and he pulled a light blanket over his sheet, he lived more easily in his body, and was even able to stretch a little, that underrated pleasure. He'd found that it was Friday. The radio news had said nothing of A-bombs or of the Apocalypse, but spoke cheerfully of little wars, assassinations, lynchings, famines, jihads, the luring but distant responsibilities he, for this personal, episodic term, simply let happen. As he shut his eyes his eyelids felt cool.

Gracie Lundgren had come down with rotten leg. It was terrible for poor Gracie, but it was not his fault, at least not legally his fault. Dory and Loretta would have none of that, and regarded him with loathing, their lips stiff with disgust. On the whey field they slid her stretcher into the high Army ambulance. There was not much hope for her. He knew if he could see her she would forgive him, and maybe he could cut out the rot with his jackknife, even though he knew his knife was dull because he had been cutting nickels in half with it. Cutting nickels in half was something as reprehensible as masturbation. Dory and Loretta wouldn't think of letting him touch her again, or even see her, so for a moment he thought of forcing them to let him into the ambulance, but then he remembered that the knife idea was just a show he'd put on anyway, and they knew it. His shame was intolerable.

Awake, sometime in the night; a bell-like muffler sped up the street, the muffler of a huge, slow-turning engine, each mighty, cavernous explosion steadily belling after the next, a vibrato of purring gongs.

"John? John?" In dim, down-hall light from the door, Bonnie's tall figure came floating toward him. This was detectably more real than the field where Dory and Loretta stood guarding the ambulance. The dream shame, identified as merely that, began to dissipate in the enormous reality of Bonnie here, now. It still held, somewhat; the shame of their disapproval was too strong to go away at once, but it was fading into the puzzlement of interpretation. Then Bonnie's real hands were on his naked shoulders. "John?" she asked, half whispering.

"Yes," he said, meaning total agreement, and pulled her down to him, her cheek coming next to his cheek a little hard, as if she'd fallen. Her hair and cool ear were perfumed. He pulled his covers aside so that her body lay next to his, but there was a meaty feeling about it that was not quite right.

"Wait, John!" she whispered urgently. "No! Please! John!" Her breasts were soft and firm on his chest, then she pushed away. "Wait a minute! Are you awake?" She really disagreed with what he wanted, he was beginning to understand. He kissed her on the lips, soft lips and sweet watery breath, but her mouth moved too busily against his and she was saying, "No, no, wake up, please! You've got to help!"

He lay back, but like a miser wouldn't let go of his treasure. For the moment she was willing to accept these terms. "It's Urban. He's asked for you. Can you get dressed and come with me?"

He let her get up and she turned on the bed lamp, her white nightgown falling back down over her legs.

"I thought I was in Paradise," he said.

She smiled quickly and then stopped, shaking her head. "It might be serious. Are you willing to come?"

"Okay."

"Let's get dressed and go to him, then."

He met her in the front hall and hobbled along with her to her car, which she backed out into the dark street—carefully, he noticed.

"His housekeeper called. He wanted Oval. She said she had to stick her head out the window and yell up to the roof. He's on the roof."

"Why does he want to see me?"

"Because Oval's not here, I guess."

"What have I got to do with Oval? I'm just an innocent bystander."

"Maybe he took a shine to you."

"So he's sitting on his roof just before the end of the world and there's something he's got to tell me?"

"What *do* you believe in, John?"

"Constant floating guilt."

"Be serious." They were driving along a curving boulevard below a hazy half-moon and muted streetlights. "We're almost there," she added.

"I am serious," he said.

"Do you believe in God?"

He discarded one flippant answer after another. Not so's you'd notice. God who? I believe in many gods. Our Father who aren't in heaven?

"Do you?"

"Well, no, I guess not. Actually I'm pretty neutral on the subject."

"Oh, John, there is a force for good in us! You'll see!"

The Church Ovarian Apocalyptic was no wider than the bungalows on either side of it, but was tall, with a steep roof and a steeple, a Little-Brown-Church-in-the-Vale sort of church, with a small residential wing at an angle to the church part. Several cars were parked in the space formed by the angle, and as they got out of Bonnie's car he saw people sitting quietly in a circle on the grass. A dark young woman came out of the church to greet them, saying, *"Madre,"* and *"Dios,"* and other prayerful things in Spanish, which made him think of his old refrain, *agua caliente,* and then, *He maketh the deep to boil like a pot.* "Come quick!" she said, and led them into the dark church and up narrow winding stairs to the base of the steeple, a little lookout with wooden railings all around. Out on the far edge of the ridgepole someone straddled the sharp roof peak.

"Urban! Urban!" Bonnie called. "What are you doing out there? Come back! Please come back! We love you and care for you, Urban!"

"Send the kid over here. I want to talk to him," Urban said in a normal voice.

"No, no! You come back, Urban! We are one with the Universal Mind. God is love and forgiveness! Christ Mediator died for our sins! Now you just squinch yourself back over here, all right?"

"Legget thegge weggomeggan leggearn eggin seggileggence," Urban commanded. *"Let the woman learn in silence with all subjection."*

"Urban, you come on, now!"

"But I suffer not a woman to teach, nor to usurp authority over the man, but to be in silence. I Timothy 2:11–12."

"I'm going to come out there after you! Or I'll call the Fire Department!"

This brought a bitter laugh from Urban.

John started over the railing, wondering why he was doing this. Maybe he was still showing off for Bonnie. Only the bandage on his right knee seemed to restrict him at all, as though the rest had healed. The night was chilly, the roof tiles cold. Bonnie plucked at his Ike jacket, trying to make him stay, but he paid no attention. He placed his hands on the ridge and inched out toward Urban, Bonnie still forbidding him to do so. I'm just a-squinchin' on out, he thought with a touch of hysteria. The roof was a steep cliff on either side, and the tiles clinked loosely as he moved along. The dark roofs of trees and somnolent houses seemed far below.

He came up to Urban as if each were on horseback, or maybe on the same horse. Urban wore his Army Air Force uniform—ribbons, hashmarks, wings, insignia, garrison hat and all. In the hazy moonlight, or the beginning light of dawn, John saw that he had been a staff sergeant, that there were several battle stars on the pale ribbon of the Pacific Theater and that among the ordinary ribbons were those heavy ones, the real ones. Though it had been the general instinct to throw away and forget the uniform, or to use up what could be used, like his own Ike jacket, its cuffs soiled by grease, he could not deny the sudden and surprising rise of emotion borne in him by these signs. The flattish tissues of Urban's wounded face reflected what light there was, the mouth and eye holes black.

Urban's housekeeper called, *"Urbán! Urbán! Qué te pasa?"* And

Bonnie called too, asking for rational behavior in some upset manner or other, her words like chimes.

"My belief is it all got out of hand," Urban said. "Which don't rule out the Leggord's vengeance, even if Heggee fucked up. Would that make Heggim less pissed? Oval says different, he says none of it has to do with Heggim and it's all some mistake or something, and the Leggord is some kind of a nice guy who's not going to take it too hard. I can't get my mind around that. Now you been to college—what's your belief?"

Their perch on the roof peak, the loose tiles and this question seemed equally precarious. He had no impulse to explain belief he had never formulated in the first place. If he was here to talk Urban off the roof he would have to be skillful and inventive indeed, and it was probably mental laziness that made him reject that path. He could only be sincere, for better or worse—the easy way that probably wouldn't work. As the light gave a blink toward increase he saw with a complicating apprehension that beneath the skirt of Urban's blouse was the familiar brown leather holster for the service .45.

"I'm not sure what I believe," he said with a fatiguing sense of inadequacy.

"You can't not be sure of what you believe," Urban said. "You can not be sure of what you think but you can't not be sure of what you believe."

"I'd like to get you and me down off this roof," John said.

"I want to know what you believe. I ain't going to get mad, no matter what it is, so spit it out."

"In college I never studied in order to believe anything. When I read philosophers or theologians it was just to find out what they believed."

"What kind of critter are you? A man's got to put it all together and come up with an answer!"

"I guess I'm still trying to put it all together."

"You ever kill a man?"

"I don't know. Maybe. We just fired at areas, where they told us to."

"You ever see dead men?"

"Yeah."

"You ever see a man die?"

"Yeah."

"How?"

Maybe he was here to stall Urban, who hadn't mentioned the end of the world; maybe Urban was asking to be stalled, and talked to, so he told him about the patrol through the scrubby woods where the terrified Okinawans had hidden shoulder to shoulder for days and the ground was covered with shit so close together they had to step in it, big piles and little baby poops and dysenteric splashes and drips and clumps of shit everywhere. Was he trying to be amusing? Somebody, while they could still speak, said that was fear shit, it smelled worse than regular shit. The spirit of that shit got into their bodies and clothes and hair. The 105s were going over them with that rushing flutter that was so loud you always thought you had to be able to see the shell itself, but you never could, and they all confessed afterwards that they were most afraid there'd be some incoming because there was no place to hit the dirt and they'd have to dive straight into shit. Somebody said as for himself he hadn't had an un-fear shit since he got on the boat in Seattle.

Then he was, for powerful reasons signaled first in his throat, putting off what he'd next seen. Maybe it wouldn't be good for Urban, or for himself, to tell it. He'd described the thing before but never in anything like these crazy circumstances. His constricted throat was telling him that he might not be able to tell it this time because he might be surprised by some terrible significance he'd always overlooked.

"Hey, man," he said. "What are we doing up here?" His eyes were wet and his voice was full of uncontrolled-sounding passion he didn't trust because he might be putting on an act for Urban, to show him he cared for him and his life beyond all of his theories.

Urban stared at him through his mask. "Then what?" he said.

"We came out of the woods and went down to the shore, on the rocks, and sloshed our feet in the ocean."

"Yeah?"

"The squad leader was pissed off and kept yelling at us, but in a little while he came down and sloshed his boots around too. Then somebody noticed these civilians a couple hundred yards up the shore, on a bluff over about a fifty-foot cliff, throwing what looked like clothes off there. You'd see a guy in a white shirt and dark pants go over somewhere and come back with a bundle of what looked to us like laundry and he'd toss it over, and others would do the same thing. Then a woman did the same thing and jumped off the cliff herself. That's when it dawned on us what the bundles were."

"Sure," Urban said.

"They were afraid of us. I don't know what they thought we'd do to them. I mean, Americans, for Christ's sake."

"Oh, yeah," Urban said. "Just a bunch of Boy Scouts."

"Some of us probably were Boy Scouts. I was eighteen and so were the other three replacements. We'd only been in Able Company a couple days. Anyway, we started over there. The rest of the company was up on top someplace and there was no firing. The 105 rounds were going in about five hundred yards farther on. 'Crazy Japs,' we were saying. The only ones I'd seen before were dead, sort of khaki-colored all over, dusty and faded-looking, like they'd always been that way. But the idea that those civilians were alive and throwing their children and themselves off a cliff, as busy as if they were doing an ordinary job or project or something, mothers and fathers just throwing their kids down onto the rocks, that was insane in a way I'd never even thought about before. In my life that just never happened, so all the time we were going over toward the cliff I thought what we had to find was just laundry.

"Some of them weren't dead. The cliff wasn't high enough. One kid about ten years old had a bone sticking out of her leg. It was a girl—I saw her bare little pouch when I turned her over. She was making a constant thin whine, as if she never had to take a breath, and for a minute I couldn't figure out just how to pick her up. Henry Reppert carried my rifle and web belt. Her leg was black—I've never seen such a bruise. We carried the live ones up where the rest of the platoon was, and the medics came along. I never found out if any of them recovered."

"So it does no good to say it wasn't your fault," Urban said.

"Well, it wasn't my fault."

"You think you're any different from anybody else?"

"I didn't make it happen!"

"Yeah, and you wish it never happened, but that kind of contrition won't do you no good. You got to pay seventy and seven times for every *pimple's* worth of pain you caused. You think just because you're sorry it means a rat's ass to the Leggord? You going to plead your own case? You think you can plead innocent 'cause you were just a poor little dogface obeying orders? You think Heggee gives a fart in a whirlwind whether you're American or not? You think ignorance of the law is an excuse? It don't make sense at all if any shit-for-brains guardhouse lawyer can argue before the Leggord! You tell Oval that. You be sure and tell him. Tell him he was a friend to me and it's no fault of his I can't get my mind around all that forgiveness crap he dishes out. Tell him I respect him as a man, but the Leggord's no candy-ass. You tell him that!"

John's response was defensive and imperious. "Look!" he shouted. "I respect you because of what you've been through and I respect you for feeling some guilt about it, but why go ape? It's fucking self-indulgent to think the whole fucking world's guilt is on your head!"

"It ain't something I *think!*" Urban yelled back, the corners of his mouth slot turning white with each word.

Again John answered, shouting, sense having given way to simple intensity. Since they both knew what was meant, the words didn't matter. The names they called each other—"Punk!" "Asshole!"—hadn't the precision of insult and weren't taken as such. The double-talk of righteous anger.

The light was growing. John resisted looking at his watch because the subject of the Apocalypse seemed, along with the pistol Urban wore, more dangerous than argument. The roof seemed to fall away more steeply as the tiles turned pink. The roofs of Tulaveda, descending to the west, began to define themselves, palms above them here and there, the darker masses of trees not yet quite green. The air was dusty, as if just waking up. He supposed there were people in this town who got up to go to work, who made a living and were not gaga over Ultimate Answers.

He was still angry at Urban, but after the shouting it was the anger one had for an exasperating friend. "Anyway, why don't you tell Oval yourself? I've never even met this character."

Urban looked at his wristwatch. Down in the street, cars were starting up and moving away. A man carried a sleeping child, a woman another.

"Well," Urban said, "I guess I'm all washed up as a preacher. I got myself out on a limb and sawed it off again. It just don't make any sense, none of it."

"Come on, let's go back, then," John said.

"Naw. You go on, buddy," Urban said in a kindly voice. "Take the women down with you."

"So what are you going to do?" He reached out and put his hand on Urban's shoulder, feeling the fabric shoulder strap and brass button.

"You wouldn't think of grabbing on, now, would you?" Urban said mildly.

"What are you going to do?"

When he took his hand from Urban's shoulder Urban lifted the flap of the holster and eased the handle of the pistol, but didn't draw it.

"Hey, come on, now!" John said.

"You tell Oval I couldn't take it no more, that I never could get the hang of all that love shit. I'll come to Judgment wearing the uniform of Satan so they'll know me and can cut the orders right there and then."

"Hey, come on, now!" John said. A symptom of his incompleteness, or immaturity, he thought, was his consistent belief that other people weren't as crazy as their actions indicated. He was also intolerant of staggering drunks and the pickers of fights. His own scheme of rationality was the only one he was large enough to tolerate. So it was forbidden that Urban shoot himself; Bonnie and the young housekeeper must not have to cope with it. Once this imperative was clear he didn't have to think, and as in sports had no hesitations and could feel no pain. He grabbed Urban by the front of his blouse, getting shirt and tie in his fist as well, pulled him straight up against himself and at the same time, as Urban's arms came up to shove him, picked the pistol out of the holster and let it fall. It clinked two or three times on the tiles and was gone.

At that moment fear returned, along with a weakening pain in his knee that made everything worse. He held Urban in a bear hug that was overly powerful, fear seeking to annihilate danger, and he remembered the story of the wrestler in Minneapolis who killed the burglar out of panic, and how his father had disapproved. Maybe he was having a relapse of some kind, signaled also by his babbling apologies, explanations and advice, such as if they fell off the roof they'd probably just break a leg, or their necks, and become living vegetables. Urban wasn't listening, and in fact John wasn't listening to himself very carefully. Gradually he released Urban, found that Urban still straddled the roof in a stable fashion, and began to inch his way back toward safety. Urban, whose mouth slot was closed like a scar, and who seemed to be thinking deep thoughts, followed.

It was nearly broad daylight when his back touched the base of the steeple and Bonnie and the young housekeeper pulled at him, hindering his planned, careful, painless climb to safety and making it none of those. Urban came along slowly, silently.

"Loco!" said the young housekeeper. *"Por eso no entra en razón!"* When Urban climbed over the railing she cried and grappled with him, calling him sweetheart and crazy. Urban said nothing, even when she lifted him right off his feet. John then saw what hadn't been apparent to him before—that without his history and his passion Urban was really a very little man.

The housekeeper, whose name was Maria, and Bonnie both acted as if they wanted to beat Urban up, or at least give him a spanking. They wouldn't let go of him and kept shaking him all the way down the stairs. John stopped to look for the pistol, which he found in the dirt below an exotic red-leafed hedge he couldn't name, and followed them into the residential ell of the church. The pistol was loaded with wartime steel-cased cartridges. He unloaded it in the vestibule, field-stripped it and decided to keep the barrel, which he put in his pocket. He followed the cries and admonitions of the women into the kitchen, put the dismantled pistol and the cartridges on a counter and shoved them back out of the way. His knee felt freer than it had, but also wet, the wetness blood that had come through his pants.

The women had Urban in a chair and were arguing with him, though he was silent. Maria was removing his uniform blouse, while Bonnie held up his arms and pulled him forward or back in order to make this possible. John's hands were filthy, so he washed them at the sink, using dish soap, then wiped them on a dish towel.

Bonnie said, "I've got to be convinced he won't do anything till Oval gets back."

"He'll be okay," Maria said. "I'll watch him. I don't let go of him." She straddled his chair, grabbed his head and put his face between her breasts, saying harsh, chiding endearments.

"Urban!" Bonnie said. "Will you not do anything dumb till Oval gets back?"

"He means 'okay,'" Maria said. "He has no sleep. He'll sleep for two days. Don't worry." She pulled him to his feet, saying, "Beddie-bye now."

John said that he had the barrel of the pistol, in case anybody wondered about it. He looked at Urban carefully, but there was no response at all. He didn't know what Urban thought about what he'd done—whether he'd rescued him or betrayed him, not even permitting the poor desperate fucker the right to blow his brains out.

"Muchas gracias," Maria said. "He is in . . . He owe you." She took Urban away, carrying his blouse, hat and tie. Urban wore the empty holster. In another room they stumbled on stairs, Maria talking.

"He didn't talk for over a week last time," Bonnie said. "Oval gave his sermons for him, but of course the church was mostly empty."

They seemed to be waiting for Maria to come back.

"What could he have said?"

"You mean Urban?" Bonnie said.

"No. Oval."

"I don't know. I had to teach the LCD class from ten till eleven."

That would be, from his reading, the "Live Christ Daily" class.

As he moved from behind the table Bonnie saw the blood on his knee. She rushed to kneel before him and roll up the leg of his suntans. "You tore off the bandage and it's a mess! We'll get you home and fix it."

Maria didn't come back. "She said she wouldn't let go of him," he said. "Maybe she means it literally."

Bonnie looked surprised, as though she'd just understood the obvious. "Yes, you're right. She's Catholic, you know. She doesn't believe any of it."

He puzzled over this remark as they went out to Bonnie's car. Meaning that to Maria, the Catholic, all these God ideas of vengeance, love, forgiveness, harmony, etc., were best left in church for the authorities to puzzle over, while she herself stuck her man's blasted face between her breasts and held on. Maybe.

On the drive back to the parsonage Bonnie was at first silent and then began to make little chirps and sniffs, and he saw that she was crying big, Bonnie-sized tears. As big as peas they formed, glinted like opals or pearls and found smooth ways down her smooth cheeks to the corners of her lips.

"You want me to drive?" he asked.

"You are good, John!" she said. "The way you went out there and talked with him, and hugged him and brought him back! It's the power of Love again! And I love you, John Hearne! I love you for your love! I'd do anything for you! Anything!" She sniffled and swallowed and cast him bright, glistening looks.

He was startled by this and had nothing to say, but after a moment decided that she probably meant a sort of general anything, a sort of being-very-nice anything. In his limited experience when a girl said she loved you it meant that sooner or later, even if certain legal or religious requirements had to be met, she meant things uterine, that you had been chosen for that mortal process, but with Bonnie he wasn't sure about this. He couldn't be sure and he was shy, as if the worst thing in the world would be not to have understood exactly what she meant.

At the parsonage she insisted that he take a bath, and afterwards redid his bandages. Was there anything she could get for him? Did he want to go back to bed or stay up? Would he like something to read? There was the church library, but maybe he'd like some magazines. *Life? Time? The Saturday Evening Post? Collier's?* What could she do for him? He was special, good, wonderful; she was at his service. She had no assignments today; would he like to see Tulaveda? The ocean? There were many interesting sights to see and places to visit. Would he like to go to a matinee? *Bambi* was playing at the Pearl Theater on Pasadena Avenue. They could take a picnic lunch and go up to Sierra Madre Park in the National Forest. Also there was the Municipal Art Museum, the Tulaveda Museum of Natural History, or they could go see all the sights in Hollywood: Grauman's Chinese Theater, and the studios and all, and maybe they'd see a famous star walking down Hollywood Boulevard as casual as you please. Or they could go to South Tulaveda and see the motorcycle races on the dirt track—would he like that? Or tonight the midget-car races in the Rose Bowl in Pasadena. They could eat at a drive-in—did they have those in New Hampshire, with the waitresses on roller skates?—and see all the fancy custom cars. They could go to the carnival at Del Rosa and ride the Ferris wheel. They could go over to Ozzie Rittheuber's estate and play croquet or watch television or go swimming in the pool (except he couldn't, she supposed, with that knee)—she and Oval had keys, and could just walk in anytime.

"That's the Rittheuber of the Church of Something, Biosophic?" he asked. At this point he was shaving and she was sitting on the edge of the high bathtub.

"Yes, that's Ozzie—G. Oswald—Oval kids him that the G stands for God. He really made it big in the New Metaphysics. He's had some marvelous cures and is such a powerful preacher. The people just flock to the Cathedral of Gladness."

"They don't flock so much to CSW, then?"

"Oh, we're different—sort of basic, you know. More conventional. Oval doesn't make the claims Ozzie does. I mean we're all on the same side, so to speak, but Ozzie claims he's three separate persons and can appear at three places simultaneously. Oval wouldn't do that."

"He wouldn't."

"No, he wouldn't do that."

"Does he believe Ozzie can do that?"

"Maybe Ozzie can. Who knows? There's no doubt he's a Christed person—he's given hope to so many."

He rinsed off his razor, put it in his kit and put that into his musette bag. Bonnie handed him a clean white shirt—Oval's. She hadn't, truly hadn't, understood his reluctance to borrow it. It was too long in the sleeves, but he rolled the cuffs up onto his forearms. In the borrowed shirt he felt that his neck, where the unfamiliar collar seams crossed it, was another man's neck.

In the kitchen Hadasha Kemal Allgood and Thelma, without seeming to pay attention to each other, were having cereal and orange juice. Thelma had forgotten her bib, so Bonnie got one and put it on her, first making her stand up so she could twist her dress around straight. Thelma smiled. Bonnie put bread in a large, many-slotted toaster and got coffee going.

"Thelma's going to school today," Bonnie said, mainly, he saw, to remind Thelma, who got all excited and looked often up into the corner, stretching her mouth. "So we're going to wash her hair, aren't we?"

A pale wash of milk lightened Thelma's underlip and chin. "Shampoo!" she said. "Shampoo! Shampoo!"

"She likes that word," Hadasha Kemal Allgood said.

After breakfast, while Bonnie was washing Thelma's hair, a large Chrysler station wagon arrived out in front and sounded its trainlike horn. Since no one responded to it, John went out to see. His first impression was that it was full of large balloons, but soon they became the heads and faces of mongoloids, hydrocephalics—so many imprecisely focused eyes. The driver was a middle-aged Negro wearing gold-rimmed glasses. As John went around to the driver's side the man got out of the car to meet him, smiling, worried by this new face but trying not to seem as worried as he was.

"I'm Washington, transporting the children," he said. He wore a dark blue pinstripe suit, a dark blue tie and white cotton gloves, the kind that had one button at the base of the palm.

"John Hearne," John said, and held out his hand. There was the nearly imperceptible hesitation before the snow-white glove rose to meet his hand. "You've come for Thelma?"

"Yes, for all the unfortunate children, bless their loving hearts!" His diction was careful and hearty, with the excess of unambiguous good-will that was essentially servile. John had trouble making small talk against the grain of his thoughts, but before there was too much silence Bonnie brought Thelma out. Her bowl-cut blond hair was wet, but she was happy. As Washington helped her into the back seat, moving another wide child to give her room, she waved, smiled and seemed the most conscious of the passengers.

"John Hearne—Washington Johnson," Bonnie said. Washington Johnson shook hands again and bade them good day in his Negro voice that had a glassy ring in it, and drove off, the large heads swaying backwards in the mild acceleration.

"Washington and his wife are in the Church," Bonnie said. "He's a mortician. Such a lovely person, and so is Ertrude. They're the only colored family we have."

"Does he always wear the white gloves?"

"Oval asked him about that. Yes, always. He says the embalming chemicals do something bad to his hands."

Or maybe, John thought, Washington Johnson would rather offer a snow-white hand to those of doubtful inclinations, not a Negro hand, especially one that had been contaminated by the dead. The question was why Washington Johnson would want to be in the Church at all. Not for business reasons, certainly, because nowhere in his country, John knew without having to think about it, would a Negro be allowed to prepare naked whites, especially naked white females, for the grave. He wondered if Bonnie, the believer, would ever have asked why Washington and Ertrude Johnson wanted to be in the Church. But of course he, faithless John Hearne, was automatically discounting belief.

While Bonnie got ready for the day, he walked in the lush rear garden between parsonage and church. *I walk* (walked?) *in the garden alone,* he heard in memory, *while the dew is* (was?) *still on the roses*—

from Camp Washonee, a YMCA summer camp, when he was twelve or thirteen. He found that he was walking pretty well; his joints had progressed until they felt about the way they used to on a Sunday after a high school football game. *And the voice I hear, falling on my ear, the Son of God is call-all-ling . . .* Beyond a stone arch was the Church of the Science of the Way, miniature gray Gothic that because of its solidity and the surrounding vegetation seemed too ancient for Tulaveda, California.

But what did he really want to do today? Bask in admiration? That was always nice. He would like, realizing that he didn't want to talk to Bonnie all that much, to spend the day lazing with her somewhere in deep privacy, naked, their voices meaning nothing. She was the most beautiful woman he had ever touched—excessively, lushly, hugely, almost impersonally glamorous—and he an immature young buck sneaking in where he didn't deserve to be but, oh, Lord, taking advantage of his luck. That was all; grab it when you could. Did the rest of them have faith and guilt and all that? He had millions, maybe billions, of the long years in which all living matter grappled and slimed and reproduced. He would turn her rosy, melt her into honey—no, something less viscous, more transparent, gaseous, her long thighs helium, her uterus a flower, her belly a heap of wheat set about with lilies, her two breasts like two young roes, that are twins, which feed among the lilies.

Some form of calculation, its terms ethereal, metaphysical, led him down the hallway past the bathroom. The door was open, humid air wafting from it, and the tall goddess stood toweling beside the gurgling tub. Ordinarily he would have glanced and passed by in minor embarrassment, but his glance met hers, and she, who of course had been the one who had left the door open, looked into his eyes and made no gesture of modesty. He could go on, or he could stop; it was a pretty, it was a lovely, it was a generous choice to have given him. All this in a thousandth of a second as he traversed the portal. He stopped, but it was still a gamble as to her intentions as he turned back to her. She gazed calmly into his eyes and toweled the nape of her neck below her piled dark hair. She was the most naked woman he had ever seen. The borders of her were lined by light, the peripheries of her, the subtly concave planes, the dawn-downy fields, the bright hemispheres of her umbered into dark. She let down her hair and fluffed it out, watching him.

"What you said you wanted to do," she said, her voice in awe of its meaning. "Do you still want to?"

"Yes."

"Go to your room and I'll be there in a minute."

Oh, God, her prows—she wasn't a Chris-Craft, she was a catamaran, swift in the blue Pacific. In the room his clothes were whisked away by dusky Nubian naiads, her slaves. He was young Apollo—no, Dionysus, son of Zeus, ready to be worshipped, the firm male beauty so waitfully imperious it trembled of its own commanding power.

She entered in her white nightgown and with a submissive shrug let it drop in slow, diaphanous folds from her fair shoulders and walked, almost awkward with modest lust, to him whose intentions were manifest within that imperative, that taut bright fleshy lance . . .

Oh, cut the shit, Hearne. He sat disconsolately on a stone bench, his pants painfully constricting his fleshy lance. Across the gravel path a lizard observed him with Barney Google eyes. Maybe it was a skink, a name not conferred in awe or wonder.

25

She heard the radio news—Gabriel Heatter and H. V. Kaltenborn, those cranky, portentous, unmistakable voices. The Sunday New York papers, the *Herald Tribune* and the *Times,* came to Leah on Mondays and she picked them up on her regular Tuesday shopping trip. She had become aware of opposing forces in the world, and along with that orienting perception, of stupidity in the larger affairs of man. But how had she come by her ideas of the right and the decent? Some maybe from John Hearne, but not all. What should she think of a country, once the admired ally of her own, that wouldn't let people out of it? She felt the sad regression of hope, the smudged ideals, the madness engendered by power.

The year 1948 had begun with Mahatma Gandhi assassinated by a member of his own religion who thought he was too tolerant of another religion. In Prague, Jan Masaryk was found dead below his office window. Suicide? Why should the lip curl at that? Because murder was much more normal in such an affair. In South Africa, Malan took over and made race the obsession of the state. But in her own country, in the South, were laws, and in the North, customs, that reinforced this obsession too. The States' Rights Democrats nominated Strom Thurmond for President because of Truman's civil-rights policies. The Russians (or was it the Soviet Union?) decided to starve Berlin until it came under their rule. The U.S. government indicted the U.S. Communist Party leaders for conspiring to overthrow the government by force. Henry Wallace became the candidate of the Progressive Party and welcomed the support of the Communist Party. Truman was practically doomed to lose to Dewey. A jet plane went nine hundred miles an hour. A rocket went three thousand miles per hour at White Sands, New Mexico. Truman issued Executive Order 9981, integrating the armed forces. The draft was back for nineteen- to twenty-five-year-olds. John Hearne would have to register. The Jews and the Arabs were at war. There was the "Iron Curtain"; nations pouted and had tantrums like willful little boys.

She didn't read all of the huge sheafs of newspapers, but she began to read *Time,* and she always went through *Life.* Jean Dorlean was always telling her, as if they were having a continual argument or discussion, what she supposedly wasn't aware of in this cynical world. She learned about the Kuomintang, the Comintern, the Truman Doctrine, Dean Acheson, Chiang Kai-shek, Hiss, Chambers, the Hollywood Ten, Gerhard Eisler, the House Un-American Activities Committee, Elizabeth Bentley the Spy Queen. Madame Kosenkina jumped out of a second-story window of the Soviet consulate in New York.

Thousands died in traffic accidents every week. Her country was turning mad, frivolous; its most popular song was "Buttons and Bows." All was confusion, dread, sanctimony, disappointment, and all these things that had been peripheral to her because she was a child, and not responsible for them, grew over her like a huge storm of knowledge and concern she had to see as part of her own fate.

Ernst Zwanzig worked on his clay bust of Thomas E. Dewey, which was later to be cast in bronze, or he made his sketches of dancing Yvonne in her gauzy curtains, while Cynthia watched. Dibley would never go near, but nakedness was all right in the name of art, wasn't it? Did Ernst Zwanzig sign those sketches with the name of his dead teacher? Why had Jean Dorlean told her this?

She came upon Sean Patrick and Kaethe Muller in the lake, next to the raft, she floating in his supporting hands, her legs around him. What they were doing was so plain, so obvious, their disengagement when they saw her so fake and silly because there were their swimming suits on the raft. Why would she care what they did? Maybe, because Jean Dorlean was always talking to her, they thought she might tell him. But if he knew so much, as he claimed, he ought to know anyway. That he might know and not care was a concept new to her, another possible discovery about the indifferent and unloving world.

There was never a card or a letter from John Hearne.

Jean Dorlean kept finding her when she was alone. He had apologized for what he'd said and done before—apologized to Dibley, too, for upsetting him. He didn't seem as small or as freakish when he was sincere, and she began not to mind the interest he took in her. He knew a great deal, and wanted to teach her. "Where do you go to school?" he asked, meaning what college, and was astounded when she said nowhere. She began to believe that he was not flattering her for some devious purpose, and that he no longer patronized her. There was a feeling of equality that was disarming, though she was still wary.

One day he asked her for a sailing lesson, putting himself in the position of the beginner, so that she could teach him. He wasn't bad at picking up how to sail, but of course he had to give the standard confession of technical incompetence, which she knew meant overweening pride in other talents.

The wind was light and steady. After having him tack and jibe for a while she had him steer across the lake as closely into the wind as possible, watch his sails for luff and try to find the point of compromise.

"Ah," he said, "the inevitable compromise." But he did it well enough. He had a sturdy, muscular little body furred with reddish hair and she couldn't help, for an unbalanced moment, thinking of what it would be like with him. She was startled, though she gave no sign of it, that he knew what she had just thought—a connective glance, like a touch of antennae, nothing said, the idea immediately rejected by her.

He said, "Kaethe Muller is not my girlfriend, I hope you know. She said you saw her going into my room one night, so you might have got that impression."

Dory said nothing.

"I don't know why I have this compulsion to tell you things," he said. "Too damn many things. Oh, well. As for Fräulein Scharführerin Muller, we saved her, for our own reasons, from having her tits nailed to a barracks door—literally. And I'm her nursemaid at the moment. Does that make sense? I guess I tell you this because I don't want you to think of me as a cuckold."

Dory said nothing, so he shrugged and went on. "Since you won't ask it, I'll answer the question that ought to have occurred to you. I'm in what we call 'intelligence,' and I'm summer nursemaid here. You have your crew and I have mine, and may the two eventually disengage with as little publicity as possible. So how's that for candid? Do you deign to answer? To bless my existence with a little curiosity?"

He had trimmed his beard. He was getting sunburned on top of his head.

"Are you being sincere, or not?" she said. "What have these people got to do with the government?"

"Oh, you think they're sort of third-rate clowns, is that it? Dory, let me tell you that the war was fought by clowns, the camps were run by clowns. Only the victims didn't look funny. As for me, I hate this job and wouldn't mind if all my charges melted away like the Wicked Witch of the West, but now our clowns are in a war with their clowns and we use what we've got. Christ! Am I being sincere? How old are you—eighteen? Nineteen? I'm thirty-five and I can testify that most of the people on this planet are clownish swine. I hereby testify to that contemptible truth."

He did seem in pain; he didn't like what he'd said.

"You mean the people here are all Nazis?"

"In their souls they're Nazis. Haven't you heard the key words and phrases? They just don't like Hitler anymore—he was a carpet-eater, right? I'm not saying that they're all equally guilty, it's just that they don't, any of them, feel any different than they ever did or ever will. Did Werner brag about his father? Did he mention the *Ritterkreuz*—the Knight's Cross with oak leaves or whatever it was—and that he honorably fell in battle? *Heil* whoever! Actually we believe the Baron either deserted to the Russians or let himself be captured, and that he's very much alive and of some importance in Eastern Germany. The *Schutzstaffel* were not always as they seemed. So we have his son. Does he care? Will he eventually cooperate with us?

"And another thing. Werner wasn't just a little kid in the *Volkssturm,* he was an SS cadet, Klagenfurt, class of '44. And here's the sick part; when it was revealed to Himmler that the Baron had made his separate peace with the Russians, his son—this is typical Nazi logic—was used for revenge. He was posted to the *Totenkopfverbände* at Dachau. It was typical of the Nazis to feel sorry for themselves for having to murder so many people. Their sensitive souls suffered, don't you see. They were afraid a ten-foot pile of corpses might dehumanize them. What a pity. So Werner was posted there to punish his father, and given rather nasty work to do. We plucked him out of there when the place was liberated in April '45."

"But is he all right?"

"Meaning sane? I don't know. I imagine he's harmless enough. Even if I can't stand him, I must say the poor bastard's had a rough adolescence. And there's Sean Patrick, who was in the *Ausland SD* from 1942 on, a British-maddened Celt, and there are none as thoroughly insane as the Irish insane. Yvonne's husband is also alive in Eastern Germany and they're in contact with each other, through friends of ours. Anything else you're incurious about? Zwanzig is simply the pretentious con man he's always been, and the Princess is Werner's aunt and guardian. And she's a real princess, Dory—as real as any princess has ever been real. Kasimir is her servant, no more and no less. But, Dory, don't ever forget that these people are *real,* in the sense that the world and all its murdering swinishness is real. Do you understand? Christ, I still don't know why I'm compelled to tell you everything. Maybe it's like washing my dirty hands. Maybe it's that I want to corrupt you. Are you just innocent? Are you wise? You're not innocent. What the hell are you, anyway? Where do you get off being what you seem to be?"

On his own authority he came sloppily about and they headed back. She loosened the starboard shrouds and told him to let the sail out going downwind, and the wide, no-class boat eased toward Cascom Manor. A half mile away, next to the boathouse, Dibley watched, straight as a post.

"I don't know why I seem to be anything," she said. "I'm just myself. I've lived in Leah all my life and I just graduated in June from Leah High School."

"You appear to be honest. You're invulnerable to the shoddy beast I'm vulnerable to. And I can't believe you're that young. You don't act like a young girl."

"In Leah I'm not a young girl." At this moment she didn't feel like a young girl, she felt the mental and cultural equal of the mature, experienced man who wanted to tell her things almost in the way of confession. He said she was honest, and she honestly enjoyed his appreciation, but there was something wrong, something untrustworthy in this direction. Already she seemed to have traded something valuable for mere pleasure. But she enjoyed being admired and flattered, who didn't? And this man had been out in the wide world, the real world, where he had been hurt and made bitter by evil.

When they beached the sailboat Dibley wasn't there.

"That was fun," Jean Dorlean said. "Take me out again when the wind's stronger, will you? Do you think I'm getting the hang of it?"

In the warmth of his strange admiration she said yes, and she agreed. Though he looked at her tan legs, though when he'd been a little drunk he'd held her for a moment against her will, the power she'd felt in him was, as a memory, growing benign. And he represented the government of her country; she believed that. She might not be going to college but she was a student, and listened and observed. Flattery was praise you didn't deserve, and he hadn't said anything about her she didn't deserve.

But she would not let this person haze into the warm softening that meant friendship, understanding, generosity without suspicion. She was vulnerable, but she knew she was vulnerable, and the knowing was a warning and a strength.

That afternoon she picked up the Princess, who had gone to Boston to see a doctor, at the Leah depot. In the car she told Dory with her usual candor that she was not going to be pregnant, though Robert had hurt her horribly.

"He *hurt* you?"

"Alas, it is psychological," the Princess said. "I desire to arouse men but I cannot bear to have them handle me. Because Robert was so shy, and a virgin, I could not believe he would turn on me as he did."

Back at Cascom Manor she seemed her usual self. Dory thought, judgmentally, that if you were going to have hysteria, why didn't it matter in the end? It had certainly bothered Robert. Or maybe it didn't really bother him so much anymore, and he went around telling his friends about it, exaggerating, bragging how he grabbed the prick-teaser and put the wood to her whether she liked it or not. This way no one came out of it with any credit at all, but one could always think the worst.

And now there was the business of Debbie and Werner again. Werner had long ago given up on Cynthia, but in him was a constant need to impress, so now instead of insulting Debbie he treated her with politeness and a sort of gallantry that had no deprecating humor in it that Dory could see. Debbie was charmed and made happy. Her expressions didn't even look like hers. Dory had never seen her smile like that, never in all her life seen that proud, demure lift in Debbie's neck, that glow of importance. All of her new gestures and poses were felt, yet they looked like the exaggerations of acting. Her coquettish glances, which may have been caused by shyness and tremulous sincerity, were so obvious they caused pity, a kind of horror; Debbie was not witless, so she must be insane.

But that was Dory's own judgment. How much of it came from aesthetic prejudice—that Debbie was too fat, that Werner's strange misfitting body and personality precluded real feelings? The judger was no beauty herself. No, it was that Werner had treated Debbie badly once, and once was enough. No one changed. She had never seen anyone change. Your opinion of someone might possibly change, but the person never changed.

To Debbie it must be such a romance. The poor young American girl and the handsome European count with a tragic past, and then, in spite of their vastly different backgrounds, the things they suddenly find they have in common . . .

He had pulled Debbie's buttocks out of her bathing suit, the harsh red finger marks too near the places where touch meant violation, called her a cow in German, and a slut in English, to her sister. But what could her sister do? And did her older, loving, protecting sister want to make trouble, or would she let things ride and hope for the best, just hope for the best?

26

Bonnie wore a slippery light dress of pale green with strange liquid highlights that appeared and disappeared, a cloth-covered pocketbook to match, a red coral necklace and red pumps, both of which matched her lipstick exactly. He thought of the over-lush fragility of cut flowers.

They drove up into parched mountains that were composed of reddish dirt covered by scrub brush turning gray, where the only permanent feature was the curving shelf of the highway. Below in yellow haze were the cities of the plain, all one city; then, beyond the haze, the blue ocean. They drove northwest until the highway began to descend toward sparsely inhabited hills starved for water. They passed a scarred hillside where rows and parabolas of houses were being built all at once. Looking at this dusty, marginal world made him uneasy, as if he were responsible, or in danger along with the deprived trees that had been metered their water. The feeling was not so much of thirst as it was of suffocation. In spite of the glinting energy of passing cars, the unfocused sunlight and all the building—fragile, minimal sticks above thin slabs—it seemed a land of children who would eventually be called home from play.

They descended further, into a cityless suburb of small homes and pampered shrubs, until the land greened somewhat and they could see the ocean. "Here we are," Bonnie said, and stopped at a restaurant, or roadhouse, with the look of walled secrecy on the street side. They went through its darkness, however, and came out on a bright patio from which they could see the blue Pacific. Here were widely separated chairs and tables, all with an expensive, cared-for look, of redwood, heavy linen and silver. "This place is special," she said. "People come here all the way from Santa Barbara."

He decided to have a beer and had to undergo the self-exaggerated humility of having to show the waitress his driver's license in order to prove himself twenty-one, which made him feel, as usual, that he was cursed by youth, that he was going through life but not quite of it. If he were, say, twenty-six, the ideal age, he and Bonnie . . .

"I was just thinking," Bonnie said. "Since you're so much better—it's a miracle, isn't it? And don't think our Healing Echelons had nothing to do with it! You could get a job with Oval at the Produce Co-op."

"Yeah, maybe," he said doubtfully, trying not to sound ungrateful. The waitress brought him a blue blazer and tie, so that he'd conform to the decor. He put on these public garments and felt regionally nautical in his brass buttons and also camouflaged, a little more secure.

She instructed him upon their meal, the specialty of the place, a mollusk called abalone, whose flesh had to be pounded with a mallet. "Have you ever had it?" she asked.

He noticed how the other people in the restaurant tried not to stare at her, and how in low voices they discussed her, wondering who she was.

"I've had baloney," he said, "but not abalone."

"Ha, ha!" she laughed. Other people smiled to hear her laugh. He was not just observing the most beautiful woman he had ever seen, he was sitting at a table with her, looking for a moment at her teeth, pearly utilitarian incisors and crushers thrusting from pink gums, and thinking all at once how there was an idea of perfection even in such a randomly limbed, toed and fingered and leaking a creature as a human. Her perfect skin must indicate a perfect soul; there were others in the room who thought so.

Her skin was translucent; he could see into it, where there was rose, ivory, even a trace of blue . . .

"You're not listening," she said. "What were you thinking about?"

"I was thinking about the color of your skin."

"Oh, *John,*" she said. In her blush came darkness before color, some of the shimmery green of her dress, too, and the unpowdery texture of a flower petal, say a white lily slashed with blood red.

The abalone had the texture of scallops and the taste given it by the chef.

She wouldn't let him pay for anything—really wouldn't—and when they left the restaurant she flattered him by asking him to drive, saying the wine had affected her. She would tell him where to go. In the car she sat close to him as if on a high school date, her hand lightly on his arm and her vivid knees high because of the drive-shaft hump. Whenever she pointed she first squeezed his proud muscled arm. How friendly and meaningless was the garden land of southern California; it was all vacation, the houses playful, the cars toys, the trees and flowers fakely pretty. Nothing seemed to matter very much. The slave-smooth purr of the engine was nice, and her hand on his arm was praise. With this kind of going he didn't want a destination, but she asked him if he wouldn't like to see Ozzie Rittheuber's estate, Gladland, which wasn't far from here.

He thought it a defect in himself that he wasn't purely curious about things like this. He didn't want to meet a man who claimed he could be in three places at the same time. What could be said to such a person? Even to say hello would be a form of lie.

"Ozzie probably won't be there," Bonnie said. "But we'll have the run of the place anyway. You really ought to see it."

"Ozzie's in three other places?" he said.

She laughed, though she punched him lightly on the shoulder to show her disapproval.

They were leaving, on a broad avenue, a neighborhood of kept-up lawns and small prideful houses. The boulevard strips became bleached and dusty, the vacant lots and acres sparsely covered with grass that looked tough as wire, and olive-drab bushes that were barely making it. Then, on the right, beyond a pale adobe wall, were the tops of lush trees. Bonnie said, "Here we are, if you want to."

They came to a wide wrought-iron gate in the adobe, the iron word GLADLAND forming part of its grille. He turned in, resigned to this visit, and Bonnie got out and opened the gates with a key she took from her purse. When he drove through she closed the gate and made sure it was latched and locked. They were on a black asphalt drive between columns of funereal arborvitae. Bonnie got back in the car and they drove another hundred yards and came to an adobe mansion with many low roofs of red tile, a cloisterlike columned porch among green shrubs and trees all foreign to him. She said jacaranda, African tulip, pride of

India, hibiscus, bougainvillea, bird of paradise, poinciana—names that were familiar but without images. Even in their presence, her hand gracefully pointing, they were all one heady excess. He parked the car and they went into cool long rooms full of flowers and heavy wooden furniture, long tables and upright chairs that looked uncomfortable and out of place. He'd never seen television in a private house, only in bars, but here was the brown box with the gray porthole.

A gray-haired woman in a white robe drifted past them, smiling benevolently but not quite in specific recognition.

"Ozzie's mother," Bonnie said when the woman had drifted on. A young girl, maybe twelve, also in a white robe, followed Ozzie's mother, carrying white bath towels. She smiled the same smile and seemed a smaller, earlier version of the woman. Over a metal door was a red glass sign, not illuminated but readable, saying, ON THE AIR. "Ozzie's radio studio," Bonnie said.

They passed into a room of deep carpeting, deep couches and easy chairs where all the colors were warm tints of rose. "The Life Room," Bonnie said. "Ozzie has classes here. Everyone glows."

"You're glowing," he said.

"And so are you, John. Isn't that clever? Ozzie teaches that we absorb color, sort of like chameleons, so it's important to have life-colors, what he calls the bio-colors, when we open ourselves to the Life-Mind. Sometimes he uses the mauve room, which is calmer. It depends on the class. It's just fascinating, really. For the children he sometimes uses the green room, to calm them and make them understand the oneness of life forms. The Life Room is for the deplenished in spirit."

They traversed these rooms, then left the coolness of the mansion and crossed a lawn, avoiding the swaths of a sprinkler, to the pool, which seemed jagged until he recognized it as a huge cross in pink ceramic tile which made the water a warm gray, as if the pool were full of smoke instead of water.

"I wonder if you could take a dip with your knee," Bonnie said. "We could take a short dip, I bet. I can't stay in the sun because I'm not supposed to have a tan on the assignment I'm on. I'm supposed to look pale and sophisticated. La-di-da."

Ozzie's mother swam a slow sidestroke along one segment of the cross, the young girl walking along above her, carrying towels. "Ozzie's mother and her granddaughter—Ozzie's sister's child," Bonnie said. "They're wearing white, so they can't talk. White is silence."

"Oh," he said.

"White is the color of infinity, purity and restfulness. You're real calm and silent, then, and everybody's the same."

"The same?"

"Old and young, male and female—all the exact same. All differences are filtered out by white, which is all colors reflected at once, you see. The whole spectrum—red, orange, yellow, green, blue, indigo and violet (you know how to remember that? Think of a man's name: Roy G. Biv) —all received and translated back to the Universal, so in white we are one with the Vast Loving Silence."

Bonnie led him to the bathhouse, a small version of the main house. In its dim interior were shelves of one-piece bathing suits, all white, all the same except for size. "Can we talk if we wear these?" he said. "Can we splash and giggle and do cannonballs?"

"Oh, John," she said, and went behind a partition to change.

Her white suit did not change or conceal, at least to his infidel eyes, anything, and while their suits didn't cause silence in Bonnie, she did speak thereafter in a lower voice. She rose from the water gleaming, and twirled, shedding diamonds; the cotton suit when wet was so transparent he looked away from her unselfconscious nipples and shadowy triangle. The suits were thin and institutional, as if out of the thirties when much skin was covered but everything beneath the cloth was clearly defined. But it was Bonnie herself who was transparent, guileless and sweet. Exposed to her in the sun while she arranged an umbrella to keep her skin ivory, he felt that his cupidity was stealing something valuable from him. He preened, thinking what a figure he cut, soaked bandages and all, yet how dishonest he was in his friendliness toward her. She had paid him back ten times for the accident on Los Robles. Her transparency was the truth, his salacious thoughts evil, his cynical thoughts in error. How nice to believe that. How nice to believe anything. There was evil in the world, evil everywhere beyond thinking about, murderous child-killing evil. He believed in that, so why not believe in its opposite? Why not believe in the goodness of her screwy beliefs? Men had used Bonnie and hurt her, who was good. He was not of that evil, so he entered the delicious slide of his own seduction. Farewell logic, farewell intelligence. He shivered with loss.

They lay on the grass at the periphery of a sprinkler's reach, fine droplets sometimes touching them as the swath came around. She lay in the shade, he in the sun, and she looked at him, her eyes luminous and meaningful. He looked back steadily and they didn't speak, a weighty moment. She reached for his hand and put it on her breast. "We are one," she said softly, "one and indivisible in God's infinite love."

It was lovely, but he could only play at it. He tried. He could almost make it into the invulnerable sincerity of her world. At least he saw, for an instant, what it would be like. Imagine the benevolent answers, the impervious optimism, Our Father who aren't in heaven. He leaned over her and kissed her on the lips, chastely, he thought, but Satan rose in him at once and he moved too far over her. She pushed him away, not ungently, and said, "It wouldn't be love."

"Why not?"

"We're not right for each other that way."

"I'm afraid I can't get the ways separated," he said.

"I hope I didn't tease you, John. I didn't mean to. I do love you, John, for what you are, but . . ."

How flat the world went. She was right, of course. Friendship and the kind of love she meant were not enough to banish sudden boredom, loss, borderline anxiety. He wanted to own her altogether, inside and out. If he couldn't have all of her he didn't want any of her. A little boy in him pouted despicably.

"I mean I hope I didn't make you think we could be lovers," she said, worried for him. "I guess I shouldn't have got us into these baptismal suits. I can see that now. I always thought they were too thin, but Ozzie says the early Christians went naked into the waters—a symbol of death and then rebirth in Christ. But I guess you don't believe in that so much, so we just look sort of naked and it must have seemed that I was trying to arouse you." She reached for his hand but changed her mind and quickly took hers back.

"It's okay," he said. "You don't have to do anything to arouse me. I just think of you and I'm aroused."

"But is that all you feel?"

"Is it a sin?" he asked evasively.

"We don't have sins. I mean we might use the word, but a sin isn't something positive, it's just a negative, something without love."

He'd been hearing that word so much it began to veer toward a nonsense sound—a children's game with a word. "So what is love, then?" he said. "Wouldn't I love you if I made love to you?"

"I've been made love to without love. I've been loved without being made love to. I've been made love to with love, too," she said seriously.

"I'd love to make love to you with love, too," he said.

"Oh, John!" She laughed, but she said, "You can't 'make' love. You either love or you don't love. Only God made love, as He made us all, as He made the lamb. He is our Shepherd. We are enjoined in His Spirit and in Christ to love."

"Bonnie, you know what shepherds do to lambs?"

"Love and protect them."

"So they can eat them later."

"Oh, John, the meaning doesn't mean that. It doesn't go that far. They protect them from getting lost and from wolves."

"The wolves are trying to make a living too."

"Where did you ever get so bitter and cynical? Was it in the Army? Or because of your lost father? I was bitter once, too, but Oval and CSW saved me."

He almost asked her if Oval was her lover, who made love to her with love, but at that moment Ozzie's mother and granddaughter appeared, the granddaughter with a tray holding four tall glasses of orange juice. They sat down, Indian fashion, and offered the orange juice, their silence and loving smiles.

He and Bonnie sat up, so the four of them faced each other, all wearing the identical translucent bathing suits, sipping orange juice. He tried to smile, and perhaps did, but he couldn't close his eyes or look away. What the old woman and the young girl proffered to his captured vision were the details he mercilessly catalogued. The grandmother's skin hung from her bones in the bunched, mottled, soiled-looking patterns of age, her pubic hair a snarled gray patch, her long dugs flat against the sides of her belly. The granddaughter's skin was pearl smooth, her breasts barely beginning to swell, her plain young face simple and unfinished. Her expression, like her grandmother's, was doctrinal, unnatural, too sweetly uncaused. In her child-slim crotch he saw the simple fold of her and looked away toward Bonnie, where he had to note the rose surrounding her thimblelike nipples. He asked himself what he should be seeing, anyway. The young girl seemed to be joyously examining his forehead. The old woman seemed fond of her life and condition, proud of all of them, in love with her orange juice. His own eyes were openings to his consciousness, unfiltered. What was he supposed to notice or not notice?

Bonnie's toenails were enameled blood red and her little toe was homely and bent, with a small sallow coin of bunion. Sunlight, diffused by haze, pressed upon his head and shoulders. The random droplets from the sprinkler were pinpricks. Bonnie seemed as pleased and satisfied as the two other females, and he had a boy-shame of being here in their moist, indulgent aura. It was not a man's life to be so surrounded by them. The immodest way they presented their near-nakedness to him was in itself female. Surely they must be aware of his criminal eyes and ignoble thoughts.

When the orange juice was finished the old woman and the young girl, still in silence, went back to the mansion and he could stretch and yawn like a dog.

"Look out," Bonnie said. "You'll break something."

They went to the bathhouse and got dressed. When Bonnie came out of her cubicle, shimmering in green again but with straight wet hair, she said, "I'm so sorry if I did anything to lead you on. I really didn't mean to. I just wanted to be friends and we can love each other, can't we? Without the other thing?"

"Sure, Bonnie."

"You have your little girl in New Hampshire and I'm much too old for you."

"And you've got Oval."

"It's true I love him, but Oval won't touch me."

"He must be out of his mind."

"He says he's my teacher and he won't take advantage of that."

"He *must* be a saint."

When they got back to the parsonage in Tulaveda a tall man came out on the porch. He was lanky and his clothes seemed to be held up by odd ridges of bone and muscle. The clothes themselves were cheap, gaudy and wrinkled—yellow pants and a green sports shirt, tan-and-yellow shoes. His face was pale and lean, his lips full, with a sweetly worried look.

"Oval!" Bonnie said. "You're back!"

John remembered what he had forgotten to remember, the pure, handsome innocence of the face. It would substitute candor for all cleverness, even for intelligence. It proclaimed that it would, that everything would be seen, always, that nothing was worth concealment or indirection, ever.

"Hadasha told me your name and that you were from New Hampshire," the man said in a tenor voice that was suddenly more familiar than his looks. "Are you from Leah? Is your mother's name Martha?"

"Yes," John said. He was at least three persons at this moment. He had time to think this, with a lurch of disembodiment. He was his own self, with all his grown history; a half-person in another's white shirt; a small child bound in memory and the choked paralysis of wonder that had in it some resentment—an emotion he was not all that familiar with and which made him think of his own victims, as if he were one of them—some hurt, unhappy child he might have snubbed or been mean to, or a girl he had abandoned, like Virginia Hadar, who wondered why he never wrote to her.

"Come in," the man said. "Bonnie, you come too."

If this awkward-looking man was his father there were certain immediate judgments he had to make. For one, the fellow's clothes were tacky, from another class than his. This was of no great importance but it was a fact. The five-year-old wouldn't have known or cared; the ten-year-old would have noticed. Who would ever buy brown-and-yellow shoes, the brown all gingerbreading?

They went into 601-B and through to what was probably 601-A, the other half of the parsonage where Oval Forester's office was, and what seemed to be classrooms, folding wooden chairs glimpsed in passing. In the office was another portrait of Christ, heroic and kind in thorns, gazing out of mist. Bonnie sat on a leather couch, next to him, while Oval, or whoever he was, his posture and expression indicating worry and concern, walked back and forth before a large wooden desk. He looked too young, an aging youth, his face simplified by its lack of reserve. His hair was an almost dyed-looking black above his high pale forehead. Maybe he was a more imposing man when he didn't have an explanation or a confession to make.

"Do you know John's father?" Bonnie asked.

"You've recognized me, haven't you?" Oval, or Sylvan, said to John.

"I think so," John said.

"I was told you'd been adopted by Amos Sylvester and taken his name and it would be best if I bowed out of your life altogether. That was ten years, thirteen years ago."

"Amos?" John said, a half-uttered bubble of strange laughter.

"But you call yourself John Hearne."

"It's my name," John said. "Did my mother tell you all that?"

"Yes, Martha wrote that to me."

"It figures," John said.

"She said he was a marvelous father to you."

He couldn't think of anything to say. It seemed perfectly logical that his mother would have said that Amos was a marvelous father.

"Don't be too hard on her," Oval, or Sylvan, said. "She must have wanted it so much she decided it had to happen, so she just said it. She tends to do that. She really means well. She's a fine woman."

"I always had the impression she was a fucking liar."

"Hey, Johnny. Johnny."

"Oval?" Bonnie said. "You're all upset and you're making me upset! What is it? What is it? Are you John's father?"

"I'm sorry," John said. "I'm a big boy now. Ancient resentments and all that. But if you used to be Sylvan Hearne, how come you're now Oval Forester?"

"I didn't want to leave you, Johnny. I loved you more than anything in the world."

"Yeah. Okay."

"Oval?" Bonnie said.

"You had to live with your mother. It's the law. And then when Amos wanted to adopt you . . ."

"We can forget that part," John said. "The whole idea is a little nauseating."

"I don't blame you for blaming us. But we always loved you, Johnny, both of us, no matter what."

"Oval!" Bonnie said. "I don't understand! Is it true? And all the things about truth? You never would have told me?"

"Bonnie, dear," Oval, or Sylvan, said. "I'm sorry. Of course I'll explain. I took a man's place, that's all. He was afraid and I was too old to be drafted, with Thelma as a dependent, so I took his name and he took mine. It doesn't matter. The Good Lord knows who we are."

"And you were drafted?" John said.

"I enlisted in the Navy as Oval Forester."

"She told me it was Amos made her cut off any contact with you."

"Be easy on her, Johnny. She wanted something else. She wanted the best for you."

"It's amazing. You can't disbelieve everything, no matter how cautious you are," John said.

"That's so true," Bonnie said. "You've got to believe something. Oval never was your real name. How can I believe anything now? What happened to Thelma when you went in the Navy? Where was your wife? How did you get away with it? Is it true at all?"

"My wife was long gone by then, and his mother—Oval Forester's mother—took care of Thelma. I had a monthly pay allotment sent to her. I couldn't tell you because the man who's called Sylvan Hearne has a family now. Only he and his mother know the truth. Listen, Bonnie, dear, please. He's the kind of person who'd have been destroyed in boot camp, let alone in combat. Some people just can't do what you have to do in the service. They have talents, but not that kind. As for getting away with it, who cared in 1942? The country got its sailor."

"You could have trusted me," Bonnie said. "There's something wrong with all of it."

"Do you want proof? Here's my son who recognizes me from another life. There's an honorable discharge from the Navy in that drawer there with my thumbprint on it. Maybe it was all a lie, but I don't think God would chide me for it, even if my reasons weren't so noble. I wanted a vacation from a boring job and also, I have to confess, from taking care of poor Thelma, bless her heart. So I got to cruise around the Pacific for a couple of years on a submarine tender. Meanwhile Thelma got loving care from a grateful woman. Does the Lord judge me a cheat? It's not for me to ask."

Bonnie got up and went to a window, where brownish gauze curtains made the light seem old. "It sounds possible," she said. "It sounds noble, too, except for leaving Thelma. It's just that I can't believe you wouldn't have told me. There's nothing I haven't told you, nothing. I bared my soul to you and you weren't even the person whose name I called you. All the time you had a secret from me."

Oval said in his sweet, light voice, "Dear Bonnie, no one hates secrets more than I do. If it was a secret it wasn't my secret, it was his and his mother's secret. As for me, I'm Oval now and I'll always be Oval. When we bared our souls to Christ and to each other I was Oval."

"Oh, I don't know! I don't know!" Bonnie cried.

A preacher's grave tonality came into Oval's voice. "Let us put our faith in a loving, all-wise, all-powerful God," he said. He went up behind her and put his hands on her shoulders. "A God everywhere present, knowing we are His children, made in His image and likeness, whole and complete in His eyes. With such faith our names, our worldly goods, our reputations, are nothing, for we will be our true selves, linked to the inexhaustible forces of the Infinite Mind of the Universe."

John could see that Bonnie was not convinced; while she wanted to be convinced, she kept finding herself unconvinced. Her shoulders softened, then grew straight again. She turned, her mouth drooping, questions shading a face pretty even as it pouted and felt sorry for itself.

He listened with an irritating sense of loss, as if coins were falling out of his hands into deep water and he couldn't ever get them back. Oval—it was better to think of the man as Oval—kept talking Lord, God, Christ and love, love, love. John, if he ever had to name the man, his father, would call him Oval as a sort of necessary evasion, the way he always used the word "love" as if it had quotes around it.

Soon Bonnie let herself be calmed. She put her head on Oval's green chest for a moment as if bowing to a superior force. In the quiet of this brief ceremony Thelma came thumping in. "I'm a bee!" she said in a throaty voice like a burp. "I'm a bee!" Evidently Thelma had learned at school how to be a bee.

"Yes, they're coming," Oval said. "I've got to work all night tonight getting the trays set up."

"I'm a bee coming!" she said. She took John's hands in hers, her lopsided head squashed with delight, her amorphous body parts galumphing. "I'm a bee coming, John!"

This, by God, was his half-sister, his sister, flesh of his flesh, who wanted to play ring-around-the-rosy, good nature spilling from a leaky vessel. Here you are, Thelma, a foundering ship, whoever built you, and here is your half-brother, son of an untrustworthy mother and this implausibly pseudonymous saint whose voice, he believes, is linked to the inexhaustible forces of the Infinite Mind of the Universe.

Thelma's skewed blue eyes looked gleefully into his, one more accurately than the other. "John wih hep you, Daddy!" she said.

"Come, Thelma," Bonnie said. "Let's get all the finger paints off you. Let's get all cleaned up so we'll be nice and neat." Bonnie's idea was to leave father and son alone to catch up on the lost years, but when they were alone they found it hard to look at each other. After a silence long enough to have become meaningful, the father said, "You must have got this address from Estelle."

"Yes."

"Did you remember Winota? Did you meet anyone else besides Estelle? She's such a wonderful person." His smile seemed too pleased, his lips bowed to the point of recurve.

"I remembered being pretty happy there," John said. "I met Estelle's niece, Gracie Lundgren, and Miles Wagner. His parents said you were 'a clean man.' "

"George and Ada Wagner! I had some wonderful friends in Lou' Qui Parle County!"

"My mother told me once that you were 'playing around' with Estelle. Was that another of her lies?"

"You're still back there, aren't you, Johnny? I don't blame you. I guess you got a raw deal, all right. I met Amos Sylvester once and he seemed like a pretty mixed-up sort of fellow. The question about Estelle I can't answer because, forgive me, Johnny, that's her business."

His father's version of the divorce, which John hadn't really intended to get into, was that Martha was simply "bowled over" by Amos Sylvester. Also she was sick of Winota and wanted to go East—you couldn't blame her. She was twenty-six years old, a pretty and lively young woman, and she felt she was in a dead end. Who could blame her for having those feelings? She'd go to Minneapolis a lot with a friend of hers, Esther Peterson, just to be in the city. Meanwhile, Estelle Lundgren was living with them above the *Herald,* and one thing led to another and people began to talk. After Martha went away with Amos, Sonny Hilberg got him fired from the *Herald.* Estelle didn't know that, so don't ever mention it. Anyway, he took off for California, like half the people in the country, it seemed. Those were hard times. When he got a job in San Diego he wrote to have Johnny maybe spend some time with him, or at least keep in contact with him, but Martha thought it would be best not to, that Amos was his father now. "I didn't have much money, and in a way I guess I wanted to believe it might be best for you, but I missed you, Johnny. I always did."

There was still that fading, this amiable man washing out before his eyes. Resentment seemed wasted, too complicated for such pale and kindly good nature. But he had to answer his father's questions, filling the blank places, wondering how to sum up his childhood in Leah, where he'd navigated by dead reckoning among willful children and childish adults. Well, he got here somehow and it wasn't all that bad, even if he had been eager to go into the Army. Georgia, Okinawa, the end of the war, Japan, Fort Dix, the university, no major yet. Yes, Martha was fine, Amos his usual pain in the ass. No real complaints.

He didn't go back to the long seasons of dread and evasion, when the world of adults seemed insane and he hid with books and fantasies of rescue. He had some friends, later, when old enough to have the time with friends. There were lots of fights, embarrassments, but maybe that was normal. High school was boring, dumb, avoidable a lot of the time because his mother was always ready to sign excuses, no matter how dishonest.

His father's wide blue eyes stared at him, unselfconsciously avid, and he thought: What good would this father have been? At least there would have been no broken glass, gin fits, howls, unpredictable giants crashing through doors, a child with no place below a roof to hide. Imagine abandoning your own child.

Oh, well, he got through those years all right, and here he was. There was no way now to tell what kind of person he might have been.

At supper Bonnie told what had happened with Urban Stumms. She was subdued, and didn't make John quite the hero she'd seemed to think him at the time, as if she might now know the real truth about what had happened on the roof peak. His father (Oval, he thought: Oval) thought it a brave and responsible thing to have done, and said so, praising him, the praise a faint music for another time.

"I'll stop in and see Urban on the way to the Co-op," Oval (his father) said.

"I'm a bee coming!" Thelma said, and John understood that she'd meant lima beans. "John wih hep you, Daddy!"

So he did help. They drove in Oval's '40 Buick to the Church Ovarian Apocalyptic and Maria let them in, relieved to see them. "He sleeps, maybe," she said. Oval went on upstairs and in a little while returned to the kitchen.

"He's coming with us," he said. "He's getting dressed."

"You watch him," Maria said, meaning that Oval would know how to watch him.

Urban came down buckling his belt and shaking his head like a stunned creature, expressionless in his scar tissue. Goo had run out of his eye slots, so Maria dampened a paper towel and delicately wiped it off. In the process an eye glinted at John. "Hi, there, sport," Urban said, meaning it was okay but maybe they had further business to discuss.

At dusk they parked next to a factory building that was so long it diminished in haze toward the vanishing point, steam venting from it here and there, lighted windows at odd places. The long building rumbled and hissed as it slept by its railroad siding. A watchman nodded to Oval as they entered the gate and crossed a catwalk into the vaulted interior of the place. Here was the freezing machine itself, a girdered cube two stories high. Oval turned on more lights. There were two narrow doors on this side, one at each corner, refrigerator doors with frosted hatch-wheel closures, neither more than four feet high. Above one someone had written in chalk on the board-and-batten siding: OVAL'S FOLLY, and beneath that: ABANDON HOPE, ALL YE WHO ENTER HERE. Above the other door the same wit, perhaps, had written: ARBEIT MACHT FREI.

Oval paid no attention to these signs. "Trays and more trays," he said. The trays he had trucked from Seattle were stacked beside the freezer, at least a hundred of them. They were aluminum, about ten feet long, just wide and deep enough to accept frozen-food packages. Several battered lockers stood next to the trays, and Oval searched through them until he found surplus Air Corps flight suits that fit Urban and John. They were alpaca-lined, with hoods. He also found them Air Corps lined leather gloves and fleece-lined leather flight boots. Urban muttered about never having thought he'd have to wear such shit again. "Suit, flight, lined," he read from the labels. "Gloves, flight, lined. Boots, flight, fleece, fuck." But when they were all outfitted he bent to enter the thick, four-foot door, into a brittle arctic world, the iron-secret world of below zero.

"The fans aren't on full," Oval said. "But don't let your skin touch anything. Poor fellow lost the tip of his nose."

They were in a small space surrounded by trays hung on drive chains that were like motorcycle chains but bigger, the chains weaving through large and small sprockets. Next to the door was a slot with a rubber flap, where the packages would enter the machine from a conveyor belt and fill the tray positioned there at the time. "Then they go up through the machine," Oval said with no pride of inventiveness, his voice smaller and higher, as if frozen in transit. Frost flowers grew on the chain links and I beams near the door and the package slot. "But they bend and buckle and break sometimes. I never know where or when it's going to happen and it doesn't make sense."

He led them up a narrow iron ladder to the next level, where the chains and sprockets took the trays horizontally. Here the trays had twisted and torn themselves from their hangers, and at least one chain was off its sprocket. "No reason for it," Oval said. "The chains are in sync, the sprockets all free. Why does it run perfectly sometimes and other times it eats itself up? Don't ask me." He'd gone from lithium-based grease to cold-weather aviation lubricants to powdered graphite, but that didn't seem to make much difference. In a day or two the lima beans would come by the billions and they'd have to run night and day. A hundred women up the line would be culling, blanching and boxing lima beans and they had to be frozen immediately, right now, this instant. Some would go into another freezer on hand trucks but this machine had to function. And it had to be helped and supervised all the time. "You can stay inside about twenty minutes at the most, then you have to go outside and thaw for ten to get the feeling back in your fingers," he said. He took them higher, up near the roof where the fans blew across the Freon coils. Up here the trays were turned in an arc so that they could proceed around and down by stages through the back of the freezer, where each paused at another slot and a plunger disgorged the packages onto hand trucks that were then wheeled to the main storage freezer. It was here, though, at the roof level, where the worst carnage could happen. He dreamed, Oval said, of metal coiling and wrapping over and around itself while the pure, clean lima beans were torn from their boxes, bruised and thrown down through the machinery. "A waste, a terrible waste," he said in sorrow. In his hood he looked like a mourner, like a monk, pale except for flushed fever spots on his chilled cheekbones.

They walked single file on narrow planks bolted to I beams. SECTOR 3, a small sign said. There were five sectors in all, and in each was a kill switch for the main drive motor.

That night they repaired chain with replacement links, and wrestled with, removed and replaced twenty trays. After a few minutes the simple act of fitting a wrench to a nut became difficult, as though their own hands were mechanical claws directed inefficiently by remote control. The metal, too, behaved strangely, almost as if it were fused, brittle as glass, so that a careful, mounting pressure of torque was necessary, rather than a sudden force. This was not just the severe cold of outdoors in winter. In spite of the constant wind it was stifling, alien, of another magnitude altogether. The rules of physics no doubt applied here, but what should have been the simple, learned rules no longer wholly applied, as if this were an alternate, crystalline universe, their breath wisps of dusty ice.

On one ten-minute break they sat on piles of folded cardboard cartons, John and Urban smoking cigarettes. Urban said he was going to have to rent out his church. "Even if anybody comes tomorrow I'd be useless," he said. "I'm going to do something else for a while and rethink the Ovarian Doctrine. Something's wrong there, Oval. It's knocked the shit out of my calculations."

"Work here with me while you meditate," Oval said. "Let this be your wilderness."

John looked closely for humor or for the slightest tinge of patronization but found none. They were both pastors, fellow professionals in the mumbo-jumbo business, and evidently weren't about to have arguments over doctrine.

"Also," Urban said, "Maria's knocked up, she informed me around noon today, so I've got to make an honest woman of her."

"Why, that's wonderful!" Oval said. "Congratulations, Urban! Maria's a wonderful woman! She'll make you so happy!"

"Happy," Urban said with a bitter laugh. "That'd be the worst sin of all." He looked at John, not unkindly but it was hard to tell, and said, "You can safely give me back that pistol barrel."

"Okay," John said.

"I suppose I appreciate what you did even if it made me look like a damn fool," Urban said.

"Well, I . . . ," John said.

"Course I wouldn't have looked any less a damn fool if I'd blown my brains all over the neighborhood."

"Now, Urban, old pal, that's all in the past," Oval said.

On breaks they took their wrenches and crowbars out with them so their tools would warm a little and not suck so much warmth through their gloves. On another break Oval seemed nervous. He looked here and there, to the right of John and to the left of him, and said, "What about you, Johnny? The job pays well—a dollar-ten an hour, time and a half after forty hours, double time on Sundays. You might have to put in a lot of hours, but that's good money. You can stay at the parsonage and save rent and take a peck of dough back to school with you. What do you say?"

John thought for a moment. The man was wholesome, like Jack Armstrong, the All-American Boy, or a lankier Superman, good and simple. He was afraid he'd found out what he could find out about his father. He could not dislike him, but then nobody could. It was all too easy. When his motorcycle was fixed he should pay for the repairs, sell it and take a bus somewhere, maybe straight back East. His far past now contained few mysteries, and they were probably disappointing. It was all too easy. "Okay," he said unexpectedly, "if I can chip in for groceries."

Oval was terrifically pleased. He reached out, put his arm around his son's shoulders and gave him a manly jerk of a hug, cold air exhaling from their clothes.

He had agreed to Oval's, Sylvan's, his father's, offer, and one of his reasons, if a vague one, was ridiculous, and it was Bonnie, not her friendship but a sort of unminded beauty worship or star worship he judged to be puerile, like that of a fan in a fan club. He had never felt, would never feel, adoration. But there she was, still shimmering. She said she loved him, placed his hand on her breast and kissed him, a mystery. Yes, but that wasn't it; maybe he didn't know why he said okay. Maybe he just wanted to be agreeable.

At three in the morning they let Urban off at the Church Ovarian Apocalyptic. Maria was up, waiting for him, and John's irreverent thought was that Maria's ovarian condition, though not quite apocalyptic, was at least real. And then of pale, dimming Dory, who might have been in the same condition but wasn't, and his unexpected lack of relief when they'd found she wasn't. He must send her a card or a letter, because he'd said he would.

When they parked beside the parsonage Oval was exhausted. "Oh, Lord, I'm tired but Your Work must be done," he said. Before tonight he'd been driving for two days with little sleep, that taken beside the road, but he had to prepare a sermon for the morning. He sighed as he turned off the engine. "There's no reason for you to feel you ought to come to church," he said. "I'm not sure what your beliefs are, Johnny, but I know you're a loving person."

"I believe Our Father aren't in heaven," John said.

"Oh, ha! That's the way you used to say it! I remember! Out of the mouths of babes, huh? Well, maybe you were right! I think I'll use that in my sermon tomorrow!"

John washed up, changed his one remaining bandage and took his loving self to bed. He woke at noon, so he did miss the sermon. That afternoon Bonnie told him that Oval was just as happy because it hadn't been one of his best and John's presence would have made him nervous —his judgmental son, the college boy. Oval had, he'd told her, only two semesters at Mankato State and later his necessary courses at the New Metaphysics Seminary, and most of those by correspondence. Yet, John thought, he'd been a newspaperman, and his article in *Avatar: A Quarterly Devoted to Metaphysical Thought* was literate in its language, if eclectic to a fault in its literary figures: "Consider your soul an internal-combustion engine firing on only three cylinders . . ."

He walked down Los Robles to a drugstore and bought some post-cards of Tulaveda, featuring royal palms and an adobe mission he hadn't seen, the sky bluer in the photograph than he'd ever seen it. Back in his room he sat down to write one to Dory, thinking casually that she loved him, thinking that he casually thought she loved him, thinking that he was a shit to casually think that she loved him. "Dear Dory," he wrote, and her name grew powerful, making him remember a dream of last night in which she'd been floating solemnly alongside him, maybe in water, and she'd embraced him with one arm and with the other reached right up his anus, hand and arm easily, weirdly, normally slipping in farther and farther, up his large and then his small intestine the way you put on a long sock or glove, her whole arm going up inside him until she firmly grasped his "tripas"—the operating dream word. There were always words in his dreams.

Dear Dory,

How is Cascom Manor this summer? I'm here, about to become a professional lima bean freezer. You know how I love lima beans. See you in Sept. Let me know how you're doing.

love,
John

Dear Mother,

Got out west okay. Have a job freezing lima beans. See you in Sept.

love,
John

Dear Gracie, Loretta & Miles,

Fond memories of Winota and your hospitality. Located my father and have a job freezing lima beans. Cold work in a hot place. How are you all?

Best,
John

Dear Estelle,

I found him. You were right, he's a nice fellow. Working with him in a lima bean freezer this summer.

Best, & thanks,
John

Little spoor-tracks, he supposed, easily thrown. Lies only of omission; once you got down to it, it was easy to get these promises out of the way.

27

One day a cool northwest wind flowed tirelessly over the shoulder of Cascom Mountain and stippled the lake with whitecaps. The tamaracks hissed, and even the morning clamor of birdsong was hushed by the push of air.

At breakfast Jean Dorlean reminded her of her promise to take him sailing in a good wind, but of course she had already remembered it, wondering, with a little thrill like a gamble, if he would remember.

After the breakfast dishes were done and the tables set for lunch, Dibley came near her, as if he were forcing himself against another kind of energy, closer and closer to her. She stood at the desk in the hall, making a list of things that had to be done, and done, and no doubt done again. He tried to speak: "Today," he said, unable to utter the words that went with it.

"Today?" she asked.

"You should stay here."

"Why?"

"Stay here," he said, little white bumps moving along his jaw. He had stepped in front of her to stop her, but he couldn't explain. "Stay here today," he said.

"Why, Dibley?" she asked. "It's okay, you know. It's okay."

"No," he said.

"Nothing's going to happen," she said to reassure him, thinking that he was jealous of Jean Dorlean. She put her hand on the side of his face where the muscles clashed. There were little pebbles under his skin. Her touch immobilized him, as if he were caught—as if he were a goose caught by the neck, knowing that struggle could be fatal to it. She removed her hand.

"You," he said. "No." He shook his head.

"I promised, Dibley. I'll be back in a couple of hours, before lunch. Don't get upset. It's my business, isn't it?"

He nodded, but he said, "Stay."

"There's a breeze, but it's not that strong. Are you worried about that? Say something. Say anything."

Jean Dorlean appeared, ready to go down to the lake. Dibley looked at him, and at her. There seemed a kind of alien glee in Dibley when he said, "Werner killed a toad," as if Werner, or the toad, were in some crazy way Jean Dorlean.

"How?" Dory said.

"Stepped on it," Dibley said with that strange grin.

She didn't want to think about Werner and toads. She didn't feel anything different about the day. She would be busy in the afternoon, but she saw no problem with a couple of hours of sailing. The boats were beamy, sturdy and relatively stable. Debbie was going to be washing the downstairs windows on the porch, she on the outside and Cynthia on the inside, and Dibley was going to mow and edge the front lawn. She'd be back before they were through. She said this to Dibley, irritated that she had to. She was going to give a guest a sailing lesson; could she have a couple of hours off? She just wanted to go sailing for a while.

Jean Dorlean said nothing. He wore shorts, sneakers and a sweater, which seemed right for the day. She went to her room to get her own sweater and they went toward the beach. Dibley had disappeared. When they were out of hearing of anyone else, Jean Dorlean said, "Your bodyguard didn't want you to go, did he?"

"He's not my bodyguard," she said. "I don't need a bodyguard."

"Now don't get touchy," he said. "I take it back. It's a glorious day and you're a lovely girl to give me a sailing lesson."

That tone reminiscent of John Hearne.

On the lake the boat came alive, bucking and thrusting along. She sat amidships where she could give him quick advice if he needed it, such as to let out the sheet when they began to heel over too far. It was clean and bright on the water, and the wind was such a simple force, steady from the west. They did a beam reach toward the south-southwest, diagonally across the lake, the boat's energy surging through and over the waves.

"Have I got it?" he asked. He looked thrilled and tense, grinning at his task.

"Pretty good," she said. "When we get opposite that point, come closer into the wind for a while." She pointed across the lake to a promontory dark with pines.

"In other words, steer more to the right," he said, and she nodded, though he would find it a little more complicated than that.

What was it she wanted from him? The attention of intelligence, but not just the live workings and emotions of any intelligence. It was a different mystery because he was a man. There was the power, the choice, the sweet vulnerability of that power. It could admire her and need her approval, even want and need more than that; it could be in real pain because it couldn't have everything. That would not be good, but the possibility of the possibility was fascinating. Admit it; if that fascination was the reason, it was dishonest to be alone with him.

The wind purred in the shrouds and stays, the bow slapping into every fifth wave or so, the wake a hiss. He said, "You have a boyfriend, I'm told."

She admitted that. They spoke of John Hearne as if he were a stranger to them both. Jean Dorlean's words didn't define what the subject really was. His words were not as important as the real subject. All that was said was for the purpose of her pleasure and her license, because of his admiration, to answer with easy, becoming modesty.

"You are really something," he said. "I don't mean to patronize the state of New Hampshire, but I didn't expect to find the pearl of great price in these rural byways."

Easy, she thought; he shouldn't ruin it with obvious flattery.

When it was time to go back, he suggested that instead they go have lunch at the Casino, at the foot of the lake. "Surely the others can feed themselves one meal," he said. "Have you *ever* not done your duty? Say the hell with them, for a change." He said he'd brought his wallet, so he could pay for lunch.

She'd told Dibley she'd be back for lunch, but what did she owe Dibley? Something else could "come up." It certainly happened with others all the time. And with this wind it wouldn't take long to get back; the boat would go like a train. She still thought about it.

He'd wanted to know about John Hearne. She didn't tell him that there had been no card or letter, and that because of this the whole significance of John Hearne was fading out. But then she was surprised by her sudden resentment; she could hate John Hearne. She could kill him for making her feel so badly, for so long.

"Well?" Jean Dorlean said. "Remember, I'll be taking an eye off my charges, too. Do you really believe Kasimir can't cope with one minor meal? What's it going to be, anyway—potato salad and hot dogs? Oops —*salade pommes de terre et saucissons?* Dory, relax! The universe will go on functioning without you—for at least a couple of hours!"

She felt her mouth smile at his smile. He was a small man, but bigger than her, and sinewy, a man. She saw the bunch of him, the bulge there, and knew that he saw her glance, which made her feel naked and a little shy and embarrassed. He was not embarrassed at all, though not lewd about it, or about anything. Nothing would embarrass him. Neither was he overimpressed, or callow, or shy. He was not made insensitive by his wild needs. The worst thing a man could be was to be unsure of himself in that self-conscious way. He could be unsure in a deeply moral, deeply honest way—like the conflict between his real feelings and the work he had to do for his country.

She did say yes, and they came about and sailed to the Casino, which had a sort of sandwich shop for a restaurant. It was twelve-thirty, but she wouldn't think of Cascom Manor. To hell with Cascom Manor! It felt like falling. They both had a western sandwich and a Coke, as if she were on a date with the older man.

At two o'clock, when they were halfway back, the wind died altogether, then came in small puffs, died, came on again, and they didn't get back until five o'clock. She was worried, but he said, "To hell with them, Dory. Are they all going to croak without you to take care of them?"

A storm was coming from the west, a shutter of tarnished steel that by its immense height diminished Cascom Mountain and the long hills of its range. The storm seemed more substantial than the granite mountain, as if to demonstrate the real force of nature, the earth itself nothing to its magnitude. Within it red fires burst and went out, all in silence. She would have to check the Edison and Aladdin lamps, the wick lamps and candle holders. This storm went halfway around the compass and couldn't miss them. She would have to make sure that all the windows were shut.

They drew the boat up on the sand and tied the painter to a tree.

"Let's take a quick swim while we can," he said.

"No."

"Let me kiss you, then," he said, and when he put his arms around her she put hers around his body. Her face pressed into the springy beard to his alive lips. It wasn't real at all. She really didn't feel like kissing him, though she was doing it. "I've got to get back right now," she said in a voice that sounded to her dreamy, and which might even be misconstrued as a promise. God knew what it really meant.

As they walked up to Cascom Manor his hand floated gently, oh, so lightly, on her hip. She wondered how much of anything he'd said was meant. And how could she find him attractive? He was not attractive and yet she felt the warmth, the dreamy softness in thinking of him.

"Dory," he said, "I know this is ridiculous, all of it. I'm seventeen years older than you are, but I've fallen in love with you. Listen, I take back every cruel, snide remark you've heard me make in the presence of these clowns, these dregs of the war. They affect me that way. I'm really not like that at all."

She said nothing, thinking this over. Had it been said with difficulty, or with ease? They reached Cascom Manor walking side by side, not touching. The Princess, the Zwanzigs and the Patricks, without children, were sitting on the porch watching the coming storm.

"Oh, Dory! There you are!" the Princess called. "We were so worried! We missed you! Are we prepared for the approaching storm?"

"There are plenty of candles and oil lamps if the lights go out, but I think we'd all better close our windows," Dory said.

"Dory thinks of everything! What would we ever do without Dory?"

Faintly they heard Cynthia's violin.

"And where are the others, then? Where are Werner and Yvonne?" Marta Zwanzig said.

" 'La Gioconda' is probably at the concert," Jean Dorlean said meaningfully, then looked at Dory, as if contrite about having said such a thing.

Marta Zwanzig ignored it. She reared back on her chair and then rocked ponderously forward onto her feet and stood up. "We must shut our windows!" she said.

"And I must go to the children," Mrs. Patrick said. As soon as she left the porch, Kaethe Muller came around the corner of the house. Sean Patrick looked up at her and she licked her lips. Jean Dorlean looked at Dory, a sardonic look, and shook his head. He said, "I wonder where the rest of your crew is."

Could Debbie be with Werner?

"Let's go look for them," he said, assuming what her thought had been. "Not that it's all that urgent, I'm sure."

The storm came over the house like night, though it would be hours till true dark. Lights came on down hallways, in rooms. Then, with a tick like the breaking of a stick, lightning took out all the lights. Simultaneous thunder was more pressure than sound, as though it bowed out the walls and windows.

From the landing she took an oil lamp and lit it with the matches she had put on the table next to it. "Foresight. Efficiency," Jean Dorlean said. "Are you frightened of the storm?"

"No more than I should be," she said.

Werner's room was empty, and looked as though no one had been in it since Debbie had made it up that morning. His silver-mounted hairbrush, his combs, orange stick, clippers and fingernail file were aligned on the bureau as if for inspection, the bedspread neater and more taut than Debbie would ever make her own bed.

In the hall Cynthia and Yvonne had come from the dark to the lamplight. "Have you seen Debbie?" she asked them.

"Not since this morning," Cynthia said. "She quit doing the windows and went off with Werner. She said if you didn't have to work, she didn't." Cynthia then looked at Jean Dorlean. She looked him over, as if evaluating him part by part, no opinion expressed.

"Do you know where they were going?"

"Sailing, I thought. But that was this morning."

"Were they back for lunch?"

"No, they weren't. Oh, Dory! Are you awfully worried?"

"I don't know. I guess so. The other boat was there when we came in, so they must be around here somewhere."

Then she smelled gas, just the faintest hint of that heaviness, and knew what it was. She hurried downstairs toward the kitchen, leaving her lamp on the landing and proceeding in near-darkness. Something, maybe the concussion of thunder, had put out the stove's pilot light and the kitchen was dense with the leaden odor. Jean Dorlean opened the windows while she turned off the gas at the tanks outside. The storm was beginning to pass over to the east, and rain came in little flicks of spray, nearly horizontal; there would be leaking at the western dormers. When the gas had cleared out enough she lit a single-mantle Coleman lantern, turned on the gas and relit the pilot, thinking that the pilot-light system was illogical in that it substituted real danger for a minor inconvenience. She would not have done it that way.

They went to the living room to check on lamps and candles. The Zwanzigs were there alone with an Aladdin lamp whose mantle was mostly covered with carbon, an orange stream climbing its chimney. She turned it down so the carbon would burn off, and Marta Zwanzig said, "We didn't know if it should turn up or down."

"Let's start upstairs and go through the whole house," Jean Dorlean said. "Might as well not have to worry. Okay?"

Kasimir shouted from the kitchen, *"La vapeur! La vapeur!"* They found him in his white smock and chef's hat, with a candle. Steam and a jeering note like a blue jay's ricocheted from the sink, and the faucet screamed. She ran outside and again turned off the gas at the tanks. Though steam kept hurtling into the sink, soon there was a slight tonal fall to the blue-jay scream.

"La vapeur!" Kasimir said.

"Pas de l'eau," Dory said. *"Pas de l'électricité."*

"Je n'aime pas cela!" Kasimir stated, took his candle and went up the back stairs like the little boy in the ad.

"My God, I forgot," she said. "The pump's off. I can't remember everything. And there won't be any water. They'll flush the toilets. They're helpless. I've got to tell them how to turn their lamps out when they go to bed." She heard her complaining voice from the hollow of her head.

He put his arm around her, gently. "Come on, let's go find the kids," he said. She let him lead her upstairs.

Debbie was in none of the dark, low-ceilinged little rooms on the third floor, where the rain drummed. She wasn't in the empty room on the second floor, where Dory let Jean Dorlean put his arms around her. He put the hissing lantern on a table next to the unmade bed. She was sick of looking for Debbie, and also anxious about her, and tired. The anxiety was such that its relief would only be unhappy. Debbie would resent being found.

"There, now," he said, holding her. His hands knew her back, where their warmth felt needed, or welcome, or familiar. She put her face up, and it was kissed, the strange fibers parting for his lips. How gently he wanted her, but how actual was the hardness of him. It was the gentle wanting that appealed.

"I love you," he said, as if he knew every smallest meaning of the word, every large and small meaning of it, and meant each one.

Time passed, standing there. He said, "Let's disappear ourselves." She said nothing, which could mean anything.

"He left you. What do you care for him anymore? You know it didn't mean much to him or he wouldn't have just gone off . . ." His words were not so much an argument as a lullaby, a nuzzling murmur, voice and breath against her skin. "Let's turn out the lantern," he said, and reached over and turned it off, so that its light and hiss began to fade. He pulled up her sweater and blouse and knelt down a little to kiss her breasts.

This was going to happen if she wanted it to. It was real, though it couldn't be real. No, it would not be. It was not her real, her best self standing here, the one she knew each day. John Hearne had nothing to do with it. To hell with John Hearne. "No," she said. "Don't. I'm sorry . . ." God, she was all wet, even so, even considering it, even thinking about it.

"I need you," he said, not stopping anything. "I love you, Dory. Please let me make love to you . . ." That went on, and soon she knew that he wasn't going to let her go, that she was a prisoner, that he would take whatever he wanted no matter what she did or said. She felt in him a new temper, a cruelty.

"Let me go!" she said.

"Oh, Dory, Dory, please," he said.

"Stop! Let me go!" But he was not going to.

In the light of the Coleman lantern appeared Dibley's ice-pale face, and then Jean Dorlean jerked and slumped down and away from her. "Oh, God," he sighed hopelessly. Dibley stepped forward and kicked him hard in the stomach, and a thin liquid gushed out of his mouth. She heard it. She thought: I'll have to clean that up.

She left the lantern there. Dibley had his Boy Scout flashlight, and she followed him, her bodyguard, but it was all unrepairable and horrible now. Everything was, and she had caused it.

Dibley took her to her room just as the lights came back on. He looked at her like a judge, disapproving and even angry. "Don't you know him?" he said. "Don't you know anything?"

He meant: Don't you know who really loves you?

"I guess I don't," she said.

Kaethe Muller appeared in the doorway. "Hah," she said, looking speculatively at Dibley, but that thought was unimportant. To Dory she said with an official lack of emotion, "It is best you find your sister. Unless she has gone home? She is with Werner Ganz-Lengen? That is the question. A boy who has been through much, and can be . . . eccentric. Not meaning to frighten you, but best we look for them. This we all agree."

"Eccentric?"

"Sometimes, *ja.* Meaning like condition red? Shell shock? In New York he is in the care of a doctor."

"You mean he's dangerous?"

"More . . . unpredictable."

"Unpredictable," Dory said, cool before the shock of its implications.

"Dory!" Cynthia called as she came down the hall. "They think we ought to look for Debbie!" Yvonne was there too, standing quietly.

They all went along the hall, Dibley leading. They met Jean Dorlean coming out of the bathroom. He stood against the wall, impersonal as a stranger in a public building, to let them go by. Kaethe Muller said, "Jean, have you found Werner?"

"Der Tod sei unser Kampfgenosse," he answered, and she made a hissing, dismissive sound with her lips.

Dory left them and went downstairs, Dibley at her side, her mute champion, her fingernailless protector, rigid as stilts. His allegiance seemed his pain, but what could she do about his queer love? She could say that it was her right.

Dibley took his olive-colored Boy Scout flashlight from his belt and tried it; it seemed brighter after its rest. Dibley said, "Boathouse?" The rain had stopped, so they left Cascom Manor behind them and went toward the lake.

The wind had gone down but the lake was still unruly, like a basin that had been tipped and righted. One of the sailboats was not at its mooring, so was probably ashore down along the pines somewhere. The boathouse was empty of all but its usual nautical tack—oars, paddles, lifesavers, paint and tools. They looked on the loft, up the plank ladder. Cobwebs and sawdust, no one.

"Where could they be?" she asked, hearing and feeling the taint of plaintiveness.

They went down the shore and came upon the loose sailboat. Dibley tipped most of the water out of it, pulled it up on the sand and tied its painter to a bush. They could get it tomorrow.

They went back to the house; no one had found Debbie or Werner. She and Dibley checked the station wagon, the cellar, the library. It was still so wet outside she couldn't see how they would want to be outside. Everything was soaked.

They turned on the water heater and went around turning off kerosene lamps and blowing out candles. It would be so good when this anxiety had passed, when Debbie came back from wherever she was.

Dibley was hurt when she said he ought to go to bed. He was her right hand and protector, wasn't he? But he was beginning to make her even more nervous with his intense, mute connection to her, as if she had something deformed on the end of a leash and couldn't let go. She felt unfair and ungrateful, but she couldn't help it.

Dibley scowled, turned and went toward his room. Her legs were trembling and she had to sit down somewhere alone, where she couldn't be seen trembling so. She locked her door and lay down on her bed.

Time had passed awake, then not-awake time had passed; which went slowest? The stunned time of half-sleep. Maybe Debbie had come back by now, one in the morning. She would go to her room and find out.

As she passed Werner's room his door was open upon darkness, that other element, but something caught her eye, a shape wide where a woman would be wide, and she first thought: Well, I'm hallucinating again, imagining Betty Salmon in every dark place. She looked again. Something was there, in the very center of the room, but it wasn't standing; it floated, turning.

If it was real it couldn't be Betty Salmon, unless her mind had crossed over into another dimension. It had to be some tangible thing, unless she was mad. Things could bite the mind as well as the hand and arm to the elbow—what she would have to risk to find the light switch inside the door. If she turned on the light she might see what could hurt by being seen. It masqueraded as a choice—Betty Salmon, or whatever that bulk there really was, accusing her of some terrible omission of pity. As if she were placing her hand in a mouth she reached inside for the wall switch and pushed in its lower barrel.

It was Werner, his face black as a prank, his toes just off the floor. The rigid line of the rope angled his head quizzical. Not a squiggle of movement in him, just the slow turn as the rope pulled to a new tension and length. A straight chair lay on its side and the light fixture had been pulled down from the ceiling, but the old solid-copper wires had held enough. She yelled for help and tried to hold him up against his weight, but he was too flexible, so she held just legs that bent perversely, together or one at a time, the upper weight remorselessly beyond her strength. His clothes were dripping wet and cool. She went to the door and yelled for help, complaining and crying like an outraged child.

Dibley was there first. He opened his jackknife and cut the rope, part of a sailboat painter, and the body came down into their arms in an awkward bunch, half held, and thumped its several parts to the floor. For a moment they looked at the cyanotic face of the first dead person either had ever touched. The noose Werner had fashioned for himself came loose easily; it was actually a hangman's knot, a strange skill to have.

"Artificial respiration!" Dibley said, and turned Werner over on his stomach, but their frantic looks at each other confirmed the toylike uselessness of that old rhythm they had learned as children on sunny beaches. Dory cleared the dark lump of tongue and Dibley sat on the legs. *"Out* goes the bad air, *in* comes the good air," he sang as he pressed forward and sat back, but he might as well have been sitting on a side of beef. There was no pulse, no breath. The half-open blue eyes were as coolly inert as marbles.

"Has somebody called a doctor? An ambulance?" she cried to the others at the door, complaining of their helplessness. They all stared with the dead expression of horror, keeping their distance. Kaethe Muller shouted angrily in German, and then, to someone, "I told you so! Stupid to bring him here!" Yvonne came forward, her hands out as if to hold something, but couldn't make herself come all the way.

Dory pushed through them to the door, moving them aside as if they floated in water, and went downstairs to the telephone. Mr. King was the part-time chief of police and the only policeman in Cascom. She had the normal thought that he would be asleep and it would be an imposition to wake him just because Werner was dead. When the operator asked her what number she wanted her voice failed for a moment at the prospect of explaining what had happened, of introducing that subject into the normal world in the middle of the night. Her child voice would have to say death, suicide. But maybe Werner wasn't really dead. She said the number and heard the ring. Soon Mr. King, sounding grumpy, answered. She said, hearing tears in her voice, that she was Doris Perkins at Cascom Manor and a guest had hung—hanged—himself and he might be dead or not. A doctor. Artificial respiration.

"All right, now, Doris. Keep calm. Dr. Winston's on call for the Cottage Hospital in Leah. I'll call him and come right over." His fatherly voice almost made her whimper, because now she could resign. He would be strong, with authority and age, and would come here from the real world.

When she returned to Werner's room, Dibley was sweating as he mouthed the old phrases. *"Out* goes the bad air, *in* comes the good air." But no air moved at all, and it became clearer and clearer that Werner was dead. They gasped when Dibley stopped and got up. "He's dead. There's nothing," he said.

The rule was that no matter the lack of response you continued artificial respiration until the doctor arrived, but that was after a swimming accident. Maybe this was different. She knelt and tried for a pulse at Werner's neck, but there was no motion, no new warmth. He might have been made of rubber.

A note was on Werner's bed, in foreign-looking handwriting, with strange *r*'s and *s*'s, but as regular and legible as an exercise: *We were playing and she said and tolerated lewd remarks that enticed me to believe she would submit to my advances, but when I acted upon this assumption she became insolent and abusive. Being grossly unattractive she had no right to put on airs, so it was necessary to teach her a lesson.*

She read this, its stunning logic excluding for a few seconds the knowledge that it referred to Debbie.

Mr. King had arrived before Cynthia and Yvonne, unaware, found Debbie on the couch in Ernst Zwanzig's studio. Cynthia became so hysterical and inconsolable she seemed in her continued screaming perverse. Dory didn't believe in such hysteria. For herself, she acknowledged fact, no matter what it was; her own weaknesses came and then went away as she assumed control over herself. Dr. Winston came from Leah and eventually calmed Cynthia.

The State Police came—two troopers in their creased, hard-cloth uniforms, near-identical giants with large pistols angled from black holsters. In their presence the guests became quiet and attentive.

Her mother and father came, seeming smaller than she remembered them to be, as if compressed by their summons and its cause. They were both rational; her mother shuddered with grief and sucked in her breath, but wouldn't make another sound. Her father, in his black mailman's boots, stubbed his toe on a throw rug and had a small limp thereafter. Neither held her responsible because they felt that she, like they, had come among powerful strangers. She saw that she would have to take care of them, and that she couldn't resign just yet. She could not stop moving. And as for Cascom Manor, it was against her nature to leave loose ends and she couldn't think about what had happened, or make sense of it, with all kinds of tasks undone, with messy incompletions here and there and under her feet. She went to the Princess's room and found her attended by Yvonne and Mrs. Patrick.

"Dory!" the Princess cried, "I am so terribly sorry!"

Dory could only nod her head. The Princess's skin, rarely in the sun, was smooth and yet as old as a primitive religious painting, ivory on canvas, the grain visible. Her eyes were out of control, jumping from one part of Dory's face to another, as if she might find an answer in her brow, or chin.

"Werner was a sick boy," she said, a plea. "We thought he was better, but he was a ghost."

Mrs. Patrick shuddered so that her teeth clicked together several times.

"Marie," Yvonne said to calm her, and for a while they were all silent. The Princess, still in her nightgown, leaned back in the bunched sheets and pillows, the other two sitting on the bed.

"Princess, perhaps you had better dress," Yvonne said in her half-smiling voice.

"Yes." The Princess stood, and with her usual lack of modesty let her nightgown fall and then accepted the clothes Yvonne selected from drawers and wardrobe. Mrs. Patrick also attended her, combing and arranging her black hair. While this was going on the Princess said, "Dory, as soon as everything is . . . settled, we will be going back. There will be checks for all your salaries for the rest of the month."

Debbie's too? she had to think, always a prisoner of detail. She said, as if she had to dare anything to try to upset her own iron composure, that she'd have Dibley help her close up Cascom Manor, if he would, when the time came. The Princess was startled, and looked at her closely for a moment.

"How we trust you, Dory," she said. "But . . ."

"It's all right," Dory said. Already she was constructing the near future in which she would enter upon duty and live for its satisfactions. Tonight there would be transportation, who in what car. Tomorrow Northlee Hospital, where the bodies would be taken, then Balcher's Funeral Home in Leah, after what she had already been told was a mandatory autopsy in such cases, according to state law. Tonight there would be room in her father's car for Cynthia, Dibley and herself. Or she could take the station wagon and their things. That could wait. It was already tomorrow, though, so she would have to organize everything now. She would have to take care of her mother and father. She could take the car tomorrow while they were at work, but would they go to work? There was even, in the center of all calculations, the spread and mattress of the couch in the studio, soiled beyond redemption.

In the next few days she was told more than once that she was "a pillar of strength." She kept busy, organized everything, took everything to its conclusion. On Friday, Cascom Manor was closed, drained and locked. "Dory's been a pillar of strength," her mother said after the funeral on Saturday.

Cynthia didn't come to the funeral, though Robert and Dibley did. Three of Debbie's classmates came—the dutiful ones, that type. The others who came were relatives, their cars full of casseroles for afterwards. Her family didn't go to church except for occasions like this, and weddings. Reverend Gile knew Debbie well because she'd baby-sat for them, and was moved beyond sonority by her "loss."

Sunday evening, when everything immediate had been taken care of, the casserole dishes washed and ready for their owners, she went to bed at eight and woke at four in the morning. It was windless in Leah, black and still, no difference between closed or open eyes. Fragments of dreams nudged her memory, but they were just states of mild emotion decorated with little friezes of this or that—leaves, a bell, a sail. She could not go back to them, and felt bittersweet regret for their loss.

She and Dibley simply hadn't thought of Ernst Zwanzig's studio, and she couldn't think of a single reason why they hadn't thought of looking there. This vacuum was disturbing. It was like reaching out for someone and finding that your hand had been cut off at the wrist. There was no explanation. Debbie might still have been alive, her wrists and ankles wired to the couch frame with coat hangers. She might have been alive then, her panties stuffed in her mouth. It must have been some time before she died. No one had accused Dory of negligence or lack of care, but that disappeared studio, its growing bust of Thomas E. Dewey—how had it not come into her mind? It almost seemed deliberate. It wasn't the sort of thing she did. While Debbie was in torment. It was not good enough to be honorable and conscientious. Good was not enough. It might be better to be dead than to lie here with the black air pressing like cloth against the eyes.

If she could go back to those mildly interesting dreams, whose faint nostalgia somehow preceded Debbie's agony, she might get some relief. This situation was without hope. There was nothing she could do to stop it. It was intolerable. It was like nausea but there was no way to kneel at the cold bowl, no place to shove a finger. Time refused to pass; what good if it did?

How sweet and inevitable was sleep. She woke again at eight, unable to remember how sleep came and erased knowledge. Her arms and legs were warm honey, a delicious fatigue not weakness but a willed dissolution.

She woke again at noon, lying in sweat no more substantial than she was, beaded with it, the sun in the wall hot on the backs of fingers weak as flagella. Thereafter when she slept and woke she didn't look at the time. She went to the bathroom, that delicious languor everywhere in her, in bladder and sphincter, in heart and spine, and then, hardly waking, she melted into bed again.

Her mother called through the floor register, but seemed to be calling through fog. She thought she might answer, but not now. In a minute. Her mother came into her room and stood there. She saw the woman, almost. Her eyes had melted out of focus, and didn't want to come back.

"Doris?" her mother said. "Doris?"

She believed she said to her mother that it was all right.

"Doris?"

Please leave me alone for a while. But the voice she used didn't have any sound because nothing came to the throat. She didn't want her voice to wake her.

"Doris, what's the matter?" her mother said. "It's been two days you been sleeping. Ain't you hungry?"

"Mmm," she answered, risking a hum. "Mmm, mmm, mmm-mmm," she hummed reassuringly. Surely her mother would understand that reasonable answer.

"Pa and me are worried about you."

In sudden irritation she said out loud, "Please don't wake me up, Ma!"

"You can't sleep the rest of your life!"

Her mother's cry focused her. Her mother was ugly with unhappiness, gray dishwater in her eyes, her mouth set with hurt. This was no thing to have caused.

"Oh, Ma," she said, whereupon her mother made small percussive sounds as meaningful and senseless as fragments of dreams.

Once her mother whipped Debbie home with a dog leash, Debbie's bawling mouth in memory as big and round as a bushel basket, as loud as a bronze bell. Debbie, who looked so strong, was weak, and feared pain to the point of fainting when it was spoken of. She and her mother both knew this; she didn't know how much her mother had been told of Debbie's torment—knowledge that had come to her instantaneously, her perceptions seared with knowing, her sister's hand, the dislocated fingers flowered out, the deep punctures in the shy, stretched skin of the arches of her feet. Other impalements so thoughtfully deliberate they caused a vertigo of transference into the punisher's mind. The slime of lust; what you can understand has soiled you. Debbie whipped home, Debbie slapped by her older sister once, twice, three times, the cause forgotten, the impulse still vivid.

On the blade of the dagger were the words *Blut und Ehre!* When he was finished he went to the lake to cleanse his hands and clothes.

Because Debbie was dead and forever mute, all that had happened in those hours was gone forever, as if it hadn't ever happened. We don't live very long with another's agony. It goes away. If a tree falls in the forest, no one to hear it. For moments at a time it could seem so, and was such a familiar trap, because with a smirk it revealed itself a fraud the more vicious for its sly offer of amelioration.

Her valedictory had so stupidly proclaimed some self-flattering "deep chord." Here was irony, the opposite of opposites, John Hearne's humor. *Being grossly unattractive she had no right to put on airs.* Could she find a flaw in that logic? No. *So it was necessary to teach her a lesson.* She thought of John Hearne, and of all soiled writhings on the verge of cruelty. She had been used, and she saw them together naked, as if she were cleanly away from her body, up near the ceiling someplace, while the two animals jerked in each other's meat and mucus. She couldn't understand who she had been then.

28

That evening Oval got a call. They were coming. Ten thousand bushels in the morning, more on the way. He turned from the phone and revealed this information. Thelma was all excited. "John wih hep you, Daddy!"

Oval said, "We'd better be there at seven, Johnny, so we can get you and Urban officially hired before the avalanche hits."

It was more like a tsunami, a rise in the ocean that might have been only six inches high but when compressed into an inlet or an estuary showed its force. From that morning on was a time of no time, days and nights indistinguishable. Oval made out "watch bills," evidently a Navy term, for them all. There were three others on the crew: Tex, an amiable forty-year-old man who told jokes and, like many who had no sense of humor, could be very funny; Jack, a young TJC dropout who was a semipro boxer on the side, and his buddy, Les, who at twenty-two had a comfortable roll of fat just around his middle, above his belt, and who knew Dianne, or Streaky. "You ought to try her," Les said. "She's been through the gang at Jimmy's."

"She gobbles the gerbil," Jack said.

"Which is to say she eats the bird," Les said.

"Aw, she's a good kid."

"She's ginger-peachy, positively."

"She used to be a brunette, but now she's a big-league blonde."

"How you know?"

"I seen her jim-dandy. Ain't you?"

"Seen it! I ate it!"

And so on, until Urban and Oval came out in swirls of cold and Jack and Les went in. Tex had the easier duty, on that watch, controlling the conveyor belt. John, during his break, was bolting hangers on the new trays. Tex said, "There was a young lady from France, who boarded a train in a trance. Everyone fucked her, except the conductor, and he came off in his pants."

Oval wouldn't rest with the others but was continually checking motors, temperatures, the counters that measured the number of packages entering the machine and the numbers that came out the other side. Urban, as if in answer to Tex's limerick, said, "And Adam was not deceived, but the woman being deceived was in the transgression. I Timothy 2:14."

Tex said, "There was a young monk from Paree, who went into the garden to pee. He said, 'Dominus vobiscum, why won't the piss come? I must have the CLAP.' "

"Do I have to listen to this crap?" Urban asked.

Things were going smoothly for the moment, the white boxes of Fordhook lima beans moving remorselessly down the converging tables to enter the one conveyor belt. Inside the machine each tray paused, if the timing was right, just long enough to be filled, then the conveyor belt was supposed to pause long enough for a new tray to get into position. Without help this didn't always happen, and when it didn't, the slightest lack of attention tore boxes of the new warm beans apart so they slithered out onto the floor and froze. Usually they waded in lima beans, and when the footing got too bad they shoveled them out into GI cans.

Normally three men were inside the machine. One supervised the loading of the trays, another was stationed at the sector 3 trouble spot, and another watched sectors 4 and 5, where he could spot any malfunction in the ejection plunger system, which actually worked pretty well. Communication was by shouting against the fan and wind noises and the icy squeal of metal under stress. When the machine stopped, a bell rang and everyone who wasn't numb helped make repairs. The bell also called workers from the orange-juicing section down the line, a less feverish operation, to come with hand trucks and help take the flow of boxes from the conveyor belt. Their irritation and disdain were always apparent.

Days passed, or nights; it made no difference. The Indian Pony, repaired, was returned to the parsonage, and he insisted on paying for the new parts—Phil the mechanic hadn't charged for labor. Bonnie didn't really take his paying for it very well. His and Oval's irregular hours, the time they spent at the parsonage in exhausted sleep, seemed to make her morose and quiet. When he did see her, in passing, she had a dark look about her, as if she had been misused and was resentful. Then Thelma got a bad cold with bronchitis and Bonnie had to take care of her as well as all of the church activities, such as the prayer schedules of the Healing Echelons, the Live Christ Daily classes, the Library of Spiritual Help, the visiting lecturers—Prince Grégoire Ushant on "Perpetual Youth," Dr. Addie Walmberg on "The Lord's Humor" and Rev. Dr. Pierce G. Pierce, D.D., on "The Dynamic Healing Power of Thought." She also had to give comfort and counsel to those church members ill in spirit, mind and body. Hadasha Kemal Allgood, lost in his scholarship, wasn't much help.

Oval's preoccupation with the machine, John began to understand, was not just an involvement of pride in his invention but a concern for the flow of the beans themselves. He was hurt by stoppages; the bright green cells, rich and perfect, were sacred, and when they were bruised and wasted he was responsible for that loss, the sustenance of the world diminished because of his lack of skill and understanding. He brought damaged boxes home with him and cooked them for himself because no one else wanted any. He expressed no pleasure in them but piled them steaming on a plate with a bit of butter melting down through them and methodically ate them all. Bonnie, who grew more and more grumpy about everything, said he was going to turn green if he kept it up. When he finished he said he had to get back, that Tex sometimes didn't pay enough attention. It was his and John's turn to have eight hours of sleep, but he couldn't sleep. Things were going too well. They'd processed a thousand dozen boxes in a row, with only a hundred boxes damaged. Something had to give way, something he didn't understand or might not be there to prevent.

He'd touched his wrist to a link of chain and had a raw sore there big as a quarter, which he wouldn't bother to bandage. He hadn't shaved and his jaws were gray, pepper and salt.

One night Bonnie called Oval at the Co-op. He was in the machine at sector 1. John was just about through with a break and went in to tell him and take over.

Oval came back stooped and distracted. Thelma was worse, he said. Bonnie had a doctor come see her and he said she should go to the hospital. Her lungs were congested. So Bonnie had taken her to Tulaveda Municipal and called from there. Thelma was terrified by hospitals. It was irrational but how rational did you expect the poor dear to be? People didn't always know how to treat mongoloids, and mongoloids could be as unhappy as anyone on earth. If only they didn't feel so much pain. If only their threshold of pain was on the level of their intelligence, not their emotions. It wasn't fair to them; nothing was.

John looked for Thelma's face in Oval's, but saw only the blue of the eyes, if that blue could be separated from expression. Even in his doubt, Oval's face, surrounded by the furry fringe of hood, was open, stalwart and virtuous, like an ideal hero of, say, 1926—a pen-and-ink drawing of "Glenn Goodheart, the Guide," in an adventure book for boys. His own face, as he'd seen it a few minutes before in the men's-room mirror, was smoothly youthful but a little lopsided, as if it strained against itself in equivocal ways. There was a resemblance to Oval's in chin and mouth, but his own seemed less readable. He wondered if Oval had ever snarled and fought.

Oval climbed the iron ladder to sectors 2 and 3, leaving him in charge of the incoming boxes. The trays filled, rose, paused for the conveyor belt as he guided the boxes in across the threshold, sometimes having to pull one or two out to keep them from being crushed. The machine chirped of stressed metal as the open teeth of the sprockets took to the chains. The frigid air moved, a wind without freshness. He clapped his wooden hands against his thighs when he had time, but whatever help that gave to his circulation was never apparent. Just as Jack came in to relieve him he missed a box at the threshold, letting it be sheared in half, so he carried half of the severed box out with him, the warm beans steaming until the heat of Tulaveda extinguished their mist. He took off his gloves and put his numb fingers into the warmth of them. It was true they were perfect, each a separate life, a seed containing within it every characteristic of a wholly new plant. He didn't even know what the plant looked like, but there had to be, he thought, a pod of some kind. He knew very little about them except the beans were supposed to be good for you if you could get them down. Too bad they had to turn grayish and claylike when cooked, because in this fresh state their green wasn't unattractive. They were clean, like good air, even though he had waded in millions of them. Tex, imitating the military labeling of their clothes, had once said, "Beans, lima, Fordhook, many, fucking, too."

Yet they didn't cloy by appearing in multitudes. He put one to his mouth and bit lightly into it. The center was like a nut, a giving, flexible resistance until it softly snapped. It was conceivable that this fruit, or seed, might be prepared in some edible way, not boiled to the pallor of a corpse, with the flavor of wet cement. It was interesting to him that he thought "it," not "them," as if there were no threat of inundation now; not, at least, to his throat.

He put his grimy flight gear in a locker, went to the office and punched his time card. In the parking lot his Indian Pony stood next to Jack's A-V8, an admirably neat and shining black roadster Jack had told him was "chopped and channeled." It also had Edelbrock heads and four carburetors, which allowed it to lay out black strips of rubber whenever Jack left a stop sign.

He rode his faithful but tame Indian Pony out onto Pasadena Avenue and over to Los Robles, then up the hazardous rising mile of Boulevard stops to the parsonage. His new sealed-beam headlight was much brighter than his old bulbed one. He wanted a bath, something he'd never really craved in this way before, even in the Army, having always been content enough in his grime and grunge. Maybe it was a symptom of growing older, that you pampered your hide. It was also a cosmetic urge, this time, because a beautiful older woman whose feelings for him were problematical might be there, and who knew what the possibilities were? To make anything really possible was not something he'd work at, or knew how to work at. The possibility was just there. He was tired, yet hard from work, his tendons and muscles firm in ways he would never visibly flaunt but were deliciously prideful.

Bonnie's car was in the side yard. He parked the Indian Pony and as he came up onto the porch she rose from the darkness of the swinging couch that was suspended there on creaky chains. Her eyes and cheeks glinted in the streetlight. Those were tears. He came up to her, his excuse to see if they were the tears he knew they were, and because she seemed helpless, or at least passive in her unhappiness, he put his arms around her. Hers came around him. "Poor, poor Thelma," she said.

Could it be that he had forgotten Thelma's illness? It was true that he had set it aside, as if it were his to categorize. He knew of it, but could place it here or there.

Bonnie's head was on his shoulder. The cloth strap of her brassiere crossed her back, reminding him of a piece of boy knowledge gained not so long ago, when he was about fifteen: you could get your hand into a bra easily from above, but not from below.

"She's so sick and unhappy and lonesome there. Would you go see her tomorrow?"

No force in the world could make him go if he didn't want to, and he didn't want to.

"All right," he said.

"You're so sweet," she said, and kissed him on the mouth.

But he didn't want to go, and hadn't resigned himself to going. Beauty was so strange in its effects, taking away, as if it took away breath, time to equivocate. This was true even of beauty wrong in dimension and circumstance. She was not really possible, not for him, but he still held her.

"You'll be off work again at seven tomorrow night," she said. "You can go see her for a while then."

"Yes," he said, and thought: You put your hands on a woman and in just a few moments, if you don't move them over her, you might as well have your hands on upholstery. The hands forget.

"John? Are you going to let me go?" she said with a little laugh.

He let her go and looked at his wristwatch, his military Waltham that he liked to look at, as if time, neatly indicated by the glowing green numerals and sweep second hand, were on his side, a passage toward an undefined but inevitable state of happiness. It was ten-thirty; he'd have to be back to work in eleven and a half hours.

Bonnie said, "I'll make you something to eat, if you want."

"I want," he said, "a bath. My pores are clogged with powdered graphite, ozone and cold sweat."

"And lima beans?" she said with a grimace.

"I think I'm getting friendly with them—we've been through so much together. You know I don't want to visit Thelma."

"It can't hurt you!"

"Then why am I scared?" he said as they went on down the hallway into the kitchen.

"John, she's just a human being, a child."

"I'm frightened by imbecility."

"Thelma's not an imbecile, she's a kind and loving person!"

" 'The coward dies a thousand deaths, the brave man only one.' "

"I know you're brave, John."

"Bonnie, I may not go."

"She wants to see you. She loves her brother."

"You told her I was coming."

"Maybe I did! She was frightened! She needed something to look forward to!" Bonnie's face went soft and out of focus. "I didn't mean to manipulate you, if that's what you're angry about. I was just thinking of Thelma!"

He offered her one of the beers he'd stashed in the refrigerator, but she shook her head. "You make me feel guilty," she said.

"What do you think you make me feel?"

"I'm so sorry! We shouldn't feel this way toward each other, none of us! Something's gone wrong with CSW, with the Divine Harmony we should manifest—that the God of love is the Lord of our lives. Oval's crazy over that machine and his lima beans, and I'm not good enough to take his place. I can't always show love and tolerance. When the doctor was explaining about Thelma I could see his lack of care. I could see it and I couldn't forgive it. He meant that it would be just as well if she died and he said it right in front of her, as if she couldn't understand. Because he said 'bronchial,' and 'renal,' and 'mortality,' she wasn't supposed to understand. He as good as said she wasn't worth all the effort. I can't forgive it!" She put her long hands on her face.

"Are they doing anything for her?"

"She's terrified of the oxygen thing they stick up her nose. She knows what they feel. She may not know all they say but she knows what's really important. Oval said once, 'The mind is only the tail—the soul is the dog.' "

"What's Oval going to do?"

"He's off work in the morning, so he'll see then. I don't know. But how lonely she must be tonight! We're praying for her, all the Healing Echelons. If you know a prayer, John, if you believe in anything, pray for poor Thelma."

Soon Bonnie said good night, and he took his bath. Again he put Thelma and her problems aside. He couldn't do anything about Thelma anyway, and to pray was such an alien idea, so much against his morals, or something that felt very much like morals, that the request made him freshly aware of the insanity he'd fallen among.

He didn't feel that the day was over, so he dressed and rode down Los Robles to Concha, guessed left and followed Concha until he came to Jimmy's Palace, a standard sort of bar in a little square building with a red neon sign. There was the familiar worry about having to show his identification, but this time Les saw him come in, so it was all welcome and introductions. Jimmy himself shook his hand and brought him a draft on the house. Dianne, or Streaky, about whom John had faint but lustful thoughts, had, it seemed, forsaken Jimmy's and now hung out at the Baccalaureate Club over near TJC. Too bad, Les said. Les had to be at work at 1 A.M., so John had a couple more with him and his friends, who talked of cars. Les was restoring a '33 Cord, Pete was putting together what he called a "Chevroplane," a '32 Chevy body, chopped and channeled, of course, with a '36 Hudson Terraplane straight-six engine, highly milled and modified because it had great tolerances. Joe was dicking around with a '34 Packard straight-eight roadster with a stroke as long as your goddam leg he'd paid two hundred and fifty bucks for. Les suggested that John's motorcycle would look less ridiculous if he cropped the fenders; right now it looked "grandma." Pete changed the subject by asking if they'd all registered for the new draft law Truman just signed. John hadn't heard about it, and when told that everybody had to register felt a small twist of apprehension, which soon passed. "You're a vet," Les said, "so you'll be 4-A."

"You hear he also intergrated the services?" Joe said.

"He what the which?"

"Intergrated the niggers. No more nigger outfits."

"Ninety-sixth wasn't a bad outfit, I heard."

"Well, it's going to be all intergrated now, thanks to Harry."

"I'd hate to be a spook in my old outfit. Captain T. N. Jones ate niggers for breakfast."

"I hope old Harry knows what he's doing."

A connoisseur of these inflections, John found them strangely nonvirulent—but then the subject was usually brought up by the virulent, and it hadn't been here. From the jukebox came, again, a song he made a note to listen to carefully sometime: "Hey, Okie, tell Arkie Tex has got a job in Californy . . ." It went on about orange-juice fountains and streets with curbs of gold. But there was an actual orange-juice spigot at the Tulaveda Produce Co-op, provided with paper cups so you could drink orange juice anytime you wanted some. And all the lima beans your heart desired—fact and myth in this peripheral land.

Les got up. "I got to go freeze my nuts," he said. "I ain't happy till I'm up to my ass in lima beans, same as John here. Right?"

John left then, too, and rode back up Los Robles in the cool midnight air, passed the dark house where Bonnie lay sleeping and climbed a mile or more up toward the Sierra Madre until the town ran out. He stopped and looked down at the lights of Tulaveda. The muted streetlights kept their night vigil throughout the town, defining its planned avenues, streets and pretty arbors. When were all the people—Okies and Arkies and everyone—going to go home? He could not define the principle of impermanence here. It was not just that the town was built upon dust, that he stood on the side of a mountain made of dust, or that all of its water came from far away, through tubes—which seemed as strange as if the air to breathe also came through tubes—and yet water was sprayed everywhere for frivolous and cosmetic reasons, the supply unlimited. Timbuktu on its parched sand would seem more permanent, or a base camp in Antarctica. Maybe it was a matter of effort. There was no weather here, the sun always pale in a pale sky, the air nothing but there. No wonder it was a place of toys and goofy simplifications.

Maybe the freezing machine was a bit of needed reality—one of Sylvan Hearne's remembered Winota winters when the wind from Canada was so cold a touch of skin to metal meant instant necrosis—its purpose to serve the honest, unpretentious lima bean. Of course, the machine held worrisome secrets from its inventor, but that too was at least real.

The next day, after Oval had been to the hospital, they sat against the lockers and had a few minutes to talk. "Bonnie says you might go visit Thelma tonight," Oval said. "That would be so kind and thoughtful of you."

"Maybe I will," John said.

"You know she's very sick this time. She always gets these colds, but lately she's had other complications, too. If they can get her to breathe a little better we'll just bring her home and do what we can for her. She's dying, you know. We've known it for a year or more. She just hasn't got what it takes to fight off sickness. Something's missing. Something Marge and I didn't manage to give her. I don't know. She's always been such a happy child, a loving child, and she has such a marvelous talent for drawing."

"And your wife, Marge—she just ran away and left it all to you?"

"Poor Marge. She was too sensitive, Johnny. She just couldn't take it. She meant well enough, and she tried, but some people just aren't up to what life deals them."

"Don't you ever say anything bad about a woman?"

Oval was surprised by the question. "What do you mean by bad?" he said.

"Like a selfish bitch?"

"That's just a name. Names don't mean anything. The fact is, I respect, love and adore women. I'm not saying they haven't given me a lot of grief, but most of that was my own fault. They have warm, generous hearts, bless them. They want to give. Their blessed gift is in giving."

He'd been hearing a familiar echo in Oval's voice, and it was Bonnie's voice—the lilt, the accent, the mild descending order of the phrases. He wondered which of them imitated the other, or if their common sweet refrain of love, over and over, humorless, clear-eyed, high-minded, pretentious and sincere, had somehow homogenized their manners and their voices. Urban Stumms, who now came frosted and lurching from the thick door of the machine, seemed more a creature of his world.

Oval got up, zipping his worn flight suit. It wasn't quite yet his time to reenter the machine, but of course he said, "Take a few more minutes, Johnny. I'm warmed up," and went in.

"Thirty-two thousand on this watch," Urban said. He unwound the wool scarf he had to wrap around his face because of the scar tissue. John examined the stiff mask for the pure white of frostbite but found none this time.

The machine had been running so well they'd gone to two men inside instead of three. Les oversaw the conveyor belt, and up the line in swirls of steam from the blanching, rows of women in white smocks bent over the flow of lima beans.

More than a week ago he'd given Urban back his pistol barrel. Because Urban had become so dutiful and even proprietary about the machine and its production, he'd stopped thinking at all about Urban and suicide. Here, it seemed, was a worthier enthusiasm than self-punishment. The man who had burned Tokyo and seen Jesus Christ in a Kawasaki Ki-61, who had tried to murder Christ with twin fifty-caliber machine guns, now seemed happy in his duty. Maria was pregnant with his child and that, too, must have made him reconsider doomsday. Details of the wedding were being worked out, as was Urban's current faith, for that matter. He and Oval, when their breaks coincided, discussed this in serious, private voices.

At six o'clock he was in sector 3 when a sprocket stopped turning and immediately lost several of its teeth. The chain slid from it and the trays began to tilt. He hit the kill switch just before the trays began to bend, which would have made them unusable. It was luck that he'd been looking in the right direction, and in fact happened to be staring at the sprocket that froze, because he'd been thinking about how to avoid going to the hospital and in dangerous ways wasn't really doing his job. It was just luck. Even as the teeth sheared and fell he was not quite there, but then he was, and was able to act.

"A number two sprocket!" he shouted down through beams, trays of white boxes, chains and hoarfrost. The fans still roared above him but the chirping of metal had stopped. Urban pushed a thirty-six-inch pipe wrench up the ladder and climbed after it to help him loosen the sprocket's two-inch nut. It would not loosen. They'd had enough experience to know that the next thing to give would be the welded frame it was mounted on rather than the more easily replaceable shaft, so they called for a blowtorch. Oval came up with a new sprocket. Just as his head and hands appeared he missed a rung of the ladder and the sprocket rolled along the plank and went over the side, down into the machinery. "God*dam*it!" Oval cried in exasperation.

"I'll get it," John said. Urban had given Oval a look, just his slits and dark pupils visible.

"We'll need a torch to unfreeze this one," Urban said.

John went to the end of the plank and let himself down a story and a half on beams and chains, thinking of Charlie Chaplin in *Modern Times* and how it wouldn't be quite so funny if the machine started up. He crawled back along the floor in six inches of snow and luckily found the sprocket, then had to swim backwards to get out again. He was about at the end of his ability to control his hands when he got to the secondary hatch, the one with ARBEIT MACHT FREI over it, and let himself out into the hot air of late afternoon. The bell was ringing. Oval was about to enter the other door with a blowtorch and a hammer. Then the bell stopped ringing and Oval's head jerked around toward it. His mouth opened and he uttered a groan of sad disappointment, as if he were saying, "Oh, no." He pulled at the spokes of the locking wheel on the door. The silence of the bell meant that the machine had started up again. John ran up to help him with the wheel, and as they entered, the bell began to ring again. Oval ran across the heaps of lima beans to the ladder and shouted, instantly hoarse, "What happened? What happened?"

At first nothing answered but the mechanical wind. Oval dropped the torch and hammer on the frozen beans and climbed the ladder, John behind him. In sector 3 were too many people, soiled green flight suits crowded on the plank, shoulders pushed against the machinery. Jack looked around, surprised by Oval's shouting. John pushed ahead of Oval, who seemed unable to move forward and yell the one question at the same time. John expected to see someone hurt, flesh and clothing crushed between sprocket and chain—fingers, a hand.

Urban turned away from what he was doing and straightened up, staring at Oval. "Take it easy," he said. "It's okay, Oval. We had to go forward a few inches to free the shaft. Take it easy, now."

"What! What!"

"We heard John go out the other hatch. Everybody was accounted for." Urban pushed past John to get to Oval. "We thought you heard us say what we were going to do. You said something just before you went out, didn't you?"

"Oh, my God," Oval said, finally understanding. "Oh, dear God."

"You got to take it easy, Oval." Urban looked up at Oval and Oval bent down over Urban, exhausted, his jaws bluish white.

"You go take a break. We can handle it," Urban said.

John still had the sprocket, which he handed to Urban.

"You go on out with Oval," Urban said to him. "Too many bodies up here as it is. Go on, now. Go on, skipper," he said, gently pushing Oval toward the ladder.

Oval went down. John followed and brought up the torch and hammer. "Tell him it's okay," Urban said.

Outside, Oval sat on the pile of corrugated boxes, slumped back against a locker, still trying to catch his breath. "Whew," he said. "Whew. For a minute there."

"Me, too," John said.

"Aren't you off soon, Johnny?"

"Why don't you go? I'll stay on," John said with a hopeful, dubious yearning for the opportune.

His father looked at him. He didn't know what the man was thinking; he just looked at him neutrally, as if thinking long thoughts not necessarily about the moment at hand. There had been more than a little panic in the man. For good reason, maybe, if there ever was a good reason for panic. Yes, but who was John Hearne to judge anyone? Under the steady gaze of the blue eyes his attempted excuse not to go see Thelma shivered and fell away. It didn't matter what anyone thought; he'd said he would do it and because of that it would be intolerable not to do it.

He stood the Indian Pony in the visitors' parking area, next to a cement wall so if it fell over it wouldn't fall all the way over. He was in a slightly traitorous way sick of the motorcycle because apprehensive of its dangers. Right now he was more or less generally apprehensive. She would recognize him, and then what?

At the desk in the lobby he asked for her room or ward, which he'd neglected to ask Bonnie or Oval about. People came and went, not sorrowing or crying, though some looked pinched and flushed. He took the stairs rather than an elevator. Stairs were only tiring if you walked up them instead of running lightly. He ran, but was not in a hurry. At the nurse's station he asked for her. Was he a relative? "Her brother," he said. How sweet, the nurse seemed to imply. She took him to a large room where there were eight or ten beds, none of the others occupied. Thelma's was surrounded by movable partitions.

"See? See? A visitor!" the nurse said. Thelma stopped making a thin, airy sound he interpreted as a mild whine of hopelessness. She was a heaped, bloated-looking mound on the narrow bed. Her round face was yellowish. From an ordinary-looking welding oxygen tank, except that the gas bubbled through a suspended jar of clear liquid, came a rubber tube that was taped to her forehead, cheek and upper lip before it went up her flat nose.

"She stopped taking out her nasal catheter," the nurse said. "I don't think she knows what it's for but it must give her some relief."

"John!" Thelma said. The nurse left.

"Hello, Thelma," he said. "How you doing?"

She held out her short hand, her thumb like a huge peanut. Her hand was dry, grainy, substantial, and had the ability to grasp. It took him away, into himself, then became less intolerable, his hand mostly forgetting what it held.

"I thick, mawful thick," she said. He guessed she was glad to see him but she was distracted, trying not to be.

"I know, Thelma," he said.

"I cwy'n I can hep it!"

They didn't like her whining, of course.

"When can I go home, John?"

"I don't know. When you're better. When you feel good."

"I fee good *home,* John."

He recognized the feeling that had once been for him white clouds passing over green and blue Minnesota. She'd felt good at home, so a kind of logic he could name but no longer believe made perfect sense to her. She panted shallowly, her tongue visible.

"They want to make you feel good so you can go home," he said.

"I draw pichures for you."

"Beautiful pictures," he said. Her grasp on his hand relented and her hand went back to her side, the bulb of flesh below her arm flattening on the sheet.

"I don fee good, John."

"I know," he said.

He wondered what she knew about her fate, or anyone's. She always seemed to know just a little more than he thought she did. The talent she had was like a sharp light that must in some ways illuminate the murk she'd been condemned to at birth, or at conception. She understood space and the positions of planes and lines in space, then had the really rare ability to translate three dimensions into one, deliberately losing certain qualities for the sake of art. Maybe that wasn't intelligence but it was a brilliant understanding, a brilliant sacrifice most of the people in the world could never make.

"My gonna die, John?"

He thought of saying, We're all going to die, Thelma. But that wouldn't do. "No, don't think of that," he said.

"See Mama John Bonnie Daddy in heaven," she said. Her hand went to the tube taped to her lip and grasped it firmly, as if she'd forgotten what it was.

"Don't touch that," he said quickly. "Don't pull on it."

"My node itch it."

"It helps you breathe. Don't . . ."

She pulled the tube out. It was longer than he'd thought—nearly a foot of it, slimy with mucus. She coughed and gasped as she rubbed the red place on her upper lip where the tape had been. He looked for a button of some kind that might call the nurse, but couldn't find one so went out into the hall.

"John! John!" Thelma called, then began bawling what might have been the same word. The nurse was not at her station and he looked peculiar half running down the corridor. Visitors in civilian clothes looked at him. He nearly ran into the nurse coming around a corner. She put a hand to her strange hat, blue with white wings, pinned to her brown hair.

"She's pulled the tube out," he said. He followed her back to the room. She immediately turned off the oxygen and he noticed something as strange as anything he'd noticed lately; stamped into the side of the iron-brown tank was a swastika and some words in German.

The nurse zipped the tape from Thelma's forehead and let the tube go down to the floor. She said, "The doctor said if she pulled it out again not to call him, just leave it out."

"Can she breathe all right?"

"Oh, she can breathe. She's just got to learn not to pull it out. We'd have to put her in restraint and she sure wouldn't like that."

"Sowwy!" Thelma cried. "Node itch! Can hep it!" She was embarrassed and guilty—he'd seen that look before. She panted, her meaty tongue looking like something she didn't want to chew and swallow.

The nurse looked at her wristwatch. "The doctor's going to be here pretty soon anyway and he'll look in on her. We don't like the jaundiced look she's getting."

"How long?" he asked.

"Twenty minutes. Half an hour. Are you going to stay?"

He looked at the nurse carefully, for the first time, because she asked him that question. She was a little older than he was, with heavy down on her upper lip and chin, traces of acne and the luminous, dark-rimmed pretty eyes that quite often went with skin problems. Her starched white uniform was a perfect blankness, snow too bright to look at. All of these things made her seem deeply female. He'd looked at her too long, and she blushed.

"Are you going to stay?" she asked again.

"Do you want me to?"

"Well, we're not absolutely sure how well she's breathing. I can get a mask if there's any trouble." She glanced at Thelma, who turned her head to the side and back, her habitual look over her shoulder. She was listening to them, though.

"You can't put that catheter back in?" he said.

"No, the doctor does that. It's unsterile now anyway."

"I'll watch her, then," he said.

"She's your sister?" the nurse said, frowning because she wished she hadn't said such an unprofessional thing.

He was about to say Thelma was his half-sister but that seemed at the last second mean. "Yes, she's my sister," he said. The nurse was competent and slim and reminded him a little of Dory.

"John ith my *brother,"* Thelma said, startling the nurse so much she became tense, as if her authority were in doubt.

"Now, can she breathe comfortably without the oxygen?" the nurse said.

Thelma coughed and drooled, but went on breathing. "Don fee good," she said. The nurse nodded professionally. She took a cord and push button from a side table and plugged it into a wall receptacle at the head of the bed.

"We couldn't use the call button with the oxygen because it might cause a spark," she explained. "If she has any trouble use the button, all right?" She left, walking self-consciously, he could tell by her purposefulness.

Thelma breathed out loud. He found a chair and sat by her side, holding the hand she put out to him. She breathed and rubbed her nose with the hand that held his, squashing her face with their hands, getting them wet.

He understood her words more and more, though they changed according to how they were combined. Sometimes she lisped, sometimes she dropped consonants, sometimes she left out articles; there was a pattern to it, though, he was discovering. A word used as one part of speech changed when used as another even though it wouldn't in his language. Hard sounds became soft, long vowels became short. Some words, though still ghostly in her voice, she carefully articulated.

What if she were his seventeen-year-old sister and hadn't this curse of fog and bloat upon her? She would be a trim blonde girl with honest blue eyes and they could talk freely and evenly, equally, to each other, no mysteries or tensions because they would be brother and sister, twin perceptors of all the bothersome complications of the world. Imagine having a sister. What questions they could answer for each other.

Thelma spoke to him, saying her daddy loved her and would come take her home. She would see Grandma Hearne, too, and Sylvan. Bonnie would give her a shampoo. Her dog Skip would come back. Her friend Alfie, too. When you died you went to heaven and were never sick and nobody was mean to anybody.

She said she knew she was retarded, that she had a condition that made her unable to do things that others could. She could read and write only a few words. She was proud of her drawing because she could really do that. She knew she didn't look like other people, except Alfie and some of the children at her school. She knew she couldn't go to real school, she couldn't ever get married, she couldn't have a job and make money, as other people did. Her daddy said that in the next world she would read and write as well as anybody and be beautiful and run like the wind. "Run lye win. Run like uh win. Run lika win," she said, trying it, looking at him. The phrase seemed comfortable, something he might say himself.

Her intelligence seemed as precise as any, her knowledge of the truth as deep—at least of this world; the other world was a myth so comforting to her it didn't bear thinking about.

She half sat up. Suddenly her throat grew thicker and with a bray like a goat she projected a dark liquid toward the foot of her bed. She seemed as surprised as he was, but then he saw that her surprise was that she couldn't get a breath. Some engine in her body was still explosively pumping out the dregs of a thick, tea-colored liquid with an odor like phosgene gas, or lewisite—the one that smelled like frying onions. He pushed the button.

She couldn't get a breath. She was suffocating with her mouth open to the same air he breathed without effort. He didn't know what to do. He could run out into the corridor. He could wait. He could yell for help. Her eye whites were yellow and he was afraid blue had begun to stain her fingers. He'd run away from plenty of things in his life and if he tried to do something for her now it might be the wrong thing. He wasn't a medic; nobody could blame him if he did nothing. He grabbed her and turned her on her side, trying to get her over. It was like trying to move a boulder sunk too far into the ground—all round and nothing to get a good hold of, but he finally got her face-down over the side of the bed and slapped her hard on her round back. Her johnny didn't fit all the way around her. The pimples on her back were surrounded by blue. She'd powerfully soiled herself, he could smell. The dark liquid shook from her mouth in drops and strings. Tracheotomy, he thought; get out your jackknife and operate. There had been a famous case in the infantry when a GI had saved his buddy's life with a knife and the barrel of a fountain pen. Christ, he might put her out of her misery, too. *Medic,* he called silently, for Christ's sake!

When they pulled him aside his hand tingled. The nurse and two orderlies or doctors pushed him out and drew the movable partitions closed. He heard them talking and muttering in there for a long time.

One of them had a voice that carried. "Simple catarrhal jaundice." "Yeah, but . . . ," the other said. "Aspirated vomitus." He could understand that. "Acathectic?" "Hepatogenous." "You think so?" "There." "How long was it?" "Three or four minutes," the nurse said. "Brain damage?" Incredibly, a laugh. "I didn't think of that. We'd better use a tent this time." "Give her mutter mutter mutter."

At least he didn't have to do anything. The tea-dark, onion-smelling stuff was on his shirt and down his right pant leg.

"Get her cleaned up," one of the doctors said.

The nurse came out carrying a bundle of bedclothes in one hand, away from her uniform. She stopped, startled to see him right there. "She's all right now," she said. "She's breathing all right now."

A child's urgent whine of pain came from behind the partition. "Liver's sensitive," a doctor said.

"Let me say goodbye to her," he said, and without waiting for an answer pulled the partition aside and went in. They were not ready for visitors. She lay spread out on her back, gray folds like rhino skin on her knees, an enormous hairy complex leading to her belly, where chafed red skin showed through the tangle.

"Hey. What? You should wait outside," one doctor said. He pulled her stained johnny down over her belly, a small tablecloth over a boulder. The stench was sweet, like licorice. He went around the doctor to where her head was, and thought she looked at him. He said her name but she went on whining, one eye definitely not seeing him, the other maybe. "Thelma?" he said again.

He was past horror. She didn't by her freakishness violate anything worthwhile, but was, he could see, a small center, bright as a distant candle, which knew it was itself and that it was alone. For a moment everything came together for him. If she were lost she would be lost to herself forever, her self and her talent condemned not by any fault of hers or any lack of brilliance and resolve. So purely lost. It was a void so perfect it had taken him all his life to understand it. She was herself, indivisible. Oh, Hearne, figure this out. If lost she would be lost forever to herself. It was all so final, a clarity so immense it disdained grief or sorrow. How could his father not know this?

He put out his hand and touched Thelma's coarse blond hair. Her skull was foreshortened, like a gourd. "Thelma?" he said. She whined and murmured, far off somewhere. His sympathy was beyond tears, pure and terrible.

"She's disoriented," one of the doctors said. "Best not to stimulate her now." Both doctors were embarrassed and wanted him out of there. "Tell her father she's had a small episode, possibly petit mal. She has so many degenerative symptoms now. Best to check on her in the morning." This was speech caused by unease—simply authoritative chatter.

The other took it up. "Ordinarily hepatogenous jaundice has a very good prognosis, but in her case . . ."

"All right," he said.

He met the nurse wheeling a narrow, cloth-covered rack toward Thelma's room. She stopped. "Did they tell you you had to leave?" She was furious.

"They suggested it," he said.

"Oh, I could spit!" she said, and went on.

He took the stairs, floating down on busily independent feet. His motorcycle took him through dangerous dark streets and by the time he reached the parsonage his perfect understanding of the meaning of life had faded into the textures of the evening—streetlights behind perfumed trees, clouds of invisible moisture, suspicious cars at stop signs. He would never forget the moment of his insight, but he would never be able to explain it to himself, or re-create its exaltation.

29

Dory doesn't exist in time, or even too strongly as "Dory." She has no friends, deserves none and wants none. She has become a connoisseur of languor, its varieties and degrees. For the first time in her life she has nothing, nothing, to do, and her response to this new condition is torpor, semi-coma, the inner glimmerings of nearly voluntary shallow dreams. There are rules for these dreams; they are all interesting and not unpleasant, or she will shut them off and not let them come back. She is alone in them, neutral and aware. In them are qualities she has felt or sensed on earth: snow and sand, water and ferns, certain forms of light—textures that cause, through the sensual dream-body that is hers, almost disembodied moods. Stone is marvelously historical, like a long bare ridge of Cascom Mountain, granite or granodiorite, with lozenges of white felspar embraced in it. She moves, or just her eyes move, over miles of complicated, undulating stone, about a yard above it, and it forms pictograms for her interest, created and interpreted at her pleasure. Nothing is by accident. The textural variety of the granite and its aggregated specks of quartz and mica, garnet and felspar, is of course random, random as creation is, but she sees the march of the British Empire, invasions of China, flotillas in the Sea of Japan—arms, faces, weapons, boots, ships, horses, all ancient and true and relieved by time of all but a carefully neutral historical interest. Nothing is in human terms, only in the frieze of history before it screamed in terror and pain, before she learned that it was all agony. There is danger here, so the melting begins and the stone is gone, turning like lead to quicksilver.

Water is defined by flow, sometimes by wind, but only mild wind. No storms are allowed. Nothing is unexpected. She is not "she." It is sometimes hard to control all of this and at the same time have no responsibility for control. Only in this liquid state can she deny it.

When her mother brings her food, sometimes her mother places it directly into Dory's mouth, using Dory's politeness as a method in feeding her. Sometimes her father stands silently in the room. They don't threaten her; her weakness is powerful and makes them go away.

So "she" exists, inexplicably in their terms, being more careful than they can imagine.

30

Oval was home, cooking lima beans while Hadasha Kemal Allgood sat at the kitchen table. He lifted the cover of his saucepan of lima beans, which gave off a humid, slightly fishy odor, and peered in.

John went to wash up. When he returned Oval was poking a fork into the steam. He brought one bean out, bit into it carefully and nodded. "Anyone want some lima beans?"

"You really like them?" John asked.

"They're almost all I want to eat anymore. Here." He brought one out of the pan on the fork and moved it unmistakably toward John's mouth, the green seed coming at him, behind it the man balancing it carefully, with the calm intensity of an adult feeding a child, even the way the mouth imitated what it wanted the child's mouth to do.

He had to take the plump green seed on his tongue. It was hot, smooth and firm, with a bland, watery flavor that was almost no flavor at all, as if the bean were a sort of light pebble, food in name only.

"Phaseolus limensis; Phaseolus lunatus," Hadasha intoned.

John bit into the flesh of the one bean. Its blandness, which had always suggested the inedible, such as gray clay or wet mortar, now grew in authority, blandness becoming a subtlety that encompassed space, or distance. He thought of the koala bear, who ate one food only, the leaves of the eucalyptus, the texture and flavor of which must be so perfect to the koala bear no other food could even be imagined.

Of course he must be hungry; he hadn't had anything for over eight hours except for a cup of orange juice from the spigot at the Co-op. But there was a change in him, a little sea change near the center, somewhere, of choice, not just of mind but of something more like temperament. There was the good in the seed, the life-good in its increments, flavor a mist surrounding value. He took a small plate from the cupboard and accepted a portion of them from Oval, a finite number of them, thinking of China during famines, when merchants counted out rice by the grain rather than by the measure.

Hadasha said, "The proper Linnaean terms seems to be *Phaseolus lunatus,* though Webster's says *Phaseolus limensis.* The common kidney bean is *Phaseolus vulgaris,* though by analogy one wonders why Webster's doesn't call it *Phaseolus renalis* if they're going to do that sort of thing."

"They should never be overcooked," Oval said. "Never, never. It ruins them. It ruins their *separateness.* Try a little butter. They don't actually need it, but they like just a tiny bit of salty nuttiness from the melted butter." He stared and nodded as John took his advice, then added, "I like to eat them with a salad fork. I think the shape of a salad fork is best."

"A little boat shaped like the moon, a half- or quarter-moon," Hadasha said. "Specifically a pinnace, a light sailing craft used as a scout or a tender. Also, figuratively, a woman, a mistress."

"What a name for a bean," John said.

His conversion was neither immediate nor, at this point, total, but the beans didn't grow in his mouth. They became separate from each other, less a pile or a crowd.

"Not that they aren't good no matter what you eat them with," Oval said. He didn't seem to hear Hadasha's scholarly remarks; names really didn't mean much to him. He took another damaged package from the refrigerator. "But they deserve more. They remind me of the perfection of the universe. They speak to me of the universal. I become them. There's something sacred, a sacred trust. I'm not sure. I can't abide throwing them away. When we have to shovel them out I can't abide the idea they'll become garbage. Each its perfect, separate oneness. I just can't abide it." He put a small amount of water in his saucepan, adding a pinch of salt. "That's just habit," he said. "They don't need salt. They get a touch of it from the butter anyway. I'm going to stop putting salt in the water." He poured out the water and started over, saltless.

Hadasha smoked one of his Houri cigarettes and sipped his coffee. "I'm only a scholar," he said. "All I care about is my work. My enthusiasm is engendered by a minor god. I reduce, I discard interpretations; the fanciful juxtapositions sound like mere errors to my prosifying soul. But our teacher"—he nodded toward Oval—"invests the smallest of these with passion."

Silent blue flame bathed the bottom of the pan. Oval hadn't been listening to Hadasha, but to the little ticks along the bottom of the pan as the water heated and began to change its form. He held the torn box of lima beans at the ready, a gaunt figure in a green sports shirt with flowers, little red propellers, printed all over it, and yellow slacks, the material unevenly faded and flimsy, as if it had once been starched but had lost it all. His shiny blue socks seemed as thin as tissue paper over his ankles, and his shoes were shiny black oxfords, the ones he must wear to church on Sunday. There was no suggestion, in the gaudy colors, of any thought or choice, and there probably hadn't been.

A telephone rang somewhere in the parsonage, then stopped ringing. Bonnie came into the kitchen. "That was Urban," she said. "He says Jack got into a fight and broke his hand, so he can't come in tonight."

"I'll go," Oval said.

Bonnie looked at John.

"I'll go," he said.

"No, I'll go," Oval said. "It's my responsibility."

"You're too tired," Bonnie said. "You're too tired and worried about Thelma. You stumbled on the threshold when you came in tonight. Your eyes are bloodshot. I won't let you go."

"What difference does that make?" Oval said, turning back to his saucepan.

"That I won't let you go?" Bonnie cried, hurt to tears.

"No, no, dear," Oval said to the boiling water. "The rest. The rest of it."

Bonnie ran up behind Oval and grabbed him, pink sweater sleeves sliding up her pale round arms. "You can't do it! John's young and he can do it! Sit down and I'll get you something decent to eat! Sit down, now!" She pulled him away from the stove, their legs awkwardly tangling. One of Oval's legs buckled and they nearly fell together to the floor. On one knee, holding Bonnie to keep her from falling all the way to the floor, Oval looked again to his steaming saucepan. Bonnie cried.

This, after a second or two, began to have in John's mind the eternal quality of a vignette. He left the kitchen, got his Ike jacket for the cool night air and rode down Los Robles to the Peg o' My Heart Drive-in, where he quickly ate a sandwich called a Hammurabi—ham and, he supposed, Babylonian barbecue sauce—laying it down on an honest base of lima beans. He had no business even thinking about Bonnie, whose concern for Oval was on another plane entirely, near to a desperation he was probably not capable of.

He rode on to the Co-op, suddenly remembering Thelma, poor Thelma, whom he had forgotten again. Would that cold forgetfulness always lie in wait for him?

On a short break around eleven that night he and Urban were out together. Urban unwound the scarf from his rigid face. Some animals seemed to grin when they didn't; others looked fierce when they weren't. In Urban was the dangerous quality of a beast who was, if silent, unreadable.

But he spoke: "I don't see what she wants with me. My disability pension? My GI insurance? She knows I'm a freak and a nut. She could get rid of the *niño* easy enough—I offered to pay for it."

John could hear the words, but from behind the scars came only a glare. He said to Urban, "She acts like she loves the shit out of you."

"I know about a doc in LA he'll do it for five hundred, a real doc, too, but she acts like Baal is in the Church if I mention it. She wants to have the kid. We got hitched yesterday at the Town Hall, so no matter what happens the kid won't be a bastard, but what she wants with me, I don't know. I don't know why she ever climbed in my bed. The mackerel-snappers are funny that way—they don't think it's much of a sin to fuck. Well, she got caught. I thought I was dreaming the first time she came padding up the stairs in her little bare feet. I thought it was before the war and I had a face and clean hands, more or less. I was a Baptist then, a young stud from the Ozarks with the Devil's rod hung on him like a bloodsucker, like a viper bit him in the crotch and wouldn't never let go."

"Why don't you think she loves you?" John said. "Women are funny that way, I've heard."

"From Oval, yeah. He's been banging my ear about it. He wants to marry us in his church as soon as the lima beans slack off. He says he wants to consecrate our union in the love of Christ."

"Do you love her?"

Urban held out his hands, to show them. "With these? You can't see the blood on them, but I can."

"Well, aside from that, do you love her?"

"The love of Christ! The Christ I saw with my own eyes is a different Christ than Oval ever dreamed of. He's fed up with all this love shit. He's sick of the two-legged devils that play with fire."

Urban looked at his watch and sighed with resignation much gentler than his words. It was time for them to go back into the unforgiving winds of the machine. John wondered how Maria made love to the burned man. He wondered if she kissed him on the slot of a mouth and caressed the terrible mask.

At one in the morning he was working sector 1, guiding the warm boxes into the frozen trays, when he felt, rather than saw, a new tension in the chains. Urban had just come in to take over for Les in sector 3, and had gone up the steel ladder. Tex was outside. The tension he felt was like a hardening of the jaws, no other symptoms, and then it seemed to have passed. His trays moved with their normal squeaks and pauses, so it must have been his imagination, a squint of the eyes, some thought unrelated to the machine broadcasting itself into the outer world. The inner-outer world here, created and chilled for *Phaseolus lunatus.* He wondered why Dory had never answered his postcard. The others had. His mother had sent him ten dollars, which he'd in no way requested. He'd had a card from Gracie, Loretta and Miles, and from Estelle Hilberg a note on engraved stationery. "Give my love to Sylvan," she'd written. Oval, no longer Sylvan, had smiled ruefully at that. But not a word from Dory. He felt guilt, like a blush; had he treated her so badly, so meanly, that she wouldn't write to him? He never knew the rules. He wondered if he'd ever know them. Maybe her answer had been lost in the mails, but he knew better; the ordinary processes of the world were always more efficient and predictable than you wanted to think they were.

The machine stopped. The bell clamored faintly through the package slot, the fans whined far above, where Urban was shouting, so he couldn't make out the words. His hands were numb but could still grasp the ladder rungs. Urban's shouting seemed too urgent and he heard the word "help," which made him afraid. He ran along the plank in sector 2 and up the ladder to sector 3, where Urban and Les were huddled together, looking at something they both held on to. It was one of their hands but at first he couldn't tell whose. Les was saying, and had been saying, "Oh God damn it Jesus oh Jesus oh fuck God damn it," continuously in a soft, furry voice. "God Jesus damn it all . . ." It was Les's hand that they both looked at. What was left of the glove was still on it. "Jesus fuck it shit damn it," Les crooned. It was his left hand, not bleeding very much, just oozing from the ragged palm of the glove.

"We got to get him down the ladders," Urban said. "He already fainted once." The shortest way was down to sector 4 and out the back hatch in sector 5. They guided Les to the first ladder and manhandled him down, one on each side, dragged him by his clothes along the plank and then down the ladder to sector 5 and out the hatch. He fainted again for a moment as they let him down onto the cement floor. A cart pusher was sent to the office to tell the watchman to call an ambulance. They got out of their flight suits and tucked them under Les, a sleeve under his head.

"I didn't feel nothing," Les said. He held his hurt hand in the other, squeezing it. "Christ, it felt kind of funny, so I looked and that was the first time I knew what the fuck happened. Jesus, I guess I slipped a little and stuck it right in a fucking sprocket. I was so numb anyway."

"I should have relieved you sooner. I was a couple minutes late," Urban said.

The watchman, having called an ambulance, came with a first-aid kit. John cut off the rest of the glove with his knife and there the hand was. Les had his thumb and two-thirds of his little finger left. They dusted sulfa powder on the stumps and put on a pressure bandage, tying the strings tightly. The carts were already rolling by with the packages of lima beans. "Starting to sting now," Les said. It was starting to bleed, too; the bandage was already a red ball. "Shit," Les said. "It's really starting to sting."

Urban felt for the artery but any pressure made Les yelp. "Christ, let her bleed!" he said.

"I should have relieved you sooner," Urban said.

Tex had found them by going all the way through the machine, where he'd seen the blood on the planks and on the white packages. He took off his flight suit and put it over Les. "Shock," he explained. "Don't want him going into shock."

John gave Les a lighted cigarette, and Les, looking very gray and sick, said, "Hell, I got a thumb and part of a pinkie, so I'll still be able to hold a butt."

"Hell, yeah," Tex said. "Anyway, you still got your good right hand."

"I guess you never noticed I'm a lefty," Les said.

When the ambulance came Les walked to it, the attendants close beside him. The watchman said he'd called the plant manager because all accidents had to be reported immediately. They were to leave the machine off, the fans on, and be back at eight in the morning.

"Did you call Oval?" John asked.

"You live with him, don't you? Why don't you tell him."

The cart pushers who normally took the boxes from the machine would help the other cart pushers take the beans from the line.

"Oval won't take this too well," Urban said. "But you better not wait to tell him."

They dawdled at the lockers, though, trying to talk themselves through what had happened. "The poor bastard," Tex said. "What's he going to do now? He sure ain't going to play the piccolo."

"There's three fingers in the machine somewhere," Urban said.

"He ought to use the rest of his GI Bill," John said.

"He says he ain't college material," Tex said.

"I should have relieved him sooner. If I'd only . . ."

"You put your ass in the gears, the gears don't say, 'No, thanks,' " Tex said.

John said he thought he'd felt a difference in the chains around the time it happened, but that was impossible.

"No," Urban said. "You had a premonition. If you'd trusted it you might have saved his fingers."

"You know I don't believe in that kind of thing."

"That kind of thing don't care if you believe it or not. If I relieved him one minute sooner he'd still have all of his hand."

"You sound like it's your fault. It's not your fault," John said. "It's not my fault and it's not your fault."

"Yeah, and Christ loves us all," Urban said.

John got back to the parsonage at two-thirty. A light was on upstairs, but he wasn't sure whose room it was. He didn't want to tell Oval; it seemed a dangerous thing to do. Maybe he was having another premonition. He tried to think that Oval might as well get some sleep, but that didn't work, so he went up the stairs, quietly on the thick brown runners, trying to get his mind made up. Light came from a door down the hall, but from the first black open door at the top of the landing came clear voices.

"Please, please, my dearest. Please, my dearest heart." It was Bonnie's voice, small with pleading.

Oval groaned. "Don't, dear. Please don't."

"I love you. I know you love me. Don't you love me?"

"Of course I love you, dear."

"Then it's right. It's right. I know it's right."

"Oh, God," Oval groaned.

"Is it me? Is it anything I've done? What can I do?"

"No, no. It's wrong. It's just wrong. I'm too old for you. There's

Thelma, there's my faith in doubt. My spirits are in chaos. It's not you, dearest—you're beautiful and true in Christ's love. But not me, not me."

Bonnie sobbed.

John turned and carefully went back down the stairs. He went to his room, shut the door and lay on the bed. His spirits were in chaos, too, else how could he be disgusted at himself for hearing what they'd said, at the banality of their words, at his jealousy of his father, at his father's pitiful, idiotic hesitation?

She was in the wrong room. She should say that to him. He was a voyeur, an impostor sneaking into his father's place, entering her soft, feathery thighs. It was as if he were in a car skidding on ice, yearning for the way he wanted to go but forced by momentum sideways, toward danger. They were both real, the two upstairs, existing separately from him, having their own intense feelings, no matter how he judged them. They could die of their feelings, saying the same dumb words and dying of them.

He saw Dory, so clearly she startled him. She watched him. She needed him but was suspicious. She couldn't trust him. The dark, waterfowl eyes saw the truth of his unfaithfulness and were sad. "What truth, damn it?" he said out loud, but of course got no answer. But this was all his own imagination; he hadn't seen a ghost or had a premonition. He could be wrong about everything. Right now she might be in the back seat of Robert Beggs's father's Plymouth. Stop this. She wasn't a virgin anymore, so there was no mystery. They'd leave the dance at the Casino, park, and pretty soon they'd be in the back seat and she'd think, what the hell, it'll feel good and the bastard that seduced me is out in California screwing Streaky the bandanna girl, which he might very well have been doing under slightly different circumstances. Yes, it was Dory, slipping off her panties as she had only for him.

Toward waking he dreamed that Les was taking his baby's temperature with a rectal thermometer. Les pulled it out and tried to read it but couldn't because of the fecal matter on it, so he casually stuck it in the baby's mouth to clean it. The baby just looked goopily at his father and licked his lips. Perfectly normal. John Hearne observed this, but was not neutral. He suggested to Les that no matter how customary it was to cleanse a rectal thermometer in your child's mouth, there was a danger of infection. The dream chose not to have Les respond.

He awoke in broad daylight, in his clothes and boots, still grimy from the machine, remembering that he should have told Oval about Les and about being back at the Co-op at eight. It was nearly eight. He found Bonnie in the kitchen.

"Thelma died," she said, and sucked in her breath. She looked faded, her jaws pale and her eyes congested and weepy. Thelma was to him then a tiny point of light, just winked out, nothing at all physical, purified of all that. He tried to make an appropriate sound. He'd known her only a short time, with much repulsion, which she'd seen and forgiven, but in her knowing him there had been no change at all, just the assumption of the best in him, no beginning or ending.

"When did it happen?" he said.

"I don't know. Oval heard this morning. He's gone to the hospital, but he didn't have to."

"I'd better get down to the Co-op," John said. He told her what had happened to Les.

"The poor guy! How awful!" she said, then thought for a moment. "I hope Oval can take that too."

There were two suitcases by the door and two thick wardrobe bags over a chair back.

"Yours?" John asked.

"I was going to leave."

"Why?"

"For selfish, terrible reasons!" she cried. Still making little sounds, she picked up her two suitcases and half ran down the hallway and up the stairs.

The plant manager and Tex were waiting at the machine. "Where's Forester?" the manager said. He looked out of place and even more impatient because he wore a seersucker suit and tie and if he touched anything he'd get dirty.

"His daughter died last night, so he went to the hospital this morning."

"Oh!" The breath went out of him.

"I think he'll be in soon," John said. While they were quiet he had time to notice that there were fewer women on the lines. The cart pushers were a little less frantic at the conveyor belt, too. Perhaps the season was dying down.

"When he shows up . . . . when he comes in, come and get me." The manager went off toward the glassed-in offices.

"His daughter was kind of . . . slow, wasn't she?" Tex said in order to get things into the proper perspective.

"Yeah."

"Urban told me not to tell no freak jokes in front of Oval."

"Where is Urban? He ought to be here," John said.

"Ain't seen hide nor hair of him."

He wasn't immediately concerned; people showed up and sometimes they didn't show up. Sometimes they had reasons and sometimes they didn't. Except that Urban Stumms was not that tolerant of the affairs of men, fixed as he was upon revelation, not coincidence.

Meanwhile he and Tex lounged upon the corrugated cardboard by the lockers, putting in their time for pay. Tex, wanting to change the mood of the moment, said, "Feller says, 'Doc, ah took them suppositories, but for all the good they done ah maught's well shoved 'em up mah ay-us.' "

Urban had mentioned his GI insurance. Strange for an Ovarian Apocalyptic to keep up a life insurance policy. What was a Nazi oxygen tank doing in Tulaveda Municipal Hospital? From the machine, "Oval's Folly," came the lower-register hum of the fans, hardly audible through the insulated walls. ABANDON HOPE, ALL YE WHO ENTER HERE. Maybe the chalked words gave him the premonition, if that was what his vision could be called, because the event had already happened. The premonition was of his discovering it. He put on his cold-weather gear. Tex said, "I'd never go into that goddam contraption unless I had orders," and watched him.

The latch wheel, not having been turned for six hours or more, was impossible to turn, the iron dogs probably frozen into their slots in the frame. He got the thirty-six-inch pipe wrench and levered it through the spokes until the wheel gave and the door was free. He entered in a brief haze of fog, hearing now the higher whine of the fans that caused the constant unfresh wind. His skin tightened immediately as he lost surface warmth. Urban, in his flight suit and boots, lay on a bed of loose frozen lima beans, his hands at his sides. John went to him thinking accident, emergency, the urgency of it swelling his arms. Hoarfrost glittered over Urban, equally on his clothes and skin. He tried to lift Urban's head and shoulders, but he was all one piece. There was no question of life still burning somewhere within this piece of stone. He lifted him, wondering again how small and light he was, put him under his arm as if he were a branch, or plank, and took him out of there.

Tex came running. "Holy mackerel," he said in a normal voice, "it's Urban."

In the moist heat Urban's scar tissue grew furry, as if the mask grew fine white hairs, but then the hairs melted at their tips. John laid him down on the cardboard. Webs of frost glinted for a while in the eye holes, the uneven nostrils and the mouth slot.

Tex went to the office to give the alarm, to shift responsibility and to gladly tell the news. John looked down at Urban, the face as simple as a child's drawing of a face—two eyes, two nostrils and a mouth. Or a mask from the Solomons, a white devil god, implacable and malevolent.

A worn effigy in white marble on the lid of a sarcophagus. He had seen dead men, women and children, some bloated into caricatures, faces painted on balloons. They had all by their extreme silence been full of power.

Oval arrived when everyone had gathered around. When he saw what they were looking at, and understood, he knelt beside Urban and put his long hand on the cold forehead, pressing and measuring the shape of it. With his other hand he cupped Urban's jaw. It must have been like handling ice. Oval, his own clean jaws inert, removed his hands and stared at the moisture on his palms.

The police came this time. One, in civilian clothes, said after examining Urban that he might, by the cant of his head, have a broken neck. The police went inside the machine and examined the iron ladder and the carpet of lima beans. They came out quickly, shuddering with cold, and did husky little jigs to warm themselves up again. John had assumed that Urban had committed suicide, that the man haunted by fire had deliberately chosen ice, but now had to think again. They found Les's three gloved fingers in the map pocket on Urban's thigh, and when they lifted him and took him away, the shape of his body on the cardboard was printed dark with moisture and studded with the jade green of lima beans.

Oval stared at the three frozen fingers and the tip of the other one. It was the first time he'd heard of Les's accident. "His left hand?" Oval said. "He was left-handed."

"He used to be," Tex said.

Oval looked around at Tex as if he'd said something in a foreign language, in tongues, Oval's expression opinionless except for distant wonder. But his breath came short and a dark vein in his temple pulsed rapidly.

"I'll go see him. I've got to tell Maria. I've got to," he said to himself. "I've got to do these things. Oh, faith, faith." He looked out of himself, focusing on John. "Johnny?" He swallowed twice, unable to speak, so held out his arms to the machine, meaning would John take over, nodding the question.

"Sure," John said.

Oval got up, a little crooked, as if he had a pain in his back, and left.

John reset the alarm bell and he and Tex ran the machine until it was empty of packages. The plant manager came by and said that the committee, by phone, had decided to shut it down now and dismantle it later, in the off-season. He said to tell Oval there was still a job for him in maintenance. "He's a good man, but he was just a little over his head when he built this Rube Goldberg." When Tex was out of hearing he said, "You Oval's nephew or something? Maybe we could find a place for you."

John said he had to go back to college, but thanks.

For the next three days Oval spent much of his time sitting in his car, which was parked under the tangerine tree in the parsonage yard. He didn't want to talk to anyone but it was known that he was preparing himself for the memorial service for Thelma and Urban. Bonnie took care of the rest, such as the notices in the papers and helping Maria with Urban's obituary. Urban had indeed suffered a broken neck, had probably been paralyzed and had then frozen to death. Internal evidence, such as the amassing of blood in the abdominal area and in the brain, confirmed this.

Urban had also kept up the full ten thousand dollars of his GI insurance. Because of this strange fact John had the dark thought, never spoken, that Urban might have taken a deliberate header off the ladder. Maybe domestic seductions had been threatening the purity of his guilt. Again he felt that at least he understood Urban's uncompromising view of behavior better than that of the Church of the Science of the Way. He would stay for the memorial service because he had to—duty toward the living. He didn't expect to hear anything but the usual, the comforting, everything he could never believe. In churches, when he had to go to churches, during prayer he could never bow his head; he gazed horizontally, because it would be hypocritical not to, with the visual acuity of a scholar in an alien culture. It was as if, at funerals especially, he wrote in his head his own stern oration, which had nothing to do with God.

While he waited he sold his motorcycle to Phil the mechanic for a hundred dollars. This gave him in all nine hundred seventy-four dollars, which he put in traveler's checks, more money than he'd ever had in hand before, enough to make him think of buying a car and driving back. But in the end, remembering the daunting expanses of his country, he bought an airline ticket. The DC-3 would make just seven stops and he would be in Boston in a day. He'd take a train called the Peanut north to Leah.

There was still no note from Dory, and when he thought that maybe she had seen through him and was no longer interested in him, he felt caught out and hurt, a strange, fading regret, as if in another life he had not behaved honorably.

31

She wants no expectations. She wants *not to expect.* Her mind is reluctant. She prefers to retire from what she has learned she is—offspring of the race whose qualities she prefers not to have. That seems to her beyond argument. How cruel she is to her mother and father. She can't explain it to them because it is too dangerous; in her previous life all she did was explain; now she knows they don't want to know what she might explain. John Hearne just disappeared, but that's all abstract, his business, human business.

She watches varnish cracks and bumps, a map of a thousand villages.

She is not lost; she is deliberate in everything. If only she could will herself out of this house, literally imagine her body away from the people she makes unhappy.

Dr. Winston has been called—unheard of. Where is the blood, the fracture, the fever? She won't eat, Doctor. She won't get up except to go to the toilet.

Can't you discuss this somewhere else? All humans squat and strain, so what? Stuff their craws, brag, strut, fuck, kill and squat again. Danger. Danger. There is a perfectly valid reason for choosing one state over another. She chooses sleep, carefully. The connotations of nearly every dream or waking vision are human, creations of the human. Arguments are dangerous to peace because they are human. To retire is not, Mother, to hate you or the human race, just to have understood it and its games. Monopoly, sex, war, torture. Red Rover, come over—a memory of a memory of enthusiasm, unregretted.

When he first put his hands on her breasts, how stupid that pleasure was, because she didn't suspect his contempt. There is no pleasure in humiliation, memory multiplying the horror of having been a fool. Danger here, but not the greatest danger.

Cynthia, right here now, says it was all because Yvonne was of royal blood, bar sinister, and was so gentle, but when she left she was just polite. Summer is over, that quick lifetime. How are you, Dory?

Robert, on the chair, asks, How're you doing? Dibley stands near the door, biting the edge of his thumb, his elbow in the air.

We love you, Cynthia says. We want you to get dressed and come with us. We're going to climb Cascom Mountain and eat lunch at the top. Robert has his father's car. It's a beautiful day.

Yvonne took Cynthia to the studio because she suspected Debbie would be there, and didn't want to go alone. Why didn't she get Mr. King to go, then?

If we are all vile, what difference does it make if we're tortured? We deserve the agony. Goodbye.

Dory? Dory?

She must escape into an idea that is fascinating but emotionless, a landscape of the will. Her father varnished that trim board long ago, but sunlight and heat have created on its surface the most delicate cracks and shapes and continents, each meaning precisely what it means, only to change into another, even more convincing precision. In the distance, through mist, is a pagoda with winged roofs, gilded dragons and trees so old their leaves have never been green. It is all ageless, cool and inhuman, just visual. There is no sound, no tinkling, no bonging, no wind, though it is real. Now it is a forest and it is impossible to find one delicate branch that even suggests a dragon or a winged roof. There is a bird of paradise, and another, and a golden tree snake. Beyond is a wooded hill rising into cloud, all ancient and amber but not monochrome because amber and its variations are all the colors there are in the spectrum of this ancient world.

A varnished board. They are gone. Her scream of exasperation was not directed at them but came out of her for its own reasons, like vomit. Go away, Ma. I'm being sweetly, passively reasonable. If you say I need a bath I'll have a bath, but you will not force me into attending your unhappiness. I don't want to hurt you but I am in constant danger.

32

One reason he'd never even entered the Church of the Science of the Way, a minor reason, was that he didn't have the proper clothes. He still had the use of the Indian Pony, so he rode downtown, found a men's shop a little more conservatively Eastern than the rest and bought himself a dark sport coat, slacks, shirt, a tie with narrow regimental stripes and brown loafers. This costume would do on the plane, too. He was, after all, a debonair young blade and who knew what adventures lay ahead? That mood was fleeting, as if it were something he'd grown out of, or something he'd regretfully lost.

He caught Oval on one of his trips from his car to the bathroom or the kitchen, and said, "I guess I'd better go back East after the services."

"So you're coming to church?"

"Yes."

Oval nodded.

"Why do you sit in your car all the time?" John asked him.

"Because I don't know where I should be."

"What do you mean?"

"Maybe I don't belong anywhere. I've failed at everything I've eve tried." Oval said this as if it were a simple matter of fact, and went on t his car.

Bonnie had been watching from the kitchen window. She met John i the front hall. "What did he say?" she said.

"He said he'd failed at everything he'd ever tried."

"He's so wrong! John, I've tried everything to get to him. I'm jus frantic! I'm afraid for him. He tries what he can't do, that's his trouble He never thinks about the things he can do, he just does them and neve thinks they're anything special. Who can talk to him? I've tried, bu what have I got to give?"

"I don't know," he said, thinking that he shouldn't be having thi conversation, that it wasn't a proper subject.

"So like the dumb twerp I am I got mad and went to pack up an leave. That was a help, wasn't it? He's got all these terrible things on hi mind and because he won't take what I offered I act like a jilted hig school girl. God!"

"But you didn't leave."

"I couldn't. All the time I was packing I knew I couldn't. And the he heard about Thelma and I felt so *cheap.*"

Cheap was what John Hearne felt, too, for the reasons of his continu ing intolerance and his own departed, petty fantasies.

He was still in this nervous state at ten of eleven the next mornin when, dressed in his new clothes, he walked through the back garde toward the small Gothic church. He felt empty and vulnerable, a moo that could surprise him when any small accident, or a bit of norma cruelty such as a cat playing with a lizard, reminded him that th universe was absolutely indifferent and merciless. In this state he didn' know what he would do. From what impervious calm could he listen t sorrowing friends speak of the dead? He could run away; whenever tha option came to mind it was as if he had already run away, and anothe small shame was marked against his soul. Soul? Temperament plu history; what you think of yourself; the entity that computes all of th pain you've caused, measured in *cruces;* what goes to heaven to mee Mama Daddy Bonnie John.

Villa Mesa Street was yellow with the monotonous glareless sunligh of Tulaveda. The cars in the small parking area and along the stree were all clean, probably washed for the occasion. He stood on the side walk in the shade of a mulberry tree, on dried purple bird shit, watching the dressed-up people gravely going into the church. To enter a church, rather than to pass by a church, was as unnatural as looking into another person's shoe. There were churches and shoes everywhere, but to look into one, to see where the toes bulged out the leather and the bunions smoldered in the incense of foot, or to see where people professed belief unto death in something they had never seen—that was too strange and personal.

Washington and Ertrude Johnson, approaching the church, were dressed in somber, shiny black. She was gaunt, with bent calves, and heels that protruded like spurs. With them was a large male child who walked heavily and looked about with the lopsided eyes of retardation. There was Phil the mechanic, his wife and two of their older children. The matronly woman in a purple dress and black shoes was, he recognized from the brochures, Dr. Addie Walmberg, who lectured upon God's humor. Maybe they were all there, Oval's and Urban's colleagues, such as the Rev. Dr. Pierce G. Pierce, D.D., and Prince Grégoire Ushant, the ninety-five-year-old in the thirty-five-year-old body. A tall man in his sixties, wearing a clerical collar, climbed the steps. The people of the congregation looked scrubbed, dressed up, glowing and ordinary.

He went among them into the religious hush and the pious dimensions of the church. The holy vault rose over the intent people who sat on heavy wooden benches. At the gable end of the arched vault was a tall stained-glass window in somber reds and bottle blue around a yellow cross. Clerestories above the stone pediments in the wooden arches made the light on the floor of the church seem to have no source because it cast no shadows. Some architect had known how to make the most of what height and length he'd been allowed. The pulpit, or podium, was carved from a once-bright wood like oak, now brown under cracked varnish. The people came at least once a week into this room purely designed to erode their judgment.

Flowers were everywhere in sconces, the tall, amputated funeral flowers that people thought beautiful, broad scents and gaudy tints among fairy ferns. He had always thought them—snapdragons, chrysanthemums, gladiolas, dahlias, irises, daffodils, gardenias, whatever they were, the whole sweet cloying panoply—an aesthetic hypocrisy before the honest rotting dead. Thelma and Urban had been cremated and weren't here, of course, but perhaps those scents were once more useful than symbolic—like, say, Worcestershire sauce, created to hide the taint in meat.

He observed from the last row, in his health easily patient and silent, letting all this pass. They were here today to absolve the living, to give good news, to sift out of the dust an invincible optimism, 'cause, man, we need it! Oh, bullshit, Hearne; this ceremony cares not for you or your opinions.

There was Bonnie, at the harmonium, her large breasts official, her narrow waist at attention. The pedals began to clunk like a distant pump, and then the treble whine of a hymn familiar in melody made thin slices, or narrow golden threads, of sound. He didn't know where he'd ever heard the hymn; it was as if he had inherited that sequence of notes from ancestors.

Oval stepped to the podium, the pants of his blue suit wrinkled at the lap, and said in his plain boyish tenor, "We will turn to hymn number one thirty-three."

People reached for books in the racks before them, so John did too. In the rustling of pages, the muted creaks and coughs as the docile made ready, he quickly scanned the first verse of the hymn and found it undangerous.

For the beauty of the earth,
For the beauty of the skies,
For the love which from our birth
Over and around us lies,

(refrain)

Lord of all, to Thee we raise
This our hymn of grateful praise.

But he was unprepared for the voices, which without hesitation soared, a gale of voices at sudden confident force. These motley people surprised him into an insecurity of emotion he quickly prepared to control, if he could. It was not just their wholehearted unison, but their skill. Every space in the church sang and answered with song. He missed, in the purity of the sounds, a verse and refrain, but then read the next as they sang.

For the joy of ear and eye,
For the heart and mind's delight,
For the mystic harmony
Linking sense to sound and sight,
Lord of all, to Thee we raise
This our hymn of grateful praise.

The joy of ear and eye: where did they come by such plain language, dangerous to him? Linking sense to sound and sight, alliteration okay in these circumstances. This might mean too much, too clearly. Thelma and Urban, blessed and cursed by perception.

For the joy of human love,
Brother, sister, parent, child,
Friends on earth, and friends above,
For all gentle thoughts and mild,
Lord of all, to Thee we raise
This our hymn of grateful praise.

Pierced by invincible cliché, his proud judgment faltered and stumbled not toward belief but toward appreciation. This brought tears to his eyes, real messy hot tears that swung back and forth in his lids like bilge in a boat.

He would not allow it; his was a true and justified arrogance.

Oval said, "Let us spend a few moments in silent memory and prayer," and bowed his head.

The silence contained echoes without source, a sigh as if a great mouth breathed over the church. The innocent wind of voices, still so clear in memory, seemed to have swept from him some of his resistance. In defense of his status as an observer from the real world he looked at people, the backs of heads and partial profiles. There was Maria, in black, in the front row with an older man who wore a pencil mustache. Three men in American Legion uniforms sat behind them.

Throats cleared here and there, and a child's plain, reasonable voice asked, "Why are they? Why are . . . why are they?" and was hushed.

Oval raised his head and the people raised theirs. Oval blinked several times, as if his eyes hurt, his lids clenching down to meet the muscles of his face. He said, "Pastor Rittheuber—Ozzie Rittheuber—of the Church of Love and Triumph, Biosophic, was a great favorite of Thelma's. She called him Uncle Ozzie, and for her he always had a smile and words honest and gentle, in the manner of the Christed soul he is. He has asked if he might share with us a few of his thoughts."

Oval stepped back as a squarish little man in a silver-gray suit sprang lightly up the two steps to the low proscenium. His motions were all quick, his steps short. He stood beside the podium, arms akimbo, staring fiercely at the congregation, as if angry at them. Left, right, center, his head turned and precisely stopped. He let the silence last, so that his angry look could cause the proper wonder. He looked like someone's middle-class uncle who happened to be angry, but by his stylized motions he also signified that this was to be recognized as a performance. When the silence could last no longer he accused them all. "Have we come here to *grieve?*" His high voice rang as though it came from a greater distance, like a shout through a culvert. "To *grieve?"* A long pause in which his face cleared, feature by feature, until it was happy, a little lip smile left as if he heard distant sounds that reassured. "Oh, no! Let us listen, in a vastly different spirit, to Isaiah: *Give unto them beauty for ashes, the oil of joy for mourning, the garment of praise for the spirit of heaviness.* For I have news of Thelma Forester! Yes! I have good tidings! I saw her last night, clear as a star . . . Oh, I was sad; I grieved. That sweet, afflicted soul, cut off in her seventeenth year. Can we not say, as Paul did in his Epistle to the Galatians, *The fruit of the spirit is love, joy, peace, long-suffering, gentleness, goodness, faith, meekness, temperance?* Who will not say that our Thelma was, then, of the Spirit? Of the meek, a princess; of the long-suffering, a gracious queen; of love, temperance, peace, goodness, faith; yes, even joy, a soul royal to a fault . . ."

This went on until it might have been forgotten that he had said he'd seen Thelma last night. But just as his praise began to be repetitious he jumped, like a child playing hopscotch, to the edge of the stage. "I walked in a dream last night; I walked in the valley of the shadow of despair, asking, 'Why? Why this child? What force caused her to be born in sacred innocence, blameless, yet cursed with her condition?' Oh, people, in my sorrow I had fallen into the gravest of error: I doubted.

"But then, my very soul downcast, there came a light in the west. What was it?" Ozzie looked up over his shoulder, flinched as if he looked into a blinding light, raised his arm against it, his expression saying that it was the light of joy, joy too great to bear. " 'What is it?' I asked, and a voice answered, 'Do you doubt?'

"And I said, 'Yes, Lord, because of the tribulations of a child.' And the Lord said, 'What are seventeen short years next to eternity? Would I forsake my own child? Behold!'

"And the mists of darkness parted and I was in a castle, in Florence, in a vast studio full of light, where there were easels and canvasses, and by a great window were the Master and his pupil. It was Leonardo, the great Leonardo, in a robe of rich velvet, his noble visage shining with genius and with admiration for the work of a young girl who modestly yet with great joy stood next to her easel and listened to the Master. She was blond, and tall, and richly dressed, and her eyes were of the purest blue through which intelligence shone warm and vivid as the sky on a summer's day.

" 'Thelma!' I cried. 'Thelma Forester!' but they heard me not. The quiet joy of that scene, in which genius and an apprentice of true talent were inspired, both, by the creation of beauty! The quiet joy, the lasting joy, the love of the valuable, the triumph! Yes, the *triumph* over pain and suffering, that is what the Lord showed me in my dream. What He has made is indeed marvelous and beautiful, but the final message is triumph itself and the literal transmigration of flesh and blood. Thelma *is* there, in rooms of light, as beautiful of mind and body as she was in this Vale of Tears beautiful of soul!

"And so I have come, as the Lord bade me, to give news not of loss but of triumph. Do we grieve? No! Do we doubt the Lord's intentions? No! Oh, Thelma, dear, we are all so happy for you, though you can't hear us, for we are, to you, but a fragment of a fragment of a dream, a wisp of forgotten pain, a fond, dim long-ago of loving friends, a blink of memory. Someday, perhaps, we will meet again, when we too are radiant and beautiful."

"Oh, *yeah,*" Washington Johnson said.

Ozzie paused, beatific with certainty as he looked over the heads of the people toward the rear of the church, where his Florentine castle was, or where God was, his gaze moving from one wonderful vision to another, each more glorious than the last. He said, "*God so loved the world, that He gave His only begotten Son, that whosoever believeth in him should not perish, but have everlasting life.* And also: *Another book was opened, which is the book of life.* And also: *God shall wipe away all tears from their eyes; and there shall be no more death, neither sorrow nor crying, neither shall there be any more pain: for the former things are passed away.*"

After a meditative moment, Ozzie backed up, turned and came down the two steps to his place in the front row. Sitting with him were his mother and his niece, Hadasha Kemal Allgood and a high-backed, platinum-blond woman who may have been his sister or wife. These observations, too, were to John a defense against sentimentality and disgust. There had been his own vast, cold revelation as to Thelma's fate, which had seemed chilling and grand, though he couldn't quite remember why. But this costume fantasy of Ozzie's left, after its initial surprise, a feeling of dilution. Thelma did die, all by herself. She did it. Don't forget that.

And now Oval; what news would he have of Thelma and Urban? As he came forward to the podium John thought it an error, probably a typical error, for his father to follow Ozzie, a professional who delighted in performance. He'd never heard his father give any sort of presentation except for brief flows of sincere jargon. His father, he thought now, instead of Oval Forester: Sylvan Hearne, father of John Hearne and a failure at everything he had ever tried, including his frigid temple dedicated to *Phaseolus lunatus.* Wrinkled about the lap, tall and skinny, with a weak, sweet, outdated handsomeness, his tie already turning over inside its knot to show its folds, his eyes damp, bothered and shy, he stood there and tried to clear his throat. No one would ever call Ozzie a "saint," because Ozzie was too clever, so they probably called his father a saint because he wasn't too clever.

He was certainly nervous. "Thank-thank you, Ozzie, for your lovely and reassuring vision of Thelma," he said, stuttering a little. John felt concern among the people. The voice was weak, as if there weren't enough breath behind it; heads tilted slightly as the people tried to hear him. "We will now turn to hymn forty-five, 'Lord of All Hopefulness,' " he said.

Bonnie pedaled the harmonium, and over its clunking the sweet whine of the reeds grew into another familiar melody. Again the voices soared until the church was full. He read the words inside a windstorm of voices.

> Lord of all hopefulness, Lord of all joy,
> Whose trust ever childlike, no cares could destroy,
> Be there at our waking, and give us, we pray,
> Your bliss in our hearts, Lord, at the break of the day.

At the end of the hymn, its conceit being that morning, noon, evening and night represented birth, maturity, old age and death, the voices hushed, then sang "Amen."

His father looked at him across the church, over the people. "I would like," his father said, "to speak . . . to say a few words about my friend Urban Stumms." He could hardly be heard. He surely must have known that nothing failed like inaudibility, and that the act of trying to hear what could barely be heard was irritating. Maybe he just didn't have the breath. He paused for a long time. There were things he must be expected to say, that he knew he had to say. He glanced at John again, and then away.

"Uh," he said. "With us today are Urban's widow, Maria, and her father, Mr. Dominguez. I'm not going to quote any scriptures and I don't want to be sectarian in any way. We are all God's creatures. Urban was going through a crisis of faith, not in his stern God but in matters of sect and doctrine. Maybe he was right, and his confusion necessary and right. Who are we to say? I see that many of you here once belonged to the church he led, the Church Ovarian Apocalyptic. You will all know that Urban could forgive anyone but himself. He was basically a kind and loving man disturbed by what he had to do during the war. He wanted to be purged of that guilt and all we gave him were honors and medals. I see there are members of the Legion Honor Guard here today because Urban was a brave and decorated airman. He had fifty missions. Over Tokyo his face was burned nearly to the bone and to the bone in some places. I just want to tell you these things if you don't know them. There was no lightness or gaiety in his life. He loved his wife Maria and would have loved his child, but his own happiness was something he could never believe he deserved. Why should such a man . . ." Here the words faded into little sounds and edges of consonants. ". . . bowling and play golf, but he . . . trivial . . . forgive himself . . ."

John strained to hear the words, because his father looked at him. He could tell by the people around him that most had stopped trying to hear and merely accepted the dim sound of a voice as part of the ceremony. But his father looked at him and moved his lips as if audible, reasonable thoughts were being communicated. *Speak up!* John silently commanded. He pointed to his ear and shook his head. If the man had no voice he shouldn't speak. This was impossible and embarrassing. It was senseless.

So why did he care, being only an observer? Maybe what the man wanted to say he shouldn't say, so the compromise was a mumble, demonstrating another failure. Everyone in the church was upset, or John felt that everyone was upset. Maybe this was a form of speaking in tongues; instead of mad ecstasy a dribble of little sounds, parts of phrases, orphan words. Maybe the people in the front row could hear, but he didn't think so. This disaster seemed willful. But fright, or any emotion powerful enough, could take away a voice. Maybe failure itself could do it, compounding itself.

No one moved. Finally the wounded man up there, his father, couldn't seem to move his lips anymore. His jaws frozen slightly open, he stared as if in the power of some startling, final idea.

Bonnie began to pump and play another hymn. Ozzie Rittheuber went up on the platform and put an arm around the taller man's shoulders.

"Our beloved friend and pastor is moved beyond words," he said in a voice so clear it was refreshing, as if everyone had suddenly recovered from deafness. "Let us bow our heads in prayer," Ozzie commanded, and immediately began: "Oh, Lord of joy who hath taken our two friends, Thelma and Urban, to live with Thee in radiant harmony, unconfused and guiltless, made beautiful and whole, how can we begin to thank Thee for Thy divine goodness? *These are they which came out of great tribulation, and have washed their robes, and made them white in the blood of the lamb.* We know there is unhappiness and cruelty in this world, but there is none in the next. Here we must struggle against the forces of evil, but in that fair land there is no evil. *There was war in*

Heaven: Michael and his angels fought against the dragon; and the dragon fought and his angels, and prevailed not. Lord, we thank Thee for the comfort of knowing that our departed friends, though far from us now, will greet us in our turn, when we cast off our own earthly scars and flaws and are reunited in the vast light of Thy love. Amen."

Bonnie played the harmonium, creating a mesh of incandescent little wires of sound that had in it a meant discordance. Some signal he didn't catch, maybe the music, told the people that the ceremony was over. They all rose to their feet and the chief mourners, Maria and his father, came up the aisle. As they came toward him he looked at them, but they were blind. They were followed by Maria's father, the three members of the Legion Honor Guard with their caps under their shoulder straps and then all the people who had been sitting in front. He watched them as they passed, waiting for his turn. Bonnie still played. He wanted to be gone from here but there were questions and responsibilities, so when the aisle opened to him he went instead to Bonnie and waited behind her, watching her arms under the cloth of her suit and how the padding in the shoulders rose and fell above her real shoulders. She seemed institutional and efficient, her haunches pulsing with muscle as she pedaled wind into the bellows.

When all the people had left she turned on her revolving stool and looked at him. She was bothered and unhappy but she tried to shake all that off. "You caused it," she said. "I suppose it wasn't all your fault, but you were the cause of it."

"Me?"

"He's afraid of you."

"Nobody's afraid of me," he said quickly.

"Lots of people can be afraid of you. I'm afraid of you, for instance."

"For God's sake, why?"

"Because you're judging all the time. Because you're from the East and go to college and think we're a bunch of crackpots out here. But it's more than that, it's the way you are. You never open up. We give you everything and you just sit there *digesting* it. It's as if you think we're all fixed and never have any doubts, which isn't true at all, and you're just sort of *documenting* us."

"I'm sorry. I don't know how not to . . ."

Hadasha came up to them. "Where was Oval going?" he asked.

"Going?" Bonnie said.

"The ladies are setting up the tables. Maybe he went downtown to get something," Hadasha said, and left busily on some kind of errand.

In the back garden, tables had been set up with white tablecloths, and women were bringing pitchers, covered platters, crustless sandwiches under cellophane, silver, paper cups and napkins. At one side people were lined up to sign the guest books, and a few had begun to help themselves to the food. He and Bonnie could see that the '40 Buick was gone.

They went to the parsonage to see if there was any explanation, and found a note on the kitchen table:

Dear Bonnie,
I'll be back in time to take
Johnny to the airport. Driving.
Love, Oval

"Driving?" John said.

"He drives, that's all. When he gets really upset he just goes off alone and drives and listens to the gospel station."

That information given in her usual bright, teaching manner, Bonnie's eyes grew wet. "That's what he says. I don't know." She took a Kleenex, pressed her eyes and blew her nose. "I want him to be happy. He saved my life. How can I help him, John? It's so frustrating!"

"I don't know," he said. In a way he couldn't imagine how she could be so taken up with a man as old as his father. No, it wasn't just the age, but the fact that the man was his father, who had lived his life and gone into history, prologue to John Hearne, whose story this was.

"Are you all packed?" Bonnie said. "Do you have Thelma's pictures she drew for you?"

"Pretty much. Yes."

Bonnie looked in the refrigerator. "The freezer's all full of guess what," she said. "Lima beans. You want one of your beers?"

"Sure. You have one, too."

"Of course he failed with that lima-bean machine. He was a machinist's mate in the Navy, so he thought he was an engineer." She opened two bottles of his Pabst and poured them into glasses. "Did you hear anything he mumbled today?"

"Some of it," he said. "What I heard sounded pretty good."

" 'Pretty good,' " she said. "See what I mean? That's a judgment."

"I mean he didn't go on about meeting in heaven and all that crap."

"Crap! Why is it crap to want Thelma and Urban to be happy? Don't you want to be happy?"

"Yeah, but do you believe all that stuff?"

"I believe it's beautiful and it made me cry!" And she began to cry.

"Bonnie . . ."

"Well, I don't care! No, I don't—we don't—exactly believe in the resurrection of the actual body the way Ozzie does, but it's still beautiful to think so, isn't it? How can you be so cold and so superior?"

"I don't think I'm so superior. I just don't believe all that stuff. I don't think it's true, that's all."

"What's true or not got to do with it? Who cares about that? It's how people *feel* that matters! Do you think we should have told Thelma she was going to die, period? Just turn into nothing? Would you have told her that?"

"No," he said.

"See? It isn't much fun, is it? None of it!" She began to hiccup and click her teeth, a kind of sobbing.

"I'm not cold, either," he said. He felt that she was good and so, cause and effect, he grew unhappy over her unhappiness. Cause and effect; he never trusted his own tears because he suspected they were there to congratulate him upon his nice sympathy and generosity—at least partly, but a taint was still a taint. Her lips gleamed and were slack, so he took two steps and put his arms around her.

"Oh, John," she said. "I'm sorry I said you were cold. You're warm and good, I know." She kissed him on the mouth, her unhappy lips wet as mucilage. In her shoes she was taller than he was, so she bent toward him, a beautiful, aromatic continent of woman.

They stood holding each other for a while, but because there didn't seem anything to do next, they finally sat down at the kitchen table.

"My face is a mess, I know," Bonnie said. "I've got to put in an appearance out there. Then I've got to go to Maria's for a while." She stood up to go fix her face.

"I'll go with you if you want," he said.

"Why would you want to?"

"Because you might want me to."

"That's so sweet, John."

After the affair in the garden, run by the ladies of the Healing Echelons, they went to Maria's, the apartment connected to Urban's church, where her relatives ate and talked and seemed very polite and careful, as if confused by the cultural aspects of it all. All the men wore narrow mustaches. There seemed no grief; it was Bonnie the men all looked at, quickly and then away. Maybe they had been less careful before she arrived.

By dark he and Bonnie were alone in the parsonage, Hadasha having found a ride to Fresno to see his mother.

They had another beer, which seemed to make Bonnie more talkative, and he wondered if it had made her mildly drunk. He could never really believe in drunkenness in others; they always seemed to be imitating its symptoms rather than having them.

"So what do you feel?" she said. "Like you're a sort of explorer out here? Like you're doing research on the natives? Because I could tell you all kinds of things. For one thing, hardly anybody's *from* here—we're all from someplace else, like you, so maybe it's the sunshine that does it. Is that what you're going to say in your report? But why shouldn't we try to make it nicer here than it was back there, wherever it was?"

Again there was an edge of resentment. When he didn't answer quickly enough she finished her beer and went out to the kitchen to get another, still talking. "Why shouldn't we? In a way it's like going to heaven coming out here—at least until you find out what it's really like. You want another beer?"

He'd followed her, and said he would. They went back to the brown living room, its brown velvet drapes pulled against the windows. The amber wall lamps suggested an antechamber in a mortuary, the monochrome of formality and unuse. In the deliberately somber room Bonnie placed her glass on a crocheted doily, then took off her suit jacket and folded it with care. Her white blouse, frilled at the neck and wrists, took on the amber light. He felt their aloneness in the house and the danger of words. All the death that had been considered today made him feel that this was a dangerous place in which he was quick and strong.

Bonnie looked at him and said, "Are you always thinking and not saying what you think? What are you thinking right now, for instance? I mean really thinking?"

He thought. She leaned toward him from the davenport. He sat in one of its matching chairs, leaning forward too. "I can't catch up with thoughts," he said. "But I remember thinking that I felt alive. I was thinking that. You really want to know?" Danger here, a constriction because he might be about to lie, and then nothing would matter. Maybe his thoughts would be what he said, but in the choice of whatever words he might say was an area of untruth. One spoke to manipulate; there was no way to get around that, so every word had in it the lie of choice. "Bonnie, do you really think you can know what somebody else is thinking? We're alone inside our heads, like we're alone when we're dead."

"How can you live like that?" she said. "How can you live in a world like that? What's the reason for going on living in a world like that? It's all selfish and hopeless!"

In the amber light, in the brown room, she was like an ancient picture in rotogravure, a beauty of another age, time separating them as much as their ideas of the world. The handsome blond Christ over the mantel gazed over their heads, suffering serenely.

He wanted her to come back from that distance and at least listen to him, so he said with some exasperation, "But do you actually believe Ozzie can be three places at once? Do you believe Prince Grégoire Ushant is ninety-five years old? Do you believe in prenatal astrobiology, the Healing Echelons and the Ovarian Apocalypse?"

"I believe in belief!" she said defensively, tears glinting in her unhappy eyes.

He felt responsible for the tears and leaned forward earnestly. "But what's wrong with just living, as long as you can?" he said. "Why do you have to have all this mumbo jumbo in your head?"

"Your trouble is you can't love!" she cried. "You don't know what love is!"

This might be true, but she had changed the subject. Urban had said to him on the roof peak of the Church Ovarian Apocalyptic, "You can not be sure of what you think, but you can't not be sure of what you believe." Did that make sense to Bonnie's way of thinking? It seemed purely backwards.

"Tell me what love is, then," he said.

"If you don't know I can't tell you."

"Just because I don't use the word all the time?"

"Don't you ever say what you really feel?" she asked, her words distorted by gasps of unhappiness. He thought of an umbrella suddenly going up, that sound and instant shroud, as if a black dome had appeared over her. In his guilt he went to her and put his arms around her. She moaned, partly as if in pain or frustration, but then melted against him.

"I'm so un*happy!*" she said. She kissed him hard on the lips and then turned her face away, though she still leaned into him. They were like this for a long time, while his guilty feelings were slowly overcome by love, or lust, or whatever demanded further union.

The telephone in the hall rang and she got up, rubbing her eyes, and went to it with long graceful strides, her hips and legs too thoroughbred for him, beyond his ordinariness.

After a while she came back and said, "That was Oval. He's two hundred miles up the coast, in Cambria, he says. Just driving," she said with a grimace. "Ho, ho, just driving. He'll be back tomorrow, so don't worry, don't worry about a thing!"

"It's okay," he said. "He'll be back, won't he?"

"I don't know anymore."

"My mother always said he was 'charming and irresponsible.' "

"Charming? Oval?" She tried to laugh but couldn't quite do it. "He's not irresponsible, either. He's just exasperating." Her expression changed into the oblique near-squint of a certain kind of curiosity. "What's she like, anyway? How could she say that?"

"What's she like? She's untrustworthy, but I didn't always know it."

"What's she look like?"

"She's small, blond and supposedly cute, or she was once. No, she's still cute, I guess, for her age. She's forty-two and still cute. The main thing is that she thinks she's totally above the law. Any law of God, reason, or even of physics. I can't really explain such a creature. She thinks she's great, charming, generous and that she's to be totally forgiven for any possible errors. Her promises mean nothing. Words, unless they praise her, mean nothing. She told me when I was thirteen how she cheated on Amos when she went to some kind of convention, and how great this guy was, how satisfying he was—that he reminded her of my father. I mean she is strange. Once she called me, when I was nine or so, into the bathroom where she was in the tub. She proceeded to stick her rear end into the air to show me her bleeding piles. It seemed very odd to me then and still does. Sometimes I wonder how I can be related to someone whose customs are so different from mine."

Those were actually his thoughts, connected instantaneously to the words he surprisingly uttered. But if your mother did this sort of thing, and you were nine, it had to seem, in a way, normal.

"She showed you her hemorrhoids?"

"Yeah. Maybe Amos didn't want to look at them. Don't ask me. They were *her* hemorrhoids, so I guess they were the most important hemorrhoids in the world."

"But you must not like her."

"I don't trust her, that's for sure. I don't think she's got any limits, somehow. But in her fashion, if everything goes according to her rules, she's very generous, and always has been. She wants to make everybody happy. Figure that in."

"Do you like her?"

"The word doesn't seem to apply."

"It's good she left him."

"God knows," he said. He wondered why he'd told Bonnie about this, except that it had seemed an antidote to his sneaky desires, a change of subject. With it came relief from all of the implications of his cheap urges. Poor Bonnie, whose life was complicated and her own. If she let him have her she wouldn't be her best proud self. It would be a sort of relapse, and who was he, anyway, to presume that she might want him? By her own words she wanted his father.

"John," she said, "I'm sorry! I didn't mean it was good your family broke up when you were a little boy! I didn't mean that!"

What she did then he couldn't at first believe because he still had some lingering faith that he knew something of the mysteries of women and their logic. Were they not somewhat rational in their urge to give? She tipped off her shoes with her toes, came to him and pulled him to the davenport's wide lumpy cushions. They lay side by side and kissed, the weight and exotic substance of her beside him, her perfumed white skin and dark hair astoundingly offered. She held him, saying nothing, until his hands presumed too much and she said, "No, no." But after a longer while she let his hands do what they wanted. He looked up again at the serene Christ in the Protestant room, his own secular fingers fishing for things—a garter belt, strange rig for catching eels, silken skins from pale depths where there were caverns. He knew she would wake from this unbelievable trance and stop him; his trembling would give him away. But she didn't. Surely she would now, but she didn't. Then, when he was about to enter her, she said in a whispery voice, "Not here. Let's go upstairs and I'll put in my diaphragm."

Toward morning he withdrew from her as if from a soft fist and went downstairs, his naked and responsible self, to gather up the glasses and their clothes, destroying evidence for what court? He took her clothes up to her room, where she lay in the lamplight. He reached out and touched her hip, letting his hand flow down the slim increase of her belly, ivory shading to pearl, to silk, a live, smooth thing. She turned onto her back, her knees drawn up and open, her caverns rimmed with silky fur. He eased himself into her like a thief.

"Oh, John, John, I love you," she murmured, her cool hands feathering his hips and back. "Yes, yes, good, yes, yes, more like that, oh, God, you fill me . . ." She had to speak while he was in her, having to signal with her voice all the changes. He wondered if a man had taught her to do that, or if some, or most, actually talked their way through it. He remembered clearly a fantasy from very early childhood in which women were passive, safely entranced so they could be touched everywhere and could not speak at all, so they could never object to curious little hands.

But while her voice instructed, it didn't complain, and over his skin flickered a near-painful ecstasy that interfered with language. Maybe her habitual chatter was part of her exotic, freaky perfection—the proving flaw that allowed this beauty to be his.

And now her vagina ran with his semen, her perfect waist was measured by his common hands, her breasts printed by his lips. Nothing of her was not for his use and pleasure.

"Don't go back East," she said. "Stay here, why not? There's a hundred colleges around here. You can cancel your airplane ticket easy enough."

"And stay here?" he said, meaning the parsonage.

"There won't be a parsonage very much longer, or a CSW either, I'm afraid. The people here are wonderful, but no new ones seem to come in. I don't think Oval can support it much longer. I'm sure that's what he's driving around thinking about."

"What will he do, then?"

"I think he wants to be a farmer. Why not?" she said in exasperation. "He's tried everything else in his life. I'll tell you what he's good at. He's good at getting people to love him and trust him. That's what he's good at."

She sighed and slid her arms around him. "Anyway, look," she said. "We could get an apartment, or rent a little house. I've got six thousand dollars in the bank. I'll work and you go to school. If anybody objects we'll say you're my brother."

He got up on his knees to look at her, wondering how in the world he had the right to touch a woman of her kind. It was as if it weren't John Hearne whose desire she once again aroused, but a whole class, or generation. She was meant to be the mother of the race, the rose of Sharon, the lily of the valley. Thou are all fair, there is no spot in thee.

She touched him and he seemed to snap taut, like a sail in a jibe. "Oh, my!" she said. "Come, come, oh, my God! Wow! Wait a minute. Slower. Easy. Eeeeasy. Oh! Oh! Oh! Oh! My God, I had about ten in a row. My God, you've got muscles. I *love* muscles. Feel those muscles! What an arm! What a neck! The muscles in your back, they're like arms inside your skin! John, you're just beautiful with your clothes off!"

He loved her but he watched and listened, making his usual internal comments. She offered him a life, for a while—maybe she meant much more than a while. Every night in her arms, the constant luxury of her astounding beauty, but a beauty that was official, or universal, defined by some vast cultural authority he wasn't sure he approved of. No matter, he was enthralled, insane in his tissues, spent but knowing how soon he would not be spent. He would live with her and listen to her describe her pleasures. What a simple life, no idea of a future, just flesh and passion. California as the everlasting rainless present.

"No, stay. Stay in me," she said. "I know a place for rent. I've been kind of looking in spite of myself. It's over on San Jacinto Road, sort of a little bungalow, I know who owns it. It's got a bedroom that could be your study, and another one for us."

Thinking of the life she offered made him want a cigarette; he had to pull away and look in his clothes for one. She watched him, waiting for him. "Give me one, too," she said.

They smoked, that grownup hiatus in which one could consider all things. She gave off energy that seemed to come from him, too, as if rays came from their nakedness and sharpened their eyes. Next to her all other women would seem like midgets, runts, culls.

"I've lived without a man too long," she said.

A man? A strange abstraction that didn't quite seem to apply to him.

"Don't you want to?" she said. "Wouldn't it be lovely to sleep together every night?"

"You really mean it?" he said.

"If you want to. Do you, John?"

He couldn't make up his mind. He couldn't understand why he couldn't make up his mind. The reasons for not staying here and sleeping with a goddess every night were vague yet looming. He'd told Dory he wasn't looking for "romance." He told her that clearly, and meant it. But why hadn't she written?

"But you won't, will you?" she said.

"I don't know. I know I want to."

"Why don't you, then? Because you promised your little girl-woman in New Hampshire you'd come back to her? Do we have here a specimen of the honorable man? Is she prettier than I am? Just because you seduced her you feel responsible, is that it? You deflowered her, you cad, so you're going back to make an honest woman of her."

"Maybe, someday."

"Someday! The first thing you'll do when you get back is jump in bed with her. Then she'll get pregnant and you'll get married. It's the same old story. And pretty soon you'll be fooling around with your friend's wife, or some woman or other. I know how it goes. And meanwhile she's got a full-time job taking care of babies. Do her a favor and don't go back."

"Maybe you're right."

"You don't believe for a minute I'm right. You think she's pining away for your fantastic personality and your perfect body."

"Maybe you're right."

"Oh, John. Well, you do have a perfect body."

"Thanks."

"All night I loved you more than Oval."

Window light was just overcoming the light of Bonnie's table lamp when they heard Oval's car come into the yard. He insisted on hurrying back to his room, and she seemed wryly amused by his flight.

The light in his room grew like an accusation. Morning light fed his familiar critical demons, now with a breathtaking half-memory. He opened the drawer in the bed table and there was the card he hadn't mailed to Dory because he was going to write her a letter instead. The forgetting of it, the false memory of having sent it along with the others —how false was it? In what way false? Because she had deserved more than that flippant message, his conscience had made him not send it. But what quality in him had made him not write the letter? He trembled with anxiety and shame. What she must think of him. It was intolerable and it could not be undone.

His father drove him into Los Angeles to the airport. His night driving seemed to have cured some of his nervousness, but he looked pale and a little grimy. The wrinkles around his youthful eyes were deeper, with more minor ridges and valleys. On the Arroyo Seco Parkway he took a breath and said, "Johnny, I don't deserve such a fine son. You were so kind to Bonnie and Thelma. And Urban, too. He thought the world of you. Did you know that? You're a good man, no matter who raised you."

You're a seaworthy ship, Jonathan. Sure. You're a submarine.

The plane wasn't ready, they were told, because they were trying to fix the hot plate so they could serve hot coffee on the flight. He led his father to a bar partitioned off from the rest of the terminal building by a low fence of beaverboard, and ordered a rye and soda. His father ordered a Coke.

Bonnie had come down to the kitchen tying her bathrobe, flashing them a pretty, pink-nippled breast. Then she kissed John and hugged him, comradely, sisterly, motherly, and hoped he and his wonderful girl in New Hampshire would be so happy.

The rye tasted like pencil lead, the soda water like water without water's protoplasmic necessity. His father was shy and quiet, but after a silence he said, as if he had to speak, "We'll miss you, Johnny. You were a great help and strength to us, you know."

"Me?"

"It's been a time of trouble and sorrow, and you were there. Bonnie told me when I came in how you were so loving to her last night."

"Loving to her? What did she say?"

"Why, that you made love to her. It's all right. She loves you and wanted to give you what you wanted."

Christ, what he needed was Leah, dark under its hills, where men and women kept their own guilty counsel. His father said, "What's she like, your girl in New Hampshire?"

"Small and plain."

"I'm sure she's intelligent and beautiful."

They were silent, Dory a powerful wraith, non-benevolent, with stricter requirements than all this amorphous love and forgiveness.

His father said, "I know I'm never going to make it in the ministry. Ozzie wants me to edit a new magazine for him, *The Clarion of Love and Triumph.* And they want me to stay on at the Co-op, Lord knows why after what happened. But I think I'd like to go into farming."

"Raising lima beans?"

"Wouldn't that be something? There's a farm and some rental land up around Marysville I heard about."

"What about the Church of the Science of the Way?"

"It's fading, Johnny. It just can't make it with only twenty families. They'd have to tithe just to keep up the mortgage and they couldn't afford that."

"Would Bonnie go with you?"

"If she wants to. Lord, I guess I was the only man who was kind to her at a time she needed it. But I've wished myself on enough women, Johnny. It's always been bad luck for them. Anyway, Bonnie's too young and pretty for the likes of me. I'm twenty years older than her, and a failure at that. I couldn't even manage to keep my own name I was born with." His father was silent for a while. Then he said, as if recklessly, "Johnny, you rode your motorcycle all the way to California to find out what your father was like, and I'm sorry you found out."

"I'm not sure what I found out," John said quickly, exasperated and saddened by the man's humility, which seemed such an easy pose. What had he found out, anyway? That he, John Hearne, was the result of a union between a monster of ego and an addled saint? The sweet, feckless, awkward man who sat across from him had once in unsaintly heat impregnated a pretty, improbably egocentric blonde named Martha Gustavson, who, by the dark bypassing of ineptitudes, by the Grace of Fecundity, had produced a male infant. How that infant came to be John Hearne, whatever John Hearne was, was a vaguely unsavory mystery, an embarrassing sort of progression leading to here and now. He, John Hearne, was inside this person, the one that surrounded him and through which he perceived the world. All this, at this moment, seemed unbearable.

And now he sat nervously, culturally superior before his father, the failure who aren't in heaven, his name not even his name.

"Look, Johnny!" his father said, all at once eager. "See that fellow, the big man there? That's Mike Mazurki!"

John looked where his father looked and sure enough, there was a big man in an ice-cream suit whose craggy, hoodlum face was instantly familiar, though he wouldn't have thought of the name. Through a hundred minor parts had moved that predictably ominous mug.

His father was marvelously excited and pleased. "At least we got you to see a movie star!"

The plane was ready. A squeal came from the loudspeaker and a high male voice read off a progression of landings generally northeastward: Phoenix, Albuquerque, Tulsa, St. Louis, Cincinnati, Albany, Boston—a progression somehow retrograde, toward a harsh twilight.

As they got up, he with his new suitcase, there came a business with lemons and oranges. A blond girl and four boys equally tanned and handsome, all in Bermuda shorts, came running across the concrete floor. At first he thought the girl was Streaky, or Dianne, because she wore a halter made of red bandannas. Her suitcase opened and at least thirty lemons and oranges came out rolling and bouncing, the lemons erratic little footballs among the rounder oranges. It wasn't Streaky, but she screamed and they all stooped and scurried among the people and chairs after the lemons and oranges, their laughter a pitch below hysteria within this most wonderful and desperate event. As she reached beneath a chair occupied by an older woman, one of the boys skillfully tweaked the knot of her halter, which fell away. There was more laughter, including hers, her bone-white breasts hugely swinging, and then John saw that she wasn't amused, that what he had thought was her laughter was above the allowable pitch and she was crying. She picked up the bandannas and spread them with both hands over herself as she ran alongside a wall, or partition, probably looking for a rest room. The way she had to run, bearing the awkward burden of her breasts, made him think of Thelma. The boys, contrite but still helplessly unstifled, as if under the spell of perverse hilarity at a funeral, went on picking up the lemons and oranges.

His father walked with him to the airplane, where it stood canted skyward, and embraced him, hard arms beneath slippery cloth; in that quick embrace he thought of nothing but how strange it was. They waited, saying nothing, for the passengers ahead to climb into the sloping fuselage. As he was about to board they shook hands and his father said, "Don't worry about Bonnie. We'll take care of each other. We'll both pray for your happiness, Johnny." The care and urgency in the callow, handsome face was deserving of all of his attention and was pitiful. "Johnny, we are all one in God's infinite love. I know that so well! I know you don't believe what we believe, but I know it so clearly in my heart!"

The stewardess was waiting, as was an attendant who wanted to roll away the stairs. The starboard engine gave the tearing, metallic, screaming cough that was the beginning of power, and then so did the port engine, which blew all their words away. In his father's face was the sweet grin of failure. Another handshake, quick but infected with longing, and John entered the silver airplane.

33

Her mother, with her sad bony face, had come into her room sometime during the languor of sleep.

"Doris," her mother said, the name tentative and guilty because whenever her mother said her name there was the implied accusation.

She didn't sleep all the time. She got up to eat sometimes, and to go to the bathroom. In the bathroom mirror she looked gaunt and transparent, the eyes of the girl in the mirror larger and nearly black, as if they wanted to merge into one cyclops eye. She listened to Debbie's radio, which her mother had brought into her room, and read *The Leah Free Press,* which her mother brought up to her after her father was finished with it.

Her mother said, "He come in Friday, on the Peanut. It's been three days. How come he ain't come to see you?"

That needed no answer.

"Don't it make you wonder?" her mother said.

It was morning, her mother and father about to go to work. The car idled down on the driveway. Once the information her mother brought her might have been interesting, more than just interesting. When she'd first retired she thought her rest would be temporary, like a vacation—just a while and maybe she could get going again, more or less, and at least not seem so queer, as if she were sick.

"I told you Everett Sleeper seen him," her mother said. "He never come to see you or let you know he was back."

"It's okay, Ma. Go on, now," she said.

"Oh, I don't know," her mother said unhappily, and left the room. Her steps on the narrow stairs, the way she turned her feet a little toward the wall, her hand on the rail, had been familiar in the house before she and Debbie were born. The car crunched down the driveway.

Now she was alone. Some of the things she'd done at first seemed strange. Once she went to Debbie's room and stuffed a pair of Debbie's pink panties into her mouth, as much of them as she could jam into her mouth. The silky cloth turned harsh and absorbed all of her spit. It was impossible to scream; all she could do was make an *urr, urr,* almost intimate in its lowness, no matter how desperately she tried to scream out.

The voices of Cascom Manor were still with her and seemed the voices of the world, telling her what she hadn't once minded so much that she'd known. "So one wog bumped off another wog"—the assassination of Gandhi, in January. She had seen John Hearne in January, downstreet, she in boots and mackinaw, and they'd said hello. When you were small you had to trust, but would you trust your life? A bird lands upon a hand able to crush it at a whim. Why? "Masaryk, the typical fool! Of course the Bolsheviks threw him out a window!" "Now the Semites are hooking noses over a piece of desert. May they eat each other up!" "That rube in the White House—what a chance to use the bomb while he's the only one who has it! Tell them to leave Berlin alone or else! Pouf! There goes Moscow!" "Now, Malan—an intelligent man, with a will!"

Oh, those voices, the world having its constant tantrum. "They are beginning to understand just *who* fought for Western civilization!" Who was Dory Perkins to have opinions counter to these? Her mother and father never seemed to notice the news; it was none of their business. Her mother's cousin, Everett Sleeper, had seen John Hearne step down from the Peanut, though. That was their kind of current event.

But the others—the bitter, gloating voices. The Jean Dorlean who called himself a "democrat" and who was as snidely pleased and as superior as the rest. The ways of the race. She would ponder for a longer time whether she would join all this cruel incompetence, in any fashion. There had been others, legions of them, who had decided not to. Betty Salmon. Debbie had not been allowed to choose.

After all this time the weight of anxiety was not constant. It was fickle, now, and waited for the right moment. All of what she saw and expected turned rotten, the sunlight rotten, its heat rotten. She could wonder at it, that the world which she knew to have been beautiful at times, in which were people she had thought she loved, was now intolerable. It would be better not to be part of it. She herself had coyly fished for praise while Debbie screamed. She had been despicable. There had been a time when the knowledge of cruelty was not intolerable, but now it was. The hands of her race were in it, her own hands in it. The vanity—imagine the strutting, the self-importance, the stinking rotten humor. Imagine the stupidity of its preaching and teaching. There was her window, now, gray sunlight on trees shaking like maggots.

When John Hearne got off the Peanut, once called the Penultimate when it had been a fast express to Montreal, he thought how Leah, of all the towns in the world, was the one he least wanted to be in. The tall elms around the station, though dignified and handsome, hung their grayish leaves far overhead in an inexplainable attitude of threat. Leah was the town in which he'd cried, run away, lied, stolen, shit his pants and done all the other cowardly, needful, arrogant and self-pitying stupidities of childhood. Maybe Winota, with a certain sweet candor, had forgiven, but Leah, the elms implied, remembered everything.

He stood on the undulant red bricks of the station platform and watched the Peanut—a steam engine and three grimy passenger cars—huff and hiss and move away. It was a warm September afternoon, getting on toward dusk, and the air was all the sweeter for a sniff of cinders. He was prepared to walk the mile or so to Amos's house—up a block to the Town Square, then down Bank Street. The suitcase was a little awkward but that didn't matter. He could walk all the way back to Boston if he had to, turn around and walk back. There were no limits to what he could do with his misplaced strength.

He hadn't gone a hundred yards when Paul Columbard stopped beside him in a '38 Plymouth coupe so dented and pounded out along its side and fenders it had the texture of a used paper bag. "Hey, Johnny!" Paul said, so he went around the Plymouth, put his suitcase behind the seat and got in. Strange that even now, after the war, when they had all supposedly grown up, it could still be taken for granted that Paul was at his service. A large, heavyset, crumpled sort of fellow with a sweet nature, Paul Columbard had always done whatever John Hearne told him to. It had been an odd responsibility he hoped he had never really betrayed.

They went first to Futzie's to have a beer. Paul had been married since June to Natalie Dionne, and wanted to know if John had ever seen, or used, what were called "French ticklers," a form of condom that might have been just a mythical element in boy culture but which supposedly had an end like the snout of a star-nosed mole and drove women mad.

"Doesn't she like it plain?" John asked.

"Yeah, yeah. I just thought . . ." Here Paul sensed John's disapproval and changed the subject. "You heard about Debbie Perkins?"

"No," John said, and was told what Leah knew. It had happened at Cascom Manor, in August.

"What about Dory?"

"She's at home, I guess. She had a nervous breakdown, is what I heard."

"Christ, I better go see her."

Paul's look asked, but John had no definitions. Nothing was steady. "Well?" he said, meaning that Paul should drive him "home," which Paul obediently did. John promised to come to supper some weekend when home from school.

Then, after Paul let him off in front of the neatly kept house on Union Street, came the distractions. As he entered the back door and stepped into the kitchen he heard a low, rasping human sound coming from the living room. Glass crunched under his shoe. The kitchen, looked at now because of the soft crunch of glass into linoleum tile, became clearer than its mere expected continents and seas and was wrong, dusty and scummed across surfaces. The glass was the remains of tumblers and more than one gin bottle, their thicker bases intact here and there, the square bases of the bottles frosted glass. The refrigerator door was open an inch upon an insistent hum. He stepped delicately across the floor into the dining room, which was intact, and into the living room, where he found Amos lying, too long for the davenport so that one knee was on the floor, breathing the noise he had heard.

He went back and closed the refrigerator door, then came back to make a judgment upon Amos and the anarchy implied by this situation.

Amos, unshaven, dirty along his seams and in obvious disrepair, slept. John quickly went upstairs and through the rest of the house. Martha, along with certain critical possessions of hers, such as suitcases, jewelry and half the contents of the bathroom medicine cabinet, was gone.

Dory's house was dark, hovering over there in the dusk. He called and let the phone ring a long time, but no one answered.

He went downstairs and swept up the glass, thinking that this act of responsibility was logical because when he left he'd have to traverse this floor. When the sweeping was done, however, there were other choices, or imperatives, he couldn't seem to avoid. He had to go into the living room, arouse that dangerous consciousness he had from childhood avoided and find out what was going on. Then again, he really didn't have to; he could go somewhere else. Something sustained him against his urge to run away, perhaps many things. He would think more about this when he had the time, but now he went, deliberately, to poke a snake.

Amos was more of a mess than he'd thought. He reeked—the word hit the brain directly through the nose—of booze, urine and thin vomit. His oily forehead was hazed with yellow, his narrow mustache a wavery line of ink across his shadowy lip. Shaken carefully awake, he came into a sort of passive hysteria, no real force in it. Martha had been gone for two weeks. She left a note. She was gone, gone. Amos blubbered, he sat up and clasped his face with long but childishly dirty hands. He produced from his side pocket the now-grimy note.

> Dearest Amos,
> I have fled with my life's love, my passion.
> It is all beyond my strength. I'm so sorry
> for my poor Amos but it is written in
> the heavens that I must follow my Prince.
> Affection always,
> Skytop

"Skytop" was her version of what Amos often called her: "Shylock."

Amos, in his self-pity and dramatic dissolution, didn't treat him as Johnny Hearne, but as an authority, neutral in this matter. It had all of the revolutionary quality of a dream.

"Let's get you cleaned up," John said, finally, and half carried the long, disjointed parts of Amos upstairs. He helped him off with his soiled clothes and got him into a tub of hot water. *Agua caliente.*

He was about to go down and make some coffee when the phone rang. He picked up the upstairs phone and said hello.

"Johnny? Johnny? Is it *Johnny?*" It was Martha, sounding far away, crying. "Oh, Johnny! Oh! Oh!"

"Okay," he said. "What's up?"

"Is Amos all right?"

"He's okay."

"Is he terribly upset?"

"Yes, I guess so. I just got here and found him passed out and the place pretty much a mess."

"Johnny . . ." He recognized in her voice a certain calculation—that this was a welcome answer—but she went on crying and said that she was in a hospital in Rochester, New York, where "they cut my *organs* out."

"They what?"

"They cut all my *organs* out."

He managed to get more information. It was her womb and other related parts that had been removed. Her Prince, a Celotex salesman, had abandoned her; she was broke and they were kicking her out of the hospital tomorrow. He and/or Amos was to come get her. He got a telephone number, said he'd consult with Amos and call back.

Amos, his long hairy knees in the air, received this information with, at first, horridly vociferous and weepy satisfaction, called her the expected names and then commenced to sob and writhe gigantically, water sloshing all over the floor.

They drove all night, John driving Amos's new 1948 four-holer Buick, on the same roads he had taken in daylight on his motorcycle in June. Amos had never let him drive any of his cars before, but his driving now was, after all, part of the revolution, part of the year.

At the hospital the next afternoon Martha, all made up, looked tragically from her pillow and said with quivering longing, shame and vibrancy, "Amos!" Amos said in the same mode, "Martha!" and they kissed and cried.

They stayed in a hotel that night so John could get some sleep, then took two days coming back. Once when they'd stopped in a restaurant to eat and Amos was in the men's room, she said, "Well, I guess this has taught *him* a lesson!"

"Who?" John asked.

"Amos," she replied.

John drove all the way, the two lovebirds in the back seat, Martha's orgy of self-incrimination something John could not help but admire for its effectiveness and its mendaciousness.

"I'm so *weak,*" she said once, in the triumph of her power, "but, oh, my two strong men!"

Error, John thought. *Error.* Amos sulked for several miles, a bull pricked hard by the invisible, the quick, the agile cruelty of what he needed. She'd meant to say what she'd said. Sooner or later the Celotex salesman, too, would emerge into their chaotic discussions, but for now her crinkly cute frailty forbade that. Not an error, no. She hadn't been able to convince a seven-year-old prisoner that she could alter reality, but Amos, who was not growing up, was another matter.

Lord, John Hearne was just the chauffeur, sir, ma'am. Let the miles pass. The biggest Buick floated on, finally, thank the Universal Mind, into Leah. That was why he'd been back three days before he'd really tried to get in touch with Dory.

She wondered why those three days should intrude upon her rejection of the world. The three days seemed petty, but there they were, even if she didn't care. She wouldn't answer the phone, which rang for a long time. When it stopped she was instantly weightless, smooth, forgetful.

The rapping brought her away from peace, where she had been among leaves in warm colors unlike the slaty near-nausea of what her eyes were forced to open upon. This room, this bed, that window—how ominously boring was consciousness. Behind the screen, hunkered on the roof in his obscene strength, surrounded by a golden outline thin as a crack in glass, he pressed forward, rapping his imperious knuckle as if on her skull.

He looked in as deeply as he could, suffering from Dory-fear, or fear of mortality. He thought he saw her in there on the narrow bed among runnels of sheets or blankets, too dangerous to speak to in that nest. "Dory?" he said anyway.

He named me that. What arrogance.

"Is that you in there?"

After a while he said, "Well, we never did talk much."

That tone. Humor that was the worst sort of self-protection.

"Hey, Dory?" he said with Dory-fear again, the fear of permanence.

She had no answer.

"I heard what happened and that you didn't take it very well. I don't mean you should have taken it *well,* you know. Can I come in?" he asked with Dory-fear again—Circe-fear, Athena-fear, the fear of entrapment. Anyone could look upon conventional beauty, but the effect of Dory's oddness was unpredictable. There was the memory of enthrallment—not of its power, just a simple warning.

He slid the wood-framed screen together and removed it.

He slipped into the room and stood over her, then leaned down and pushed her hair away from her face. She could resent, somewhere, this invasion, but the shouted commands were heard in other places, in the halls and passageways of another dungeon.

"Your hair," said the prince, "smells like an old tennis shoe."

She was all bones, her skin milky across her cheekbones, her arms soft, the muscles gentle rubbery connectors he could follow with his fingers. Her brown eyes looked at him, or he could see too deeply into them, their close-together force seeming to ask a question, but she wouldn't speak. He lay down next to her.

—As if he had a right, and gathered her to him with, she recognized, benevolent intent—strength's intent, which could change without losing power. She felt like pieces floating in water, not whole, so she couldn't feel that her weakness had a right, or deserved privacy. He was huge and hard as wood, trying to be gentle.

"Do you mind if I tell you everything that happened to me this summer?" he asked. She didn't answer. It was her old habit of not answering, not, she thought, because of anger, or irritation or dislike. He put his hand into her pajamas and felt her belly and hipbones, his warm hand tickly as a soft brush. "You're too thin," he said. "Are you sick? I heard you had a nervous breakdown, whatever that is. I suppose my mother knew all about it but she chose not to write to me about it. What am I supposed to know, anyway? I got back three days ago and I called but nobody answered and then I had to drive Amos over to Rochester, New York, to get my mother, who ran off with a Celotex salesman and had a hysterectomy. Does that explain anything?"

"You don't owe me anything," she said.

"You spoke to me. I heard you. I wrote you a card, I really did, but it never got mailed because you deserved a letter. Does that make sense? And also I found my father and my half-sister, a mongoloid. I sort of got to know her and then she died . . ."

His voice was like a cat's purr, her face in his throat. She recognized the tone she resisted but she began to drift. Her hair probably was filthy, which ought to have been meaningless. He gathered her watery spine to him by way of her hips and she began to fade into a dream. Mongoloid? Hysterectomy? Sister? From what shadowy past had those words come? But unlike her other dreams this one forced her out of ease. The universe was inside immense space that also was the universe, which she could never understand, now composed of planets of ancient beige and rose, all the world-sized and larger globes connected by roads like rays and all dangerously important. She was in charge of the switches but she wasn't good enough to handle it, so right before her eyes the whole universe blew up.

"Okay," he said.

"The roads!" she cried.

"Okay," he said, and felt her slip off again into the inert steadiness of sleep. Her tears and snot lubricated the hollow of his throat. She was so thin and light and alive he wanted to cure her with his touch, which seemed to him invincible, but he was afraid to disturb her now. He was in her bed, in her family's house, without permission, but it was all right because he was responsible and he never threw anyone away.

Except, you faithless intolerant child, those you have betrayed. But not Dory, at least not yet, and not children. No, and he was here, now, in this narrow bed, his woman sleeping beneath his arm, in an aura of steady and faithful poverty, in the mild funky odor of continuance and survival, so he betrayed no one and could himself drift into the hours.

Urban Stumms, though definitely known to be dead, frozen and then burned to a grainy powder, came steadily up the stairs, his mask of scars gray as steel. A friend in life, though a fierce one, there was no reason for him to be a threat now, was there? Dead as a doornail, croaked, finished, *todt, shinimashita,* he came as a threat dressed in a black suit and heavy black preacher shoes. Of course John Hearne in his strength could take the small man easily except that Urban's rage was righteous, he was insane, his valor was proven, and he was dead.

He woke: that dream could be endured because he always lived with fear and the sense that he was a betrayer. If he could admit to just how he had betrayed Urban and all the rest he might come to terms with his treachery. He would not count strangers who had asked too much of him, at least not yet, but there were those in whose good estimation he falsely stood. Even now he thought his simple presence could comfort her.

She slept. He hadn't slept, except for his dream of Urban, if that could be called sleep, for a long time, so he matched his breaths with hers until her breaths proved too short for his, and then they descended into separate places.

She came near the surface, remembering "mongoloid," and "sister," which allowed him something she hadn't known or expected. He had always been too dangerous in these ways, his gentle sleep even now seducing her resentment, making her feel that her resistance was unfair or petty. His even, alien pulse was at her lips, not alien so much as necessary, its separateness necessary. Then she descended easily, believing she would return for another breath of that consciousness.

Something woke him; he knew by the dim September light that an unexpected amount of time had passed, so he let only his eyes expose him, as if he were in the woods and in danger. Her mother stood in the doorway, not five feet away. She had been there a while, the precise instruments of survival informed him, and now stood in fierce surmise, pending judgment. Her narrow dark eyes were Dory's, but Dory's after a long, long voyage, her skin worn and pale, her shoulders bent, a silent and honorable woman. Without admitting his knowledge of her presence she stepped back into the hall and closed the door, sealing her only daughter in the room with whatever fate, for good or ill, John Hearne might cause her.

Dory was awakened by the change in his metabolism and then more clearly by the sound of the door.

"It was your mother," he said.

She was still coming awake, pushing away the leaves of her dream, an interesting dream she all at once could not remember.

"Christ, it's five-thirty," he said, getting up and shuffling into his moccasins.

"It's all right," she said. He stopped and looked at her—instead, she supposed, of jumping out the window. His chinos were all wrinkled in diamond and slash shapes because they had sweat together.

"At least she had to see I had my clothes on," he said. She felt musky and stale and damp, her hair clotted. She hadn't had a bath in days and she could smell herself, which came with memories rimmed with shimmery pleasures and embarrassments and pride. For him she shouldn't be like this. She got out of bed and stood up, dizzy and light in the bones.

"Jesus, Dory," he said. "Have you been physically sick? You look like a skinned rabbit." He reached out and held her up. Her pajama bottoms fell down, which bothered her only because she was ashamed to be in such a strangely rank condition. Sick?

"I just retired for a while," she said. "Now I've got to go to the bathroom."

He guided her, mostly by remote control, to the bathroom. Mr. Perkins looked up from the bottom of the stairs. "Hey, Johnny?" he said, his narrow, creased, shadowed expression all one hard question. The bathtub began to fill. "Hey, Johnny? Come down and have a ale if you want."

They were friends, but Mr. Perkins was the father of a young daughter, after all, and in the present circumstances this could not be ignored. He went downstairs and was treated by them not as a child or as an irresponsible randy youth but as if he were a doctor to whom they described Doris's symptoms. He drank Genesee ale from the can and nodded sagely. Some poet or philosopher had said that as you grew older you didn't rise to the level of the world, it fell to your level, which seemed to be happening here and to have been happening all this strange year long. If he were the authority God help the poor people, God help them all. Mr. Perkins looked friendly, grateful, then as if he had been slapped and resented it but couldn't quite figure out who had slapped him, then sad, then again grateful. Mrs. Perkins looked into

John Hearne's soul, and surmised. She knew more about this business than her husband really wanted to know.

John Hearne's prognosis was guarded and careful, but his recommended therapy was clear: he would try to get Doris up and out of the house, talk to her and feed her and try to get some meat back on her bones. This was what he told them, but there was the question of what he might be getting into. There was the question of his possibly being flattered because these adults had delegated so much authority to him, a former child.

He did a strange thing: he went back to Amos's house and into the living room, where Martha was ensconced in afghans and lace on the davenport, a brave, twinkly convalescent, and asked Amos if he could borrow the Buick this evening. It was the first time he'd ever asked Amos directly for anything. Amos was startled, and said yes, hedging his mercantilism or whatever by adding that it would be all right if John would first go to the store and get two quarts of ginger ale and a bottle of aspirin. Martha glowed and preened, as if through this transaction all of her dreams had come true, her two men actually talking to each other, asking favors of each other. Now don't blow it, John thought; for once please leave it. But of course she couldn't, and said, "My two men! Isn't this happy? Aren't we all so happy?"

"I'm going to take Dory Perkins out," John said quickly. "She hasn't been out of her house in weeks."

"How sweet of you, Johnny!" Martha said.

"Just don't wreck the goddam car," Amos said, mollified by the mention of another female. What simpleminded psychology these children danced to. Amos took out the keys to the four-holer, holding them at first, for part of a second until even he saw the error in it, up in the air as if asking a dog to beg. John took them, with thanks, at waist level.

Dory felt her weakness when she stood up to get out of the bathtub. He'd said she looked like a skinned rabbit. She'd skinned rabbits herself when her father brought them home, the downy fur and the weak skin that wanted to tear into handfuls of red-bordered fluff. In the mirror were the black eyes against pale skin, angled white collarbones. She wasn't red like a skinned rabbit, but the air, warm and humid as it was, seemed to abrade her nakedness.

Her mother waited for her in her room. "He wants to take you out. He borrowed his stepfather's car and he wants to take you to supper at the Cascom Inn."

"I'm not hungry," she said, not meaning that she objected to his wanting to take her out, or to her mother's wanting her to act more normal again. But her mother's face turned loose and grayish and she began to cry.

"No, Ma," she said, "I didn't mean . . . Why do you want to make so much of it? I'll be all right."

"You ain't all right!"

"You want me to go out with him?"

"You got to get out of the house. You got to wake up. I don't know what he wants with you. I don't know how serious he is about you. Has he growed up yet? I don't know." Her mother dried her hair, violently, Dory's neck wobbly under the thunderous flopping of the towel. She put Dory's hands on the towel and said, "Keep that up," then picked out clothes for her and put them on the bed. The patterned beige dress she'd bought at Trotevale's in June seemed to have grown into folds and bags, so her mother got out a skirt and blouse and fixed the skirt band with a safety pin so it wouldn't fall down. "You don't look so bad, but you got to fill out some," her mother said. "Anyways, he knows you been sick." She combed Dory's hair and pushed at it. "I got to cut your hair again."

"A nervous breakdown," Dory said. "Is that what everybody says?"

"God knows what they say. I never said it. Will you try to eat something at the Cascom Inn?"

"It's a pretty fancy place," she said, and her mother was grateful for this, wanting to smile with her against fancy people like those of Union Street, the rich, the spoiled who could pay all that money to go out and eat.

Her breasts were small in her bra, her stockings looser but at least not baggy. She put on lipstick but it looked like a slash of blood, so she washed it off. He didn't like lipstick but she took it off for herself, not for him. Her mother thought her pink cardigan sweater might give her a little color.

"You're almost eighteen years old and you look about twelve," her mother said. "You're scrawny but you're awful pretty, too."

"Ma, you don't have to say that."

"I just feel like hugging you," her mother said, standing still, so Dory put her arms around her mother's thin rib cage and they stood awkwardly for a moment, two bony women hugging in a way more perfunctory than they felt.

It was as if down the hall in another room was Debbie, a bawling giant who might judge this affection against what they thought of her and what they'd done for her.

When she turned the corner at the bottom of the stairs he was stunned. He saw through her—through her clothes, to her skin, to her bones. That she was willing to come away, at least for a while, from her illness or distraction was an unbearable gift. Even her parents had given her into his care. Take her, our troubled daughter.

The Buick flowed along, soft and quiet as a room, and she seemed passive, even serene about it all. At his touch she slid over to him, her transparent hand on his thigh. They traveled over the long hills toward Cascom as dusk came on, going as if through the years, and he thought if he could always have this power—of the car, of her mysterious assent, of a pleasurable destination, of a looming choice that was dangerous but in his power to make—then that would be a life.

Well, he did come back, she thought, and now his nervous seriousness meant that he was thinking very hard about her and what to do with her. She touched him as he guided the car over the hills toward the lake. September was the benevolent month, the season but not the summer over, the air still luminous as the light dimmed. Even green looked gold on the far hills as the sun left, then straight to dark. He'd slid down the teeter-totter and kissed her, then in his own time just taken her, because he could. There was no murder in him that she could see, just that taking. She had watched him all her life and she ought to know. There were doubtful things, too, but he was not happy to be cruel. He had always been friends with Debbie. He might cause hurt, and had, and would, but he wanted to be fair. He'd come in a somersault through her window, neat and quiet as an acrobat, and just took her over.

But he was substantial and warm, now, at her side, and he was kind except when he was too upset with himself and had too many doubts. She was kind, too, she thought. She tried to be, and tried not to judge too harshly. But these judgments and evaluations were beside the point. No matter what he was she would let him and no other man inside her, because she had made that decision. No, it hadn't been a decision, it had been a command. No use thinking about it.

It seemed strange, in September, not to be going to school, but only for a moment until the events of the year, resonant as a long past, made all that recede. All became memory.

The Cascom Inn would soon be closed except for weekends, and they were the only ones in the long dining room, their pink table lamp making of their table and their faces a sphere of light below the dim sconces on the walls. The old inn was kept up like a museum for the tools and furnishings of a hundred years ago—spinning wheels, harvest tables, cobbler's benches, hooked rugs—all gleaming with soft, expensive taste in the half-darkness.

They knew the waitress, Sandra Kelly, who had been a class ahead of Dory, and who knew about what had happened at Cascom Manor but not about this wonderful unexpected pairing of Dory Perkins and John Hearne. Sandra was so pleased about them her bright solicitous curiosity seemed an official Leah blessing upon them as a couple. Dory was too thin, Sandra said, but we would soon have her herself again, wouldn't we? Her smile suggested secret, avaricious discoveries.

"We'll do our best," John said. He looked at Dory in the rose light. She seemed demure and fragile, her eyes for now large with a cloudy inexactitude of focus. She had such an odd little face, the closeness of her eyes belying the common reserve about such an attribute; it gave her power. She was shy and wouldn't look straight back at him.

Sandra couldn't bring him a drink because she wasn't twenty-one, so she went away to find someone else to bring it.

He looked at Dory, moving his head to get into her line of sight, and said, "She thinks we're cute. She wants to breed us."

"We've already bred," she said, seeing that this startled and amused him. He was thinking of other things to say and she could see him making up and rejecting things, the play of wary thoughts.

"Will you eat?" he finally asked, having rejected everything in that other tonality.

"Yes," she said. She looked at the menu. A salad, but not meat, not yet. Something bland and neutral. What difference did it make, though; food was not supposed to scream that it was the flesh of victims. But not red meat, not blood. Fish, shellfish. Why not a triumphant feast, as after a hunt? She had never been finicky. She ate the rabbits she had skinned and quartered, throwing away their heads and soft brown eyes. It was good meat. This perverse comparison of meat with the flesh of her sister would simply have to stop, and would stop.

He said, "You may not believe this, but I now like lima beans. So I'm a man, according to your father. You remember he said that?"

When Sandra came back, the bartender bringing John's rye and soda and Dory's ginger ale, Dory ordered sole au gratin. She knew who the cook was—Mrs. Brock, Sarah's mother—so the food would be pretty good, if she could make herself eat it.

"I'll have that too," he said. "By the way, do you have lima beans?"

"We never have lima beans," Sandra said, making a face.

"Imagine that," he said. "No lima beans."

"Squash, carrots, green beans," Sandra said. "Baked or mashed potatoes. The house dressing's got herbs in it, like little green specks. It tastes good, though."

While they ate—and she did eat something, as if boughten food were somehow purer—he told her about his father and the lima-bean machine, trying, she saw, to be funny and detached from it all, but he would come to places that surprised him and constricted his voice. He stopped, in consternation, and then said, "You go for a summer and certain things happen and they don't have to make much sense. For instance, how can I feel terribly sorry for my mother when I can't understand her constant dishonesty? She ran off with some jerk she practically created, for Christ's sake. She's been married to Amos for fifteen years. Granted, he's a kind of jerk, too, but she's been about as faithful as a bivalve. When I think of her operation I get sympathy pains, for some reason in both feet, but in another very peculiar way she doesn't exist."

"She doesn't exist? What?"

"Well, if you're talking to her and you realize that you don't exist—at least not in the form you think of as real—then pretty soon you have the feeling that she doesn't exist, either. But then I have to think that she is real, and she's nearly forty-three and here she's had a hysterectomy and she ought to be upset, and is upset, and all I feel is some slightly gory pains in my feet."

The Princess was forty-three, too, she thought. But of course princesses were out of time.

"But my sister," he said. "My half-sister, Thelma. She had this real talent. She sounded like she was talking through a sponge but she told the truth. She could draw . . ." He was thinking of Debbie, too, and the two victims got mixed up, as if the death of one were linked through Dory Perkins and John Hearne to the death of the other. Dory's sorrow and guilt loomed over him and he remembered his moment with Thelma of near-religious certainty, power without sense, and all of this paralyzed his throat, a static, motionless seizure.

She approved of his seriousness—whatever strong feelings kept catching him unawares. He said, "Let's go to Cascomhaven after. Would you like to?"

"I'll go anywhere you want."

At Cascomhaven they sat on the dock to look at a sliver of moon. The weather had been so dry the lake was low and they could let their feet dangle, watching the small, moon-tipped waves slide noiselessly beneath them. He told her what lima beans were named in Latin, and went on from there, not telling her quite all, she could tell, about Bonnie Forester.

"I have the feeling I'm just making up a story," he said, "because I'm telling it to you. But everything I say happened did happen. I'm not making up events, you know. It just changes."

"That's what everybody does," she said. "Like your mother."

"Please don't tell me I'm like my mother," he said with a small laugh and a touch of irritation.

She didn't know how to answer that, so she didn't say anything. She looked out at the broad lake, in which Debbie's blood had been dissolved from the clothes and hands of her murderer. How the pale cloud had dispersed, cell by cell, into the cold lake.

He said, "You can't blame yourself for some madman, Dory. Some German. You knew there were murderers in the world. You've got to go on living."

She didn't answer that.

"Jesus Christ!" he said.

"Debbie didn't go on living!" she said in sudden anger. "Can you just lecture me? Where did you get all the authority?"

He put his arm around her, like a yoke, and she struggled to get up.

He held her, thinking his touch must heal, but she struggled against him like a bird whose frantic wings he tried not to damage.

She couldn't stand it. She fought his easy power as hard as she could, thinking of scratching or biting, the superficial irritants that were all weakness had.

"Dory," he said as if to a willful child.

"Let go of me!" she said. She was crying and hated it. "You don't own me! What do you want, anyway?"

"I want you to be reasonably happy."

"You want what you want! What have I got to say about it?" She would just as soon die anytime. Pouf, there goes Moscow. He let her get to her feet, and stood beside her, looming like a bully. She was ashamed of her yelling and yet she believed in what she'd yelled.

He said, "I don't want you to be crazy."

"Tough!" she yelled. The word didn't truly represent her but she couldn't think of words that did, and in a red fit of frustration she pushed him off the dock. He grabbed her to get his balance but then saw that he couldn't and tried to push her back upright so she wouldn't fall in too, but it was too late. The water was not as cold as it had been in June but she began to shiver immediately and was really weak. She reached out for help and he picked her up easily and waded the rocky bottom to shore, then up the steps toward the cabin.

To his strength she weighed little, not much more than the gravely hurt child on Okinawa, the girl child with her leg and God knew what else smashed, who signaled her consciousness with a whine of agony. He'd seen her smooth ivory little pouch, a sign of mortality and commonness, a twinge at his heart. He never knew what to do with the weak and the wounded but to carry them, and what good was that? He was not of the Healing Echelons. He knew what to do with men; you looked them in the eyes and things got sorted out. If they didn't know what to do you told them what to do. If they were killers you either put them out of their misery or got the fuck out of there. But what did you do with women? And this one, a complication of desire and fear, humor and anger, who was an object, too. He was made by her to feel the risk of intolerable loss, but he believed that to own her was to be owned forever.

She stood wrapped in a blanket while he knelt at the fire, a beach towel over his broad shoulders, a smaller towel around his waist, like Tarzan, his golden thighs and calves defined by fire into their hard, classical blocks and lines, all mobility and strength. She was cold clear through, trembling to the marrow, ice to the fire of his energy, so chilled she didn't dare move for fear of moving the air. She hadn't been able to undo the safety pin at her waistband, or do anything, and he did it all, matter-of-factly, as though they had no secrets and had never had any secrets. He squeezed out their clothes in the kitchen sink, rigged clotheslines across the room and hung out everything they had worn. Their shoes, wallets and his wet traveler's checks and cigarettes he arranged on the hearth.

She warmed slowly, opening the blanket away from him, to the fire. She'd never been modest; it wasn't that. "I'm sorry I pushed you," she said. "That was dumb and I can't even remember why I did it."

"You thought I needed a swim," he said. "You didn't care for my advice."

He sat back casually on the couch, the place of examining and taking, where she'd lost her singularity. "My mother wants you to cure me of all this sleeping business, isn't that right?" she said.

"Dory, I want to."

"Then everything will be all right."

"Easy," he said. "Come on, now."

"So what do you want? Why did you come back?"

"Because I wanted to," he said. "I mean because I had to."

They made up carefully, only little slivers of resentment and shame left, as those little slivers and twigs and grains were always left, no matter how they tried to forgive. They lay down together, no tentative looks or hesitations. He was being careful about what he said to her but he acted as though he owned her body, which she supposed he did. She could tell that he had decided that she was too ill, or fragile, to do to her what he wanted to do, as if it would be too physical and momentous for now.

"You're a ghost," he said. "You're all sticks and fog. I want you to get your muscles back and then you can push me off the dock all you want."

She had no answer to that, but his bulk was heated and gentle, and after a while she let him know that she wanted him to do what he wanted to do.

At midnight they put on their damp clothes and he took her home.

The next day he went to Mrs. Pulsifer's and registered for Selective Service, then got Paul Columbard, since Paul had Saturday off, to drive him around to look at secondhand cars. He bought a dented black '36 Ford two-door sedan for two hundred dollars. It visibly used oil, but aside from a little smoke ran pretty well. It didn't stop very well, with its cable brakes, but he was used to watching for obstacles.

There had been no rain for weeks, and fires had run out of control in Northlee and to the west, so everyone was cleaning up brush around houses and cabins. A few days later he and Dory were at Cascomhaven doing this, Dory unable to keep herself from dragging away the brush he cut and gathered. The old man with his scythe was cleaning up the sparse hay along the road, his stone often calling *agua caliente, agua caliente.* John had to go back to the university in a week, if he was going.

He watched Dory drag away a pile of dead branches, steeplejack and spiked blackberry stalks. Her arms were scratched and she was creased with sweat and dust, but if work was to be done she had to do it. So did he. It seemed to him that they should work like this all of their lives—that terminal, mortal shiver, though the years ahead seemed to stretch out forever, give or take the Apocalypse.

At dusk they washed up in the lake, naked, soaping each other with shameless, proprietary hands. Lord! They handled each other's rubbery cold exotic protoplasm, and swam through the cool libidinous primeval like horny squids—his terminology, which she would find doubtful—and he thought how she never haggled, she never bargained. She could resent, and probably should. He asked her if she wanted to get married, she said yes, and he thought how she would frighten him all of his life and make him careful, because he would have to pretend that he was better and stronger and more honest than he really was. But she was his woman and she would have his children, who would never be abandoned or betrayed. Never. Surely the decent and responsible could have their stories too.

Made thoughtful by this exchange, they went up to the cabin. She'd said, "Yes," because he really meant it, but her even-sounding "Yes" was not simple assent, it was something like surrender. She had loved and admired him ever since she was eight years old, but even if all that puppy love and infatuation and the way he owned her now seemed to obliterate sense, sense was still there. She knew what it meant to make such a decision. It meant the years, the years, for better or for worse. She knew what it was like to be a parent; she knew her mother's life as if she had been a sister to her, of the labor and the losses. She knew more than he did about the long years of vigilance, the way through a vain world toward Homeland.

Now he came to her, just to her, and he was for this moment perfect and beautiful, the creation, she knew—but this knowledge washed away unregretted—of all the dreams and fantasies that at this commencement must begin to slip away into the past.

34

It is one of their anniversaries, another warm day in September when the summer people have gone from the lake and they have it all to themselves. The small green canoe sails trembling on its sensitive, skittish keel. It now has a name stenciled in light blue letters on its bows: *Phaseolus lunatus.* Its sail is now white Dacron, its sheaves and cleats stainless steel and bronze, but the pretty hull, made in Maine so long ago, is still the same.

"Do you remember," he asks, "your dream about the Canadian soldiers?"

No, she can't remember, and he is always doing this to her. They are heading toward Pine Island on a port tack, to have a sort of picnic. Somewhere near here, she does vaguely remember, she told him about a dream, but sometimes it seems as if they must have led separate lives, because she remembers what he doesn't and he remembers what she doesn't.

"Do you remember 1948?" he asks.

"That year," she says. From Pine Island they will be able to see where Cascom Manor once stood—now a series of A-frame condominiums John Hearne is partly responsible for. But she remembers that year all right, when the dregs of a distant war washed like a tsunami around her and her sister, and the world became precariously balanced upon a point of terror. She is the compulsive historian of the family, the active political one, whose composure can most easily be shaken by distant events. Her children, now grown up and away, have always lived in this world; they were born into it, and survive as if they are mutations who have adapted to the loom of Apocalypse. So far she too has survived, as has the man who steers the little boat on the mild blue lake. Mild for now, anyway. "Yes, I remember," she says, thinking that he still feels proud of himself because, thirty-six years ago, he kept his word and married her.

"It wasn't such a bad year, was it?" he says. "Harry Truman won, didn't he?"

He, too, thinks about the world and his country and the history he has witnessed. He can't define his country because it is the air he breathes, the water (becoming acidic, oh, woe) he swims in. In a way, he and Dory are his country. He even has a battle star for having fought for it—three days hearing the rattle of distant guns, a walk through shit, a time to carry a wounded child up a hill; there are better and worse records. But his country, his life—how can he define it, them? A black man or woman can now take a leak in Utah; that's no small thing. Hold on to that.

There were more wars, in which we lost, or almost lost, the feeling that we were the loved and the good. Only by comparison, a doubtful form of logic, can we feel righteous now. The world does seem, as Dory says, to be in a state of jihad, the sects at each other's throats everywhere. The rational and the decent, where they are found or dare to speak, are the first to be shot. Theocracy, in all of its linguistic disguises, is ascendant, newspeak triumphant in the service of dogma. Urban Stumms, who no longer comes toward him in his dreams, heavy-shod and implacable, would share the joke of terror as peace; that is what the two-legged race has come to, Urban. What happiness there is must ignore the inevitable; but of course it can. Now: the blue lake, a light breeze, the austere September sun, Dory who is still alive.

The little boat heels slightly, its wake leaving a smooth, turbulent hush among the waves, its energy understood but still miraculous. His companion in the bow examines and judges, a miracle of continuity and passion not so well understood.

When he thinks of 1948 and of his father, now dead, it is always of that hushed moment when, with the calm intensity of an adult feeding a child, the man who did not believe in names brought toward his tongue one common, immaculate lima bean. In that vision innocent of dogma and intolerance he will always believe.

Dory watches him, thinking how the gray-haired, still young-looking man at the tiller has not really had the life he wanted and expected. When Amos died in 1951 they came back from the university to take over—temporarily, they thought—Martha's financial and business affairs. He has always considered his involvement in business merely temporary, secondary, but of course it is life itself that is temporary. He has been, like his partner, John Cotter, one of those detached, ironic scholars of the counting house who cultivate odd skills, such as the casting of a fly, and who have odd and irreverent opinions unrelated to their professions.

The only one of their parents still living is Sarah, her mother, who is seventy-two and in good health. Better, perhaps, than her own. That chill.

Martha, after Amos's death, had an active career as a woman of leisure in which she traveled, fell in love with Adlai Stevenson, among others, bought a garage for her Indian chauffeur (they have a photograph of the Sylvester Garage, a white cement-block structure in Bangalore), and ended up after many travels and romances in Sun City, Arizona, where her heart stopped at seventy-four as she piloted her canopied golf cart down a residential street.

Cynthia and Dibley have passed from her ken, though Robert Beggs still keeps his father's store, now a "superette," in Leah.

"Coming about," John Hearne says, and she ducks her head to let the wooden boom pass over. He has put up with her worries and causes, always as a self-proclaimed ironic observer, though she knows what he believes. Once, in Washington, D.C., they watched the Vietnam veterans throw away their medals and he wept, an act which placed him firmly in his generation.

Pine Island is now, partly because of her efforts, a state reservation. The hurricanes of 1954 blew down half of the great trees, but others have grown up to take their places; it is a sign of age when you know how fast a white pine grows.

He comes neatly about again, lets the sheet go and ties up on a root, surely not the same one, and they go ashore beneath the trees that are like the sighing masts of a schooner. After her mastectomy in June he asked to look, and looked, and said with his quick tongue, quicker than truth could ever be, "Look, Dory. Bilateral symmetricality has never been one of my fetishes."

How can she understand someone who talks this way? But he did mean it; he told the truth. Now if it is such that she is cured and doesn't have to die just yet . . .

Is the world more beautiful for its being at risk?

It all depends upon the risk. He left her once, for a while, because of a fight, or a series of fights, the cause actually forgotten by both of them. And then there was Mary Denny, but he doesn't like that subject at all; it gives him pain to think how she was hurt, the bastard.

Her left front is as smooth, he says, as a boy's, so he must be half queer. She will never care for his humor because it sounds insincere, though he doesn't seem to be. Can time alone prove such a thing? It is like trying to catch a grasshopper.

She opens the hamper and brings out the wine, glasses, sandwiches, salad, silver, napkins and condiments, and puts them on the blanket. She has known him for, let's see; when would she first have been aware of the boy across the backyards? At, say, three? Then she's known him for fifty years, half a century. How can there be any secrets left? What is the mystery?

"Our wounds," he says, touching her ghost breast, where there is none. Her arm is strong enough again. The pines move far overhead, massive and opinionless. Across the broad lake, below the long hills, is Cascomhaven. The little green boat quivers and shakes at its tether. Nothing has ever been exactly right, exactly in control, but she would rather be here than anywhere.